CASTIEL

KINGDOM OF FAIRYTALES
SEASON THREE

You all know the story of your favorite fairytale, but did you ever wonder what happened after the fairytale ending? Well we know. Not all afters end up happily, sometimes the real adventure starts much later...

Following famous fairytale characters, eighteen years after their happily ever after, the Kingdom of Fairytales offers an edge of the seat thrill ride in an all new and sensational way to read.

Lighting-fast reads you won't be able to put down

Fantasy has never been so epic!

KINGDOM
OF
FAIRYTALES
URBIS PRISON
SHIPLEY
THE VALE
AZREN
BADALAH
DESERT
KISBU
DRACONIS
ZHORE
MOSA
ABORIA
ELDER
AIRE
SKYLA
URBIS
AZURE
ENCHANTIA
EMERALD CITY
OZ
FLORIS
TULIS
THE FORGE
ARCADIA
RENAIS
MELFALL
ATLANTICE
ANTLA
W
E
S

ISBN: 978-1-989997-25-3
Enchanted Quill Press

Contaact the author at www.enchantedquillpress.com
Cover by Enchanted Quilll Press
Interior Formatting by Enchanted Quill Press
Editing by Rose Lipscomb

KING OF WOLVES

26TH FEBRUARY

The weather was perfect for a run. It was cold enough that most people would need a coat, but not me. Winter season wasn't entirely done yet, but the cold never bothered me. I ran a bit warmer than most, and it had only gotten worse over the past few moon cycles. I didn't need to heat my small hut anymore as I was always warm. My fast-paced jog meant I was already sweating, even without my shirt on. The chilly winter breeze was perfect as I chased the lithe wolf, still beating me in our last turn toward home.

Running was simple, like the people of Elder. We lived in harmony with each person playing their role assigned by our leader, The Red. We traded for what we needed, and everyone took care of themselves. I'd never really known any other sort of life, but the one I was given suited me, preferring as I did, to live my own life with my own rules. I took care of myself and didn't need anyone else to do it for me.

Since I was fifteen, every morning and every afternoon, I'd jogged around the local woods. At a full out run, I could do the southern trail before breakfast, and as long as I got out before the sun started to set, I could make the northern trail before it got completely dark. Both paths allowed me to monitor the woods between the two peoples of Elder. Three seasons ago, Red ordered me to start making the runs I now do daily in trade for items I didn't have at my hut. At the time, I refused, but now I do it without needing to be reminded. The Red had asked me to keep an eye on the wolves, but I felt something more than that. I belonged in the woods and running made me feel alive, not that I'd ever tell her that.

I preferred the simple life of the forest to anything else. Where there were no machines for people to fight over, no money to be used, and every person you met didn't use magic. In fact, not many people ventured here at all, and that was the way I liked it. I hadn't actually ever left the borders of Elder, but I had no reason to. All I knew of the outside kingdoms came from the few outsiders that ventured into Elder when I was growing up in the tree village, and they didn't make our forest a stop on their way through. They always worried about what might be lurking in the woods, which for the most part, was nothing. Almost every day I was alone as I crossed the pathways that I ran. Well, I wasn't completely alone; I had my wolf beside me.

The young wolf raised his head into the air and sniffed. Taking a deep breath, I took in the fresh forest air also. I could smell the faint scent of a river, elderberries, and a rodent of some sort nearby not to mention my wolf friend.

"Not today," I told him, sure that he wanted to chase whatever prey it was. "I'm always in enough trouble as it is."

The wolf shook his head. I was pretty sure that was his way of saying he didn't agree with me. It wasn't his butt getting in trouble every time he decided to eat something he shouldn't. The Red would be knocking on my door, scolding me and making me make retribution for his latest folly. *He's just a wolf.* Grabbing a pine cone off the tree I just passed, I took aim and hit the wolf on his head as he pounced in front of me.

"Not today." I tried to add more authority to my voice.

The wolf dropped back alongside me and nipped at my leg. He knew we didn't get supper until we finished our run.

Running in the big bad forest seemed to intimidate most people, but not me. I loved the fresh air and all the scents of the world around me. It was pure. It was nature: not metal or magic, just life. Contrary to what everyone thought, the evil forest was just a forest. The area I patrolled was the safe zone between the wolves and the tree people. No one crossed it on purpose, and the few that I found just needed to be set back on track because they were lost. It was a simple job and something I actually liked, but I'd never tell Red that.

A wolf howl in the distance made my companion perk up his ears, but I kept on my track. It wasn't anything to worry about. I have no idea when it started, but I'd always had a deep connection to the animals in the woods. That howling wolf was at least two towns away. It wasn't going to come anywhere near us and the buffer zone I patrolled. The wolf beside me whined as he didn't have the same sense as I did.

"It's not a problem," I reassured him. The wolf trusted me and kept pace with me.

As I scented another smell, the wolf veered again to the left, like he was going to go off to chase something else again.

"Beat you home?" I challenged, raising an eyebrow at my companion. The wolf yipped his agreement. Without hesitation, the wolf took off.

The trees passed by as I quickened my pace to catch up with the blond wolf. He was fast, but I knew he was pushing it. This was the max speed that he could run. I was just getting going.

Within moments I was neck and neck with the wolf. He whined as he noticed me beside him, jumping the logs that littered the forest floor and ducking the low-hanging branches. I grew up in the woods, and this was like home as much to me as it was to him. Elder was mostly forested. Only the southern region had farms, but I didn't need to patrol there. The wolves stuck to the forest, and so did the tree people I grew up with.

Ten more strides, and I pulled ahead of the wolf. He nipped at me but wasn't close enough to get a piece of me. As I ran faster, he wasn't going to get a second chance.

The wind and trees whipped by me as I ran, easily dodging trees and bushes. As I pushed faster, it felt like I could be a bird getting ready to take off. I was part of the forest just like every creature around me and the wolf that still pounded behind me at my heals. I focused on my pathway home and picked up my speed. This was home, and I knew every last piece of the woods I was running through.

The scent I smelled before hit me harder, and I knew

exactly who it was. Just as I burst through the pine trees that kept my small place hidden, I saw her at my doorway.

I skidded to a halt, and my wolf friend ran past me. His tongue was hanging out as he turned back to mock me while he ran full force into the hooded person standing outside my doorway. Her back was turned to us, but it didn't matter. Red was agile and nimble as ever. She sidestepped the wolf barreling at her and let him run into the door, knocking it open.

"I see some things never change, Castiel," Red commented as she turned to me.

Honey brown eyes assessed me like I was being analyzed from head to toe. Red had a way of doing that to everyone. She didn't need words, just a look, and I was back to being a boy of only eight winters.

Anyone not from Elder would have never thought to look twice at the small lady before me. She stood barely taller than a one-season oak tree. Most of the people of Elder were shorter, but Red was exceptionally short. I could look her eye to eye by my tenth winter season. Now I had to look down to talk to her, but it didn't matter. The authority that came from her made me feel like I was that little boy again, but could finally look her in the eye. I had a feeling it would be like that my whole life.

"Do I get an invite in?" She waited while I tried to remember words.

I waved my arm to the doorway, inviting her in and followed behind her as the wolf went over to my couch that doubled as my bed and climbed on to sleep. I motioned for him to move, and he finally realized Red was standing there, also looking at him. The wolf stumbled off the bed and hurried over to the corner where he slept at night when I was using the couch.

"What do I owe this visit to?" I asked as I stepped around the room and tried to hide my mess a bit. It wasn't that my place was horrible, but Red had standards. With my foot, I kicked a pair of pants under my couch.

"Does a mother need a reason to visit her son?"

I turned my back and walked over to the stove in the corner while rolling my eyes. Pouring water into a banged-up kettle, I set it on the stove while I grabbed more wood to stoke the almost gone fire. Red didn't visit without a reason, and she only reminded me that she was legally my mother when she wanted something.

"What did Nikkan do this time?" I asked as I grabbed two mugs from the cupboard and set them down in front of Red.

The wolf in the corner lifted his head and growled at me. I shrugged at him. This past week alone, he ate one of Farmer Allen's chickens, and I caught him before he could chase Miss Mary's dog into the river for a third time this moon cycle.

Red looked over at the wolf that now had his eyes closed, pretending to be asleep. I knew for a fact that Nikkan never fell asleep that easily. And there wasn't a wolf around that would sleep with Red sitting not even a sapling away. There was a reason she was the Red of Elder, and it wasn't because she made a good cherry pie.

Little Red Riding Hood was the name my adoptive mother earned. She was the smallest and youngest Red to ever come into power, but that didn't mean she was the weakest. In fact, she was probably the strongest Red for over a hundred generations. Her size had nothing to do with her power. Alone, she had beaten the curse that had plagued the wolves and tree humans. The final battle was almost eighteen winters ago, but she was still a force to be reckoned with. She was a warrior with more wolf kills under her belt than any adult alive in Elder. She wasn't someone you closed your eyes around, especially if you were a wolf.

"Was there more beyond the chicken?" Red asked as she eyed the wolf.

"Not really," I replied. Nikkan kept his eyes closed.

"I already compensated Farmer Allen. He's agreed to not shoot him on sight as long as he continues to get double the value of his lost stock."

Red shrugged like it wasn't a big deal. That was a first. It was always a big deal to Red when the wolves didn't behave.

I wasn't sure what to make of that. Red had threatened to put Nikkan down herself when he wasn't behaving. Not that I ever thought she would. She knew he was my friend, possibly my only friend. I grabbed the hot kettle and poured it over the leaves in her mug and mine before returning it to the stove. I joined her at my small two-seat table.

Red gazed at the wolf in the corner of my house. She had to be thinking something, but she wasn't speaking. I knew enough to keep my questions to myself as they wouldn't be answered. Red would tell me what I needed to know when she thought it was the right time. That was one of the hardest lessons I had to learn as a child.

I had time to just look at her as she was lost in her own thoughts. There were faint lines at the corners of her eyes. When did she get old enough to have wrinkles? I actually couldn't remember the last time we sat together. Today was unusual. She was a busy person, running a kingdom all on her own. She stopped by at least once every other week, but she never had time for more than what she came to tell me.

My fifteenth winter was when I officially moved out. We both agreed it was best I lived on my own, and I had already spent more than a season cycle building the hut I now lived in. While Red had taken me in and raised me, there was never a doubt among the tree villagers that I didn't belong with them. I might have the same dark hair as Red, but I looked nothing like her. And my hazel eyes kept everyone away from me. The color alone would do it since the tree people all had entirely brown eyes, but the golden ring around the hazel made everyone fear me. Season upon season of war with the wolves had made the tree dwellers distrustful of everything different, and I was certainly different. Not only in looks but in the way I felt. It was nothing I could explain, but I'd never really felt as though I fit in. It was probably part of the reason I decided to move into the forest, away from people.

Red had been working for the past eighteen winters to change their views, but stuff like that's deep-seated. Change takes time, and after over a decade of looks and whispers, I was ready to live on my own. Red wanted Elder to change, but it wasn't that easy. It never was, nor will it be. Especially in Elder

My first forest home had been with Nikkan and the wolves in one of the closest villages, but I soon found I didn't fit there either. My hut was a better option, not with humans and not amongst wolves, but somewhere in between. The wolves distrusted me as much as the villagers did. I was raised in the trees with the humans. I knew their ways, and I acted too much like them. I was one of them. I found the best place was on my own in the woods. My house built by my hand on my own was all I really needed— one room with a couch, table, and chairs. A little stove provided the heat and ability to cook. What more did one teen need? The best part was, it was all mine.

“I’m planning a festival in Azren six moons from today. No one will volunteer to be my envoy to Micco and the wolves. I’d like them to come too. It’s time we move forward. All that happened was a long time ago. It’s time we become one people again.”

Red looked back at me, and I could see more lines on her face. Her forehead had a permeant line across it like the lines at the corner of her eyes. I wonder why I hadn’t noticed it last new moon or the one before. She was aging, which could only mean one thing. She was losing her powers as the Red.

“You want me to go invite the wolves?” I asked as I continued to stare at the wrinkles on her.

It was hard to see her not as I remembered her, the young, vibrant Red that taught me how to fight and stand on my own two feet. The Red that showed me the only person I needed was me. The Red that, though she didn’t kiss my cuts like most mothers, but instead, told me to get back up, was the best mother she could be. She taught me how to be independent. As much as we sometimes didn’t see eye to eye, I’d forever be in her debt for that.

“Why don’t you do it yourself?” I asked, taking a sip of my tea.

Red was actually on excellent terms with Micco, the leader of the wolves. Even though he was at least ten seasons older than her, I knew that he had a crush on her. Anyone in his inner circle knew that much. While the wolves and tree humans rarely got along, Red was special. The wolves had caused much destruction and death, but she never blamed them for it. Red was one of the good tree-dwellers.

"I would if I could get away long enough. I had to slip out today just to stop by here. Sera is probably looking for me right now. There just seems to be a never-ending list of things to get done." Red sighed. She looked tired. It was beyond strange. Red never tired.

I sipped my tea more and watched her. She was looking intently in her cup like it held some grand secret. Red was never really one for sharing what she was thinking or the load she bore alone as she kept the tree people and all of Elder safe. She looked worn out.

"I can do that," I told her finally when I realized she wasn't going to add to why she wasn't going herself.

Red smiled and nodded, but it wasn't the kind of smile that reached her eyes.

"How is everything else?" she asked as she drank down her hot tea in one gulp before she stood. She was back to the leader I grew up with as she was all business now. The Red was back in full form.

I shrugged. "Nothing to report," I replied like a good soldier.

"Good." She walked back to the still-open doorway. "I'll see you in six moons time. The festival starts at dusk."

I nodded, and she left without another word. No, *I love you, son. Take care, son. Stay safe, son.* That was the mother I was used to. She didn't ask if I was coming; she ordered me to come. That was the part of her I could never get along with, but the soft, tired Red was beyond strange. I watched as she blended into the trees with her brown cape and disappeared from my view.

"You know she's crazy," Nikkan said from behind

me.

I turned around and found him standing fully naked in the corner where he had just been pretending to sleep. I groaned as I grabbed the pants I had previously shoved under the couch and tossed them to him.

“Come on, man. I don’t need to see all that.” I covered my eyes as I hoped he was putting the pants on I had just tossed him.

“What’s wrong with being natural? To us wolves, you’re the strange one with weird customs,” Nikkan replied.

I shook my head at him. We both knew the wolves in human form wore clothing. Nikkan was from one of the wolf villages. He knew that too. They didn’t run around naked unless in the furrier form. He just didn’t like clothing.

“So, why do you think Red is crazy?” I kept my hand over my eyes. The fabric rustled as he slipped on the pants and saved me from having a full conversation with my eyes closed.

“The wolves are never going to show up at some festival. Don’t you remember the stories of like thirty seasons ago when the tree people invited the wolves to come to a truce and then attacked them? There’s a reason we keep away from them. Tree people can’t be trusted.” Nikkan walked over and flopped down on my couch.

“I’m a tree person,” I reminded him, at least, I had been raised as one.

“Not even close,” Nikkan replied.

I shrugged as I sat beside him. I wasn’t technically a tree person, but I wasn’t a wolf either. I was just a human that didn’t belong in either world, and my mother expected me to somehow bridge the gap between them.

"And there's the fact that the wolves are getting sick. Probably not the best time to be making a good impression if the tree people are really extending a peace offering."

"Getting sick?" I asked. I hadn't been back to the wolves or tree villages in over a moon cycle. Nikkan went back often to check on his family.

"My father told me to stay here with you, so I don't catch it. Not sure what it is, but probably best to stay away from tree people."

Great. Not only was there distrust between the two sides, but now there was a sickness he conveniently forgot to tell me about. I looked at Nikkan. Illness with wolves was serious. Whatever caused the curse also caused very good health. Wolves aged but rarely got sick. Why hadn't he told me sooner?

"I was promised to secrecy," Nikkan replied, answering my unspoken question with his hands in the air as if he was giving up.

"So, if I'm not a tree person or a wolf you can tell secrets to, then who am I?"

Nikkan raised an eyebrow at me. We had debated this for as long as we had been friends. Nikkan was convinced I was a prince from a hidden valley of fairies since I loved the forest but couldn't shift into a wolf like him. I personally thought he chose fairies so that he could picture me with wings and sparkles. I told him I just was probably not from Elder; some traveler left me on their way through when I was too young to notice. It wasn't like Red ever told me much, nor would she answer questions. We had to come up with our own stories, which ended up being a traveling group of fairies left me.

"Not like I have a choice in this," I reminded him.

"The Red ordered me to invite them."

"And we could just get distracted for six moons and not invite them. What good will come of it? Either it's a trap on the humans' part, or the wolves will bring sickness to the tree people. Neither is a good thing." Nikkan had a harder time following rules than I did. He tolerated Red and respected her like most wolves did, but he didn't really like a single other tree person.

"What harm could it do to just invite them? Not like many would consider going." Usually, I'd be on board with Nikkan and ignoring it, but something about Red made me pause. She was different today, and I kind of didn't want to disappoint her. "Red would never let it be a trap, but like you said, most of the elders remember the wars, so they won't go. And the younger ones tend to follow the older. So, where is the worry? You know how Red is. All she wants is a couple of honorary wolves to show up, and she will consider it a success."

Years of wars between the two sides had left everyone mistrustful. Red had been the only one able to call a truce between them, and so far, she'd been able to uphold it for over eighteen winters. But the truce was tenuous at best. It was hardly as though either side put in any effort, they just kept to their own parts of Elder, but I guessed it was better than constantly fighting.

"And what if they do show up?" Nikkan countered. "What if they bring the sickness to the tree people? And worse, what if they transform? Are you willing to be the one that starts it all over again?"

Okay, he had a point there.

"And what if the sickness isn't as bad as you think. You want to be the one that keeps the tree people and wolves apart?" I really wasn't into the peace thing like the Red, but I couldn't help arguing the other side with

Nikkan. It was just something we always did.

Nikkan grinned at me. He knew how I felt about being the bridge between the two sides that neither wanted me around. Even that didn't stop him as he went to open his mouth again. He was always ready to argue. This was going to be a long night.

27TH FEBRUARY

We had stayed up way too late into the night, and when the sun rose in time for our morning patrol, I didn't want to move. I reached for the blanket to pull it back over my head and found it wasn't on me. In the corner of the room, the wolf Nikkan was curled in the one blanket I owned. I threw my arm over my eyes and tried to block the invading sunlight. Why the heck did I let him get me going last night? We were up until the moon shifted toward day, and now I had a job to do.

Slowly, I rolled off the couch and stood to stretch. Nikkan didn't even move.

"Get up, you lazy mutt," I grumbled as I took my blanket back and shook off the blond wolf hair now covering it. I placed the blanket over the back of my couch.

Wolf Nikkan rolled on the floor, pretending to be still asleep.

"Fine. I'll patrol without you and stop by the wolves. I'll tell your father you say hi, and maybe I can talk to Grace."

That was all it took. Wolf Nikkan was up on four legs and ready to go for a run. I shook my head at him. That was all it took.

Before we left, I grabbed some jerky I had stored from last week's large kill and tossed a piece to Nikkan as I began my run. With a toss of his head, he caught it. While he could hunt for his own breakfast, I didn't want to wait for him to catch and eat his kill. He chewed away beside me as we kept the jog light.

Unlike most people of the wolf villages, Nikkan preferred his wolf form over his human form, especially if any physical activity was involved since the wolf was stronger than his human side. Nikkan wasn't alone in his preference to use his wolf for strength, but in the village, most people stayed in their human form. In fact, I had found over time, most of the people preferred being human and pretending their wolf didn't exist.

The wolves had spent the better part of their existence feared by everyone, not just the tree people of Elder, but everyone in the neighboring kingdoms too. The curse could be inherited from your parents, as was the case with all the wolves under the age of eighteen winters, or could be transferred via a bite from an infected wolf. Not a single wolf in the wolf villages was there by choice. They had all inherited or had been made into wolves.

They all were at least as much human as they were wolf, and lots of them were more human than anything.

If it wasn't for the variety in hair and eye color, you'd never be able to guess who was a wolf in Elder. The tree villagers all had brown eyes, and most had varying shades of brown for hair. Wolf humans had every color of hair you could think of because it usually matched their wolf fur. Nikkan had a head full of blond hair since his wolf was blond. But it was the eyes that gave away wolves. Born and transformed wolves all had blue eyes. Even if a tree villager was bitten, their brown eyes would change color.

The curse was where it had all begun. No one knew who the first person was or how they ended up a wolf, but we all knew what came of it. One person was the start, and once he found he could increase the wolf people's population by biting tree people, he grew an army of wolves. It was like the curse just appeared. The wolves were the reason that the humans lived in the trees in the first place. It was just safer that way. I supposed that at some point, humans would have made their homes on the ground like I did, but the wolves had forced them to build entire villages in the trees. Houses, bound to the trees with rope walkways connecting the dwellings, became the norm, and while we looked strange to outsiders, living in a tree hut was as normal to us as any other house in the other kingdoms.

And then it changed further. There were too many wolves, and they were running out of food in the forest. Rather than turning back into humans and raising their own crops and animals as the tree people were doing, they chose to eat humans. The first human kill elevated the curse to a whole new level. Where the wolves once had control of their changes, they no longer could control their changes or the wolf they became. They were a danger to all of Elder.

To counter the possibility of the wolves wiping out the humans of Elder, the Red of the village went to the witches to get a spell that would make them powerful enough to fight back. That's what my mother was part of; she carried the power the witches gave to the first Red that fought back. While I asked many times as a child, my mother never told me how she got the power or how she used it to defeat the curse. But since the day she did, the wolves had gone back to being peaceful. They didn't lust after human flesh, and luckily for Nikkan running beside me, they regained their ability to transform at will.

Nikkan and I kept our light pace as the sun moved higher into the sky. Micco's village was the closest one to the safe zone between the two sides. Before our normal pathway turned back south to head back to my house, we only needed to turn north for a bit to find the wolves. It was a pathway we both knew well. Nikkan actually grew up in the village that Micco lived in.

While Elder was divided into the plains where most of the farms were located, the northern half of the kingdom had always been covered by forest. The tree people lived in cities such as Azren at the southern side of the wood, while three main wolf villages were located in the northern half of the kingdom. Micco was the strongest wolf leader and had the largest pack, which also happened to be the closest to the tree villages.

The wolves were technically under Elder law, but Micco had ruled the wolves as long as I could remember. The Red was now welcome in the wolves' villages, but my mother tended to only visit for formal meetings when she absolutely had to. She let Micco rule them as he saw fit even though they were now safe for any human to visit. In fact, when I was a child, Red would take me with her to see the villages when she had meetings. Most tree people still harbored a distrust of the wolves, but not Red. She saw the truth. None of the wolves chose to be wolves, and they were still humans, good humans at that.

We had already veered left and begun making our way into wolf territory. Things were quiet, but that was normal. The animals knew they had more predators than normal living nearby, like a whole village of them. It wouldn't take the village long to realize we were there. Nikkan, at least, still smelled like a wolf, but I was sure they would know a human was coming closer. It was best we approached the village slowly. Micco would certainly know my scent, but other wolves could see me as an intruder. At most times, their furry half would be prone to attack first and ask questions later.

As the huts of the village came into sight, I slowed our pace to a walk. The wolf village was several huts that circled around the central shelter in the middle of the small clearing. As this was the largest village, there were close to a hundred huts that circled a considerable meeting lodge.

The huts were more basic than what I had built but looked very similar on the outside. Wood was used to frame the house, and clay dirt was then put on the frames to give the hut insulation in the cold winter weather. I knew from visiting and living with them for a time that the inside had just a sleeping side and a cooking side to the hut. The rest of their lives was spent outdoors. Most wolves preferred to cook outside, too, when they actually cooked. Hunting as a wolf could feed them for up to six moons depending on the size of the kill.

We walked into the village, and not a single face

turned to stare. Everyone was trudging on with their daily duties. About two oak saplings away, three girls not even ten winter seasons old were each carrying full buckets of water from the river. Children weren't playing in the streets like they might in other kingdoms, but tending to fires, carrying wood or water, stirring pots of food, and basically doing any chore that needed to be done. We continued to walk further into the village and found most of the men in threadbare pants or shirts that had holes in them big enough for a third arm as they lay about by their house. A few men seemed to be trying to pack stuff into carts, but most seemed exhausted to the point of sleep.

The people of the wolf village had seen much better days. Even moons ago, when I last visited, they would run up to me to see if I was friend or foe before Micco stopped them. There was no fight in them now.

"We should see your father before we go to invite Micco to the festival," I told my wolf companion quietly. I almost didn't want to speak out loud, afraid it would startle the closest wolf into changing and attacking, but no one paid me any heed.

Nikkan took the lead and began to weave through the huts with new vigor. I couldn't talk with him when he was in wolf form, but I knew this had to make him feel off too. The wolves weren't tired, lazy animals. They lived a harder life than the tree people, but they could as they were stronger and always had more vigor. To see them so worn down was more than a little shocking.

"Castiel?" a large man boomed as he made his way through the people milling about. They didn't even turn to his voice as they would only a moon cycle ago. I turned to Micco calling to me. "What in the world are you doing here?"

Nikkan doubled back to where I had stopped to wait for Micco. He nipped at my hand and whined.

"Go check on your family," I said to him. "Find me when you know they're okay."

Nikkan nodded to me and took off, weaving through the people and under the legs of some.

"Son, you shouldn't be here," Micco told me as soon as he was closer.

"What's going on?" I asked as a man nearby finally noticed me. He was so thin you could tell from how his shirt hung on him he didn't have much muscle. Wolves were never that skinny. I knew for a fact that the forest had plenty of food. There was no reason for a wolf to go hungry.

"Let's talk inside," Micco replied before ushering me towards his hut in the center of the village.

It wasn't a long walk, but I couldn't help but look at the people around us. They were sick and tired. Children seemed to be doing the majority of the chores as the fathers lay around. Most looked like they hadn't eaten or bathed for weeks. I should have noticed the smell as we approached, but it seemed the children were doing an excellent job of keeping things running for the most part.

Micco stopped at the door to his hut and ushered me in. He closed the door behind us, which was a little strange. One of the reasons he was leader was that he kept no secrets from his wolves. I couldn't recall ever seeing him close his door. Now, I stood in a dimly lit room as it seemed he already had candles lit. He must have had his door closed when I entered the village.

"So why are all the wolves looking like that?" I asked as I was finally alone with him.

"We have a small problem," Micco replied cryptically.

He took a deep breath and looked around his sparsely furnished hut. His was in better repair than most, without any noticeable cracks in the wall or ceiling as several were that we passed on the way.

"Problem?" I asked, trying to get him to continue talking.

"The wolves are sick," Micco continued after he seemed certain no one was listening. "It started a few moon cycles ago, right before the new winter. A wolf here or there would black out at night time. As long as there's a sliver of the moon in the sky, they are changing. Not everyone. Just one or two here and there. They came to me to complain, and I brushed them off. We've had complete control of our wolf side since your mother saved us. I figured these people were just drinking too much and didn't want to admit it to their wives."

Micco paused to wipe his brow. He was sweating even though his hut wasn't heated. I wasn't cold, but it wasn't hot enough to make me sweat, yet the older wolf was drenched.

"I let it go. It was only a couple of the men. I didn't think anything of it." Micco wiped his brow again.

"You might want to sit down," I suggested, wondering if he was sick also.

Micco walked over to one of the chairs at his small eating table and sat down. I dipped a ladle into his bucket of water and filled the metal cup beside it before joining him. I handed him the cup. He needed to replenish all he was losing. He took a deep swig of his drink, and I had time to look at him. Micco had lost some weight. He was always a large man, at least a head taller than me, but he weighed twice as much. He didn't look sick like the few men lounging around by their huts, but he did look thinner.

"I realized too late that they weren't making it up. The wolves are sick, and it's spreading. At first, it was only eight men. Now it's close to twenty. Soon enough, all the men of our village will be infected."

"Infected with what?" Wolves couldn't get sick; how could they get infected?

Micco looked around again like he was worried someone could be listening.

"With a disease that turns them back into hungry wild wolves," Micco whispered. "Any sign of the moon and they change and hunt. They've been killing all the animals for miles, so the rest of the village is starting to starve, but it doesn't satisfy their hunger. Each night they change and keep hunting. Men come back covered in blood and don't remember what they killed or ate, and the next day, they are hungry enough to hunt again. They are turning into monsters."

Micco sounded serious, but what he was saying was impossible. The forest was large enough to support his wolves and the two smaller villages north of it. There was no way they could kill everything. I'd have sensed that on my runs. The forest still had enough animals. Maybe the sickness was more of the brain and not the moon, as Micco suggested.

"You don't believe me," Micco said as he watched me in the dim light of his hut. All the shutters were closed, and there were only a few candles burning. The drink of water seemed to bring a little more life back into him.

"Wolves don't get sick," I told him back, not agreeing or disagreeing with his statement. I didn't want to have to deal with a mad alpha wolf if I called him a liar.

"I wouldn't believe me either if I hadn't seen it with my own eyes," Micco replied. "Just over ten moons ago, I followed one of the men that had been complaining since the beginning. I figured I could find the truth, but it wasn't what I thought I'd find. He changed and then hunted. I had to change into my own wolf and could barely keep up with him. His wolf was stronger and faster than he ever was before. He killed and ate any prey he could find. You'd expect after a night like that he'd wake up at home, satisfied, but he wasn't. He was actually sicker than when he left his house. I had to carry him back. He's been in bed ever since, but each night he feels the moon and changes again. It's killing him."

Micco was so sure of his words, and I wanted to believe him, but it still seemed impossible. Wolves couldn't catch a cold or get a sickness. Part of the wolf gene was the ability to change, but the other part, their human side, was beyond healthy.

"I've been working day and night to help the infected men. I don't know how or why they've gotten sick, but they can't function as a human now. They are bedridden, and their homes are falling into disrepair." That explained the sweating, at least. "I'd ask if you could stay to help, but I have no idea how everyone got sick. I wouldn't ask for you to stay around when they could possibly get you sick or worse when night comes. They are hungry enough; you smell too human. You could be viewed as friend or prey."

There hadn't been a wolf attack on a human in over eighteen winters, but I didn't want to be the first. I actually wasn't afraid of the wolves as most. I didn't fear being bitten or even killed. Red had trained me in all forms of hunting, combat, and fighting. She didn't go light on me, and I knew I was strong enough to withstand a wolf attack. What I feared was having to kill one of them. The wolves didn't trust me just like the tree people, but something about them or the way they lived felt like home to me. If I killed a wolf, I'd never be allowed to come back again.

After mopping his brow for about the dozenth time, Micco finally stood.

"What brought you this way?"

I had completely forgotten about that.

"Red asked me to come and invite the wolves to a festival she's having in Azren in five moons time," I explained.

"A festival? Right now?"

"She wants more cooperation between the tree people and wolves. You know. Her normal stuff."

I didn't need to explain more to Micco. He knew my mother very well and knew that it was her quest to unite the two sides of Elder. She had lectured the older wolf many times before in my presence, and I doubt she stopped when I left the room. She was quite persistent.

"And she'll be disappointed if I don't send anyone?" Micco guessed. I thought the same thing. "I'll have to think about this. Right now, the women and children don't seem to be affected, but I can't send people off if I think they might have a sickness they can spread. I'll wait until closer to the festival to decide what to do. Right now, I have to find a solution for the wolves. I have to protect those that are still healthy. I can't afford for anyone else to get sick, or we could become a problem."

"Have you asked Red for help?"

Micco looked sheepishly across the room to the door and shook his head. There was a faint scratching noise.

"I didn't want to bother her," Micco admitted. "She's so busy, and I thought it was just men being lazy wolves. I didn't know it would get worse. Now it's so bad I can't leave my people alone."

Micco opened the door, and Nikkan came into the room still in his wolf form.

"Your father okay?" I asked him. The golden wolf nodded. Nikkan turned his head to Micco and nodded to him too. I looked at the old man that was wearing himself thin, trying to keep people safe from something that could all be in their heads.

"You don't think I'm telling the truth, but see for yourself. I'm not making this up," Micco said as he reached down to grab a bag before walking to the open doorway and out into the village.

I followed behind as he made his way through the closest huts. They were all mostly in working condition, but as we moved further away from Micco's hut, they were a bit more in disrepair. We finally stopped at a shelter that was on the very edge of the village. Large pieces of the roof were missing, and some of the mud for the walls had crumbled enough that there was candlelight shining through it.

"Stay out here, Nikkan," Micco ordered the wolf.

Nikkan sat down to wait.

"Nathan?" Micco called as he knocked on the door. He opened it up, and I stayed outside as the stench blew past me. Fresh air was defiantly needed inside that place.

"Micco?" a small voice rasped. "I told you to stay away."

There wasn't much force behind the voice, and I could see why. A man lay on what must have at one time been a bed. His eyes were sunk into his face like he hadn't eaten in a moon cycle, and his hair was in clumps. A threadbare blanket covered part of him, but he still shivered at the open door.

"What will the village do if you get sick?" the man

whispered, not opening his eyes as he talked.

"As they always do, friend, choose a new leader," Micco replied kindly. He sat the bag down that he brought from his house. Carefully he opened the bag to pull out a small loaf of bread. Micco broke it in half and handed both halves to the sick man.

"You don't need to bring me that," Nathan told Micco. "This would be over a lot quicker if you'd just let me die."

"Not today, old friend. Not today." Micco pushed the man's hands to his mouth. The withered old man, Nathan, took a small bite.

"What brings you here today?"

"I brought a friend," Micco explained, and the man turned to face me. I realized that I'd thought his eyes were closed, but he was actually squinting to see me. A wolf squinting was a new one. Wolves had perfect vision in wolf or human form. "Can you tell him about your night?"

Nathan nodded as he swallowed his meager bite of bread.

"Last night was the same as the night before and the night before that. It has been over a moon cycle of the same thing. My only reprieve was the night the moon was gone. I'd give anything to have more black nights like that one." The man nibbled on the bread again. He took his time chewing before he swallowed again. "I can feel the change coming, but I can't stop it. The moon calls to me too strongly. The first few times, I was able to fight it, but not now. I change at its call, and I lose me. In the morning, I wake with blood on me but no idea where it's from or what I killed. My wolf has complete control. And then, I'm weak. My human body is shutting down. The only thing keeping me alive is

Micco."

"Get some rest, old friend," Micco said as he ushered me out of the hut. "As you can see, we aren't pretending about this. I thought he was and regret not helping him sooner. Something is going on with the wolves, and I think we need help."

I nodded.

"You need to talk to Red for us," Micco continued. "I can't keep patrolling the border at night time. I have to find a permanent solution for keeping the rest of the wolves safe. When these wolves run out food, I fear they might attack the humans next, whether is it a wolf or a tree human."

I still didn't understand what it meant, but the wolves were sick. Micco needed help, and Red needed to know what was going on. As much as I didn't want to, I needed to head back to the tree village that hadn't wanted me there since I was a kid. It was time to head home.

28TH FEBRUARY

I headed into Azren on my own. The run would take most of the morning. It was strange to run through the woods without my wolf companion, but Nikkan hated the tree villages. They looked at me as an outsider and suspicious, but him, he was the enemy. He promised to be at my place when I returned, which probably meant he was going to be off causing trouble. I hated being in debt to Red as she paid off the farmers that Nikkan upset, but there wasn't much I could do. The wolf wanted to hunt, and unless I was there to stop him, he would be out hunting anything he could find.

The tree villages of Elder were a sight to behold. While we didn't trade with neighboring kingdoms and did everything on our own, but that didn't mean we were backward, as many travelers had told us they thought we would be. They pictured a rustic uncivilized place with no cities or technology. We had technology, just not the same as other places. Our technology involved pulling people into trees, getting running water into a village many oak saplings off the ground, and heating a place made entirely out of wood. Trust me, the people of Elder knew how to create.

The ingenuity of the tree people of Elder amazed me as a kid, and it still did. Until Red broke the curse eighteen winters ago, most people in the woods lived where the wolves couldn't get them up in the trees, rarely if ever setting foot on the ground. It sounded impossible to believe, but whole generations had grown up without once touching the ground. People would be assigned to do the running to the farms in the southern half of the kingdom, but only those people ever came down. The rest of them stayed where no wolves could eat or infect them.

Elder tree people had built whole cities in the trees. Their wooden homes ranged from mostly two to four levels, which connected to the homes and trees around them. Bridges connected trees and homes, and platforms were common meeting places between dwellings. With an abundance of wood, there was plenty to build with. Every house had an emergency escape route, but to go up and into the city, you had to go to specific points of entry. Until Red defeated the curse, the ways up and down were guarded, but now the guard points weren't manned. People were free to come and go as they pleased, which meant the tree village of Azren prospered all the more.

Most tree people of Elder chose to remain in the trees

even without the threat of wolves. They found comfort in the trees, and it was all they really needed. Red had a tree residence, and her office was in the trees, but she also had a small home on the ground. The cottage she owned was within sight of the tree city, strategically placed there eighteen winters ago. She wanted them to see her live freely on the ground, unafraid of the world in the woods. While some people were encouraged to join her, most people did not. Change was hard.

As I drew closer to the magnificent sight of hundreds of homes in trees all strung together, I heard the clack of wooden staffs hitting against each other. I slowed my pace.

"Again," Red growled. I didn't need to see her to know what she was up to. That sound was one from my childhood, including the clacking noise and the grumpy Red.

The clacking started again. One, two, three, and a thump. A pause and then, it repeated. One, two, three, and a thump.

"Again," Red said the same thing. Whoever was with her was holding their own if it took Red three tries to get them off their feet. "Castiel could take more hits than that before his twelfth winter."

She was using me as motivation. How nice. With her super senses, I was more than sure she knew I was close enough to hear her.

Clack one, clack two, clack three, clack four, and an oomph this time.

Whoever she was training, they must be learning. Red was a hard teacher, but not impossible. She expected you to try your best and nothing less. I remember those days, not always fondly, but at the same time, I have to give her credit. I never once feared living on my own in the woods, and that had to be in part due to her. But I wasn't about to tell her that.

I stepped out into the clearing in front of Red's house. This was going to be convenient. I thought I'd have to go up to her office in the trees and hunt her down, but she was waiting for me on the ground.

"Did you want to join in?" Red asked me, though her back was to me.

Nothing got past Red. That was part of the problem when being raised with her. Children needed to explore and make mistakes. They also needed freedom to do things without their parents knowing every last little detail. I never had that. Even if it wasn't a villager tattling on me, somehow she always knew. Red had a sixth sense I'd never understand.

"Not today," I replied as Red offered the girl on the ground a hand to stand back up. The girl shook her chin-length dark hair.

"Go clean up. I'll meet you back at my office to go over the charts on the new land divisions," Red told the girl. She didn't look at me as she turned and went inside the cottage where she lived with Red.

I knew who that girl was and that she was holding her own pretty well against Red. I was the only person that could spar evenly with Red. Just another reason the tree people were scared of me.

"I see Sera is getting strong enough to take a couple blows," I told Red as she took both staffs and leaned them against her cottage. She didn't need to go clean up. I doubt she broke a sweat. Red turned and left the open space in front of her cottage to head toward the trees.

Red didn't reply or look back to see if I was following her. I was, of course, but she already knew that. She was walking toward the trees and her office. I walked up behind her as she tugged on the rope to get the platform down that would take us up to her office. Once we both stood on it, she gave a second tug, and the whole thing rose quite quickly. As I was used to it, I didn't wobble, but I had seen more than one newcomer fall off the lifts. It was better for them to use a ladder or the new stairs that had been installed this past summer, but that was too slow for Red.

We walked over the dozen walkways that led to her office. I followed her in silence and did my best to ignore the looks I received from the tree-dwellers we passed. Of course, they all nodded and raised a hand of respect to my mother, but when their eyes fell on me, they barely hid their looks of disgust. I tried to get over it as a kid, but I was more than happy I had moved out several winters ago. Beyond never feeling the dirt on your feet, the tree-dwellers had a bad attitude if you asked me. The city was amazing. The people, not so much.

Red opened the door to her office and finally turned around to motion me inside. I walked over and took the seat across from hers at the large desk she used for everything, and I mean everything. The wooden desk was longer than she was tall and filled with piles of paper and objects she was working on, collecting, or needed to oversee. There was a piece of wood carved to look like a horse. Even more wooden pieces dotted her desk, holding down papers. Red always kept busy.

"I take it you went to Micco and invited the wolves?"

She knew I'd never show my face so soon in Azren if I hadn't.

"Micco asked me to ask you for help," I started.

"Help? What in the world would he need help with?" Red replied, interrupting me.

It was better to start at the beginning. "The wolves are sick. Micco thought it was just some wolves drinking and forgetting when they turned, but it isn't. They are withering away in their human form, but their wolves are eating everything they can find. The wolves who aren't sick are finding it hard to find enough food. He doesn't know why they are sick, but they need help. Micco and I can't protect the safe zone between the wolves and the tree people on our own. He needs help figuring out how to get them better, and even more, he needs help keeping them from doing something that will start the wars all over again."

Red placed her fingers together and tapped them on her lips as she stared at me. Her eyes assessed me before she spoke again.

"Wolves can't get sick. It's part of the whole transformation thing. Their human bodies are close to invincible."

I had heard that growing up also, but I had seen it with my own eyes. That friend of Micco's wasn't faking it. He was wasting away.

"They are sick. I've seen it." I tried to plead with her but knew it was impossible. I didn't believe it when Micco told me, and I was in the wolf village with him. How was I supposed to convince her?

"The only time the wolves ever got sick was when the curse hit them. And I took care of that. The curse is gone. I broke it," Red replied. "I saw Micco a moon cycle ago. He was fine, and the village was fine. I don't know what you're playing at now, but I assure you, the curse is gone, and the wolves are fine. I bet Nikkan put them up to it. This is probably his way to get back at you."

While Nikkan did like to play jokes on me, I knew this one wasn't a joke. The wolves needed help. They needed Red's help.

"Micco asked me to ask you for help. Does that sound like a joke? I saw that they are sick, but it is him that is asking." She had to believe that.

"Micco has a soft spot for Nikkan."

That he did, but this wasn't Micco helping with a joke. Nikkan had always been a wild spirit and drove most people nuts, but Micco let him get away with it as a child growing up. In fact, most of the time, Micco was laughing along with Nikkan. If Nikkan didn't have a father that looked just like him, one might have thought Micco was his dad.

"This isn't a prank. I promise you that much."

Red still wasn't convinced.

"Go check it out," I begged. "See for yourself." If she saw it, she would be convinced. I was sure of that.

"I don't have time to run off to the wolf village. Not right now. I have Sera to train and a festival to plan. I'm a busy person. I can't go around checking on people playing jokes on others."

I couldn't help the huff that came out. I was sure to be scolded later by Red, but she was frustrating me. She didn't have time not to help them. If the wolves were starving and running out of food, they would come south to get it. Her tree people would be on the list of their next meals.

"I didn't believe them at first either, but I saw it. They are sick, and I don't think between Micco and me that we can protect the tree people much longer. What will happen to your peace then? Festivals can wait, but the wolves can't. They need help."

It was beyond frustrating. Red still didn't look persuaded. Anger built up inside of me. Why couldn't she see they were asking for help? Was she not hearing what I was saying?

"The curse is gone." The finality told me it was the end of discussion on that. She wasn't sending help, and she wasn't going to go see for herself. I kept my frustration bottled up as I wanted to yell or maybe hit something. Red was dooming everyone by being stubborn.

I wanted to be able to change her mind, but it was impossible. The Red was in charge, and she always let me know that. She didn't take orders like the rest of us. I could get down on my knees and grovel at her feet, but she wasn't going to change her mind.

"Fine," I told her as I stood and stalked out of the room.

Just before the door closed, she called to me.

"I expect to see you at the festival, and you should have at least one wolf with you."

I shook my head as the door slammed shut. She was impossible. Unless she decided something needed to be done, she wasn't doing it. Why couldn't she listen to me for once? She sent me to the wolves to invite them but then didn't trust what I reported. Why send me? Just because she said they weren't sick, wouldn't make them better. Sometimes she drove me nuts.

The trip back down to the ground was as quick as going up. I needed to get out of Azren and the trees. My urge to hit something was growing stronger, and if I did that in the city, I'd just get reprimanded by Red for scaring the poor defenseless tree-dwellers. What about the poor defenseless wolves that needed to be protected? What about the women and children? Not a single person living there chose to be a wolf, but no, Red wasn't sending them help. Wolves couldn't get sick. That was a lie, and I knew it.

Touching the ground brought me an immediate relief

at getting away from Red. I needed out of the trees and a run to clear my mind. I had a long run back to my home, and plenty of time to think once my frustration with Red passed. I'd have to find a solution to help Micco without her.

"If you think too hard you might pass out," a sing-song voice said to me as I passed my childhood home, Red's cottage.

"Not today, Sera," I told the dark-haired girl leaning against the cottage as if she was waiting for me.

"What, did dear ol' mommy hurt your feelings?" Sera continued to mock me.

Three winters ago, when I moved out of Red's cottage, Sera moved in. I had known her since she was little as we were only a few moon cycles apart in age, and Red liked to visit Sera and her parents at least once a season. I never knew why Red was always helping them out until Sera moved in. I had suspicions, but now that I could see Red aging, I knew what Sera was to her. She was the next Red.

"There are problems bigger in this world than you and me not getting along," I told her. And really, that was it.

Sera and I saw eye to eye about as much as I did with Red. If that was any indication, Sera was going to make a good Red someday. I just wasn't going to stick around to see it. Right now, I still needed some supplies from Red, so I worked for her and the tree dwellers, but I was slowly getting my own little patch of land and plants going. It would only take a few more winters, and the tree-dwellers would be my past.

"How about a round?" Sera tossed a staff to me. I caught it with one hand and threw it back to her.

"I don't have time."

Sera caught the staff with one hand and tossed it back to me. This time she didn't wait for me to say no and moved forward to attack. I caught it in midstride and had it up to protect my face as Sera swiped down at me. The crack of the two wooden staffs hitting each other sounded through the woods around us.

"I don't..." I started to say as she swung again.

Crack. Another hit I parried away from my legs this time.

"Have...." I tried to speak again, and yet again, she kept swinging at me.

I stopped a hit to my midsection and decided instead of talking to hit back. Two quick hits in a row, and she dodged them. As I raised my staff for the third blow, she was countering with her own. I rolled out of the way and let her hit the dirt, knowing the hard ground would vibrate up into her hands. If I didn't know better, I would guess the slight wetness at the corner of her eyes were tears, but that would mean she hit the ground harder than I was expecting. With a couple more jabs to keep her moving, I made my own signature move, not something Red taught me, to knock the staff from her hand. Sera fought exactly like Red. I'd had to make up my own moves to stand eye to eye with my mother, and it made me a stronger fighter. Sera quickly placed both of her hands on the top of her head.

"I surrender," she called out before I could land a hit on her. Not that I was planning to hit an unarmed girl.

I tossed my staff beside hers as I huffed a bit. I hadn't practiced in several moon cycles. Nikkan wasn't a fan of fighting with weapons. He preferred to rip people apart with his wolf teeth. And it didn't help that not too long ago I had run all the way to Azren either.

Sera sat down and leaned against the cottage she

now called home.

"Feel better?" she asked.

I slid down the wall to sit beside her.

"A little," I admitted. I actually did. My anger to punch something was gone, but my motivation to help the wolves wasn't. I was going to go home and get some sleep before heading off to see Micco and figure out what I could do to help him, even if Red wouldn't.

"Good," Sera replied and smiled at me. "I'd hate for you to have to take out your anger on any poor innocent trees on your run home."

"I wouldn't do that," I responded quickly, though actually, I would.

Sera raised an eyebrow at me but didn't call my bluff.

"How is it possible that you two always fight?" Sera pondered.

I pushed myself back up. That was my cue to leave. Sera and I had known each other most of our lives, but I found we could only tolerate each other in little bursts. Basically, she was the annoying little sister I never had nor wanted. But as irritating as she got, she had a good heart. She would make a good Red someday.

"I gotta get back to Nikkan."

Sera rolled her eyes at me.

"Someday, we're going to have a real conversation," she called to me as I began to run.

I didn't look back as she spoke but upped my pace so she couldn't get out anything more. She was always ready to give me advice I didn't need. Not Red yet, but playing the role perfectly. As I ran deeper into the trees, I turned to give her one last look. She was still sitting against the house, staring at me. I nodded before I turned back and disappeared from her view.

Sera was a complicated person. We didn't always

see eye to eye; that was more than an understatement. Most of the time, we fought over everything. But we both understood each other. She didn't choose her future. Red said she was moving into her cottage, so that's what Sera did. Red said we train, so Sera trained. Red told her to do everything. Her life was chosen for her, just as mine was chosen for me. It would've been easier to be just a tree person or a wolf. But I was stuck outside of it all and always would be. She could understand that feeling more than ever as the next Red; she was never just an ordinary tree person. She would always be different.

The trees brushed past me as I picked up my pace to a full run. It would take a while to get home, but it was quicker at the pace I was going. I was just a kid when I realized I could run faster and longer than most my age, but I didn't understand why. Now I was thankful I could so that I didn't have to ride a horse like the others in Elders when they had a far distance to travel. I knew how to ride a horse, but riding another animal just felt odd to me.

Usually, I would've taken my time and enjoyed the run. If I hadn't run into Sera, I probably would have been targeting unsuspecting trees to hit, but I didn't need to let out any anger now. I was past that and moving onto helping the wolves. Even if Red didn't want to send help, I was going back to the wolf village tomorrow to see what I could do.

The sun began to dip in the sky, and I knew night was coming. I made my run loop a bit east to cover my typical afternoon path I'd run to keep the safe zone safe. Unlike the day before, I kept a closer eye on the woods around me. Micco said they were transforming with the moon, but I didn't want to take any chances. A stray, sick wolf was nothing to mess around with.

As darkness descended on the woods, I kept up my pace to finish my loop and make it home. Nothing was out of the ordinary for the forest. It was still full of life. I couldn't understand how the sick wolves could be so hungry, but it did mean one thing. They would start traveling more if there was food here and not by their home. I didn't want them closer to me as that meant closer to the tree villages.

It wasn't my job to keep the tree people safe, even if Red had ordered the patrols. What I was doing was keeping the wolves safe as I knew the first time a wolf bit a tree human, they would be back at war. Tree people against wolves. Innocent people got killed in wars, and my best friend happened to look just like what could be attacking the tree villages. I didn't want to lose the only family I had.

As the last of the sun faded and the moon shone in the sky, I could hear the howls. One....two....three.... four.... It wasn't good. They were closer than I would've liked. Nikkan threw open the door to my hut as I got closer.

"Get inside man before you attract the wolves."

I would have laughed at his statement being that he was a wolf himself, but I knew better than he did that they were closer than they had been in weeks. Without complaint, I ran straight into my hut, and he closed the door behind me. Scraping on the floor told me without turning around that he had pulled the couch in front of the door. Nikkan was scared, which meant this was a bigger problem than even I knew.

29TH FEBRUARY

The sun was barely up when I woke the next morning, ready to go help the wolves. I didn't want to be the bearer of bad news that Red wasn't going to help, but there wasn't anything I could do to change that. Red had made her choice, and I'd have to find another way. If she wasn't going to protect the wolves from whatever disease was spreading through them, I was. They weren't just monsters like the tree people still remembered them. They were men, women, and children. They were families. And most importantly, they were human.

"You should move back with Red," Nikkan said from where he sat on the floor. He had spent the night in his human form, waiting to have to fight the pack of crazy wolves he was sure was coming. He would fight in his wolf form, but the wolf couldn't open doors or windows.

"Not going to happen," I replied as I searched for a shirt.

"The trees are the safest place," Nikkan continued. "The wolves will come closer each night. We both know that. They will go wherever they need to go to find food. It isn't safe for you to stay here."

I smiled at him. "I'll be fine. I always have Essie."

Nikkan shook his head. My mother had brought back new guns from one of her trips to another kingdom. I had no idea what she'd traded, but the tree people had a stock of firearms and ammunition. She'd insisted I take one with me when I moved out, but it was so pointless. The thing was tucked away and never came out of the box it was in. I spent most of my time running through the woods or doing chores outside. I didn't have time to carry and load a gun. The wolves weren't given guns, so to keep it a secret, Nikkan and I named my gun Essie.

After finally finding my shirt, I went over to the lone cupboard in my house and pulled out two bowls. There was breakfast on the stove. I could smell that Nikkan had already been cooking before I woke.

"Did you get any sleep at all?" I asked. I had slept. If a wolf did get close to the house, they weren't getting in without making enough noise to wake us, so I didn't see the point in staying up as Nikkan most likely did.

Nikkan shrugged as he stood to help me dish up the eggs that were cooking on the stovetop.

"Their howls make my wolf side restless. It was better to be human. And I would've slept if someone wasn't snoring so much." Nikkan pushed me out of the way as I filled the two bowls. He took one from me and went over to my small table to set his food down.

"Snoring? I don't snore."

Nikkan rolled his eyes at me.

"At least, not as loud as your wolf." And that much had to be true. I couldn't imagine anything snoring as loud as my golden wolf friend.

"Wolves don't snore." Nikkan grabbed a spoon and tossed it to me. I caught it before it hit the stove.

"I assure you, they do."

Nikkan was too busy scarfing down his food to respond. Half his eggs were already gone.

"You know," I continued since he was too busy to talk. "If you'd stop upsetting the farmers around here, I might be able to trade and get chickens of our own sometimes, and you wouldn't have to steal eggs."

I knew precisely where breakfast came from. Now, Nikkan pretended like his mouth being too full was the reason he couldn't respond. He seemed to keep our cupboards stocked with food, but less than half of that came from Red as a trade for my service of keeping track of the woods. Nikkan seemed to bring home as much as Red did. I asked once where he got the food, but since I figured he was never going to tell me the truth, I quit asking.

As I scarfed down my own eggs, Nikkan was completely done with his and already cleaning up the last of the ones in the pan on the stove.

"So, what's the plan for today?"

I took the last bite. We weren't slow eaters. It was probably unhealthy or something, but we had stuff to get done.

"I'm hoping to go to the wolves and see what Micco has planned. You know how he is. He doesn't wait for help but starts by helping himself. There's got to be something we can do."

Nikkan nodded.

"But I still don't like you going to the wolves. Right now, you don't have to live with feeling the call of the moon or having a split personality because there's a wolf inside you that wants out. No matter if Red stopped the curse, the real curse is being a wolf in the first place. You can't undo that. I don't know a single person that wishes to be a wolf, and you're putting yourself at risk being around rogue wolves. I think you should go back and talk to Red some more and see if you can convince her by staying there. It isn't safe in the woods."

It never was, but for some reason, I knew it was the place for me. The last few moon cycles that feeling had been growing. Every plant and animal in the woods was familiar. I could hear animals far away or smell a plant that was hidden from anyone's view. I could picture each animal in the forest down to the pattern on their fingers or toes. Everything was clearer in nature, and I couldn't imagine moving back into the trees. Nature was speaking to me, and I knew what it was saying. The wolves never fully accepted me, but they still felt like home.

"How about I promise that we don't stay there unless there's a safe place for me to be. Otherwise, we come back here and block the door again." It was the only deal I could offer.

Nikkan looked like he was debating it, but I knew he'd agree. The wolves were his family, and he knew we needed to help them any way we could.

"On your word?"

"On my word," I promised him.

"Fine," Nikkan conceded.

I grinned at him. I knew he'd give in as I stood at the door and waited for him to join me in moving the couch back to the middle of the room. Nikkan came over and picked up the opposite end of the couch, and we got it back in its place easily.

With the morning light shining on the windows to our little home's doorway, I opened the door. The glare kept me from seeing as I stepped out and tripped over something on the ground.

"Micco?" Nikkan said from inside the house.

I turned on the ground and found the older man was sprawled in front of my doorway, not moving. I pushed to my feet and hurried back to where Nikkan was slowly turning the wolf leader over.

Dried blood covered his body. I was too busy smelling the eggs to have recognized the scent of blood earlier, but there was enough that both Nikkan and I should have opened the door as soon as we were awake.

"Micco?" I asked as I reached for a pulse. It was strong, and he was alive, just not awake.

"I'll fetch more water," Nikkan said as he left me alone with the older man.

Slowly, I looked the wolf leader over from head to toe. His clothing was torn, but not like he shifted with clothing on, more like someone attacked him while he was human. Micco, just like any other shifter, was stronger as a wolf. There was no way I was going to find a wolf attacked in human form unless he had been surprised. His exposed arms and legs were coated with blood, and flecks were in his graying hair. The scent smelled more like a wolf than human, so I suspected he fought back, giving as good as he got from whatever attacked him.

Nikkan returned with a fresh bucket of water. He took a rag and handed one to me as we started to wipe away the blood. I started with his leg closest to me. There was more red than flesh, but as I cleaned and dipped the cloth back in the water, I could see there wasn't much of an injury. I had no idea why he wasn't stirring.

"What happened last night?" I asked. Had I slept through all this? Micco must have either used up all his energy and was passed out, or he had to have hit his head. The water was cold enough to wake anyone.

"I don't know," Nikkan replied as he wiped more blood away. So far, I only found minor scratches that were already healing under all the blood. "I was awake most of the night, but I never heard any fighting going on."

It was slow going to get through the layers of blood. The bucket of water was becoming a deeper red with each rinse. Nikkan didn't speak further as we worked to get the wolf leader cleaned up. Each time I started on a new spot, I hoped we weren't going to find an unhealable wound. The wolves and Red needed Micco. He was the strongest and had kept the village running through all the changes over the past twenty winters. There was no one to replace him. I wiped away more blood with the cold water as it finally shocked the older man into at least a little consciousness.

"Mmmmm," Micco mumbled, stirring a bit but not wholly waking.

Nikkan threw his rag in the water and moved to hover over Micco.

"Micco?" Nikkan said as he tapped his leader's face. "Waking up finally?"

Micco opened his eyes just a slit and looked at Nikkan. He groaned as he moved his arm to push Nikkan out of his face. Nikkan moved, though I was more than certain the older man didn't actually push Nikkan enough to move him.

"Stop shouting," Micco grumbled.

Pushing up, I sat back on my feet rather than kneeling before I reached over and pushed Nikkan back too. I could see the worry in my friend's eyes. He moved to lean in closer a second time, but I held my hand out to Nikkan. Everything we cleaned showed that Micco was going to be okay.

"Help me get him inside," I told my friend, who still stared at Micco with worry all over his face.

I didn't blame Nikkan. Micco was the leader of the wolf village because he was the strongest. One thing you never wanted to see was the strongest looking weak like he did now. It would take super strength to defeat Micco, or maybe the wolves that were sick were stronger than ordinary wolves when they were in their lupine form. That was going to be more than a bit of a problem. Infected wolves with no recollection or control of what they were doing were one problem. Sick wolves stronger than the alpha was an even bigger problem. Red should have listened to me. This was a problem the whole kingdom of Elder was going to have to face.

Nikkan took one side, and I took the other as we helped Micco to stand and then hobble into my home. We set him down at the table, and Nikkan hurried back into the kitchen to get some food for him. Micco sighed as he sat down.

"Are you okay, or do I need to go get Red?" I asked.

Micco shook his head as he accepted the glass of water from Nikkan. He took a sip before talking.

"She's not here with you, so I take it that means she's not helping," Micco deduced, his voice more raspy than usual.

He was right, but I hated to tell him that. I just nodded as I couldn't think of any words to explain.

Micco nodded back to me, and his encouragement brought my words back.

"She doesn't think anything is wrong. She's planning this festival and thinks it will bring everyone together. She sent me away." I shrugged. Micco knew her well enough to know there wasn't anything I could say to change her mind at this point.

Micco nodded at me. "Don't blame yourself, boy. This is my own doing. I should have been honest with her on her last visit. I should have told her the truth."

I wasn't sure I'd have done any different if I was in his shoes. I didn't believe him when he first told me. It would've taken time actually to see the problem.

"I tried," I began, but Micco held up his hand to stop me from talking.

"I've known Red longer than you've been alive. She was my best friend's girl. She's strong-willed, and once she sets her mind to something, she's a little more focused than she should be. This festival isn't anything new. She's been wanting to do it for over ten winters now. Since she defeated the curse, she'd had one goal, to bring the wolves and tree people together. I get that she can't stop now to see what is happening." Micco took the food Nikkan brought him and began to eat. "Red isn't mean or careless. She's just too focused on the festival."

Micco ate slowly. It was like it hurt him to move any muscle, including his jaw. Piece by piece, bite by bite, he got more in him. Every piece of food seemed to give him the energy he was needing.

"What happened last night?" I asked. I didn't want to interrupt his meal, but if the state of him at my doorway was any indication, we needed to work fast to do something to stop the sickness that was spreading in the wolf villages.

Micco took another bite of bread and washed it down with the water Nikkan refilled for him.

"Remember Nathan? I was doing as I have been every night for the past two moons, watching over him. He doesn't have any family left to take care of him, and most of the wolves are now getting too scared to go near the sick wolves at night. They don't want to catch whatever is going around."

Catch? I was going to have to ask more, but I didn't want to interrupt him.

"As in all the previous nights, Nathan transformed at soon as he saw the moon. His wolf took off into the night, and I followed in my human form. We suspect that you can only catch the disease wolf to wolf, so I couldn't chance transforming until we know for sure."

I raised an eye at Nikkan. He loved his wolf form, but he might be human a bit more often now if that was the case.

"Nathan took off into the woods like he had every time. I tracked him for most of the night. He wasn't making any sense, going one direction and then another. I hadn't any idea where he was going, but I began to notice he hadn't caught any food. The woods are getting thin by the village because all the sick wolves can't help how much they are eating, but it almost seems like the animals know something is wrong and are fleeing from us too. Whatever the case, the wolf Nathan had to find somewhere new to hunt, and that's when he turned south. I chased him and used a few short cuts to cut him off. He was heading for the tree villages. I have no idea why or how he could tell there was life that way, but he knew."

Micco stopped his story to take another big bite of

bread. This time, he chewed slower before washing it down.

"I was able to stop him, but I had to fight him to do so. Wolf against human is never a fair fight. I didn't have the energy to make it back to the village and knew your house was nearby. I kind of hoped your mother would be here, and I could speak to her, but I understand."

Micco took the dried meat from Nikkan, who continued to feed his leader. Wolves could take a lot of injuries and stay alive, but it took food to make them heal quickly. If we wanted to be able to help Micco head back home, then he needed to feed and heal.

"I'm sorry she's not here," I told Micco. And I truly was. If she had seen Micco as beat up as we found him, she probably would have believed me finally.

"Is it still just the same ones?" Nikkan asked. Micco nodded, and Nikkan relaxed a little bit.

"Your father sent Nadia and Sander to your uncle's place. Right now, only two of the three villages are infected, and it's safe there. Your uncle is going to keep all the children isolated and away from the infected, even going to any of the islands if needed."

Nikkan looked more relieved to hear that his little sister and brother were somewhere safe from the sickness.

"Your uncle is doing well. I think they are better off since their main source of meat is fish, and the sick wolves can't deplete their food."

"Will everyone not sick move up there too then?" I asked. It would be hard to support two villages in one place, but it was better than being with the sick wolves who ate all the food.

"No. I let the children leave if their parents weren't infected, but they can't handle the whole city moving there. They'll run out of food. And almost a quarter of the children stayed behind since the males are the ones getting sick. There's no one to work or take care of things, so some refused to leave. I would've made them leave, but I did the same as a kid."

"Then what do we do?" I needed to help. At least the children were safe, but there were still completely innocent people at the village.

"We looked for the old cages they used twenty moons ago to cage up the sick males. We found enough for the sick wolves we have now, but if we have any more, we don't have a way to contain them. We've decided to build a wall around the village." Micco looked out the window in my small kitchen. He wasn't proud of the choice, but it was his choice.

"But that means anyone left will be exposed to the sickness every night. And if the wolves are sick, then they might attack their own family as food." Nikkan was more than a little worried about his family. I didn't blame him. This was a sickness without any explanation or way to heal.

"What choice do we have?" Micco replied to Nikkan.

Reality set in. There wasn't a right solution. The wolf villages were sacrificing themselves to save their loved ones but even more, to protect the people of Elder. I doubted the tree people of Elder would understand the sacrifice these people were making.

"But then they will catch the sickness too." Nikkan slammed his hand on my small table.

"Man, what'd that table ever do to you?"

I pointed to the crack beneath his hand to try to lighten the mood. It wasn't like Micco was forcing his people to do this. I was more than confident this was the choice of the villagers. Micco wasn't a tyrant. He was a fair leader.

"We might," Micco replied to Nikkan. "But that's the chance we have to take. We can't go back to how it was twenty winters ago. We can't go back to being killers that the whole world feared. We can't go back to fearing ourselves."

He had Nikkan there. The whole of Elder feared the wolves before. They were ruthless killers that would attack and eat anything that had a heartbeat. Many men, women, and children died at the hands of the curse. Even more, they were turned into the beast that forced the tree people to move into the trees. If word got to the people of Elder that the wolves were going bad again, they would never be trusted. All Red was working for would be lost.

"We need your help," Micco looked to Nikkan and then to me. "All the wolves able to help are meeting at the village to begin making the wall."

"The village is huge. How can you really build a wall to contain it? And what will you do once there's a wall? How will you eat? How will you live?" Nikkan was full of questions.

"I had hoped Red would help me with all the details, but we will just have to figure it out. For now, we need to protect the people of Elder from the sick wolves. And we need to do it now. We can't wait for Red to understand and believe us. We need to work now as quickly as we can to get it done. Without it, it will be back to how it always was. We will be the bad guys of the forest and hunted like the animals we turn into at the rising of the moon. I don't want that life for anyone, wolf or not. Please help us."

I didn't like the idea of caging up the wolves. I couldn't imagine Nikkan in a cage, but then again, I couldn't imagine him not being himself in his wolf form. I looked at the friend leaning against the wall across from me. He didn't like what he was hearing, but he was logical. Something had to be done, and Micco was presenting a good case.

"We will help," Nikkan replied firmly. Micco nodded to him and then to me.

"Stay here and regain your strength today," I told Micco. The older man nodded his head.

"We will head to the village at first light tomorrow," Nikkan replied, giving me the stare that looked like a challenge.

We were needed sooner than that, but I knew he was more than a little concerned about my safety. It was going to take a while of feeding Micco to get him back to full strength, and by the time we made it to the village, it wouldn't give us an entire afternoon to work before we'd have to leave to get far enough away to stay safe. We could wait another day.

I nodded to Nikkan. I didn't want to cage my friends, but it had to be done. We had to keep Elder safe.

1ST MARCH

Nikkan and I left at first light to make our run to the wolf village. Micco had taken most of the day to recover the day before with us constantly feeding him. He'd been hungrier than he looked. All of the non-sick wolves were slowly starving, and that played a role in his recovery taking longer than anyone wanted. I was a bit worried when he was headed back after such a brutal fight, but he looked so much better. We had a short afternoon to catch as much as we could for food to bring with us to the village.

By the time we approached the wolf village, I could tell everyone was already in full swing on making the fence. I could hear the noise of workers long before we made it close enough to see anything. Nikkan had run most of the way as a wolf and now had to transform back to work.

"I really don't know how you wear these things day after day," Nikkan complained about his pants. That was all he was going to put on. It didn't matter that it was barely warm enough to go without a winter coat; he was just in a pair of pants with no shirt or shoes.

"I don't know how you go naked day after day," I answered back.

"Ewe man, you didn't need to put thoughts of you going naked in my mind," Nikkan answered as we approached the village. "Fine. We're even."

I laughed. I hadn't intended that when I said it, but I got how he took it that way.

People were everywhere as we came closer, but no one paid us any mind. They continued on working. Men, women, and even the children that stayed behind were doing something. Near the edge, Micco talked to a group of men. He turned as he sensed our approach.

"Good. You made it," he called to us.

"Ready to work." I held my hand up as a gesture of greeting to the wolves with Micco. Most nodded or grunted in return as they spread out in different directions. I handed our small kills to one of them and turned back to Micco.

"Nikkan, we could use your strength cutting trees," Micco waved for Nikkan to follow one of the guys as they left. Nikkan nodded and left me standing with the wolf leader.

Since I wasn't a wolf, I didn't exactly have the same super strength of the rest of the people in town, though my strength was stronger than a tree person. I was stronger than average, just nothing compared to a wolf. Cutting the trees down was going to take massive endurance on my part to keep up as they chopped quickly. I might be able to do a few, but I wouldn't be able to keep pace with the wolves.

Nikkan always talked about being a wolf as something not to wish on anyone, but it was apparent, he loved being a wolf, and the perk of super strength and fast healing didn't sound too bad either.

"I'll start you on digging the trenches," Micco said, waving to the group of mostly women that were already digging a long hole that was deeper than a sapling is tall.

I nodded and turned to leave, but Micco kept talking.

"Two more succumbed last night to the moon."

He was barely talking loud enough for me to hear standing right next to him. The pounding of the trees into the already dug portion of the ditch was loud enough to keep most people from hearing him. Our conversation was almost private.

"Do you have enough room? Can they be put in the cages?"

Micco nodded as he looked at the people working as fast and hard as they could. The wolves were tired before this started but somehow found some reserve vigor to do this. There was a sense of urgency but more so a sense of community. It needed to get done, and they all knew that. I might not be one of them, but I wanted to help them badly. I didn't want any of the wolves to be a target for the rest of Elder to hunt.

"I just don't know if we can work fast enough. It took over a new moon cycle for the first two people to break to the call of the moon, but these last two have only been sick for less than six moons. At this rate, more than half of my camp will be sick by the end of the next moon cycle. I don't know if we're doing enough."

"You can't look at what might happen. You have to look at what we can do now. And right now, I can work. We are going to make this wall and keep Elder safe. And once Elder is safe, we will convince Red to help us find a cure. The wolves won't be the enemy, and they will get better. Every sickness has a cure."

Micco looked at the working women and nodded, but not like he agreed. He was more likely resigned to the fact that there was nothing else we could do. For the time being, we needed to fence in the wolves.

"I'll dig, and you will see. We'll have everyone protected in no time."

I reached over and patted him on then back. He was taking this hard, and I didn't blame him. He was responsible for all of the wolves. Not waiting for Micco to respond, I went over to the closest group of people working and picked up a shovel. It was time to get working.

I didn't speak to the people around me as I began to dig but, instead, lost myself in my own thoughts.

This wasn't fair. The wolves were always the bad guys. No one chose to be a wolf. No one wanted to be sick. Someone had to know how to cure them. Why did they keep being the ones that were getting hurt? I was angry for the wolves and mad for the people of Elder. The curse had lasted many generations, yet it wasn't a full generation since Red saved everyone. Why couldn't the wolves have more time being free of being the bad guys? The anger bubbled inside of me. It wasn't fair, and I didn't have the slightest idea how to make it fair. I hit the ground hard with my shovel and lifted more dirt out of the way, making my trench longer.

It was healing to just dig in the dirt. I took an end of the trench and could go at my own pace, no need to wait for someone beside me. I could dig as fast as I wanted. I might not have been a wolf, but that didn't mean I was slow by any means. And my anger fueled me to work harder.

The rhythm of digging took over. Push down into the ground. Give a little tug. Push the dirt up and toss it to the side. Repeat and keep going. Make the trench longer. Protect the wolves by making the wall. Mind-numbing, but so needed.

I wasn't alive when the curse was in effect all those winters ago, but there were a lot of people that were. Both wolves and tree people of Elder spoke of that time often to the kids as we grew up. They wanted us to know what it was like as if we would never have to face a hardship in our lives. Well, they were wrong. Something was going on with the wolves now, and it wasn't anything anyone was prepared for. Red had supposedly saved us all, including the wolves, but now there was something wrong.

Maybe that was the problem. Red thought she had saved everyone, and there would only be a happily ever after. But this was real life. Real life had bumps and turns, and it was never the same. Things changed all the time. I got that Red wanted the change to be the people of Elder getting along, but that was making her blind to the change that was really happening around her. She couldn't see the truth of the wolves right now.

I kept digging and being lost in my own thoughts. There was no need to talk as we worked because we all knew what needed to be done, and it needed to be done yesterday. The women around me worked just as hard as I did with the scooping of dirt to clear a path for the trees that would make up the fence.

I didn't want to think like Micco, but what was going

to happen if we couldn't contain the sickness and sick wolves? Would my mother be the Red that everyone talked about? The famed wolf hunter? Would she hunt the wolves that did nothing wrong but be born? They couldn't help what they were any more than she could help that she was the Red. Would she hunt and kill the people she was trying so hard to get accepted? Would she hunt Nikkan?

Part of me knew the truth. She'd have to. If the wolves went crazy and started to attack people, then she'd have to hunt them. I just couldn't picture her hunting Nikkan. He was a pain in the butt most of the time, but even if he was a crazy wolf when the moon cast its power over the night, Nikkan would still be Nikkan when the sun rose.

Before I realized it, people were breaking off from work to eat. Small groups sat on the ground, exhausted from working and hungry due to days of not eating enough and now tiring work.

"Get some food," Micco told me. "I was able to catch more food on my walk home last night, so we have stew for everyone today." Micco waved to the fire that was just inside the village line we were making with the digging. Nikkan was back, and I caught up to him in line.

"Working hard?" Nikkan looked down at my shirt.

I looked down too. I was drenched with sweat. Spring was close enough that I was overheating a bit.

"Guess so."

Nikkan got to the front of the line and took the bowl handed to him. I was up next and took the next dish. Following Nikkan, we wove out the way a little bit away from the crowd and found a place to sit in the grass. The cold ground was a nice reprieve to the hard work of digging.

"Was your father cutting trees too?" I asked between bites of stew.

I hadn't seen anyone while I worked; I didn't exactly look around. The only place I had to look was the ground.

"Yeah, they told me after lunch I'm to help install the trees we already cut and brought back."

I nodded as I chewed. The stew was filled with chunks of meat and fresh vegetables. It seemed like Micco must have had plenty of energy for his walk back to the village after being at my house nearly dead the day before.

"Did you talk to Grace at all?" Nikkan asked as he looked past me.

I turned around to see the auburn-haired wolf girl turn away from our stares and blush.

"I didn't see her working," I replied as I turned back to Nikkan.

Nikkan gave me a look like I was stupid.

"Really, man." I held up one hand in surrender while still holding my stew. "I didn't see her. Honestly. I don't even know where she was working."

"She was like only a sapling away from you as you worked."

I shrugged. That could have been possible, but I was concentrating on the dirt and digging a hole in the ground. I really hadn't seen her.

"So, you didn't get a chance to tell her how great I am?" Nikkan was trying to look around me again to look at her.

"No, and I told you I wouldn't. You need to do that yourself."

Nikkan pulled back in front of me.

"If you'd just get her to see ..."

I rolled my eyes at him. "I'm not a matchmaker."

"But you could be." Nikkan grinned at me. No way was I falling for his tricks. Nikkan was good at that. He could get most people to do what he wanted by looks and words and maybe an eyebrow wiggle. I wasn't part of most people. Nikkan's persuasion wasn't going to work on me.

"You know if you take too much more time asking her out, someone else will, and then you won't have a chance."

Nikkan's face soured at my words.

"Then set me up with her. Come on, man. That's what friends are for."

I shook my head at him as I stood up and returned my bowl to the lady by the fire. I wasn't setting Nikkan up with anyone.

Nikkan followed behind me as I walked back to where I was working at the ditch. I picked up my shovel and moved to go back to my end.

"Um... hi," Nikkan said, his voice cracking a bit.

I paused at what I was doing and looked up. Grace was standing there on one side of me and Nikkan on the other. Her cheeks flamed red, but she stayed where she was. If it had been the reverse, I was pretty sure Nikkan would've run away.

"Micco said if we work in teams of three, we can put the cut trees into place," Grace explained quietly, her face still red, and her eyes glued to the dirt at her feet.

I looked over to my friend, and there was dead silence.

"Okay," I replied since it seemed like Nikkan had forgotten about his voice.

I studied the people on the other side of the fence

line. They had already placed at least five poles into the ground. It looked like it took at least two people to hold the cut tree in place, while the third person climbed up to tie the post to the one next to it. Lastly, dirt was filled in at the base to keep it in place. It looked simple enough.

"I take it, you climb while we hold?" I suggested. Grace looked at the ground and nodded.

As long as she did her job, I didn't care how shy she was. I had a harder time believing that Nikkan could do his job with her around, but since he wasn't complaining, I was going to agree for the both of us. I had already shoveled enough for one day. My back would be sore in the morning. This would be something different.

"Let's get the first one and see if we can do this," I said, walking towards the pile of fence posts. I knocked into Nikkan's shoulder to hopefully jolt him out of his gaze he had locked on Grace.

Nikkan startled back to reality and hurried after me. We picked out one of the posts, which was at least three saplings tall, tall enough a wolf wouldn't be jumping it. Nikkan took one end, and I took the other.

"You need to snap out of it if you plan to ask her out." He was too awestruck and tongue-tied. If he wanted to go on a date with Grace, he needed to make the move as she wasn't going to.

Nikkan just shook his head, like he had forgotten his words again. She scared him that much.

"Come on, man, if you don't. I know you'll regret it." How much more did he need? This was a perfect time.

Nikkan shook his head again as we stood up and carried the post back to where Grace waited.

With a flip of her red hair, Grace glanced at Nikkan

as we approached, but then looked away with the same red stained cheeks as before. These two were hopeless. Nikkan and I had known Grace since we were kids. It wasn't like they had never talked, but sometime over the past winter, they had begun this game of being shy. It was driving me nuts when it was just Nikkan and me, but more being around both of them was worse. At least they both could work while being shy.

We all concentrated and watched the other group near us work, and we tried to do the same. It took some practice to steady the post enough for Grace to scale it. But after a couple posts, we were working well enough we could talk. It was slow going to get either Nikkan or Grace to speak, and though I told Nikkan I wasn't going to play matchmaker, I had a plan to give him a chance to ask her out, and I could make Red happy at the same time.

"Did you hear that Red is having a festival in a couple nights," I tried to start the conversation where Nikkan could take over. I looked at him and wiggled my eyebrows as we held the post in place, and Grace was scooting back down.

"Really? I could use a festival right now," Grace replied to me. She was fine talking to me, but one look at Nikkan had her cheeks red. "Something to take our minds off all of this, you know? It's been ages since there was any fun here in the village."

"Glad to hear you say that," I replied as I reached for the shovel, and she balanced my side of the post in place as I shoveled dirt around it.

Nikkan was now facing Grace. The time was exactly perfect. She wanted to go to a festival, and I needed to bring a wolf or two. Bringing Nikkan and Grace would make my mother extremely happy. He stood there looking at any place but Grace and didn't say a word.

Nikkan let go of the post as soon as he could and started to stalk back over to the next post we had to grab. I dropped my shovel by Grace and followed him.

"What are you doing?" Nikkan whispered. He was angry.

"I'm setting you up," I replied. "Now, all you have to do is ask her to go with you. Red wants me to bring a wolf with me, and I figured I'd have to drag you along, but this way, I can take you both, and she'll be even happier."

All the color drained from Nikkan's face. "I can't ask her."

He reached down and picked up his end of the post. I stared at him.

"It was only lunchtime you were asking me to set you up."

"I changed my mind. I'm not ready." Nikkan stared at me, waiting for me to take my end. "We don't have time to be dating or having fun. We need to work on this wall and get it finished to keep everyone safe."

I had the urge to shake sense into him. There was no way possible I could spend the amount of time it was going to take to build this fence with him and Grace and all their awkwardness. He needed to grow up and just ask her out. It was obvious she liked him too. What was he waiting for? Not having time was just an excuse.

"Ask her out or someone else will." I was serious. Nikkan wasn't the only wolf that had noticed Grace. She was growing up. We weren't kids anymore. She was attracting more attention every day.

"No one would dare," Nikkan replied, puffing out his chest like he was something to be feared. Nikkan wasn't the strongest wolf our age, but he was pretty smart. He could probably outwit most of the wolves if he had to fight for her, but I wasn't about to tell him that.

"What if I ask her?"

Nikkan glared at me.

"If you don't ask her by the time this next post is finished, I will," I threatened. That's what Nikkan needed. He needed to be pushed.

Nikkan reached down and picked back up the post. Instead of waiting for me to grab my side, he used his wolf strength to haul it up to his shoulders and walked it back to Grace. Impress her with strength. That worked for me. The sooner those two finally got together, the better for everyone who had to deal with them.

"So, what's the festival about?" Grace asked as we steadied the post into the ground.

"Red wants to bring the wolves and tree humans together. She's invited both sides to come to it, and I'd bet it's on the ground," I explained. "Bring the wolves and tree humans together. It's her new big project. Well, old big project, but the festival is new."

"Wolves are really invited?" she asked with a big smile.

"Yes," I replied as she took ahold of the post and climbed.

"Ask her," I whispered to Nikkan. He only glared at me.

Without much of an effort, Grace scaled the post and was tying it to the next post. Once done, she scurried back down. I leaned down to grab the shovel but took my time. I kept glancing at Nikkan, but he ignored both me and Grace. If she noticed, she didn't say anything. Shovel by shovel, we got the post into place but still nothing from Nikkan.

"My mom wanted to be sure some of the village wolves

would come." I looked to Nikkan again. He seriously wasn't going to ask her. What was he waiting for?

Grace caught my look at Nikkan, and her cheeks reddened.

"Would you want to come?"

I spoke slowly, and still, Nikkan ignored us. How much more of a chance did the guy need? He had been pining over her forever.

Grace looked at Nikkan for some sort of assurance on how to respond, and yet he still didn't say a word. He was letting himself be beaten by his own fears. She wanted to go with him; I could tell, and anyone within twenty saplings could tell.

"That sounds like fun," Grace replied, turning back to me after no response from Nikkan.

Nikkan finally looked at us, and if looks could kill, then we would both be dead. I seemed to be more his focus than Grace, but he wasn't happy with either of us. After glaring at both of us, he turned and ran from us into the woods. It was only seconds when we heard the howl.

"Will he be okay?" Grace looked into the woods.

"He'll be fine," I replied. I'd have to find Micco and tell him I was heading home and would be back to help the next day, and then I had to chase down my friend. Why in the world didn't he ask Grace to go to the festival?

2ND MARCH

I got home late the night before. The sun had already set, and I heard the howls of the wolves that Micco had locked up. It still didn't feel safe to be in the woods. I was already up and planning to head back to help get the fence made. They were running out of room to cage the sick wolves, and soon they would be running free. Micco might have been able to stop one wolf from coming toward the tree village, but he was only one person. Even together, we would need help.

After working all day, it didn't seem like we got much done. I personally worked impossibly hard, but it was such a large area we needed to fence, and the fence had to be tough enough and tall enough to withstand a wolf. I felt a bit of Micco's dismay as I left and saw that we still had at least ten or more moons of work left for just part of the wolf villages, and there were two more to worry about. We were getting closer and closer to the wolves starting a war again with the tree people of Elder.

I was up early as usual and went about making tea for the morning. I grabbed a pot to boil water and set out two cups.

Nikkan was home when I made it back, and that was a bit of a relief. I secretly worried he was wandering around the woods, hurt from me asking Grace out. It wasn't like I liked her like he did, but I did need to bring at least one wolf with me to Red's festival. I was pretty sure it wasn't going to be Nikkan. And I really did think he was going to ask her out. I set him up perfectly. And then I could have brought two wolves, and Red would've been extra happy. Maybe happy enough to listen to me for a change. At least, I could wish that.

In the corner of the room, wolf Nikkan was still sleeping. There wasn't any snoring, so I had a feeling he was actually awake, but I pretended like he was asleep since he was pretending too.

After checking the cold box, I figured out that Nikkan must have eaten the rest of the eggs we had, along with most of the dried meat. There wasn't much left to eat for breakfast, so I'd have to hope for something on the way to the wolf village. I knew where there were some berries, and I'd be able to get some bread at the village. At least, the wolves weren't eating the crops they grew, just all the meat.

Without disturbing Nikkan, I opened the door to leave. I knew Nikkan, and he was going to take some time to sulk before he came around. I wasn't about to push it. Things would be back to normal once he got done being mad. I drank my tea and left his on the table.

"So that's it? You leave without an "I'm sorry?"

Nikkan was sitting in the corner where his wolf had been *sleeping*.

"I'm sorry? For what?"

If he had just asked Grace out to the festival, I wouldn't have had to.

"For asking out the girl I like," Nikkan spat at me. He stood up and marched over to where I was standing by the door. At least, he had pants on. It was hard to take seriously someone yelling at you without their pants on.

"I wasn't going to ask her out. You are the one that wanted me to set you up."

"The key being, I wanted you to set me up, not ask her out." Nikkan glared at me.

"I set you up perfectly. She wanted to go to the festival. All you had to do was ask."

Nikkan huffed. He knew I was right. I'd given him plenty of opportunity to ask.

"Ask her to go someplace we aren't welcome? Ask her to possibly go into a trap? Ask her to put herself in danger? Do you think I'd ever purposely put her in danger? Come on, man. Wake up. The wolves aren't welcome in the village, so why would I invite her?"

I had to bring someone. Red would be mad if no one showed up and even madder if I didn't support her ill-timed festival. I secretly hoped it meant I'd get a chance to talk to her one more time and see if she would change her mind. If this had been her goal for so long, maybe she'd be in a better mood.

"If you weren't welcome, why would Red ask you to come? Also, it didn't seem like Grace felt unwelcome."

I had him there. Grace was the one that wanted to

go.

Nikkan continued to glare at me as he paced around the room.

“You can’t make Grace into the bad guy here. She’s sheltered and has no idea what the tree people are like. She’s naïve, and you can’t use that against her. They hate wolves. Don’t pretend otherwise.”

Okay. The tree people of Elder didn’t like wolves, but that was more of a distrust thing after winters of the wolves terrorizing them. The wolves had no control, and the tree people had a reason to distrust the wolves. No one won in that scenario, and each side was justified in being wary of the other. But Red was in charge of the festival. She wasn’t going to let anything happen toeither the wolves or the tree people.

Nikkan stopped by the mug of hot water I left for him. He picked up the cup and threw it against the wall, shattering the pottery into pieces as he growled.

“Why can’t you ever listen to me.” His wolf was coming out a bit as his eyes flashed at me in slits. Nikkan closed his eyes and took a few deep breaths, calming the wolf within him. When he opened his eyes again, he was back to normal.

“You know nothing about her. Why would you ask her out? Are you going to marry her? Do you know her favorite color or what she likes to eat? Do you know anything about her? Sorry if I wasn’t ready to ask her out, but why would you? She doesn’t matter to you like she does to me. I bet you weren’t even nervous.”

I wasn’t nervous and had no idea how to explain it to him. Grace was just Grace, the girl we grew up with. There was nothing to be worried about. She loved to have a fun time, and she always got along with both of us. Why would I be nervous to ask her to the festival after she told us *she* wanted to go? Nikkan wasn't making any sense.

Nikkan marched over to me and stood only inches from my face.

"You asked my girl out."

"Exactly what I did. You had your chance." What would it take to get him to ask her himself finally? I wasn't his matchmaker.

Nikkan was now seething. It wasn't like I wanted to fight with him, but he didn't have an argument to stand behind. I asked Grace out after he had tons of chance to ask her. I was trying to help him, and this was the thanks I was getting from him. Not exactly how a best friend should be thanking another.

I had no idea how to motivate Nikkan to act on his feeling for Grace. It was beyond evident to everyone that they liked each other, and he asked me to set him up, but when I finally did, he didn't act. What was left for me to do?

"I liked her first," Nikkan spat at me.

My eyes bugged as I looked at him. I didn't like Grace that way and never would. This had nothing to do with liking. Did he really think I was the kind of friend that would steal my best friend's girlfriend? It showed how much he thought of me.

"How many chances do you need? If you sat around any longer, it could have been someone else besides me asking her out," I replied, still trying to make him see sense in all it. I wasn't trying to take his girl, that wasn't actually his girl because he didn't have the guts to ask her out.

"It doesn't matter how many chances. She's spoken for."

I couldn't help it. I had to stifle a laugh that wanted

out. His declarations were at odds with how he was acting, not a full day before.

Nikkan must have guessed that I wasn't taking him seriously as quick enough, a fist was flying through the air at me. I ducked and automatically responded with a punch of my own. I kept back my normal fighting strength and just did a quick jab to allow me to back up to the door.

"I don't want to fight you," I told Nikkan. A girl was never a reason to hit your friend.

"Grace belongs with a wolf," Nikkan glared at me. "Not some half-breed outsider."

His words were actually worse than a punch. It had always seemed like Nikkan didn't care about who or what I was. Tree or wolf, it didn't matter. I guess I was wrong.

Nikkan wasn't done after my hit. He didn't stop as he moved back and started to circle just like he would've done in wolf form. I was a little thankful he wasn't transforming. I considered going outside, but it was more likely he'd transform. I'd have to fight back for real if he was a wolf, and I knew I'd hurt him. Friend or not, I wasn't letting a wolf end my life or turn me into one of them.

"We don't have to do this," I told him one last time. We both knew I was stronger. I was trained to fight, and he wasn't. This was getting ridiculous.

"Then you should have thought about that before asking Grace out."

Part of me wanted to yell at him that I didn't care if I went out with Grace or not, but the rational part of me knew that there was no way I could show up at the festival without a wolf or Red would be yelling at me. And in a fight with either Red or Nikkan, I'd take my chances with Nikkan any day of the week.

As I turned to keep track of him, I didn't notice that Nikkan had stepped close enough to hit me. I felt the hit as I backed out of the way and into the door. I grabbed the handle of the door and pulled it back, knocking Nikkan back in the process. He lost his footing and tumbled out of the house.

"Man, what was that for? All I tried to do was help you, and this is the thanks I get?" I asked, my jaw was a little sore, but I missed the majority of the hit when I backed up.

"Thanks? Thanks for messing up my life?" Nikkan grumbled from the ground in front of my house. Nikkan stood and didn't dust himself off as he was back to staring daggers at me.

"Messing up your life? Really? You are crazy if you think that I messed up your life. You're the one that ran away to live here with me." And he had. He left the wolves because of all the pranks he had played had made almost everyone mad at him at some point. I was the only one that tolerated what he did, mainly because I was part of half of it.

Nikkan's eyes bulged as he slammed his mouth shut. His face turned a shade of red before he stalked off towards the trees. He stopped at the tree line.

"If you can't see how you screwed up, then I guess we can't be friends anymore. Friends don't steal the girl of their friend."

Nikkan ripped off his pants and transformed.

"I wasn't stealing anything. She wasn't yours, or anyone's yet. To steal her, that would mean you would have had to ask her out which, if you don't remember, you didn't do."

The wolf Nikkan had the glare down as much as

the human Nikkan. With a growl, the wolf went into the trees and ran from where I stood outside my house a bit winded from our argument. Nikkan was nuts if he thought I stole Grace. I was trying to help him out. That's the last time I'd let Nikkan talk me into any favor.

Friends don't steal the girl of their friend. If he had ever listened to me for once, he'd realize I didn't like Grace as he did. Obviously, he hadn't listened to anything I had said in the past few winters as he mooned over her. I wiped the side of my face and found a bit of blood. His punch must have split my lip against my teeth.

Nikkan was crazy if he thought I was taking Grace out because I liked her as he did. Anyone could see that Grace only had eyes for Nikkan. That was probably why no one else had asked her out yet. But obviously, Nikkan didn't see that.

Life was getting too complicated. I just wanted a simple life in the woods, alone. I could live off the land, do what I wanted, when I wanted, and I'd be happy.

I closed the door to my place and began my jog to the wolf village. They needed more help than I could provide, but I knew they'd take any help they could get. I just wished I could convince my mother and the tree people to help out. If everyone made a trip up to help, then it could be finished before any wolves were running around killing humans.

That had to be my goal. I couldn't let Nikkan distract me from what needed to get done. I needed to get the tree people to help the wolves. I needed to get Red to see that her help was needed, and there was a problem. No more pretending things were fine. Red had to come to the wolves and see they needed help.

I closed my eyes and just ran. I could feel the trees around me, and it was like I didn't need my sight. I was part of the forest. I could feel it. Part of me wanted to ask Nikkan if that was what it felt like to be a wolf, but of course, I couldn't do that.

The smells of the forest made the anger in me fade. Something about being surrounded by the towering pine trees that grew around me made everything seem less of a problem. These trees had been around for hundreds of winters. Nothing made them bend and break. They didn't need to worry about their friends or sickness plaguing animals. They just grew. I wanted to be a tree. I wanted to be free of the worry of the people around me, but it wasn't that easy.

Red had raised me to do what was right, no matter what. I knew what was right. Helping the wolves was right. Fixing Elder was right. Making the world a better place was right for me and all the living things around me.

I opened my eyes to take in the sights. Winter was finishing up, and green was slowly returning to the forest. I could see animals awaking from their winter slumber, and it made me feel more like I needed to leave the world of me. I belonged here in the woods with them. But first, I had a duty to help the wolves. Until I could get Red to help them, I'd do what they needed.

I must have been running fast as the village popped into view quicker than it should have. I glanced around for Nikkan, but he wasn't anywhere to be seen. I'd have to deal with that later. A day of long, hard work was what I needed. Now was time to forget all my troubles and get working. The wall wasn't going to build itself.

3RD MARCH

I returned from the wolf village late the night before, but surprisingly there was no Nikkan in the house. Sure, he didn't technically live with me, he had a family of wolves, but it had been many moon cycles since he hadn't slept in the same place as me. I knew he was mad, but this seemed to be more than usual. While surprised to find him gone, I didn't have time to dwell on it. I had a busy day planned.

At first light, I made my way back to the wolf village. Like the previous two days, I found everyone busy working. We had been working as a team for three days straight, and we hadn't gotten around one side of the village. The village had to be hundreds of saplings long. I had no idea how we were supposed to finish the fence and then move on to the next village. There wasn't enough time to get it done as five more people had gotten sick since we started. I never voiced my opinion, but I was beginning to agree with Micco more than ever. This was getting harder and harder to do each day, feeling like we were fighting a losing battle.

I had no idea what more we could do. Micco was right in taking action, but it would've been nice if he had started several moon cycles ago when he had healthier men and less of them turning into savage animals. I had to hope we weren't too late.

I guess my spirits were less with Nikkan gone. I had seen him once since he ran off the morning before, but he didn't even acknowledge that I existed. I knew I didn't need to apologize; he was the one that attacked me, but it still stung. He was my best friend and if you really counted, probably my only true friend. He never cared that I was a tree person like the rest of the wolves seemed to, or that I wasn't a tree person like the rest of the tree people thought. I didn't fit in, and that never bothered him. I wish he'd just get over me taking Grace to the festival and move on.

The rest of the wolves seemed more than ever to be indifferent to me. I helped where needed, but without Nikkan, we didn't make a three-person team to put the posts into the trench being dug. Grace was stuck helping the women around the fires making food for everyone, and Nikkan seemed to be in the woods with his dad chopping trees.

I spoke to no one as I worked. Micco only appeared once to get everyone going on new tasks before he left. The little I saw showed that this was wearing on him. He had lost at least a quarter of his weight, and the dark lines under his eyes seemed to be permanent. I didn't know how much more his body could tolerate.

He wasn't a young wolf anymore, and he wasn't being fed.

A little after lunch was finished, Grace and I took off. We would make it back to the tree village a little before the sunset, but I knew you couldn't be too early for a festival. While Red said it started at night time, I knew that meant it started just after lunch. No one wanted to wait that long to have a party.

The walk in the woods was actually more fun than I expected. Things in the village were so tense, and the lack of animals around the town was weird for me. But now, the forest was full of chirping and small critters scurrying away as we neared.

"I still don't understand why Micco didn't tell everyone about being invited to the festival," Grace commented. "I get that there are a few sick wolves, but why should the rest of us have to stay away. We need a break from all this, too, and who doesn't like a night of games and food?"

Grace was right in that all the wolves could use a break, but she was wrong in that it was just a few sick wolves. I had to wonder if she just didn't understand what it meant that they were ill, or was Micco not telling them everything?

"Besides, what could a sick wolf really do." Grace picked a flower from a bush as we passed it and twirled it in her hands.

I nodded though I knew better. It seemed that Micco wasn't completely forthcoming with either Red or his own people if she thought that. I had to hope he wasn't hiding more from me.

"And did you see who's sick? It's all the older wolves. Maybe this is an old age thing," Grace suggested.

So far, it seemed to be, but who knew when that

would change? And really, a sick wolf, old or young, could still be a problem if they neared the tree village. There hadn't been a single wolf attack since Red broke the curse, but I knew what the wolves could do even if they had forgotten.

"Did you see Nikkan today?" I asked, changing the subject.

Grace's cheeks flushed. That was a yes.

"I kind of pissed him off...." I ran my hands through my almost black hair. It was longer than usual and flopping out of place a bit. I would have to ask Red to help me cut it straight since Nikkan wasn't coming home yet.

"He seemed different," Grace finally replied.

"Mad?"

"Hmm, no, not mad." Grace tapped her chin as she thought. "Not mad, more like sad. His dad was having a hard time keeping up with the tree cutting. Nikkan might be worried his father is getting sick like the other old men. Linus was just working yesterday, but today was too sick to work. It can hit fast when you're old."

My shoulders dropped. I didn't want Nikkan to be sad or worried, though I understand why he would. Even if he didn't call the wolf village home now, it was still his family. I'd be concerned for Red if there was a sickness in the tree village. Nikkan was a good person and a good wolf. With all that was going on, I didn't intend to add more to his plate and regretted our fight the day before.

"It really is too bad more wolves aren't coming. I think Red has the right idea. If all the wolves and tree people can see each other and not think badly, then we might be able to get along."

Grace was as naïve as Nikkan said she was, but

I didn□t want to stomp that out of her. We needed more people that believed there was a way to make our kingdom whole again. And Red needed wolves like Grace to give the tree people a chance and show them that they weren□t different.

"The last few moons have been pretty crazy," she added.

That was true, to say the least. Someone somewhere had to know how wolves got sick. It didn't happen often, but there had to be someone. There were humans and wolves that were ancient and a few witches left in the woods that had to know something. Red would know where to look if she would admit that there was a problem.

"Are you sure we won't be too early?"

Grace just kept talking. The whole way to the tree village was filled with questions and more questions. Without Nikkan around, it was like she was a completely different person; actually, she was like the person I remembered growing up with.

"You can never be too early for a festival in the tree villages."

"I hope so." Grace looked a little more nervous as we kept walking and were nearing the village.

I could hear the people before Grace could. My new hearing was growing and actually helpful. While I preferred to listen to the animals of the woods, I was able to hear humans as well as the critters that lived around my house. I slowed our pace a little with her nervousness setting in.

Nikkan was stupid for not asking her to come. She was relaxed in the woods and now could use a hand to hold. I didn't see Grace that way. It was too bad Nikkan wasn't with us. The wolf was missing his chance.

As we neared, I stopped and paused before we were seen by anyone.

“We are almost there,” I told Grace.

I was sure she could hear them also by now. The sound of music and kids yelling as they ran around filled my ears. And I could smell all the scents. My mouth was already watering, but I needed to be sure she knew we didn’t have to stay.

“If you feel scared or out of place too much and want to leave, just let me know. We don’t have to stay the whole time.”

Grace smiled up at me. She was nervous, but I could see the sparkle in her eyes too. She was excited.

Pushing back the low hanging branch in front of us, I showed Grace the festival. Bright colors and lights glowed at the base of all the trees. Booths lined pathways that wove between everything. Food venders grilled food and sent the smells into the air while goods vendors sold everything from new skirts to hair combs or children’s toys. In between everything, were groups of people playing games, chatting, or dancing to the music that played all around us. It was a sensory overload, but not in a bad way.

The tree village was usually lit up at night time, but not like this. The ground was lit with a soft glow, along with lanterns hanging from every tree. The whole place glowed as much as the people running, walking, or skipping along. It was amazing to see. The happy atmosphere was contagious, and I couldn’t help but smile myself as two young children ran past us.

“Where do you want to start?”

Grace looked all over with wide eyes. Children ran by with jars filled with colorful bugs lighting up inside them. The closest booth had a young man leaning on it, making eyes at the girl cooking the corn. And not even two saplings away, an older man danced slowly all by himself to the fast music playing. Everywhere you turned there were people having a good time.

Grace bit her lip as she took it all in. Compared to the drab sick wolves, this place was a fairy tale come true. She looked like she couldn't decide what to do.

"Food first?"

Grace nodded as she stared around in awe.

I began walking forward but noticed the crowd could easily split us apart as people made their way in every which direction. I reached back and took her hand to keep her close to me as I aimed for the cooked corn and turkey legs that were roasting over an open pit not too far away. Food was always a good way to start the night.

"Two turkey legs," I told the young woman at the table serving the food.

It was busy, and she turned her back to us to grab the food. As she turned back to hand them to me, her jaw dropped when she saw Grace next to me. Festival or not, no one was used to seeing a wolf in the tree village. This was going to be a long night. Grace turned away without noticing to watch several children ride the fast lifts to the tree and back down to the ground, so I took the food and thanked the girl before pulling Grace away without her seeing the reaction of the girl at the booth.

"Where to?" I asked Grace as she bit into the food and juice dribbled down her chin. I stepped back to the booth for just a moment for a napkin and handed it to her before we started walking away from the stares.

Dusk was settling, and most people didn't look too closely to see Grace's ice-blue eyes, but the girl with the food had, and I hoped that was the worst reaction we'd get. I know as a wolf, Grace was used to it, but the whole purpose of the festival was defeated if they were going to gawk and stare at her for being a wolf.

Grace dabbed at the juice dripping on her chin and pointed to the man doing magic just beyond the red and yellow dressed juggler who currently had eight balls in the air. I nodded and offered my arm to Grace as we dove back into the crowd, food in hand.

The magician was surrounded by children that couldn't be more than four or five winters old. They all stared in awe at him as he made his buttons on his coat disappear and then reappear. After a few more tricks, he pulled a flower out from nowhere and handed it to the small girl in the front row. Grace smiled and clapped along with the children. Her smile was making me smile too.

With everything that was wrong in Elder, Red was right in that the people needed this. It was too bad not many wolves were a part of it. They could use the break. But it was great for everyone who was there. People all around us were smiling and dancing and having a fun time. If Red wanted the wolves and humans to get along, this was by far the best way to do it.

"What next?" I asked Grace.

"I don't know," she replied with her eyes big as she looked around. Music, food, and laughter filled the air.

"Let's just walk," I suggested. Grace nodded, and I led the way further into the trees and crowd of people all having fun.

We meandered between stalls, trying a few more foods, and stopping to look at things we could buy. The wolves didn't trade much with the tree people, but I had plenty to trade, being Red's son and all. I offered to get

Grace whatever she wanted, but she was just happy to look at it as we walked past.

We occasionally stopped for her to look at items or to play a game. There was one man who could keep a ball hidden in cups, and you had to guess where it was. Another man was making a game out of guessing how many winters old you were. Grace had a good laugh at the game where a man was sitting next to a target, and children were trying to hit it to make him fall into the water below him. I had to explain to Grace that he was one of the teachers at the younger school in the village, and almost all of the kids playing were his students.

As we neared the end of one of the pathways, we found dozens of couples dancing around a fire pit. The music was loud, but the laughter and smiles were even louder. Grace smiled at the commotion.

"Want to dance?" I asked over the music.

Grace grinned and nodded. I took her hand and led her into the circle that was still spinning. The people dancing didn't pay notice to Grace's blue eyes that gave away she was a wolf and let her into the circle. We began to spin with them, marching to the beat of the loud drum playing in the band. The music picked up its pace, and we turned the other direction. We followed along with the people as we danced to the song. By the time the song ended, most of the dancers had collapsed into giggling heaps. I caught Grace as she was about to be pulled down into a group.

"That was fun," she exclaimed, a little out of breath as I pulled her from the dancers.

I led Grace back into the next row of booths and was surprised to find Red there, looking through a stand of jewelry.

"Mother?"

Red turned around and grinned at me. She came over and hugged both me and Grace. I stood there in shock as Grace began to talk with her. They chatted like old friends as I continued just to stand there and stare.

"Did you have anything to eat yet?" Red was asking as my shock began to wear off.

"We had some of those little sugar swirly cookie things," Grace replied. "Those were my favorite."

"Did you try the brown and red ones yet, those little square ones I saw a couple of booths that way?" Red pointed away from us.

Grace peered around her and shook her head. We hadn't walked that direction yet.

They continued to talk, and I took a step back. The world had been turned upside down. Sure, I had seen Red happy before, but nothing like this. It was almost like she had drunk a whole barrel of wine on her own. This wasn't anything like the mother I grew up with and nothing like the Red that watched over the people of Elder. It was more than a little strange to see her talking away with Grace, not a care in the world.

"I see you brought a date," Sera said from behind me, distaste in her voice.

Of course, if my mother was off wandering the festival, Sera wouldn't be too far behind. Lately, it was like they were attached by a two-sapling-long invisible rope.

"Date?" I asked, still staring at Red as she talked. Her hair cascaded down her back. I tried my best to remember, but I came up blank, thinking of a time that her hair wasn't tightly pulled back off her face. It was like I was on a different planet or something.

"The wolf," Sera replied, pointing to Grace.

"Yes, I brought Grace with me," I answered.

It wasn't really like it was a date. I mean, I asked her to come and all, but it still wasn't something romantic. Grace was an old friend, and being together at the festival just made that clearer. I had nothing beyond friendship for her, nothing like Nikkan felt. I wasn't sure it would be classified as a date, but I didn't need to spend my time arguing with Sera. She could argue about anything.

"A wolf? You seriously date wolves? Everyone said there was something off with you, but I think this proves it," Sera replied. She didn't seem to agree with my mother's wolf-loving attitude.

"You and I both know there's nothing different between a wolf and a tree person. They are people of Elder, just like everyone else." We had had that argument more than once growing up.

"They are animals. You can pretend they aren't different, but they are." Sera talked to me, but every time she turned to Grace, her face soured like she personally disliked the wolf she'd probably never even met before tonight.

I didn't let Sera get to me. She talked like this every time she was upset, though I really had no idea what was rubbing her the wrong way right now. Maybe she didn't like to see Red happy. I knew the wolves bothered her, but she didn't hate them like she pretended to. She just was scared of them like the rest of the people.

"They are as much an animal as you or I," I replied before leaving her standing next to the jewelry stand Red had been looking at as we approached.

"So, you guys are having fun?" Red asked, still in her cheery mood.

"Much," Grace replied with a grin.

Her smile was still rubbing off on me. It actually wasn't too bad to be walking around all the tree people. For once, they were just having fun and not giving me the glares that had plagued my life with them. Grace got a few stares every now and then when someone caught her blue eyes, but no one besides Sera was hostile.

"Well, I should let you go taste that treat I was telling you about. It's just down that way." Red waved the direction behind her and the way we were already heading.

I nodded to Red as Grace took my arm to haul me off in search of a new treat. Sera glared at Grace. If I had time to care, I'd have asked more, but I was at a festival and having fun. Sera's mood wasn't going to spoil our time, and I wasn't about to let Grace see Sera staring daggers at her.

"Nikkan's missing so much fun," Grace said as we walked away from Red and Sera.

I just nodded. Yet another thing I didn't want to deal with. It was one night. Just one night. I wanted to feel like we belonged, have fun, be normal. Sera and Nikkan could pout another time. I didn't need to think or deal with either of them.

"Which way do we need to go?" I asked, trying to get off the subject of my friend.

"That way, I think." Grace smiled at me with her infectious grin.

I let it all go and just let the festival be my focus. It was time to have fun, and I wasn't going to let anything ruin it. And that was enough to turn it into one of the most entertaining times I'd had in a very long time.

Grace and I ate more food than I knew was possible, played games that we won and lost, danced more than once to music, and found that the second time walking around the festival was just as fun as the first time.

Many people had noticed Grace by the time we were making our second loop, but few cared. Red had planned and made a festival that everyone was enjoying. Every now and then, we ran across another wolf, someone that lived or worked near the city, but for the most part, the wolves were few and far between.

Grace stopped talking about Nikkan, and I was able to put my friend and his anger behind us for the night. He chose not to come. It could have been him taking Grace around, but he was too chicken to do that. Heck, it could have been all three of us having fun together, but again, he didn't care. He was the one missing out.

So much in Elder was changing, and I was happy to see something changing for the better. The wolves and tree people could get along. Red's festival was proof of that. It was everything she always wanted.

As the night grew old, Grace and I made our way back to where we began. She planned to turn into a wolf and head home for the night while I went back to my house. I really didn't want our night to end as it was back to reality. We stood just inside the festival but close enough to the woods that the magic of the night was fading.

"You're not going to kiss me goodnight or anything, right?" Grace joked.

I smiled and shook my head. There was no way I'd do that to Nikkan, even if he was too chicken to ask her out. Grace was my friend, and that was it.

"I kind of got the feeling this was just a friends thing," Grace continued, knowing exactly how it felt.

"Nikkan would kill me if I put any move on you," I explained, and her cheeks flushed.

She had spent all afternoon and evening with me

and not a single blush. Just mentioning his name made her red as a sunburn. We both knew there was nothing between us, but she wasn't ready to admit her feelings for Nikkan as much as he wasn't ready. I could live with that.

"You were my friend before all the weirdness between you and Nikkan and will be long after that goes away. Nothing will change that," I explained. Grace grinned at me. "This was just a fun night with a friend I've known for over ten winters."

"Good. I didn't know what I'd do if you both liked me."

It was my turn to grin. She knew how Nikkan felt. Quickly she covered her mouth as she realized what she had just told me. I laughed.

"I won't tell him," I assured her. Heck, I was pretty sure I wasn't going to see him for a while as he cooled down from our last fight. If only I could talk to Nikkan or my mother for that matter without fighting.

"Crap." I turned back to the festival and searched the crowd as far as I could see. Where was Red?

"What?" Grace asked.

"I needed to talk to Red a bit. I better do that before we head back."

I needed to try one more time to get Red to check out the wolves. Possibly her great mood would make it easier to convince her. It was worth a shot. Maybe she had drunk a whole barrel of wine. I could only hope.

"Okay." Grace looped her arm in mine. "Let's go find her."

Without a single question, Grace pulled me back into the moving crowd. It was going to be harder than just walking into the crowd, but Grace didn't seem to mind. She was already eyeing up a table with desserts, though I was pretty sure I had no room left to eat. I had a feeling she was up for making another whole circle of the festival if that's what it took to find Red.

I froze mid-step as I felt something. I couldn't put my finger on it, but I felt it, like the forest was telling me something. I turned back to the woods to scan it when a woman's scream pierced the air. Everyone froze what they were doing.

Red came plowing through the crowd to a group just behind us. I turned and followed her.

"What's going on, Mauve?" Red asked, authority back in place, and all happiness gone from her.

"My baby, my baby," Mauve cried into the shirt of the woman closest to her. The other women with her pulled their children closer to them as the first woman continued to wail.

"What about your baby?" Red asked gently but not with any less authority.

"He was sitting over there," the woman holding her said, pointing to an empty blanket on the ground.

"It took him," Mauve cried hysterically into the shirt of the woman. A younger dark-haired man pushed his way through the crowd, scooping the crying woman into his arms.

"Where's Jakob?" he asked, his voice gentle but loud enough to be heard where I stood with Grace.

Everyone looked around. The child was nowhere to be found.

Mauve finally pulled her head back to answer the question everyone was thinking, along with her husband and Red.

"A wolf took him."

HEIR OF THE CURSE

4TH MARCH

"A wolf took him."

Words I never expected to hear in my lifetime had been spoken. There was a fragile peace between the different people of Elder. It had been eighteen winters since a wolf had attacked a human, and it shattered the peace in the blink of an eye. A wolf took a child.

Elder was a vast kingdom made up of plains in the south that were farmland and the woods of the north where two types of humans resided. One group was ordinary humans that lived in the trees in whole villages that were off the ground, and the other group was humans that transformed into wolves who lived on the ground. The later had terrorized the tree residents for hundreds of winters. It was only recently in the last eighteen winters or so that the curse had been broken by our leader, The Red of Elder. The wolf people now had full control over their human and wolf sides and didn't attack humans. Until today.

I felt the wind change, and my friend Grace started to shake beside me. While the villagers processed that information, Grace and I knew what it meant. War was coming for the wolves. The tree dwellers wouldn't see good or bad. Any wolf would be a target. They would be suspicious of every single wolf around.

Grace would be one of those targets, being one of the few wolves at the festival we were attending. It wasn't safe for her to be in this crowd, surrounded by hundreds of humans that were now realizing that the wolves of old were back. Tree humans would see her as the enemy, no matter if she were standing in front of them as a regular human. They'd see her different-colored eyes and hair as a sign, not of what she was, but of what she could be.

We didn't wait for the people to come out of their shock at the news. I took Grace's arm and pulled her out of the crowd of people and into the woods.

Grace tripped over her feet in the dark.

"What do we do?" she asked, her hands still shaking as she clung to me.

I kept her just inside the tree line as I stood and watched the villagers and my mother, The Red of Elder. We were still close enough that I could hear what was being said.

"We need to act now. We need to stop them before more people get hurt," someone said in the crowd.

Red held up a hand, and the people around her quieted.

"Mauve. Are you sure it was a wolf? Could he have

crawled away?"

The lady who was still sobbing into her husband's shirt pulled her face back just inches.

"I know what I saw. He was there and happy. When I turned back to check on him, I saw the tail of a wolf, and the baby was gone. I'm certain it was a wolf."

Red looked disappointed. Here we were at a festival she had spent many moons planning to bring the wolves and tree people of Elder together, and it was pulling them further apart.

"It was a wolf," another lady told Red. "I saw it too."

"Me too," another one added.

"It's always the wolves. They can't be trusted," someone yelled from the gathered crowd.

I had my doubts that all the women saw it happen, and not a single one did anything to try to stop it, but it was a crowd of people filled with the prejudices of old. Tree people and wolves hated and distrusted each other. While Red was ambitious and wanted the kingdom to be whole, it was going to take longer than eighteen winters to get rid of their prejudices. Humans couldn't...or wouldn't forget that easily.

"What are we going to do?" someone asked Red.

She looked at the weeping woman and then turned to where I was in the woods.

"I will follow the tracks of the wolf and search for the baby. A search party should be made right here to comb the woods near-by. It might not be the wolves at all. It's always possible the baby crawled away. We need to look for him as quickly as we can. It's too cold for him to survive the night out here alone."

Everyone around her stared back, but no one said a thing. I could see on their faces that they didn't believe Red. They all had their bad guy already, the big bad wolf.

“Sera will come with me to help track, but Charles and Ruth will lead the groups here to start searching around the village.”

Two people in the crowd stepped forward.

“Split everyone up into groups and fan out from this spot. Don’t leave a single place unturned.” Red nodded to the man and woman standing in front of her. “Sera,” Red turned to the younger girl beside her, who was her assistant. “Go ahead and get tracking. I’m going to gather some supplies, and I’ll catch up.”

Sera nodded her head to Red and then dashed off into the woods. Red disappeared to the nearest platform in the trees.

The two left in charge walked toward the trees and where I stood like a statue with Grace.

“We need to go to the wolf village and demand they give the baby back,” the lady named Ruth told the guy with her. “Red is too soft and blinded by her love of these animals. They need to be shown a lesson and put in their place. Once a killer always a killer. It’s time to go wolf hunting.”

“We can’t go alone. They’ll just kill us. We need weapons and a hunting party to go with us. The wolves won’t stand a chance if we all act together,” the man, Charles, replied. Ruth nodded her head, and they both hurried back to the group of people as Red descended from the trees.

Red walked back to Ruth and Charles to talk more with them, but I couldn’t just sit around and wait any longer. If they could convince her to bring weapons to the village, who knew what was coming next. The wolves were in trouble.

“We need to leave now and stop this before anyone

gets hurt," I whispered to Grace. Her eyes were large as saucers as she stared at the crowd. She had heard everything too.

I didn't wait for her to respond as I grabbed her arm and pulled her further into the woods. She stumbled along beside me as I began to run. Running at night in the woods was a problem for most people, but not a wolf or me, for that matter. The woods were a second home, and I ran through it often. Grace's stumbling was something else. She was in as much shock as the rest of the people. She tried to keep up with me, but she was slowing me down. We needed to get to the wolves before the hunting party from the village.

"You need to change so we can run faster," I told Grace.

It wasn't ideal to be running around the forest as a wolf when a whole city of people wanted to hunt wolves, but we both knew that it would be faster. If we ran more quickly, we could stay ahead of them, and that would make it safer for Grace. Wolf or human form, they'd know she was a wolf either way.

"I can run as fast as a wolf," I told her. Only Nikkan, my best friend and also a wolf, knew that about me. I could track the wolf as I ran, but that wasn't something I needed to add.

Grace finally snapped out of her shock.

"I thought you said this date wasn't romantic, and here you ask me to strip," she teased as she walked behind some bushes and began to disrobe.

I chuckled as she tossed her clothing to me and emerged as a wolf. I was glad to see she wasn't still in shock, and her humor had returned. It wasn't a funny matter we were dealing with, but it meant she was back to herself, which was a much better partner to be running in the woods with. Wolf Grace would be able to help me if she wasn't in shock. Her silky red coat matched her auburn hair she had as a human. The wolf was ready.

"I'm pretty sure this isn't romantic, but if you tell Nikkan I asked you to strip before we came back to the village, he might not understand, and I'll never have him as a friend again."

Wolf Grace nipped at me as I joked.

"So it wasn't a date?" Sera asked as she came out of the trees where she had been hiding. I knew she was there the whole time, but I ignored her.

Sera was my mother's assistant. I was pretty sure that while neither of them confirmed it, she was the next Red of Elder. Sera stood with her hands on her hips as she looked between me and the wolf.

"Are we going to track this baby stealer or not?" Sera asked.

Wolf Grace growled at Sera before turning back to me. She whined and nodded towards where the wolf scent headed further into the woods. I nodded to Grace and took off with her into the dark woods following the wolf's path.

We ran quickly, and Sera kept up with us. It just further cemented my opinion that she was the next Red. No average human would be able to run at a full pace through the woods in the dark. I had better seeing than most people, and it was the end of winter, so there was less foliage, but it was still not an easy feat.

Grace led the way, tracking the wolf by the scent it had left near the village. I could follow it too, but I let her take the lead. I was trying to pick up the child's scent, but after being at the festival, it was hard to keep all the human scents that were on both me and Sera from messing up my tracking. It was better to track the wolf. After we passed my place, Grace slowed down until she came to a full stop. We were closer to the wolf village but still far enough away that I couldn't be sure the wolf was one of Micco's. Wolf Grace looked one way and then the next. Sera knelt down and touched the soil at her feet.

"The wolf went both ways," Sera explained what wolf Grace was trying to get across.

I nodded as I looked around the night woods. Where was the rogue child-stealing wolf? My mother, The Red, didn't want to believe it was a wolf, but I knew it was. And from the looks of it, it had to be one of Micco's sick wolves. Taking a deep breath, I tried to figure out which way to go. The wolf had been here. In fact, it had been by my place several times. Its path crisscrossed itself again and again. Some of the scents were old, but some were new and mixed with the smell of my wolf friend, Nikkan.

Sera looked angry at the halt in our progress, but I knew it was anger fueled by being scared. Where did the wolf go? It wasn't like he had a significant head start on us. He had to be around, but we didn't hear, see, or smell him or the baby.

I took another deep breath and closed my eyes. He had to be somewhere. The woods were usually my friend, but this time it was failing. It was like all the life around us ran away from the wolf, and there was nothing left for us to lean on for help.

"We need to go get help from the other wolves," I told the girls. "There are at least ten different paths the wolf ran tonight alone. We need people to follow each track, or we'll never find the baby in time. We need more wolves."

Sera looked like she wanted to protest, but she didn't. She was smart enough to know it was true, even if she didn't like the wolves. She wasn't enough to track this many trails. If all three of us split up, we could only go three different ways. We needed more tracking help.

Wolf Grace didn't need any prompting as she took off into the woods again, heading towards her home. Normally, it would take most of the morning to jog to the wolf village, but we didn't have that time to waste. We were trying to get to the child in time and outrun the villagers. I didn't mention to the girls, but faintly I could hear that we were being followed by horses. The tree villagers were hunting. I didn't think they'd be able to convince Red, but it seems she didn't have the power to stop them. The only way to stop the fight coming was to get to the baby first and pray to the gods that it hadn't gotten bitten when it was taken.

It would have been nice if I had magic and could have just appeared in the wolf village instead of running, but being with a wolf and the next Red did have the benefit that we could go faster than the horses following us. When we arrived at the village, we only had a little time to get help and the baby back.

I ran straight to Micco's hut and let myself into his home. In most cases, I would have never pushed myself into a wolf's hut unannounced, but we didn't have time for formalities.

"Micco, we have to get everyone up now," I said, rousing the older man from his slumber.

After working for days on building a wall to protect the tree people from the wolves, I was sure the whole village was sleeping like the dead. But that didn't matter. We had to wake them.

Micco sat up and rubbed his eyes as he looked at

me.

"A wolf took a baby from the festival and headed in this direction. We couldn't track it past my place, and we need the wolves out there to help us find it."

Micco was out of bed without a single hesitation and yelling for the wolves to wake up with his booming voice that carried through the whole village. Within no time, the place was filled with sleepy, but awake human wolves.

"I need teams of two to help us track a sick wolf in the woods," I said to the gathered crowd. "The wolf took a tree villager baby from the festival tonight, and the tree people are on their way here. We need to find the baby before it's too late, or they will be hunting wolves again."

The sleepy eyes that greeted me warily were now open wide. The older wolves all looked at me with fear, and the younger ones were confused. While I knew the full history between the two villages in Elder, the wolves didn't teach the whole story to the younger generation until they joined the town as a full member when they got married. They hadn't lived through the winters where a wolf could be shot on sight in wolf or human form. And the stockpile of weapons my mother had would make it worse. I wasn't sure the wolves could survive another war.

Horses sounded in the distance, and I froze where I stood. They were faster than I thought they'd be. I looked into the sky and cursed the bright moon that was making it easier for them to travel than it should have been. It was the same moon that caused the sick wolf to turn into a baby taking monster.

"No one leaves the village," I changed my mind. "Let me talk to them."

Micco looked at me and nodded. He knew that they would likely shoot a wolf on sight, and I was their best bet. Wolf Grace whined beside me, and I shook my head at her. She needed to stay with her people. The wolves followed me to the partially made wall, but everyone stayed behind it as I moved forward into the woods around the wall. Sera joined me.

"We can talk with them," Sera told me.

Whatever would get them to not kill the wolves was fine by me. Usually, I would argue with Sera over her assumed authority, but this wasn't one of those times to argue. Maybe together, we could save as many wolves as possible.

We didn't have to wait long as the first of the riders approached.

"Where's Red?" Sera asked the older man that was supposed to be searching the woods near the tree village.

The man looked to the rider next to him, and they both shrugged. Anger started to bubble inside of me. If they had done anything to her, it wasn't the wolves they'd need to fear. I'd make them pay. Red was their leader, and they were going against her order, but worse yet, they did something to keep her from stopping them. My mother would have never let a hunting party go to the wolves in the day, let alone in the middle of the night. They had to have done something to her. I wanted to turn into a wolf myself and rip apart the guy that so casually didn't care for Red. Sera laid a hand on my arm, and her ice-cold fingers made me turn to look at her, cooling my anger only slightly.

"Let me handle this," she told me quietly. The anger I felt was mirrored in her eyes.

It was probably best as I wanted to knock that guy

off his horse and give him a pounding, he'd remember the rest of his life.

"Without Red here, then it's my authority you have to follow," Sera told the man who was now surrounded by more riders. Every one of them carried some sort of firearm. It wasn't safe for any of the wolves.

"You aren't..." the man began, but soon he was yanked off his horse and lying on the ground with Sera's boot heal at his throat.

"I'm the next Red," she declared, authority ringing in her voice. "And what I say goes."

The rest of the riders all bowed their heads to her.

"Castiel is going to explain to you our plan, and you're going to follow exactly what he says." Sera nodded at me.

I didn't exactly have a plan; it was time to think on my feet.

"Micco is picking his top ten wolves, and we're going to spread out to find the child," I explained. One man began to open his mouth to protest, but Sera gave him a glare that shut him right up. "The wolves can track better than any human like you or I. We need their skills as I found the wolf in question has laid almost a dozen trails for us to follow. If we track each one at a time, we won't find him by the time the sun comes up. This is quicker, and the wolves all want to help. Not a single one would hurt the child in question. I trust them with my life and the child's life."

"But they are wolves, they won't track one of their own," a brave man spoke even though he was facing the wrath of Sera.

"We don't condone biting humans and especially taking children. I have more than enough wolves that will gladly track down whoever did this and apprehend him," Micco replied. "We aren't killers, and this lone wolf will be punished."

The men on horses didn't seem to want to let me and the wolves track the rogue wolf, but Sera wasn't taking no for an answer. She nodded to me as I turned to Micco, who was already ready to dole out their assignments.

"Each wolf takes a direction. Weave in a search pattern and then make your way back. If you find anything, alert us all," Micco directed them before stepping back and turning into a wolf himself. The tree men on horses all stared in shock at the older wolf but stayed right where they were.

"I'm going with Micco," I said to Sera. She nodded, still holding the lead man hostage with her boot.

"I'll keep the village safe," she told me. That was all I needed to hear; I nodded as I took off after Micco.

It had been a long time since I'd seen the older gray wolf. And he was a sight to be seen. As alpha, he was more than twice the size of an average wolf. I was used to running with my friend, Nikkan, but he was only a teen; Micco was like a giant compared to him.

It didn't take us long to pick up one of the scents. Tracking in the woods could be hard if you didn't know where you were going, but the woods were home to both of us. Micco picked up speed off in the dark, and I followed. He wasn't going to lose me in the night. The rogue wolf had run that trail not too long ago.

Micco continued heading north. When I first heard the cry, it made me miss a step in my run, but I was able to right myself before I fell. As Micco ran in the wrong direction, I turned toward the baby. This rogue wolf wasn't just dangerous because he had no control over his wolf; this wolf was smart and had left a trail that even the alpha was going to follow. If the child hadn't been crying, we might have missed it.

"This way," I said to Micco, who was now several saplings ahead of me as he ran.

Micco skidded and altered his run to match mine without question, not like he could question me while in wolf form.

It didn't take us long to find a baby, almost a toddler, sitting in the woods. There was dirt all over the poor kid, but it didn't look like any blood. The child cried as we stopped and looked around. The rogue wolf had to be close by. I could smell but not hear him. Micco took a couple of brave steps towards the baby before I spotted the wolf. His growl shook the leaves around him as he got ready to pounce.

"East," I called to Micco, who turned his head just in time to see the wolf leaping out at him.

I didn't wait to see what Micco would do but instead ran across the woods to the child and scooped it into my arms. The wolf lunged for us, trying to get past Micco. Micco used his massive body to protect me and the child. I looked back the way we came and wondered what would be the best thing to do. Do we try to run past the fighting wolves and back to the village, or would it be better to stay away from the fight by getting up in the trees where the wolves couldn't get to the child?

I didn't have time to decide as the fight moved closer to me, forcing me to climb the closest tree. Without hesitation, I tucked the young child into my shirt and tied it tighter against my body. The baby continued to cry as I grabbed the lowest branch and hauled us off the ground. Using one hand to support the child and one hand to balance, I made my way to the center of the tree to go higher. When I knew we were far enough off the ground, I stopped and pulled the child out of his make-shift sling. He continued to cry but was quieter now that we were further away from the fighting.

Down below us, Micco continued to fight the rogue wolf. To say the rogue was stronger than normal was an understatement. He was fighting equal to Micco, and Micco was the alpha and strongest of all of the wolves. This sickness was giving the wolves super strength, and that was one more problem the people of Elder didn't want to have to deal with.

Quickly, I checked over the child. There didn't seem to be any teeth marks or scratches. He was dirty from head to toe, and his clothing was ripped in more than one place, but he was fine. I looked into his eyes, and the moon was bright enough for me to see he still had brown eyes. The child hadn't been bitten and was still a normal human. Thank goodness. Now that I knew he was fine, I anxiously wanted to get him back to his people. The sooner they saw there wasn't a problem, the sooner they would leave, and the wolves would be safe, for now at least.

I watched as Micco slowly wore down the lone wolf. It would have been a quicker fight if Micco was going for the kill, but instead, he seemed to be just trying to subdue the wolf. I only knew which wolves were my friends, so I had no idea who the rogue wolf was, but it seemed Micco did. I kept the child tucked in my arms as Micco worked away at the rogue wolf. After what felt like forever but could have only been moments, Micco had the wolf trapped and hurt bad enough it couldn't get away. I saw it was now time for me to get the child back to the tree villagers who were waiting at the wolf village.

Easier than going up, I jumped down to the ground in one motion. Micco growled at the rogue wolf, who dared to lift his head and look at the child. Wolf Micco couldn't talk to me, but I knew it was better to get the tree people away from the village as fast as I could. I knew he'd understand why I was leaving him.

"I'll send backup to help you," I told Micco, but he shook his head. He didn't want help, but he didn't have much of an option. The wolf couldn't get away; who knew what it would do next? "You plan to stay here all night like that?"

Micco nodded. I wasn't about to fight with him. I would get the child back to his people and then come to help Micco.

My return was quicker than anyone expected as all the wolves seemed to be still following trails or fanning out in the woods to search. Sera still held the man on the ground, and many of the tree villagers were on the ground now by their horses. I could see more than one was holding their weapons even if Sera hadn't authorized anything like that.

"I found the child," I told the crowd as I approached. Wolves and tree villagers alike started to chatter in happiness at what I was holding.

Sera looked up at me and nodded. She let the man at her foot go and took the young child from me. After a quick check over, she turned to her people.

"Go home," she ordered them with only the authority the next Red could have.

The tree villagers lingered for only a moment before turning around to head back to the tree village.

"Charles," Sera called to the man she had been keeping on the ground. "I'll be borrowing your horse, and you can ride back with another one of your friends that aren't supposed to be here."

Charles scowled but handed the reigns over to Sera.

She handed me the child as she climbed up on the horse. I handed him back to her once she was seated.

"I'll personally return him to his mother," she told me. I nodded as she turned and faded back into the dark trees of the forest on top of the horse she borrowed. The child calmed in her arms and was quiet before they were out of view.

I didn't wait for anyone to ask as I made my way back into the woods too. I followed the path back to where Micco was still with the rogue wolf. I paused as I neared and smelled blood. That wasn't a good sign. I took off running to help Micco, who might have been overpowered by the weird powers of the rogue wolf, only to skid to a halt where I left him.

Human Micco was standing over the body of another human. He was bending down to pick the other man up.

"Micco..." I didn't know what to say.

I knew who the man was. It was only days before that Micco showed me his friend Nathan, who was one of the first wolves to get sick. He was doing everything in his power to keep his friend alive. No matter how it went down, the sickness had taken its first wolf.

5TH MARCH

The sun was high in the sky by the time I woke the next morning. I really didn't want to get out of bed after the disaster of the day before. What started out as a fun day with a festival that made me forget all the problems of Elder ended with a reminder that Elder needed help. I was kind of wishing it was all a dream even if I knew I couldn't be that lucky.

I never knew the real details; I don't think Red shared them with anyone, but I knew that Elder was a better place because the curse was gone. The place I was raised had problems, just like any kingdom, but it was working towards a new era where the people of Elder were one people and not divided tribes. At least, that was what Red was going for the night before. It didn't exactly turn out that way.

Eighteen winters ago, Red had faced and beat the curse. While that didn't mean the wolves would be free from turning into animals, it meant the wolves regained control of their animal. They could change or not change at will and remembered every moment they were in their wolf form. As my best friend, Nikkan, had explained to me more than once, being a wolf meant having a second person in his head, he was still in control of that person. The curse was when they lost that control. Anyone with the wolf side could be called by the moon to turn into a vicious wolf that would attack humans at will.

The curse divided Elder. The non-cursed people fought and feared the cursed. Neighbors turned on neighbors. No one was safe. Nighttime became dreaded as people feared the wolves in the woods. The human-only people retreated to the safety of the trees. Elder was a different place then, and no one wanted to go back to that.

The divide was something Red had worked so hard to stop. Even after the curse was broken, people stayed in the trees, and the wolves stayed in their villages. Red could see that they needed to be one kingdom and tried her best to encourage everyone to get along. That was ruined now. All her work had gone out of the window.

What we saw last night was just like everything that had ever been described to me before. I wasn't alive when the curse happened, but I knew all about it. Most of my childhood had been spent sitting in meetings of people seeking retribution from Red for what had happened to them winters before. The curse touched everyone and devastated many families.

I groggily made it out of bed and was disappointed to find Nikkan was still gone. Three nights without him felt like the longest we had ever been apart in the past three winters. It was strange. Yes, he was a wolf, and no, he wasn't related to me, but he felt more like my family than anyone. He was my brother in every sense of the word but blood. I hated to fight with him, but I knew he just needed to cool down. I could wait for him, but it was still weird to be in my house alone.

Breakfast was going to have to be tea, and I needed to go hunting. There was close to nothing left in my cupboards, and even more so, I needed to be up and going. I didn't have time to hunt, though I needed to. Azren had supplies I could get, but I preferred to hunt for my food, and that way, owe nothing to anyone. But hunting would have to wait; the wolves needed their fence now more than ever.

I heard someone outside the door to my house and hurried over to open it. I was going to be glad to have Nikkan back to talk to. There was too much that happened, and I needed his opinion on it all. He was a wolf, but he never really acted like one. He was pretty impartial most of the time and was good to bounce ideas off. Together we could come up with some great, and sometimes not so great, plans.

I opened the door and tried not to be disappointed. Sera stood there looking at me, waiting for me to invite her in. It wasn't Nikkan, after all.

"What do you want?" I asked, a little harsher than I intended. It wasn't her fault she wasn't Nikkan, but she wasn't the face I wanted to see right after waking up.

It wasn't that Sera wasn't a pretty face to see. She was beautiful when she wasn't scowling. But we never got along the best. Somehow, she always pushed my buttons, and I did my best to do the same to her. We had nothing to be competitive about, but we still were.

I couldn't help it. Something about Sera made me want to try harder and do better. I couldn't let myself be bested by her no matter how much I really didn't care about something.

"Tsk, tsk," Sera said as she pushed her way into my house just like she always did.

Sera had grown up with me for the most part. My mother insisted on keeping track of her over the winters. Therefore, we visited her and her parents often. They were one of the few human people of Elder left living in the woods on the ground. They refused to move to the trees, and Red made sure they had a cottage protected by enchantments to keep the wolves out.

Needless to say, that made them into really tough people, and Sera inherited all of that toughness from her parents. She tended to say what she thought when she thought it, and that meant we didn't always see eye to eye. Sure, I had opinions about everything, too, but I knew when to keep my mouth shut. Sera didn't.

"I came all the way here to collect you and find you sleeping until the sun's at the highpoint of the day. You've probably missed two meals already. Bet you were planning to sleep until supper time, lazy," she said as she walked around my house, scrutinizing it as she went. She looked in my sink as she passed it and raised one eyebrow at me.

Yes, there were dirty dishes in the sink, but who cared? This was my house. I didn't have to live like Red, the perfect leader of the kingdom of Elder. My house didn't need to have everything in complete order like Red's house. I never recalled seeing even one thing out of place growing up. Red was perfect; I was not. This was my house, and if I wanted to leave a dish in the sink, I could do that. I didn't need Sera's opinion or approval.

Sera made her way back to me after inspecting my house. I just stood with my arms crossed and waited. I really didn't have time to argue with Sera. I had things to get done, and obviously, I'd overslept.

"Red asked me to fetch you," Sera finally told me, looking me over like she was checking to see if I was even dressed for the day. I was basically dressed since I had slept in my clothing the night before when I got home so late.

"Like as in, she wants me there today?" I asked.

Really? Red had great timing. I had better things to do than spend another day at the tree village. It wasn't like she needed my account of the night before. She already had Sera, who was there the whole time. I was ready to argue with Sera when she continued talking.

"I wasn't to return without you," Sera added, touching the cupboard like she was checking for dust.

Yep, Red wanted me there today.

"Fine," I said, unable to avoid the inevitable.

If Red demanded I be somewhere, I had to go. At least, for now. When I had my place completely self-sufficient, I wouldn't have to be at her beck and call. And really, I'd do anything to get Sera out of my house.

I motioned for Sera with a grand wave to leave out the door I held open for her and shut it behind us as we left.

"Race you?" I dared her once we were both outside in the clearing before my house.

Just because I had to go to the tree village didn't mean I had to waste my whole day. The sooner I got there, the sooner I could be done and back to the wolves to help them.

Sera wasn't one for backing down from a challenge,

and she took off full speed into the woods. I laughed at her head start and ran after her.

It didn't take me very long to catch up with her. Yes, Sera had the power of the Red and could see better in the daylight than the dark night before, but what she didn't realize last night was that I could go faster than we had run when tracking the rogue wolf. I only kept pace with Sera and Grace, but alone I could have been to the wolf village quicker.

Sera pumped her arms quicker as I caught up beside her, but she was unable to break away from me. She expertly jumped and ducked branches in her pathway as I did the same. Gritting her teeth, she tried to get ahead of me, but I just smiled. I wasn't going at my full pace yet; I was just keeping up with her. Knowing that we would be there soon at this pace, I decided to pull in front just a little to drive her nuts. Sera huffed and tried to keep up with me.

Racing was actually a great idea. My blood was pumping, and my brain was thinking faster about everything. The wolves needed help. Micco shouldn't have to bear the weight of their problems alone. Red needed to see that, but she didn't go the night before to the wolves. I didn't have time to ask Sera, but something was up. What did Red need from me?

Breaking through the tree line, we made it to Red's cottage on the ground in record time. She stood outside the doorway, holding a steaming cup of tea, staring into the woods. Red wasn't staring in our direction as I pulled to a stop two saplings away from her. Red continued to stare into the trees.

"Not fair," Sera said as she stopped beside me, panting from her exhaustion. I had barely broken a sweat.

Red turned to us and gave us a sad smile. She had seemed happy at the festival; I hated how she looked now. Her dream of wolves and tree humans as one burned down last night. I wasn't sure if she were back to step one, but the look on her face said she knew it was like that.

"I'm cleaning up," Sera said to the two of us as she went into the cottage and her bedroom that used to be mine.

Red watched her go and then turned back to me. Somehow, in just the few days since she had been to my house, she had aged again. It was like winters were passing each day she had. The lines on her forehead seemed more profound. Her hair might even have had a few more strands of gray in it. It was beyond strange. Red was eternally young. At least, that's what I'd always thought.

Red wasn't your typical mother. She didn't give hugs or kisses freely. She didn't make pies and cookies for you to have when you came home from lessons. She didn't tuck you in at night or tell you there was nothing to be afraid of under your bed. That wasn't Red. She was always real and honest with me. She was strong and fierce. And now, it seemed like some of that was fading along with her hair color.

"Come on in," she motioned for me to follow her. I nodded and did as she asked. "Have a seat."

I sat down at the kitchen table where I had eaten all my meals when I was a kid. Red sat in her regular chair at the head of the table. I tried not to feel like a little kid again.

"Sera told me about yesterday, but I need to hear it from you." She took a sip of her tea.

"I've been trying to tell you, but you've refused to

listen," I started waiting for Red to reprimand me for my disrespect. She only stared at me, so I continued. "Micco told me the wolves were getting sick. I tried to get you to see that. What happened yesterday was because they are sick, and you didn't care enough to listen to me."

I wasn't blaming her. It wasn't her fault they were sick, but I felt like it was made worse because she didn't believe me.

"I believe you now," she told me like she could read my mind. "Tell me all the details. I need to figure this out."

I stared hard at her. Was she just saying what she thought I wanted to hear, or did she honestly believe me? I didn't know which it was.

"The wolves need help," I started and waited a moment to see if she'd dismiss my words as she had already done only a few days before. "Some time this winter Micco found that a few wolves had gotten sick. He thought they were just making it up. Wolves can't get sick, right?"

Red nodded her head but added nothing. She knew just like the rest of us that the wolf gene made it impossible for them to physically get sick. Wolves healed from almost everything and quickly. They never had to worry about catching a cold or if they ran across poison ivy. Nothing could get a wolf sick.

"Micco ignored it until he couldn't anymore. He finally realized after you last visited him that the wolves weren't pretending. They were really sick. That's when he asked me to tell you. He showed me a sick wolf, and Mom, they're really bad."

We needed to help them, and I wanted to keep the wolves safe. The tree villagers already showed that they were ready to kill off the wolves if given a chance. I didn't want to see my friends die, and I didn't want to kill any crazy tree-dwellers either. We were all part of Elder, one people.

"What happens when they get sick?" Red asked as she watched me like I held some grand secret. It seemed that she was taking me seriously now.

"They are ravenously hungry, but no amount of feeding nourishes them; they lose weight, become weak, and are unable to work. The healthy wolves left in the villages are starving because the sick wolves eat everything at night. The available food is diminishing because it seems like the animals in the woods are avoiding the area as if they are aware of the increased risk to them. When a sick wolf transitions back to his human form, he is weak and starving. Hunting in their wolf form isn't filling them up."

Red pressed her fingers together and tapped them on her lips. She knew something she wasn't sharing with me.

"Do they have control of their wolf?"

I bit my lip. If I told the truth, she might let the tree villagers hunt them. The wolves were a problem, and I knew that even though they lived in Elder, Red would protect the tree villagers first. Red didn't need me to answer as she read my face.

"I need to talk with Micco further, but I have a feeling the curse is back."

I stared at her. What was she talking about? She broke the curse. She saved everyone eighteen winters ago. It couldn't just come back.

"Back? Not something new?"

I wanted badly for it to be something new. Something we could find an answer for. Something we could help the wolves defeat.

"No. It sounds just like how the curse began hundreds of winters ago."

I shook my head. This couldn't be happening. When the curse was active, not a single wolf was able to control themselves at the call of the moon. That would mean my friends, Nikkan and Grace, would turn into the monsters that lived to kill people. All the wolves would go crazy and hunt humans. No one would be safe.

"Micco brought out cages to keep the sick wolves in, and we started building a fence around the village to keep everyone in at night because he will soon run out of cages." I wanted Red to see that the wolves were working hard to keep Elder safe. I didn't want her organizing hunting parties, and I didn't want her hurting the wolves.

I wasn't sure if I convinced her or not as Red nodded, lost in her own thoughts. She had always been hard to read, but I think being away had made it harder for me. I knew she was never going to give a yes or no answer, that wasn't her way, but it would have made me feel a lot better.

All Micco was doing wasn't going to be enough. I thought the sickness was going to be a few people, maybe the males of the wolf village. We could contain it and then look for a cure. I could never imagine Grace as a monster. And what would happen when the fence was finished. They would all be trapped with the cursed wolves. What would happen to the women and children? Would they be prey or turn into a cursed wolf like the others?

"Sera," she said as Sera walked out of her room and into the living space of the cottage. "Your lessons have just ended. Now it's time to deal with the curse for real. It is back."

Sera looked at Red, shocked. I don't think she thought the curse was back either.

"Castiel. You will stay here until we handle this. No seeing the wolves. Not Grace or Nikkan."

My eyes bulged as I stood up and pushed my chair back.

"Nikkan and Grace are my friends."

"And wolves," she pointed out.

"So?"

She had no right to tell me what to do.

"They can hurt you or even curse you with the wolf curse. They won't be in control of themselves. You have to stay away for their sake. It's the only way to stay safe. They both would be devastated if they hurt you, and you know it."

"They could never hurt me. I know that." I couldn't help but defy her. She was wrong about the curse and how it could change Nikkan or Grace. They were my friends, not the monsters she was trying to make them out to be.

"They won't want to, but they will. The curse takes away their free will. You will stay here. That's an order."

"I'm not a child," I spat back. She couldn't just give me orders. I wasn't one of her soldiers. "You spent weeks ignoring that something could be wrong with the wolves, and not even seven moons ago, I told you to help Micco, and you turned me away. You don't have a right to tell me what to do when you spent your time ignoring it. Maybe if you'd helped Micco when he asked for help, the child wouldn't have been taken."

Red didn't stand up but just gave me the stare I dreaded my whole life.

"You aren't allowed to date wolves. They are dangerous, and you will get hurt."

"Date?" I had no idea what she was talking about.

"Grace," Red added at my confusion. "is a wolf no matter how nice she might be."

I rubbed my hand down my face as I tried not to smile. Some of my anger faded a bit. My mother thought I was dating Grace too. Couldn't a guy just go someplace with a girl without it being a date?

"Grace is just a friend, mom. Nikkan likes her. There's nothing to worry about there. Grace and I are just friends."

That seemed to appease Red a little as relief showed momentarily on her face.

"Glad to hear that, but what I said is true whether you're dating her or not. You never saw the curse and don't understand. A cursed wolf can't control themselves." Unfortunately, she wasn't done with her lecture; that started my blood boiling again. "You may be all grown up, but I'm still your mother. If I tell you to stay here, then you stay here. If that doesn't work for you, how about I'm the Red of Elder, and you will do as I say."

My anger came back completely. I hated to be ordered around, and I hated her treating me like a child. I was technically an adult and had been since the beginning of winter. It was about time she trusted me and treated me like one.

"That might have worked three winters ago or maybe even two. But I'm done following orders. I can protect myself, and who I choose to be around is my choice. Curse or not, they are still my friends, and I plan to do everything I can to keep all the wolves safe, no matter what you do."

I didn't give her time to respond as I stood and left the room. I wasn't a child, and I wasn't going to be ordered around. She turned a blind eye to the wolves, but I wouldn't do that. They needed help, and I'd do anything I could so long as I could walk and breathe. Fight or not, Nikkan was my family, and Grace was my friend.

6TH MARCH

I returned home in defiance of Red's order. I understood that the wolves were dangerous. Trust me. It was a lesson she had pounded into me growing up. Wolves are dangerous. Wolves will hurt you. Wolves fight dirty. Wolves can kill you. Always be on guard with wolves. Never be alone at night. Always be ready for a wolf attack. She wanted to bridge the wolves and tree humans together, but even Red didn't completely trust them. I got all those lessons growing up. I knew what I was dealing with, but I knew my friends.

Nikkan, mad at me or not, would never hurt me. He was my family. Grace couldn't hurt a fly if she wanted to. She was just that nice. And Micco was like a grandfather to me. The older man didn't just have a soft spot for Nikkan but also for me. He was there when I needed to talk, and he cared way more than any male in the tree village ever did about me. They weren't the monsters Red spoke about, or the community believed them to be. They were my friends.

I lost yesterday going to the tree village to see Red, but at least one good thing came from it. She finally understood there was a problem. I wasn't quite sure what she would see as a way to help the wolves, but, at least, she now admitted they needed help. The first step to solving this was getting Red on board. She was the leader of the kingdom, and the one everyone relied on. If anyone could find a way to help the wolves, it would be Red.

I wasn't too happy to hear it was likely the curse was back. Red never once told anyone how she broke the curse. I wasn't sure if it could be done again. The curse returning was a bad sign. Sick wolves were terrible, but the curse was ten times worse. I wasn't going to be happy to break that news to Micco. I don't think he wanted to think that was a possibility, but now it was. It was something we would have to face together.

My walk back from my meeting with Red at the tree village yesterday included getting some new supplies and some meat. I already had my kills skinned and drying. There was enough food to last me for a little bit. This freed me up, and I had time today to go back to the wolves and see where I could help.

Luckily, it was an easy trip back to my place after Red tried to keep me with her. I was glad she didn't try to physically restrain me. I don't recall the last time I fought with her as it had been many winters. I still don't know if I could beat her or not. If she wanted to keep me there, between Red and Sera, I'm pretty sure

I would be doomed, but, at least, Red understood she couldn't do that. Even if she locked me in her cottage, I would find a way out. She didn't have a say in how I lived my life or what dangers I chose to face.

The sun had been up for a while when I finally made it out of the house after prepping and putting my food away. It was strange not to start my day with the run around the woods to check for wolves. I figured I had more important things to do; it was fine to miss a few days. And it wasn't like the wolves were out during the daylight anyway. They attacked at night; that was part of the curse. The remaining non-sick wolves were busy building the fence, so I really didn't need to be patrolling.

As I made my way out of my house and onto the pathway that headed north to the wolf village, someone was waiting for me. I nodded to the older man as he stepped beside me to walk. It wasn't going to be a quick jog to the wolf village.

"Did Red finally come to her senses?" Micco asked as he walked slowly beside me.

It wasn't just Red that had aged many winters in the course of only a few moons. Micco was looking older too. He walked with a limp, which was beyond strange also because even though wolves aged, they always stayed in good health.

"If you include telling me I wasn't allowed to see you, then I guess yes."

Micco gave me a sad smile.

"You should listen to her. She knows what she's talking about," Micco replied as he slowed further.

I wasn't sure what to say to the older wolf. Right now, Elder was in trouble. I didn't have a solution. Red didn't seem to have a solution, and neither did Micco.

We needed to all sit down and talk together, but I wasn't sure how or when that would happen. I doubted I could contain my anger if she treated me like a kid any further. And where could we all meet? I was more than sure Micco wasn't welcome in the tree village any longer, and Red wouldn't be welcome at the wolf village. The two people that had pretty much raised me were on opposite sides, and I was caught in the middle trying to help everyone.

"I'm here to help you guys. I don't care about the danger. Red made it her mission to make sure I know how to protect myself. I can handle myself, even if she doesn't think so. The wolves don't scare me."

"They should." Micco found a fallen tree and sat down on it. His clothing had seen better days, and his ragged brown pants had more holes than I could count. He was doing about as well as the rest of the wolves. "They scare the hell outta me."

Not possible. Micco was alpha. He was at the top of the food chain. There was nothing that should make him think twice, let alone a wolf that was under him. I looked at the older man, and he wasn't kidding. He was telling the truth.

"I scare me," Micco continued.

He looked into the woods at the sound of something small digging under the leaves. I was pretty sure it was a mouse, not worth trying to catch or eat, but then again, Micco, along with the rest of the wolves, was going hungry. We shouldn't have been sitting in the woods, and it would have been better to go back to my place. I didn't have much, but I could always get more. I was about to ask him when he spoke again.

"I didn't mean to kill Nathan. I was supposed to be protecting him. Instead, he ends up dead at my hands."

“That wasn’t your fault,” I told him. And it wasn’t. Nathan had to be stopped, and we couldn’t let one wolf start a war that would result in all the wolves being hunted.

“I think I’m too old for all this. I survived one curse only to have to deal with sick wolves bringing us all back to the place we’d be better off not going. I don’t know if I can fight the tree people a second time.”

I sat down beside Micco. It was time to tell him the truth.

“Red said it isn’t a sickness. The curse is back.”

Micco nodded as he tried to smile like he was expecting that news.

“I figured.”

He looked out into the woods and sighed. Here, by my place, it was still the ordinary woods of Elder. Animals roamed around, though most stayed clear of Micco. There were chirping birds and skittering chipmunks. Squirrels chatted in the trees, and the green buds on the trees indicated spring was coming. It was a time for growth and new life, and Micco was dealing with death. I understood why he was tired, but he couldn’t give up. The wolves needed him.

“You had to stop Nathan. He was going to kill the baby. No one blames you, and I bet he doesn’t either. Just think what would have happened not only to the wolves and tree people if you hadn’t stopped him. But what about him if he had awakened the next morning from the curse and found he had killed a child. It would have devastated him. You stopped him from being a monster, and I think if he were here now, he’d thank you. You can’t give up over Nathan.”

Micco nodded as he continued to stare into the woods. He didn’t seem convinced by my words, no matter how true they were.

Being the leader of an entire breed of people was taking its toll on him. I could see it in Red now, but I could also see it in Micco. He was feeling the winters of being a wolf and alpha. I wasn't sure there was anyone qualified or strong enough to take his place if he was done. He didn't have a choice. Without Micco, the wolves would possibly go extinct.

"I just don't know if I can continue to lead them."

The wolves without Micco was just too hard for me to comprehend. Micco was the wolves. He'd been the leader as long as I had been alive and would be for many winters to come. They didn't exist without him. They needed him.

"You are the best chance the wolves have of surviving this."

And that was the truth. Micco was strong and could keep everyone in line, but he also was old enough to remember what it was like over eighteen winters ago. He was perfect for the job even if he didn't think so right now.

"We don't have enough food to feed everyone because the cursed wolves ate all the local animals, but now each wolf village has hundreds of new people to feed, house, and clothe."

"What?"

I would have heard from Red if more people had been bitten and turned into wolves. In fact, I think the tree village would be at the wolf village with guns loaded if that many people had been changed into wolves.'

Micco ran his hands through his dark brown graying hair. Those streaks had been there as long as I could remember but somehow seemed to make him look older now in his defeat. He took a deep breath as I waited for some sort of explanation.

"They kicked them out."

It hit me. I knew exactly who he was talking about. Since the time the curse was broken, many wolves had decided to move back to the human villages they grew up in. Without the curse, they were safe to be home. Some of them had been wolves less time than they had been human. It made sense for them to go home. With the curse back, that meant they weren't safe.

It was better than what I was thinking. If Micco turned any more humans into wolves, they would hunt him, and the wolves would lose. My mother might have been singing the whole let's be one people song, but she was stockpiling weapons in the tree village. I had never told Micco, but I'm sure he suspected that she wasn't going to let the curse be the same as before.

"What am I supposed to do with that many hungry wolves. Yes, spring is coming, and we can plant more food, but our granaries are getting low, and we will need all summer to grow the crops. We need meat to stay healthy. We can't live on spring crops like spinach and peas alone. We won't survive."

"I take it Elder'd farmers also cut off trade?"

The wolves made a living trading with the tree people. They provided meat, animal skins, and wild berries in trade for items like tools and grain from the plains. It was an even trade. But without animals to hunt, they didn't have anything to trade, and they couldn't buy on credit for the following season if the people were too afraid to trade with them. It's impossible to trade with people that won't come within a hundred saplings of you because they are afraid.

"Yes. We've been informed by the farmers of Elder that the wolves are on their own. We have to stay away from the people of Elder, and if one more person gets taken, whether they are hurt or not, the wolves will be hunted."

I would have argued that Red would never do that, but what I had seen only the day before told me she would. Red wasn't the same peace-loving leader I had grown used to in the past few winters. She was protecting the tree people.

"What will you do?"

Micco stared into the sky and then at the woods silently for several moments.

"I don't know."

Micco was defeated. His wolves were getting sick. Elder didn't support them, and they had no one to turn to for help. Red's need to help the people of Elder didn't extend to the wolves. She was treating them just like everyone else. To say I was disappointed in her wasn't quite adequate to express what I was feeling. She was supposed to help all the people of Elder, and if they changed into wolves' part of the time, the wolf villagers were still people of Elder. They needed her help now more than ever.

I sat with him in silence. What was there to do? The wolves were sick and cursed, and we didn't know what the cure was. Red was against the wolves when she once was their greatest champion. And Micco was forced to kill his friend to save the rest of the wolves. Nothing made sense, and it sure wasn't fair.

"Legend has it when the first curse hit, a group left and lived completely as wolves. They claim the curse only affects those that transform back and forth. If we live like wolves, maybe we will stay safe."

"I thought that you said that this could only be passed wolf to wolf. Isn't that the opposite of what you're saying now?"

Micco shrugged. "That was guesswork when I thought it was just an illness. Now we think the curse is back I've been forced to reevaluate. The truth is I don't know for sure either way. Maybe it's something to do with the transforming between forms. I only know that those living only as wolves didn't get affected."

That was hopeful—if it worked.

"But we need to finish the fences first," he expanded. "We can't let the sick wolves out of the villages, and we can't let those that don't know how to transform any more out either. Some of those wolves that returned to their homes haven't transformed since they left. I'm not sure they remember how to transform. They will be a liability, and all liabilities need to be locked up."

"And you need to stay human to make the fence," I added. That was the real problem. If his idea really would work, then most of the wolves would be fine until we found answers. But if they didn't cage the ones that were sick, nothing would matter.

Micco stood up.

"Go home, Castiel. I don't need Red mad at me. Try and talk to her again. Tell her we need help making it safe. The more people that come to build, the quicker the wolves will be separated from everyone."

I didn't want to leave him alone, but I understood. He was right. The wolves didn't stand a chance to get the walls built. They needed help. I had to go back and talk to Red, no matter if I wanted to deal with her right now or not.

Micco rose and patted me on the shoulder. He was a good leader, and I hated to see him giving up. The wolves would never survive without him.

"You're a good kid, Castiel. Don't get caught between

all this. Do as your mother asks."

I didn't say a word as Micco walked back the way he came. I wasn't about to lie to the older wolf, but I couldn't just follow what Red wanted blindly. She might not want the wolves killed outright, but she wasn't helping them stay safe. She was choosing the tree people over the wolves. The women and children of the wolves' villages were just caught in the crossfire.

I got up and started to walk back to my place. I had to think and come up with a plan. There had to be something more I could do. Heck, my mother was the leader of the whole kingdom. There had to be something she could do.

I made it almost home when I heard a branch break. Whipping around, I planned to attack whatever was following me. My knife was in my hand without a moment's hesitation as I was readied to attack. I stopped when I recognized the red wolf peeking around a tree.

"Grace," I called to the wolf. She lost her shyness and bound over to me.

I ducked as she moved in to give me a sloppy wolf lick. That might be an okay way to greet another human wolf, but I didn't appreciate being covered with wolf spit.

"I don't think so," I tsked at her. "So why are you out here? Shouldn't you be back with the wolves? If any of the tree villagers are out, they'll shoot you on sight. You should probably be going home. I'll see you in the village tomorrow after I talk to Red again."

Grace pushed me with her nose toward the way I was already walking.

"Yes, I need to head back."

I took a few steps towards my house, and she trotted along beside me.

"That's the wrong way," I told her. Surprisingly I was fine talking with wolves. I was more than used to my best friend Nikkan as a wolf. He spent at least ninety percent of his time as a wolf, so it wasn't strange to me, but it was a little hard to understand what Grace was saying. "The wolves live the other direction."

Okay, she knew that. It wasn't like I needed to explain that to her. Wolf Grace sat down by my feet and didn't move to go back to her village. It seemed like she had something to tell me.

"Fine, we can go to my place," I told the wolf. "Then you can head back to the wolves. I'll even walk you back to keep you safe."

Wolf Grace happily followed me back to my house. I opened the door and let her in.

"I have your clothes from the other night," I told her as I went over to the basket by my door and dug through it, pulling out her clothing. I set it down on the couch and walked back to the kitchen to get some water on the stove to make tea for us.

"I'll step out so you can change after I get this water heated up," I told her with my back to her as the kettle filled from the slow trickle of my sink.

"Castiel, I think we need to talk," Nikkan said as he walked into my house.

I turned back to my friend and noticed that Grace was in the corner of the room, hurrying to get her shirt on. Her back was to us, but I was pretty sure her cheeks were flaming red by now. Nikkan's eyes went straight to the corner as mine did before he looked back to me. He didn't say anything more.

The hatred behind his eyes was something I had never seen directed at me before. Without a single word, Nikkan stormed out of my house. I set the kettle down on the stove before hurrying to the door to chase my friend, but before I had the chance to chase him or try to explain, he was already deep into the woods.

"Great," I said, running my hand through my hair as I came back from the doorway. Nikkan got the completely wrong impression.

"Sorry," Grace said quietly, her cheeks still flaming. "I figured I could get dressed before you turned back around. We get pretty good at taking off and putting on clothing with all the transforming."

"Not your fault," I told her. And it wasn't. Nikkan ran off before either one of us could explain things to him.

"But he was already mad at you. I can't imagine how bad it will be now." Grace looked hurt by the whole situation. She bit her lip like she was going to cry. "I screwed up." The tears were ready to fall, and I had no clue what to do. Crying girls was Nikkan's specialty, not mine, though thinking about it, that probably wasn't true either.

"Really, Grace. Not your fault. And he will get over it once I finally talk with him. I promise. We've been friends forever. Nikkan will understand this is just a big screw up. Really."

Grace seemed to pull her tears back and nodded but didn't look entirely convinced.

"I'm still sorry." The tears were barely being held at bay. I needed to act fast to avoid anything messy.

I smiled and handed her a cup. She took the tea from me and walked back to my table. I followed with the hot tea kettle to pour us each a cup. My house wasn't too warm; I hoped the tea would be enough to warm her up from her run outside.

"So why were you in the woods? The tree people are terrified of wolves. It isn't safe for you to be running around as a wolf."

Grace bit her cheek and nodded. "I know...."

I stirred my tea leaves as I waited for her to continue. One thing Red had taught me well was how to wait when someone was talking.

"I'm scared to stay in the village," she blurted out and then quickly grabbed her cup to take a sip and not have to talk more. I just waited, and she realized I wasn't going to ask more. I nodded for her to continue, taking a long sip of my tea, too.

"Ten people fell sick this morning. If I stay there, I'm going to becoming a monster like the rest of them, or I'll end up as their food. One of the newly sick wolves killed a wolf person last night. I can't stay there. I don't want to become a monster or be eaten by one."

I understood. Part of me feared for Nikkan. Fight or not, he was still my friend, and I didn't want him to become part of the curse either. I didn't blame Grace, in the least, for not wanting to be in the wolf village. I had no idea what the solution should be, but I wasn't going to send her back to someplace she was scared to be.

"You can stay here," I told her. She wasn't sick, and I knew she'd be safe with me from the wolves or the tree people. I'd keep Grace safe.

7TH MARCH

Grace refused to sleep on my couch bed since it was my house. She said she absolutely couldn't take my bed. No matter how I tried to convince her, she just wouldn't do it. So, we both ended up sleeping on the floor. Neither one of us would budge. My back was a little sore when I woke, but I didn't care. I had enough other problems to deal with. Grace was curled up in my one blanket, looking like the wolf she could become but in her human form.

Nikkan was crazy to think I had something with Grace. As I stared at her right now, I still couldn't picture anything but being friends with her. She was just Grace. In fact, I couldn't imagine how Nikkan could see her as anything other than the younger sister she felt like. She was cute, but it was little-sister cute.

Grace stirred and then stretched, a full-body stretch cracking her neck down to her toes without opening her eyes. The wolf was ever-present in her. Slowly, she opened her eyes and stared at my very dull ceiling.

"I don't have much for breakfast," I told her as I stood up and walked into my kitchen. "Normally, Nikkan gets extra eggs for us because I don't have chickens. But he's been gone a couple of days, and I don't have any food beyond some meat and bread my mother gave me yesterday."

"That's fine," Grace said as she sat and stretched further.

I rummaged through my cupboards and pulled out the meager breakfast I had to offer. Grace sat on the floor and just watched me as she talked.

"Do you remember Mira? She was short and had that wild blond hair that was always sticking up in every direction. She moved back yesterday."

I nodded. I didn't exactly remember who she was talking about, but I had a feeling quite a few people moved back, not of their own free will.

"And Ashton moved back too," Grace added. "The village is so full right now, there aren't enough homes. Some of the guys had to stop building the fence and start some new homes."

That had to be stressing Micco out. He needed that fence built before the remaining uncursed wolves could go off into the woods to live without being affected by the curse. But he needed homes for all his wolves until they could leave. It just was a tough situation all around.

"Do you think Nikkan will come back today, and we can explain yesterday to him?"

I shrugged. I didn't want to disappoint her, but I

had a feeling Nikkan wasn't coming back for a while. It took him days to come back after I just asked her out. I could only imagine what he was thinking about now. It would be weeks if he chose to come back at all. I kind of had the feeling he wasn't going to return until he knew the truth, and if we couldn't tell him the truth, he'd never know.

"Well, he should. I mean, he just walked in here and didn't even say sorry," Grace continued. "It was embarrassing. I'm used to shifting with the wolves, but Nikkan wasn't among them. He's never gone for a run with everyone else. He's different."

Oh, I had a good feeling if he came back it wasn't going to be to apologize. I kept that to myself. Nikkan wasn't really the apologizing type as it was, but this was one thing I was pretty sure he'd never budge on. And it was going to be impossible to find and talk to him. His typical reaction when he didn't want to speak was to turn into a wolf and run away. How the heck were we supposed to have a real conversation when I had to chase him, and he couldn't speak back?

I got how Grace felt. It was embarrassing because she obviously felt the same way about me as I did her. There was nothing romantic between us and nothing to be ashamed of or for us to apologize for because nothing happened, but I doubted that was what Nikkan was going to be thinking.

And with that thought, there was a knock at the door. Grace looked up at me and quickly stood. I had no clue who would be visiting me early in the morning, let alone knocking at the door. I hoped it wasn't Red. She'd be more than a little upset to find Grace in my house.

I opened my door and surprisingly found Micco

standing there. Behind him stood Nikkan and a few more of the male wolves from the pack. They all had scowls on their faces as they tried to stare me down; four big, burly men with arms the size of tree trunks, doing their best glares. Not that they cared, but none of them intimidated me in the least. Muscles didn't mean strength. Trust me. That was lesson number one with Red. She wasn't more than a sapling tall and could kick the butt of any person: woman, man, or wolf.

"We are here to escort Grace back to the village and make sure she gets there safely," Micco explained while I stayed in the doorway. He didn't look happy to be at my house, but it was something else I couldn't put my finger on.

I looked over my shoulder, and Grace stared back in shock at Micco. She hadn't been expecting to see her alpha. I had a feeling why Micco knew Grace was in my house, but I wasn't sure about the whole escort situation. It didn't seem like Micco. He was usually more laid back. He wasn't into bossing his wolves around. At least, he never had been in the past. Maybe it was the curse.

Micco was the alpha of the wolves, but he was just a citizen of Elder. Red was the real leader. While he had some control, it wasn't really absolute or that he could be ordering people to be certain places in the kingdom. Grace was a citizen, too, and had the right to go wherever she pleased in the kingdom. Micco was overstepping his authority by ordering her where to go.

"Grace, do you want to go back?" I asked, loud enough for all the people outside my house to hear.

"No," she whispered and quickly averted her eyes from Micco and the group.

Micco was her alpha. He hadn't given a direct

command that she go back to the wolves, but he could. Unless she left the wolf village, she had to do what he commanded. It was a wolf thing. At least, he was just asking for the moment.

"Thanks for the offer, but she's staying here for now," I told Micco, but looked at the wolves behind him instead. Most of them sneered back at me, and a few made fists at my words. Micco had to understand what was I saying.

I wasn't scared of a gang of wanna-be alpha wolves. Not a single one of them stood a chance against me. I had spent winters training on how to fight and defeat wolves. It was a joke that they even thought so. It indeed showed just how much I was an outsider to the wolves.

"She belongs with her people," Nikkan spat out from behind Micco's shoulder. If Micco wasn't the alpha and in charge, I was pretty sure Nikkan would have been pushing him out of the way.

"The same people she's afraid of?" I raised an eyebrow at him in a challenge.

I looked at Nikkan specifically to see if he could understand that Grace feared the wolves. She wasn't with me to play house. She was staying safe, away from the sick wolves so that she didn't get ill or become their next meal. Grace was smart, and Nikkan had to know that much. He had spent the past two winters pining over her; he had to know this wasn't some whim. She'd thought it through. If he wasn't just thinking with jealousy, maybe he could have understood better that she was scared.

Micco seemed to understand why Grace was afraid, but the men behind him didn't. I could hear them grumble amongst themselves, but I ignored them. I focused on Nikkan. He was the only one that needed to be convinced.

"Grace came here for my protection from the sick wolves," I began, pleading with my eyes as much as I could. Nikkan had to know that protecting Grace came first. He would have done the same if he wasn't so resentful.

"No one is so sick that you have to run away," one of the men interrupted me. I didn't rise to his challenge as I focused just on Nikkan.

"Not according to her. Someone was killed yesterday in the wolf village, and she feels safer here."

That got their attention. None of them spoke for a moment. Micco seemed lost for words. I could tell that was a secret they were trying to keep hidden. I wasn't trying to get Grace in trouble with all of them, but she didn't feel safe, and they had to know it was true. She probably wasn't safe. In fact, most of them probably weren't safe. Micco, the strongest of them all, went head to head with a cursed wolf and had to fight a hard battle to win. None of the weaker wolves stood a chance against a cursed wolf.

"You told an outsider," one of the men accused her in barely more than a whisper.

Grace was now right behind my back, partially hidden but close enough to hear everything. I could feel her hand on my back, and she was shaking. It seemed I was right in that it was a secret.

"Castiel isn't an outsider," Micco corrected the wolf. "He's welcome any time in our village, and I keep no secrets from him. He's spent more time with us in the past three winters than his mother."

"He's a tree human," the same man spat out like the word 'tree human' was a dirty word. How ironic that he was acting the same way that the tree humans were acting towards the wolves.

Nothing was ever going to change if the people didn't start seeing themselves as citizens of Elder, not one kind of human or another. We were all part of the same kingdom, but it seemed like neither side wanted the other ones there. It surprised me that the wolves continued the hate when it was them that faced being killed for being what they were. I wanted them to have more compassion, but then again, they were wolves. Compassion wasn't one of their greatest traits.

Micco nodded to me like he understood why Grace was at my house. I kind of had the feeling if he didn't have all the responsibility to keep the wolves safe, he might have had an extended visit with me also. He nodded his head to the men behind him, and they all stepped back away from the doorway to my place. Everyone except Nikkan.

"But Grace needs to come home with us," Nikkan told everyone that had moved as he glared at me. He couldn't just give up.

This would have been much easier if he had stuck around long enough for me to explain to him what was going on. Heck, if he had been home, he could have slept with Grace on the floor instead of me. He could be the one protecting her. There was no way he would listen to me right now, but I wished I could go back and get him to see it the way it truly was.

"Grace has already said that she doesn't want to go with you," I reiterated her position. It went over as well the second time as the first.

"It doesn't matter. She's a wolf, and you're a human."

Nikkan was trying so hard to keep Grace from me that I almost wanted to laugh. She had as big of a crush on him as he did on her. There was nothing going on between us. I had to keep my laugh hidden as I stared back at him, or I was pretty sure the fight would turn physical as he wouldn't see the humor in the situation.

"That didn't seem to matter at any point in the past three winters to you," I reminded Nikkan.

He huffed and didn't respond. He couldn't argue with that.

Grace finally peered out from behind my shoulder. She frowned at Nikkan as he stood by himself, still trying to confront me. The other men were moving back away at Micco's command and no longer threatening to Grace. She knew she was safe and was going to be able to stay. Micco was with the men as Nikkan continued to stand on my doorstep.

"Castiel is your best friend? Why don't you start acting like it?"

The other male wolves with Nikkan now were standing a good two or three saplings away from him. A couple hid their smiles as Grace started to lay into Nikkan. Everyone knew that the female wolves had more than a little fire in them.

"You ran away before we could talk to you yesterday, and if that was any indication of why Castiel is living here alone, I get it. You must have run away before too. Instead of dealing with your problems, you pretend it's everyone else's fault. Grow up Nikkan. Real men take care of their own problems and don't have to drag five men along with them. Deal with it."

Grace moved and was now standing side by side with me just inside my house. She was just getting going, and I planned to make sure I was back far enough away to not have that anger directed at me, from either of them. I slid back a bit more, so she was now in front of me.

"You don't have the right to come here and make demands of me. I can go where I please when I please. I'm a grown woman. I don't need a man to tell me what to do." Grace looked over Nikkan's shoulder and was glaring at the men with him. "And to bring a group of wolves with you? Really?" She was now shaking her head like it was the craziest thing Nikkan had ever done.

Personally, I knew Nikkan could and would do a lot more crazy in his life, but for her, this had to be the first time she saw him act before thinking. That was a way of life for my best friend.

Grace's red hair was now flying around her as she whipped between each man behind Nikkan, and she gave them each a glare to send them on their way. Her fear of them was utterly gone since her anger had taken over.

"You should all be ashamed of yourselves. Matthean? Liam? Really? Bill, don't you have a wife and kids to take care of? Running off to help Nikkan pretend he's in charge when you all should be back in the village helping those that need new homes, and if that's all done, then making the fence. You don't have time to run off and play backup to some guy's jealousy. Why in the world are you here and not being the men you're supposed to be?"

Nikkan opened his mouth like he was going to protest, but Grace didn't give him a chance. Her anger flowed freely from the men and back to Nikkan.

"You aren't my father, and you don't get a say in my life. Go home, Nikkan."

She emphasized her last three words slowly and carefully before slamming the door shut in his face. I froze where I was just behind her and listened to the space outside my house. Nikkan must have been as much in shock as I was. He wasn't moving an inch.

"The girl isn't coming back with us tonight," Micco said loud enough for me to hear. "And she's right. We need to head back and keep building. There's still much to get done."

Not a single guy with Micco disagreed with him as they all trudged back into the woods. I heard the breaking of bones as Nikkan must have turned back into his wolf form. He gave a growl at the closed door and then followed the men back to their village.

Grace turned around and leaned her back against the door. She slid down to the ground and let out a breath like she had been holding in the whole time. Her hands shook a little as if the adrenalin had worn off, and she was back to sweet, quiet Grace.

"I'm sorry about that," she said as she covered her reddening cheeks.

"Sorry for what? Making them go away?"

I pulled her hands down so she could see my face. She had done a great job of getting them to leave. I didn't need to do a thing once she got going.

"Never be sorry for standing up for yourself. Never."

Grace's cheeks stayed red, but silently she nodded her head.

"Now, what do we do from here?" I asked, though it was more for me than her.

I wasn't sure what to do. I wanted to go back and help the wolves build houses and the fence, but Grace didn't feel safe there. So, I couldn't go and bring her back. I couldn't leave her in my house alone while I went to the wolves. What Micco needed was more help, but I couldn't offer anything like that. Unless I talked with my mother.

"Do you think what Micco said was true?"

I wasn't sure what she was talking about.

"About the wolves that turned and stayed wolves the whole time during the last curse."

She was talking about the day before. She must have overheard Micco and I talking.

"I don't know. I could ask my mother, but I'm not sure."

Grace bit her lip and nodded.

"It's not that I like my wolf form so much. Kind of stinks to be naked all the time and unable to talk to people when you can understand them. But if it would keep me from turning into a monster, I'd do it."

While I knew the wolf Grace was, I couldn't imagine her as a wolf all the time like Nikkan preferred. Grace was a girl and a human.

"It could be many, many winters before the curse is broken again. Would you want to be a wolf that long? What about the rest of your life? The last time the curse lasted hundreds of winters. You could spend the rest of your life trapped in a world you could see, taste, feel, understand, but you could never talk back. Would you truly want that?"

Nikkan loved to be a wolf, but most of the wolf humans would rather be human. To lose that side ultimately was something I wasn't sure anyone would volunteer for.

"Would it be fun? No," Grace explained. "But it would keep me and everyone around me safe. I can do that for everyone else. I want to do that."

I looked at my friend that had been around as long as I could remember. Most of her family was taken by the last curse and never recovered, hunted for the monsters they became. Her mother was left alone and pregnant with Grace, spared from changing into a beast, but having to raise a baby on her own once the curse was gone. Grace was only a child when her mother passed on. The village had taken care of her since.

It was strange to see her not as that child that pestered me and Nikkan when Red would take me to the wolf village. Grace endlessly followed us around and tried to do whatever we were doing. We spent half our time trying to get away or hiding from her. She was almost three full winters younger than me, but right now, she seemed so much older. She was making a life decision without any hesitation.

"Is that what you truly want?"

I knew she had a crush on Nikkan. If she turned into a wolf right now, she'd never had a chance to tell him. Her life as a human would be over.

"It doesn't matter what I want. That was taken away from me the moment I was born a wolf. I don't get choices often, but I know this is the right thing to do."

I tried to smile, but there was no happiness in what she was suggesting she was going to do. Essentially, she would be gone. The friend I couldn't remember meeting since she'd always just been around would be gone. Human Grace would possibly never come back.

I would have loved to change her mind, but I understood. She wanted control of her life.

"Okay. If that's what you want. But let me talk to Red first. She might be able to tell us if that's true or not."

Grace nodded as she finally stood back up, full of strength she didn't have before, a new determination in her eyes.

"Tomorrow at first light, I'll go visit Red. If you promise to stay here, I'll see what she knows, and then we can go from there."

Grace gave me a small smile and nodded. With one choice, she was possibly going to be gone forever. Human Grace would cease to exist anywhere but inside her head. My friend would be gone, and everything she had ever hoped and dreamed would go with her. There wasn't a right answer; there wasn't a good choice to make. This was life in Elder and something no one had wished to come back. Now, Grace had to deal with it, and I was going to have one less friend in the world.

8TH MARCH

I woke before the sun the next morning. Grace was still sleeping on the couch as I finally convinced her I wasn't going to use it as long as she was visiting me.

Grace had returned to her quiet self as soon as the wolves left yesterday, but that could have been because of what she planned to do. There was the very likely chance that Grace was going to be a wolf for the rest of her life. Where Nikkan loved his wolf form, Grace wasn't as happy being a wolf. It was a sacrifice she was willing to make, but it didn't make it any easier.

I wasn't sure what was going through her head, but I knew she was thinking about it after the wolves left. The curse being back didn't just mean life-changes for the tree people; it meant the wolves had to make a choice also. I wasn't sure how many would want to leave their human loves behind. Mothers wouldn't see their children grow up, siblings would never hug one another again, and couples would never be able to tell each other they loved them.

Life, once all my friends were furry and never able to speak to me again, would be different. When Grace and Nikkan became wolves, I would be alone. The tree people of Elder never cared much for me. They knew I wasn't a wolf, but I was still not one of them. They never let me forget it, no matter that my mother was the Red of Elder. I had no friends in the tree village. The wolves until yesterday were always welcoming to me, even if most kept their distance. They didn't shun me like the tree people.

It was going to be a lot quieter without my friends to talk with. Nikkan wouldn't be there to argue with me over everything he could think of, and Grace wouldn't be in the village every time we went back to visit. But I guess that wasn't completely true. I was still going to be able to talk to them; they just weren't going to be able to respond to me.

I watched Grace sleep a bit. It wasn't in a creepy way, but just in knowing that soon, I wouldn't see her human form again. Part of me was mad at Nikkan. She was never going to get to tell him her feelings for him because he was a jerk. They would never get to have the time together that I knew both of them wanted. It was hard to remember that being human would be over for her if Red confirmed what Micco had said.

And with that thought, I quietly left my house and Grace behind asleep.

My jog through the woods was quiet as a regular morning would be. I was glad to find that it was clear of wolves or the carnage of their hunger. As soon as the cursed wolves got near my place, I was pretty sure Red would send hunting parties out to keep the rest of the people safe. Both sides would lose with that.

The wolf village had more going on than either Red or I had known about. I hated to see that the wolves had been upset with Grace for sharing with me. I understood that the curse was their problem to deal with, but if they were running around and killing without memory, it was the problem of everyone in Elder. We needed to know the truth, even if it wasn't going to put the wolves in the best light.

Birds filled the air with their morning greeting as the crickets and night insects began to go to bed for the day. Sounds of nature surrounded me on every run I made in the woods, and I was thankful that the sounds were still there. I had grown used to the forest and all its sounds when I left the village. It seemed the animals kept away from the tree-dwellers as much as they stayed away from the wolves.

The run was quick as I jogged at my new-found speed. I would arrive early, but the tree city began their day early, so people were bound to be up and around—the same people that tolerated but never accepted me. Lucky for me, Red preferred her cottage, and if I got there early enough, I wouldn't have to see any of the tree dwellers.

It didn't take me long to make the run to Red's cottage. It seemed like I was getting faster every time the sun rose. I really had to wonder how much faster I could get. I was beyond a normal human, but with all that was going on, I didn't have time to wonder what it meant. Nikkan and I always wondered where I came from, but Red wasn't one to share details about anything with anyone unless she chose to.

As I got close enough to smell the hyacinths that dotted the cottage grounds of my mother's place, my jog turned into a walk. The deep floral scent was easy to pick up on as I was pretty sure she was the only one that wanted her place to smell strongly of flowers. Red was like that. She was tough, barely smiled, and yet loved to grow flowers. Hard, rough, and floral, all mixed into one. A bit of a mess of ideas all bundled into the leader of Elder and the woman that raised me. I gave up on trying to understand her many winters ago.

Red was at her kitchen sink as I stood just inside the tree line. I was well hidden by the branches and the early spring foliage growing around her cottage, and it gave me time to watch her.

The day was just beginning, but that wouldn't mean a thing to Red. She was an early riser and always had things to get done. Red was doing dishes. It seemed like an ordinary task but threw me for a loop. Red was meticulous about everything in her life. She had to be. Chores were one thing she never put off until morning, and yet here she was washing away. I watched as she soaped up another dish and then rinsed it off. I wanted to think it was just a breakfast dish but knew better. Something was up with her.

Growing up as the child of Little Red Riding Hood was more than a little intimidating. She was bigger than life, even if she was only a sapling tall. There was nothing Red couldn't do. She beat the curse that no one else could. She fought for and saved her people time and time again. She was amazing. Everyone in Elder knew her name, and heck, other kingdoms knew her too. She was that famous.

Having her as a mother was more than a little

strange, as at the end of the day when everyone else was gone, Red was just Red. What the world around us didn't see was that she never turned off the part that made people worship her. She was always in control and always looking for a way to make life better for everyone in Elder. I was pretty sure no matter what I ever did in life, I was never going to live up to that.

I spent most of my childhood trying to learn from her and understanding that I would never be able to do things as well as she could. It wasn't that she was mean or didn't try to raise me. It was just that she had the highest expectations of anyone I ever met, and those expectations were placed on me too. When I reached fifteen winters, it was best to be on my own, but that didn't mean I never saw her. I made sure to visit the village at least once every moon cycle. And one thing that never changed was Red, until now.

I wasn't exactly ready to talk to her again after our last conversation, but I needed to, for Grace's sake. One thing that didn't change over the winters was the tension between us. Red still couldn't see that she raised me right, and I was strong enough to stand on my own.

Red continued to wash the dishes, and I just stood there watching her. Life wasn't easy growing up in her shadow, but because of her and all she taught me, I didn't fear to live in the forest alone. I didn't fear my friends or the curse that was taking more wolves every day. I knew I was strong enough to handle that, even if she didn't see that.

Red was the strongest person I had ever met, and that said a lot. There were many dignitaries and leaders she worked with over the winters, and as a child, I was there for a lot of meetings. I could tell just by looking that if no one understood the power in her, Red didn't care. Her life was about Elder and making our kingdom better. She never flaunted her strength, but I always saw it. It was strange to see it fading. It was weird to see her as just a human.

Slowly, I approached her hut. One thing I knew well was you never tried to surprise Red because if it was possible to catch her unaware, any surprise could be deadly. She didn't hit to maim or injure; she hit to kill.

Red didn't look up as I neared the door. I knew from experience, the door would be unlocked. Why would the most powerful person in Elder need to lock her door? If anyone actually tried to attack her in her own home, they wouldn't come out alive.

Without knocking, I stepped into the house I was raised in. The place was small yet larger than my own home by the addition of the two bedrooms. I didn't need a bedroom since I was the only person living in my hut. Red's was also cleaner. Typically, not a thing was out of place, nor was there a speck of dust. She didn't keep anything personal around her house. Yes, there was a blanket on the couch, but it wasn't made for her or given to her by someone special. There were no pictures on the wall or trinkets on the counters. I guess that much rubbed off on me as my house was similarly plain, but at least, I had the excuse of having only lived there for three winters, not twenty-five.

"Did you forget something when you left?" Red asked, not turning around from the sink where she continued to scrub away.

I walked over and stood beside her. It felt like only yesterday I was looking up to her, and now I was more than a full head taller than her. I took up the dry dishcloth and held my hand out for whatever needed drying.

"I talked to Micco yesterday." That was partially true.

"Mmm-hmm," Red replied as she continued to wash. She was always like that. She never took the bait to start a conversation even though she knew perfectly well that I wanted her to.

"He said the wolves are getting worse, and Elder kicked all the wolves back to the forest. He doesn't have enough food, homes, or supplies for all the people that returned."

Red just continued to wash as I talked. She didn't try to explain or tell me what would be done. One thing that was always Red was that she never lied, or sugar-coated anything. She was always truthful and honest to a point. It was hard to accept as a child, but as an adult, I appreciated her honesty.

She wasn't going to offer help or a solution, so I kept talking.

"He mentioned that the last time the curse came, a group turned into wolves and didn't turn back to human. He said that the curse would only affect those that were human, not wolf."

Still no input from Red.

"Is that true?"

"Yes," she replied as she finished rinsing the last dish. I took it from her and dried it before stacking it in the same pile with the rest of the dishes.

"So that's the solution, right? They turn into wolves while we brew a new cure."

Red never told anyone how she broke the curse, but I had to imagine it was with the help of the witches. While there were few witches left in Elder, there was still some left. They had grown fewer over the winters, but were always around somewhere, if you could find them. While Red wasn't a witch, I was pretty sure that if they made the cure the first time, she could get them to do it again.

"It doesn't work like that," Red chided me as she opened a cupboard and took out a loaf of bread. Reaching for the serrated knife she used to cut bread, she went to work making nice even slices.

"Then tell me how it works," I pleaded. If Grace was going to give up her human life, I wanted to be finding an answer for her, and the sooner, the better.

Red stopped cutting her loaf of bread and turned to me. She eyed me over like she was contemplating what to tell me.

"It wasn't a potion. I don't know how it works exactly. I can't explain, but it wasn't something that can just be made. It was something deeper, different. Something I can't make," she admitted as she watched me carefully for my reaction.

I tried not to let my mouth fall open in shock. Red was the savior. She cured the wolves. She brought peace to Elder. And she didn't know how to do it again.

"Please tell me you're kidding."

Red never kidded. I knew that much, but I had to hope with her new attitude that maybe there were jokes going on too.

"I wish I could, really. I just don't have an answer. It wasn't something I could do a second time. All I can do is try to keep everyone safe." Red shrugged and went back to slicing her bread.

I had no idea what to say to her. She never told me how she saved everyone from the curse, but I assumed it was some grand secret. I wasn't expecting that she didn't know how.

Red finished slicing the loaf of bread as she placed

the pieces on a plate. She took the plate to the table before she returned to grab butter and jelly. I followed behind her, unsure of what to do.

"So, if Grace turns into a wolf, it might be forever?" I finally found words to keep our conversation going.

Red gave me a sad nod.

I felt anger building in me again. It wasn't fair. Why did Grace have to give up her life? Why couldn't she have a normal life? Red said she was keeping everyone safe, but what she really meant was that she was keeping the tree people safe. Grace wasn't being kept safe; in fact, she was giving up her life to keep the tree people safe too. The wolves had to sacrifice everything, and the tree people just complained and hid in their trees. I had no doubts. Red was protecting the wrong people.

"What are you doing to keep everyone safe?" I finally asked. "Are you helping Micco feed and house the wolves? Are you helping him build a fence? Are you helping him track and cage up the cursed wolves?"

Red bit her lip as I added more and more to my complaint. She understood my point. She wasn't keeping Elder safe; she was keeping the tree people safe. The lazy tree people that asked her to put her life on the line time and time again. The ones that only found time to complain about the wolves but never help them. Those tree people.

I closed my eyes and took a deep breath. The curse wasn't her fault. I knew that much. And yelling at her wasn't going to change anything.

"Are your friends going to turn into wolves?" Red finally asked, knowing I was holding my anger at bay.

"Grace is. She doesn't feel safe at the village with the wolves and doesn't want to be a monster."

Red nodded in understanding.

"But it isn't fair." And that was my problem with the whole situation. Grace was giving up everything, and it was likely to be for the rest of her life.

"Life is rarely fair," Red replied like she knew more than she was letting on.

I had seen Red love the wolves. She cared for them even as she made helping the tree people a priority. It was her that wanted to bring everyone together. She cared for Micco and everyone in Elder. I stared at her more and tried to see it. Why wasn't she doing more for the wolves? Why was she just letting them be taken by the curse? She broke it once, and I had no doubts she could do it again.

Red lifted up the plate of bread and offered me a piece. I took one and covered it with jelly as I sat down at the table with her.

"The only thing I know about the curse from the last time is that your friend is correct. In her wolf form, she will be free of it. The curse strikes those in human form, forcing them to turn into monsters. The witches called the curse a spirit snatcher as everything that made the wolf human would be gone."

I couldn't see that happen to Grace or Nikkan, no matter how much of an idiot he was being.

"And if she blacks out and changes not on her own? She's cursed then?"

Red shook her head. "The last time, the curse took weeks. People didn't turn into monsters night after night. It took weeks of occasional losses of memory. As long as she can remember every night and every change, she should be free of the curse. As long as she can change permanently before the first time she blacks out, she can avoid the curse," Red explained.

"And can never speak to a human again," I added.

Red shrugged. “I would have chosen the same thing if it had happened to me. I’d rather live my life in silence than kill those I love.”

I studied Red as she took a bite of her bread. She had never mentioned anyone before that she loved. I was the only family she had, and we weren’t technically related as we didn’t share blood. There was never a person in her life that I could say she loved. Micco had been her friend over the winters, and I didn’t doubt he had a crush on her, but she didn’t seem to notice.

We sat in silence and ate the bread she had. There was nothing more we could talk about. The curse was back. Grace was right, and soon my friends would be gone while we fought to find an answer without them.

Red didn’t order me to stay as I stood after finishing my breakfast with her. She didn’t beg either. She understood the truth. I was responsible for myself.

As I neared the doorway, I turned back to her.

“I’ll stay safe.”

Red nodded her head and gave me a strained smile.

“Don’t worry mom; I learned from the best.”

I gave her a grin, and she just shook her head. It was true. If Red could survive as long as she had as the Red before she defeated the curse, she was the best one to learn from. It wasn’t like I wanted to put my skills to the test, but I felt safe in the woods. It was home.

Without a second glance back, I made my way into the woods and began my jog home. My mind was processing what she had told me about the curse and no cure. There had to be something I could do, and I wasn’t giving up, it was just a bit of a shock. Red was the hero of Elder, and she didn’t have an answer. I wasn’t used to that.

It didn’t take long to figure out someone was

following me, but from the steps, I already knew who it was. There was only one human that could run as stealthily as my mother.

I changed my course slightly to pass one of the larger trees on my run home. I knew where every tree and sapling stood and which ones I could climb, hide behind, or take a few branches from to take home as firewood. This was my home and my woods. I ran past and caught the lowest branch of the tree I was aiming for, pulling myself up onto the hidden branch as quickly as I ran. I waited as the quiet follower ran past, underneath the tree I was now sitting in.

Sera's dark hair bounced as she ran. The recent cut to chin length was the main reason I could hear her. Her steps were silent, but her swaying hair that didn't seem to fit in a ponytail wasn't as quiet as her feet. I could hear the hair swish in the wind. And there was her scent. I knew she was human.

Sera kept running like she was following me, though I knew otherwise. I wasn't down there to be followed. She'd soon figure out that I wasn't farther ahead.

After she left my view, I could hear her stop. I hopped down from my tree and leaned against it as I waited for her to backtrack.

"Why are you following me?" I asked when I knew she was close enough to hear me but not be seen.

Sera walked out from the trees, not pretending to be shy that she was caught.

"I was ordered to," Sera replied. She had the same honest tendencies as Red.

"Because she thinks I'll do something to get in trouble?"

Just like Red. She sent a babysitter to keep track of me. Nope, she didn't think I was grown up yet.

"Because she cares about you," Sera replied with a huff.

"If she knew me at all, she'd know I was perfectly capable of taking care of myself. Go back to her and help out where she needs you," I told Sera. I had seen Red and knew she needed the help more than I did. Sera stayed precisely where she was.

I pointed with my finger back the direction we had come from, but Sera just stared at me. Typical Sera, she listened as well as Red did.

"Go on. I don't need to deal with your snark and sarcasm. I have enough to deal with."

And I did. I was the one that had to tell the wolves they could live as wolves for the rest of their lives until the curse was broken, and by the way, there's no way to break the curse. Not exactly the job I wanted, but I wasn't about to keep it from them. They deserved to know their fate: be taken by the curse or be a wolf for the rest of their lives.

9TH MARCH

My quiet simple hut was far from being quiet since Sera came back with me and stayed with Grace and me. She wasn't really invited, but she took no as well as my mother did. Strong personalities seemed to be a requirement for being the Red. No matter what I said to her, she was determined to stay, and I knew enough to not waste my breath trying to get her out.

Sera didn't leave me any alone time with Grace to let her know what my mother had told me. Grace took it better than I expected. She only had one request—that we spend her last day as a human enjoying it. Sera seemed to like that thought and eagerly joined in making plans on how we could spend Grace's last day as a human. I fell asleep listening to them debate what were the best activities.

The sun had just risen, and they were already back at it, chatting away, planning their perfect last day. Grace and Sera found that they actually got along great and had more in common than either of them knew. Prejudices had kept them from ever talking before, but I had a feeling it was different now. Sera seemed to understand Grace better now that she knew what Grace was giving up to protect everyone. Just like Sera, Grace was thinking of all of Elder.

I pretty much stayed out of their chatter. It wasn't like they needed my input anyway. Within only a few short moments of meeting, they figured out that their shared love of food meant I was a terrible host.

"There's a baker in Azren that has the best tarts, every flavor," Sera gushed. Graced licked her lips.

There was no way the food at my place was going to compare to all Sera was describing to her. I could cook when needed, but I preferred my life to be outside and not spent at a stove. Actually, I think Nikkan cooked more than I did, so I really didn't have much to offer them.

"If you guys promise to stay here and pack, I'll run back and get us supplies," Sera said, wagging her eyebrows at the word supplies. We all knew she meant food. She hadn't stopped complaining at my diet of bread and dried meat since she came the day before.

"I thought you weren't allowed to leave me alone," I replied. "And with a dangerous wolf."

I motioned to my dangerous wolf, Grace, and she gasped and swatted at my arm. She put on a fake pout as she looked from me to Sera.

"The curse only happens at night," Sera scolded me. "And look at Grace. She's as far from being a rabid beast as you can get. In fact, I think maybe you and I are closer than she is."

Grace nodded with the pout still on her face.

"We'll stay here," Grace assured Sera, probably just to get the treats Sera had been telling her about since the moment she arrived. I raised an eyebrow at Grace but said nothing as Sera nodded and ran off into the woods.

Sera didn't wait for us to say more. She was probably afraid we would leave without her, or maybe she really wanted to get going on our day. Either way, I was alone with Grace, at least for a little bit.

"Are you sure you want her to come with us? She's not exactly a fan of wolves," I asked, knowing Sera was too far away to hear our conversation.

Grace smiled shyly.

"I like her," she said quietly.

I nodded. The version of Sera Grace was seeing was someone to like. She was laughing and giggling. Sera was telling Grace about the world Grace had always longed to be part of, and it was just what Grace needed to hear to be distracted from real life. I personally wasn't used to Sera being friendly or agreeable, but Grace deserved to have whatever last day as a human that she wanted. It was her party, and I wasn't going to let my opinion of Sera interfere with that.

"Okay. Then let's get our bags packed and be waiting for her."

Grace nodded as her cheeks returned to their normal color.

I dug under the basket I had all my clothing in and found the two sacks Nikkan, and I used when we went on trips. I shook them both out and, thankfully, found them empty of anything gross or embarrassing.

"Here," I said as I handed one to Grace.

She was already folding my thin blanket gently. She placed it in the bag I handed her. I turned to dig through my clean laundry for a few sweaters. It was just the end of winter, but that meant the nights would be cooler. I didn't have a tent or anything extra to keep warm since I ran warm all the time, even while sleeping. Sweaters would have to do for my cooler companions.

It looked like the weather was going to cooperate with us, and the typical spring rain would hold off a bit longer. That was good news for us. I'd hate for Grace's last day as a human to be filled with rain and storms. We would have a beautiful, clear afternoon and night and time to enjoy everything we could before she chose to change.

"Sera will be back soon," I assured Grace as she looked to the door.

She bit her lip and nodded. My words didn't comfort her at all. I looked at the door, too, and realized who she was looking for.

No matter what we were doing, I was pretty sure Nikkan wasn't stopping by today or for a long time. He was mad enough to drag several wolves to our place to get Grace; I was more than confident he was staying away as long as he could. I only hoped eventually he'd let me explain it all, but that wouldn't do Grace any good. She would be a wolf, and there would be no way for her to speak to him about it to confirm my story.

"It's his loss," I told her as I found the sweaters I was looking for and tucked them into my bag.

Grace bit her bottom lip and nodded as she chewed on it. I was coming to recognize that as her thinking face.

"He's a brat, but that's nothing new. He'll come back

around," I reassured her of what I was only hoping. He'd always come around in the past.

"Why couldn't he just talk to us?" Grace asked. "Why did he have to such be a jerk?"

I smiled. She was getting as angry as Nikkan was over thinking there was more between us. There was much anger, but it was over nothing. Communication didn't seem to be their strong point.

"He just cares too much about you," I answered. "And he's always acting on instinct. His wolf side wins more than not. You have to understand that."

And that was the truth about Nikkan. Maybe that was why he and I got along for many winters. I could accept all the crazy he did because of his wolf. If he were an average human, I might have actually been the one mad at him, but he wasn't. He was part wolf, and that was a part that controlled a lot of what he did.

He once explained it to me. He had two people inside his head, him and his wolf. Most of the time, he was thinking for the both of them, but there were times it was just easier to let the wolf take over. I had a feeling the wolf took over a lot more than he let on.

She nodded. "But sometimes I wish he was more a man than a wolf."

I wasn't sure I agreed with that. The combo Nikkan was of man and wolf made him Nikkan and not anyone else. I don't know if he would be the same person more human-like. Though I would have to agree if he spoke more instead of getting mad, that would have saved us from all the drama between us.

I packed the last of my dried meat and my flint to start a fire since we'd be sleeping outside overnight. Grace took the food from me and packed it in our bags. I nodded as I grabbed a few of my hunting knives and my bow and arrows. I was tempted to take my gun too since the cursed wolves could be out, but Sera assured me we would be far enough away from all that to care.

After we had everything packed that we could think of, Grace and I waited for Sera outside of my hut. I was tempted to leave a note for Nikkan in case he came back or changed his mind early, but I didn't. Mainly I didn't want anyone else following us. I wanted Grace to have one last perfect day as a human and not one last day as a human being scolded by overprotective wolves that didn't really have her interests at heart but, more so, in protecting themselves.

It didn't take Sera long to run to the village and back. She returned with a pack of her own on her shoulder that was almost as full as our two bags combined. I held up my bag in an offer to switch, but she just shoed me away as she hurried over and pulled Grace to a stand.

"Is it easier to run as a wolf or a human?" Sera asked Grace, offering to take her bag.

"Wolf, but I want to enjoy as much as I can as a human," Grace replied and slung her pack over both her shoulders.

Sera grinned, grabbed Grace's hand, and then took off running without a second look back to see if I was following. Of course, I was. Even when she was nice, Sera was a pain to me. At least, she was friendly with Grace.

Grace and Sera ran ahead of me through the woods as Sera led the way. I kept a watch out for any wolves that could be following us, but the woods were clear. We were alone on our adventure to make Grace's last day one worth having.

They kept the pace light; probably Sera didn't want to push Grace too hard. It made for a nice run. I had no idea where we were going, but that didn't matter. I knew the woods of Elder like the back of my hand. I was at home. If I thought about it, I probably could guess where we were going, but I didn't care. Grace had made plans with Sera, and I was sure the future Red of Elder was going to make Grace's last day perfect.

Spring was finally here. The air was warmer, and some of the trees and early bushes had full leaves already on them. I could hear animals around us and ones coming out after their winter slumbers. The woods were alive and not in the same scary way the tree people talked about it. It was alive with life and new beginnings, which was ironic considering we were marking Grace ending her life.

"This is a short cut," Sera explained as we neared one of the edges of the woods.

Grace halted as she looked out at the empty fields in front of her. Most, if not all, of the wolves spent their time north of my home. Very few ventured to the south or somewhat southeast as Sera was pulling us. It wasn't like the border of Aboria was close, but it felt like we were leaving home and the evergreen forest behind us. The farm fields of Elder stretched as far as the eye could see. Grace stared with her mouth open.

Sera grinned as she stared at her new friend.

"Guess she never saw the other side of Elder before," Sera commented to me as she bumped her arm into mine.

And that was the truth for most of the wolves. The northern half of the kingdom was covered by the evergreen woods that we called home, but the south end of the kingdom was all farm fields. There wasn't a reason for a wolf to go south since they lived in the forest and hunted there. The fields of Elder had some animals but not the same hunting game as the north. The wolves couldn't survive in the south unless in they were in a tiny clan. And there was the problem of eating the farmers' animals, so they weren't exactly welcome either.

"Won't we get in trouble?" Grace asked as she continued to gawk at the fields that had yet to be tilled and planted with the new summer crop.

"You're with me," Sera replied. "You can't get in trouble." She gave Grace a grin as she took her hand and pulled her to a run again.

This time, we took off across an empty field that angled up a hill. I kept pace with them as we crested to the top, and Sera stopped again.

"You said you wanted to see the world," Sera stated as Grace stared and started to spin in a circle.

From our hill, we could see so far into the distance; the horizon became a line.

"If you look that way, you can see the tips of the mountains in Aboria." Sera pointed to the northeast. "And if we turn and look that way and our vision was better than our human vision, you might be able to see the deserts of Badalah or maybe the dragons in Draconis. Just a bit south of there, would be the walled city Urbis. No way we could see through those walls, but if our vision was better, I bet we could see the walls."

Grace shut her eyes and took a deep breath of the cool spring air. The day was getting warmer, but it was still spring. It smelled fresh and full of life blooming around Elder.

"Over there where there's a green glint," Sera continued, "is the great kingdom of Oz. I've never actually been there, but Red promised me that we would make it there sometime."

Grace bit her lip as she stared out to the horizon. I wasn't sure if she saw what Sera was describing or not, but she was trying.

"Just that way is Arcadia and their fairies. They have stone castles and don't have to live in trees like the people of Elder."

"Have you ever seen a fairy?" Grace asked.

Sera grinned. "More than one, but let me tell you, they can be quite deceptive. Not all fairies are nice."

"Just like wolves," Grace snickered, and Sera laughed with her.

Sera turned to Grace again.

"Over in that direction, are the islands that make up Skyla. Make sure to look up so you don't miss the islands in the sky. If we had time or another life, we could go there to relax and enjoy life."

I smiled at the thought. Grace seemed to be soaking it all in. Sera was good at this. I doubted I could make her last day as great as Sera had in just the past few moments. I had heard Grace say she was going to miss seeing the world, but this never occurred to me as a solution to that. I never gave her enough credit, but Sera was smart.

"And lastly is our neighbor The Vale." Sera turned Grace to face west. "You can fly on unicorns and live in perfect weather, never too cold or too hot. No more winters with snow and frozen fingers and toes."

Grace took a deep breath and slowly spun in a circle. Her eyes searched the horizon in all the directions Sera had pointed her. She wasn't going on an adventure to see the world, but Sera brought her pretty close, as close as Grace was ever going to get.

I stood beside my friends and stared out into the world also. Elder was my home, and the woods were my family, but there was much more out there. What would I have left in Elder when my friends were all wolves? Would I be needed when the cursed wolves were locked up, and I had no one left? Was it time I saw the world like Grace wanted so badly to do? Could I live her dream for the both of us?

"Thanks," Grace said quietly as she turned back to Sera.

"We aren't done yet," Sera said as she grabbed her friend's arm and led her off down the other side of the hill.

Sera turned slightly to run toward the deciduous forest off to the east of us. Grace grinned as the wind whipped past them, and they took off to somewhere new.

Again, they took to their conversation of giggles and laughs as they ran. Grace was happy. That's all I wanted for my friend. One last perfect day, and somehow, Sera knew precisely how to give it to her. I never saw Sera as someone who would befriend a wolf, but right now, there seemed to be no difference between them. They were just humans having fun.

It wasn't long before they slowed their pace. I wasn't surprised when I saw where Sera was leading us. I didn't wander often into this forest, but I knew all the lands of Elder, partly because I wanted to know and partly because of Red making sure I knew everything about the place I was raised.

Sera pulled Grace through the new woods. Grace looked worried for only a moment as they ran past the bare trees, then she fell into step with Sera and let all her worries fade away. Sera led her deeper into the woods and made sure that her approach would make Grace happy. I just smiled as I knew what we were doing. When Sera was sure we were at the right spot, she stopped and pointed for Grace to push past the bushes covering the view.

Grace gasped as she stood there in shock. A small waterfall, maybe three or four saplings tall, ran down into a pool of water that shimmered in the spring sun. The water wasn't more than chest high, but it was deep enough she couldn't see the bottom. I knew the water was clean and pure, but I just stood beside Grace as she took it all in. At the other end of the pool, the water continued to flow further down the river.

"This is where the Eldoris River flows into the Adder springs," Sera explained to Grace. "It's by far the best place to go swimming anywhere in Elder in the wintertime. The Adder Springs keep the water in the pool warm all winter long. It's not quite like swimming in the waters at the edge of Elder but much warmer."

Grace not only wanted to see the world and all the kingdoms around us, but she also wanted to go back to the ocean in the north of Elder. She had been there as a young child and hadn't been back since. Nikkan's younger siblings were already there. I shook my head to try not to think of him. It was his loss to not be with us and not our fault in the least.

Grace slowly walked over to the sparkling blue water. She reached down and touched it and then looked back at both of us in shock. She must not have believed Sera about the temperature.

"It's like really warm," she said in surprise.

That made me chuckle, and Sera smile. No one ever seemed to believe that the water would be the perfect temperature.

"Turn around." Sera motioned to me. I sighed but did as she told me without complaining for Grace's sake only.

The woods glowed in a mild green light as the sun peeked between the newly forming leaves. I didn't mind looking around the quiet spring forest, but I didn't have much time as I heard the splashes of the girls getting into the water.

I didn't wait to be invited as I turned and pulled off my own shirt before diving into the water. Sera shrieked as my splash was artfully aimed at her face. I might have accidentally or purposely put my arms out to create a large splash of water intended for her. Grace giggled as she ducked back down under the warm water.

When we were all perfectly soaked and our skin wrinkled, I was the first to brave getting out of the water to get a fire going. It wasn't near supper time, but with wet clothing, it wasn't going to take long before we all got cold from the weather, not exactly being summer yet.

"So how long have you known him?" Sera was asking Grace as I came back with my second bundle of wood for the fire that was now going good enough to keep both girls warm as they dried off.

Grace looked up at me and shrugged.

"I don't actually remember when we met. It was many winters ago."

I smiled and nodded.

"Don't worry, Sera, you've known me longer," I told her, knowing exactly where her thoughts were going.

Everything with Sera was a competition. It was hard growing up and being around her because I was probably just as competitive as she was, but I'd never admit that to her. It made for quite a few fights over the winters that didn't seem to get better as we got older, a fact Red frequently pointed out to us. Red seemed to think one day, we'd give up competing and just be friends, but neither of us was anywhere close to that yet.

Sera stuck her tongue out at me.

"I wasn't asking to see if I knew you longer. I was just wondering if she remembered your phase where you wanted your hair to look like a squirrel tail."

I closed my eyes and shook my head. Yes, of course, Sera wanted to bring that up. If she wasn't competing with me, she was teasing me, and my choice of hairstyles always was a favorite of hers.

"I completely do," Grace replied with a giggle. "But I liked his skunk phase where he had that white streak down the middle of his hair."

Sera reached over and tousled my hair like I was her kid brother. I grunted at her as I pulled back and left the stack of wood at her feet before I stormed off back into the woods to find more to keep us warm through the night.

I wasn't really mad. In fact, it was kind of nice to hear them talking and laughing. There was no worrying about the future or what life would be like for Grace. They were just two girls having fun camping out in the woods.

It didn't take me long to find what we needed to get through the night, but I took my time going back. Grace needed her perfect last day, and my thoughts were making me more than a little gloomy. It was just too sudden and hard to take. And the notion that Nikkan would soon be joining her and I'd be left alone was harder to take. Grace didn't deserve my sadness. She had enough to deal with.

By the time I made it back to our camp, the sun was setting, and the girls were already making, or rather pulling out supper for us. It seemed that Sera had grabbed every dessert she had been telling Grace about, and my dried meat was the only non-sweet thing we had to eat. I didn't take any of the sweets the girls offered me but instead sat across the fire and just watched them, lost in my own thoughts.

I knew Red wouldn't lie to me. If she knew how to break the curse, she would. But I had to think back through all she had ever taught me. There had to be an answer to fixing the wolves. It was broken once and would be again.

Sera noticed my absence and raised an eyebrow in question, but I waved her off with a smile. Lucky for me, she was focusing on Grace and making her last day perfect, but I was pretty sure the run home would be an interrogation by Sera.

As night arrived and the girls put on the extra sweaters I brought, I could tell by Grace's satisfied smile that she'd had the day she wanted, mostly thanks to Sera. That was beyond surprising to me. Sera and I had never really seen eye to eye much, but today showed me a completely different side of her. As Grace fell asleep lying against Sera, it was the perfect end to her day and life as a human.

Sera watched the fire, and I had a chance to truly look at her. It had been winters since we had been together this long and not fought. In fact, I don't think I could actually recall a time we didn't fight.

Her hair had dried back off her face from the swim, and I could look at her, no longer hiding behind the mane of hair that was usually swinging around her as she moved about. Maybe that was it. Sera never stopped moving, but right now, she sat perfectly still as Grace fell asleep. Grace was now sprawled on Sera's lap.

My nighttime eyesight was perfect and allowed me to see every last detail. I could make out the small smattering of freckles across her nose that had been there as long as I could remember. I tried not to see it, but I couldn't help but notice that Sera wasn't just a girl anymore. She had grown and changed probably as much as I had the past few winters that I had been out of Red's house. It felt like just yesterday that I left, but it had been three winters. I couldn't put my finger on one thing, but something about her was changed. She wasn't the girl I remembered growing up with.

Sera didn't look across at me as she looked into the fire like it held the answers she was looking for. I had to wonder if she was searching for the same answers I was. I never pictured Sera with friends because she was raised as isolated as I was. While she was a tree dweller, they never really invited her in. It was probably because they all knew she was the next Red, someone you didn't want to get close to because it was a job that generally didn't come with a long life. My mother was the only Red that made it past her thirty winters.

As the flames flickered on, Sera looked up at me and smiled.

'Thank you,' I mouthed across to Sera, where she sat staring at me now.

Sera grinned and nodded her head to me as she laid her head back against the tree at her back and closed her eyes. She didn't seem to have the answers either, but I was pretty sure if Red wasn't going to help the wolves, I'd just made a new ally that would help me. Together, maybe, we could save them all.

10TH MARCH

The smell of the smoke from the fire dying woke me the next morning. I had tried to get up every now and then to stoke the fire and keep the girls warm, but by the middle of the night, I was too sleepy to stay awake. I heard the snoring of the girls, so it didn't seem to matter. They made it through the night safe and warm.

The day before had been perfect. Grace never stopped smiling as she fell asleep. It was everything I could have wanted for her, and it was thanks to Sera. I never saw her as anything but annoying, but that was changing with this trip.

Growing up, she hated anything related to the wolves. She could barely tolerate Nikkan; then again, he could barely tolerate her. Most of the time, she kept her anti-wolf views to herself as she knew my mother was passionate about bringing together the two kinds of humans in the northern section of Elder, but I always saw it in her eyes. I really never knew what made her hate wolves that much, but yesterday, it was amazing how much she cared and made Grace's last human day perfect.

Slowly sitting up and stretching, I could feel the aches from sleeping on the forest floor. My one couch in my house wasn't much, but it was still better than the hard ground. I really had no idea how Nikkan did it day after day. Then again, my wolf friend preferred my couch. I raised my arms and cracked my back as I twisted left and right. It felt like everything popped back into place, at least, I hoped so. We still had a walk back to my home, which would take half the day with the distance we traveled. At least as a wolf, Grace would be able to keep up with Sera and I when we were running full out.

Looking around our meager camp told me all I needed to know; Grace was gone. Seemed she was up earlier than I was, which didn't say much since the sun was already up. I wasn't one for sleeping in, but then again, I was up half the night keeping the fire going. Surprisingly, Sera wasn't up yet, but I could remedy that.

Standing up as quietly as I could, I made my way over to her. As I pulled back my foot to give her a good kick to the bottom of her feet, I paused just to make sure she wasn't going to fight back and was really asleep. One could never be too careful, especially with a highly trained warrior like Sera.

"I wouldn't do that if I were you," Sera told me, her voice groggy as if I just woke her.

I dropped my foot back to the ground. That took all the fun out of it.

Sera sat up and rubbed her eyes. She stretched just as I had, but it didn't look like sleeping on the hard ground affected her at all.

"Which way did Grace go?" Sera asked as she sat up, no longer stretching. She looked around the forest with a quick glance.

"No clue. She was gone when I woke. Figure she had some morning business and would be back soon," I replied, moving back over to where I was sitting before.

Sera patted the ground next to her.

"It's cold," Sera mentioned.

Yes, the ground was cold.

"Where Grace was sleeping. She has been gone longer than just a moment," Sera explained like I was stupid.

I hadn't thought of that because it made no sense. Grace wasn't the kind that would go wandering off to explore by herself.

"She probably went swimming," I replied. Then again, there wasn't any noise beyond the water hitting the spring pool. "Maybe she's soaking and enjoying the warmth since the fire is low."

Sera turned toward the spring pool behind the trees where we set up camp, and then looked back at me and the fire.

"How long has the fire been out?"

Great. I could tell the look on her face meant she was disappointed with me for not staying up all night to keep the fire going. Wasn't my fault I ran warm and didn't feel it die off. She was back to old Sera, bossing me around and being overall a pain in the butt.

"I put the last piece on some time in the middle of

the night. I don't know what time."

"The ground's cold," Sera commented. "But I don't know how long."

That much was normal. The ground was always cold in the spring. Guess she hadn't slept outside in a while because she wasn't making any sense.

Sera stood up and began looking at the ground. Could she see a cold ground? That was a weird Red power my mother never mentioned. Her eyes darted around before she began to walk away.

"What's going on?" I asked as I jogged to catch up with her.

She peered over the bushes we had camped behind and looked over at the water. I watched with her but didn't see anything. Grace wasn't soaking in the water as I had hoped, but I had a feeling Sera didn't expect that much.

Sera held up a hand for me to be quiet as she closed her eyes to listen.

I listened too but didn't know what we were listening for. The forest sounded normal to me. Animals were waking for the day, and some had already been up since before the sun had risen. Yes, I had heard those birds that chirped when the sun wasn't close to the horizon, but I was used to ignoring them.

"We need to find Grace," Sera told me as she went back to her bag and began packing up everything from the night before.

"What do you mean, find Grace?"

Sera looked up at me and rolled her eyes but didn't explain.

"Pack up everything; we're leaving," Sera told me.

Orders. I hated being ordered around. I did much better with reasons, and Sera knew that. Why did the old Sera have to come back? I was doing perfectly fine with the friendly Sera that was showing Grace what an excellent last day meant. I wanted to protest, but the thought of Grace stopped me. It wasn't the time or place to argue with Sera.

I honestly was lost as to what to do. Grace still wasn't back with us. I'd assumed she just got up for a few moments and would be coming back through the bushes in no time. I had listened to the forest with Sera. No human was anywhere nearby. Did Grace leave already to change and not tell us? Was she not wanting to tell us goodbye? Sera was much easier to get along with when Grace was there to balance out her crazy.

It wasn't hard to pack my stuff as I hadn't brought much to begin with. I pushed the sweater Sera had thrown over to me and the blanket that had been covering Grace into my pack. Sera had less to pack as they ate half the stuff she had carried. She finished her bag as I finished mine.

"I'll take Grace's bag if you make sure the fire is fully out," Sera told me.

I nodded as I took my canteen and poured it on the fire. It only made a small sizzling noise as the fire was almost out anyway. I wanted to refill my canteen but could tell Sera was ready to run.

Without anything more to say, Sera stood and took the lead. She picked a direction and started a slow jog into the woods around us. The forest blurred by us as we picked up our pace to a full run, but I was getting more and more anxious as we continued away from our camp. I really couldn't picture Grace running off without us. Was it possible that she was back there, and we just left her? She didn't know this area of Elder. Sera was sure about where we were going, and if it had been the old wolf-hating Sera, I wouldn't have gone with her, but this Sera seemed more concerned than anything. She wasn't leaving Grace behind but looking for her as I was. The only question was, where was Grace. The only thing I could think of was that Grace didn't want to say goodbye to us.

"This way," Sera finally said as she took off running at a different direction.

We wove through the new trees and growth as we ran farther from our camp. There wasn't much the direction we were going but Aboria. The wolves were north, and the farm fields were south. We were heading due east. I knew we didn't need to run that direction and into another kingdom if Grace had wandered off to head home without us, but Sera was tracking something.

Within seconds of me wondering if we were going to make it to Aboria on our run, Sera turned sharply towards the south and the farm fields of Elder. I didn't stop to try to figure out what Sera was seeing as I kept my eyes glancing around the forest while she concentrated on the ground. If Grace was around, I wasn't going to have us run by her looking at the ground. My eyes needed to be looking up while Sera ran. I might not like to follow her orders, but I trusted Sera. She wasn't about to leave Grace alone in the woods, wolf or not.

As we neared the edge of the forest and I no longer needed to look around since the trees had thinned and I could see for longer distances, I finally saw what Sera was following. A trail of blood.

My heart began to hammer in my chest. Was Grace hurt? Was she taken from us while we both slept, not that she just left to transform on her own?

Sera finally stopped and reached down to touch the blood. There was more now. I didn't see it immediately in the woods, but in the fields, I could see it plain as day. Something was bleeding and bleeding a lot.

"Animal blood," she told me as she smeared it on her fingers.

Seemed her Red powers were more than a bit handy, but they still didn't explain why Grace was gone and there was a blood trail left.

"What kind?" I asked, hoping it wasn't a wolf.

Sera took another breath of the blood and closed her eyes.

"I'm not sure," she replied. "This is one of the new things I've learned this moon cycle. Your mother is better at this."

So human Grace wasn't hurt, but that didn't mean wolf Grace wasn't hurt. Sera didn't wait for us to speak further as she gave me the only answer she could and took off tracking again.

Sera led us on the run into the southern half of Elder. There was nothing but farmers and farms fields, so I wasn't sure why Grace would have gone this direction. Even as a wolf, she would have known to go north. I was glad to see she didn't continue east into Aboria, but it was still confusing. And then on top of it, if she was hurt, how did that happen? Did a farmer see her?

Sera paused as she looked around for the trail. The spots of blood were getting further apart, either the blood of whatever we were tracking was clotting, or the animal was running faster.

"When did you last see Grace sleeping?" Sera asked as she looked around.

She stopped and stooped down to touch the blood on the trail we were following. She rubbed it between her fingers again as she looked around.

It was harder to track and find clues in the rows of

a cut-down corn crop.

"She was there the last time I put a log on the fire, but I don't know when that was," I replied as I looked around too. How in the world did Sera and I both miss Grace leaving us? Neither one of us could have kept sleeping if there was a predator close enough to take Grace from us.

Sera stood and circled around again, where we were standing.

"The trail just stops," she said, confused as to why it would suddenly end. We didn't find anything in the cornfield. "Like the animal just disappeared."

I looked around and walked back to the last drop of blood. I finally saw a good imprint from the animal that was running. It was a wolf. Reaching down, I touched the print. Was it Grace or another wolf? There was only one other wolf I would suspect would follow us so far south. I looked harder at the print and knew it wasn't Nikkan. I had seen more than enough of his prints to tell him from other wolves. This print was smaller than his, and a little wolf would likely be female.

The animal we were tracking was very likely to be Grace in her wolf form, but why would she run from us? And this animal was running. If it was Grace, then it wasn't instinct but an intelligent mind running that animal. We had to not look at it like we were tracking a random animal but rather tracking a human. And it was different. If Grace thought she was being tracked, she would have been smart and backtracked to lose the hunter chasing her.

"We have to go back," I told Sera, certain that Grace was sending us a message. Maybe she was running from something. She would know enough that we would track her, but anyone else might get confused.

Sera looked at me like I was nuts, but I didn't care. She only saw the wolves as animals, but I knew better. They weren't animals but a human in animal skins. If this wolf was Grace, then it would be smart.

Sera took a moment to catch up with me as I left her. Instead of running and following the blood, I carefully followed the tracks and looked all around. We hadn't gone more than five or ten saplings when I saw the barely visible trail of the animal leading in a different direction. She had run into the field to confuse anything following her and carefully headed back into the woods.

Without a word to me, Sera took the lead to follow the trail again. I smiled at her back as she started a slower jog this time. She would never admit I had done something she didn't do, but we both knew it was me that found the trail to continue on. Someday she was going to have to see the truth that the wolves weren't just animals. They were smart and still the same human inside them.

I know the curse had people thinking that the wolves were terrible and monsters, but the wolves I knew were different. They weren't rabid animals; they were people. They could think, feel, and carry on a one-sided conversation as I had done many times over the winters with Nikkan. Maybe I had a better understanding from living with him, but I knew the wolves weren't what Sera thought. Maybe Grace could get Sera to understand that.

We continued to track Grace. This time, the tracks traveled almost entirely due west. That was a good sign that the animal wasn't heading to Aboria, and The Vale was too far for an animal to run to in one days' time. If we had been tracking for days, I would have been worried, but this was actually good. The wolf was going towards the center of Elder, at least for now.

Sera and I kept the slow pace, making sure the trail never veered from the direction we were heading. It was getting easier to follow the blood as the wolf had seemed to slow considerably, and the blood splatter was closer together. I followed behind Sera as she ran but tumbled into her as she came to a sudden stop.

We were standing in a clearing in the forest, the new spring growth already had the grass past my ankles, but that wasn't the surprise. There in the middle of the clearing was a naked body, covered in so much blood I didn't know who it was.

I didn't see a human anywhere and tried not to feel crushed. Grace would never forgive herself for attacking a human.

"Grace," Sera gasped.

There, in the middle of a field, coated with blood, was my friend. I ran over to her at the same time as Sera. We both knelt down by her and searched for any injury that could cause all the blood. Had a wolf taken her in the middle of the night? It seemed impossible, but right now, human Grace was lying before us in the woods. We never saw a human track on the whole run.

Sera patted over her friend and then had her bag open, pulling out the towel she had from the day before and their swim in the spring. She began to wipe Grace down while our friend didn't move.

I placed my fingers on her neck, feeling for her pulse. It was there and strong as ever. Whatever wolf took her, they didn't kill her, at least.

"She's alive," I told Sera.

Sera got more of the blood off Grace and finally noticed she was naked. She quickly placed the towel around her and covered her up as she reached forward and tapped her face.

"Grace," she said quietly at first and then tapped a bit more. "Grace," she said a bit louder.

Grace's eyes fluttered as she finally opened her eyes.

"Grace, what happened?" I asked as I kneeled next to her.

Pieces started falling into place. The blood was animal blood. There wasn't a wolf around. She was naked.

"Happened?" Grace asked groggily.

"And why are you nude?" Sera added, not helpful in the least, as I was coming to my own conclusion.

Grace's eyes shot open as she sat up, grasping the towel around her. She frantically looked from one side of her to the other side. Her mouth hung open in shock.

"What happened?" I asked as gently as I could. I could see the fear in her eyes as she took in all the blood. The new grass of the clearing was painted red.

"I don't know," she whispered, not taking her eyes off the blood around her. She wiped her face with the towel and spat blood out of her mouth.

"Are you hurt?" Sera asked, still not putting two and two together.

I bit my lip as I wished for her to answer yes. I had only one reason floating in my head as to why Grace was lying in the woods naked covered in blood.

Grace patted her arms and legs before finally turning to look at Sera and me. Tears were welling up in her eyes. She'd come to the same conclusion I had. Neither of us wanted to admit it to Sera, who still seemed a bit clueless.

"I'm not hurt," she answered as the tears began pouring down her cheeks. "And I don't remember last night." She stared in horror at the blood all around her.

I sadly shook my head. That only meant one thing. Grace was cursed.

THRONE OF NIGHT

11TH MARCH

Grace was cursed.

I never once imagined saying those words, let alone, thinking them. She'd already decided to spend her life as a wolf. We had run away. We had given her a perfect last day. She couldn't be cursed. She was going to beat it. But it was too late. Now, she didn't have an option.

We had put so much hope into Grace turning into a wolf to live out her life uncursed that we never imagined the horrible reality of Elder would take Grace. She was way too sweet and kind to be turned into a rabid monster with no control and an insatiable hunger. It was the complete opposite of her in real life. It just wasn't fair. The curse alone was bad enough, but this wasn't something Grace should have ever had to deal with.

While Sera reassured me that the curse took time, and it would be days before Grace turned back into an uncontrollable monster, it didn't matter. There was no cure. There was nothing I could do for her.

Grace fainted from the shock right after we all realized the truth. We took her unconscious state as a sign we needed to head back, and Sera and I managed to make a cot to carry her. It took us the rest of the day and into the night to make it to my place. Thankfully, Grace had been out the entire time.

The tree people of Elder had spent many seasons afraid of the wolves and the curse. While the wolf people always had the ability to shift into wolves, they had previously had control over when they shifted to their animal form. The curse, on the other hand, made them unable to control the monster they became.

None of the wolves wanted to be cursed, even wolves like my best friend Nikkan, who was currently not speaking to me. He preferred his wolf form, but he never wanted to be cursed. They wanted to be part of Elder like everyone else. To most of them, their wolf was just another side of them, like hair color. It wasn't a bad thing until you got the curse that took away your control. No one wanted to lose control when they could easily kill any human they came across.

My mother had told us that wolves that shifted before being cursed could live out their lives as wolves. Grace was prepared to give up any hope of living her life as a human to do just that. She was ready, but it was too late. She was now infected with the same thing that had turned countless wolves into monsters of the night. Actually, they were the reason the people of Elder fled to the trees to live in the first place. Now, Elder would be divided again. The tree people in their treetop homes and the wolves roaming the ground below, trying to eat anything they could find.

I honestly don't know what I would have done without Sera. I expected her to turn on Grace once we figured out Grace was cursed or maybe say, I told you so, but none of that happened. Sera was actually level-headed and helpful the whole time we worked together to get Grace home. I had a feeling that Grace had won her over, and even though Sera was raised a tree person, she was now seeing the wolves differently than she had been taught. Grace had shown her that light.

After making it back to my cottage situated right between the land the wolves currently lived on and the land the tree people lived on, we put Grace to bed. She hadn't woken the whole trip and was still out. Sera explained that the curse would be draining, but it was harder to watch than I could imagine. Grace already looked sick and exhausted to the point she was sleeping through the day.

I needed to rest before deciding what to do next and lay down to sleep as soon as we had Grace situated. Sera refused to leave me with Grace and kept guard all night. By the time the sun rose, Sera looked exhausted and almost as bad as Grace. Either it was the knowledge of being cursed or the sickness taking over as Grace's skin had paled a bit since the day before.

With me now awake, Sera finally lay down to get some rest herself. I tried my best to be quiet for both their sakes as I started to prepare breakfast and got lost in my own thoughts.

My mother, Red, was the leader of the people of Elder. While I had gone to her for help breaking the curse, she said she didn't have the answer. Part of me wanted to yell at her. She was the Red, and she had broken the curse before, but one thing I always knew about Red. She didn't lie. If she didn't know how to break the curse, then she didn't. I was left having to think about it on my own.

It would have been nice to have my friend Nikkan to help me come up with ideas, but he was still not talking to me due to a misunderstanding with Grace. She was my friend, but he thought there was more going on between me and his long unrequited love. If he only could open his eyes for a moment, he would see that Grace was as crazy for him as he was for her.

"Castiel," Grace said weakly to me from the couch as I was getting breakfast made.

I turned to her and found she was struggling to sit up. Sera was asleep on the floor as I made my way past her.

"Save your energy," I replied to Grace quietly as I kneeled down by her. I tucked her back into the couch comfortably. "I'll have breakfast done in a few. Just rest."

"Castiel," she called my name again as I moved to stand. "You should have left me in the woods. The farmers would have taken care of me for everyone. I don't deserve to live."

Sinking back down to the ground beside her, I grabbed her hand and stared into her eyes.

"You deserve to live." I put every ounce of truth I had behind that statement.

Grace bit her lip as it began to tremble.

"But all the blood. I'm dangerous. I killed someone."

Tears began trickling down her face.

"It was animal blood," I told her, but that didn't seem to stop the tears that were now running rivers down her face. "You didn't hurt anyone but an animal. Just a normal meal, right?" I gave her a smile and a wink to try to lighten the mood.

"This time," Grace whispered as she finally wore out her energy from trying to sit up and let herself slip back down to lying on the couch.

"Sera, and I won't let you harm anyone. You don't have to worry."

She closed her eyes but didn't seem convinced by my words. Her breathing slowed as she drifted off to sleep again. I placed her hands on her chest as her breaths became shallow.

Within moments she was back asleep. I stared at her for a few moments before standing and going back to my kitchen.

How in the world was I going to break the news to Nikkan? He already hated me because he thought I was dating Grace. Would it matter that I wasn't after she got sick? He was never going to forgive me for not protecting her.

I heated up the skillet and got ready to fry the eggs my mother had given us on our way through town. Once it was all done, I'd wake Grace to eat, but it seemed she wasn't going to spend much time awake.

As I went through the motions of cooking, I couldn't help my mind from wandering again.

Where did the curse come from? Red had explained to me as a kid that it had been around for hundreds of winters. Everyone in the villages, wolf or tree-human, knew that. But no one spoke of why or where it came from. Maybe defeating it had to do with that. Or perhaps it could be beaten by the same witches that gave the Red their power. Someone had to know something; it was just going to take some searching to find and talk to the right person.

First, I was going to have to talk to Red again and try to get some more answers out of her once I figured out what to do with Grace. Red had knowledge that other people didn't have, and even if she didn't know how she broke the curse winters ago, she still did it. It might just be stuck in her head, and if it wasn't, Red was an excellent place to start. And there were books in the village. There had to be more knowledge. But I wasn't leaving until I figured out what to do with Grace. She was weak right now, but I didn't trust she'd be okay if I took a run back to Red for the day.

Grace's crazy talk of wanting to be killed was just that: absurd. Being cursed didn't mean she was dying. It meant she was sick. I could see it as it hit her hard in the last day, but that didn't mean we couldn't help her. While Sera didn't especially like wolves, I could tell she was on my side about this one. We needed to save Grace. She was too sweet and innocent to be taken by the curse.

Watching my friend sleep and suffer from something she had no control over made my mind wander to Nikkan. Yes, I was mad that he was acting like an idiot, but that didn't mean I didn't care. In fact, with all that was going on, I cared more than ever. I wanted him to stay safe and this stupid curse to stay as far away from him. The last time the curse came, they didn't know how it was spread amongst the wolves, so I had no idea how to go about keeping Nikkan safe. If he were with me now, I'd beg him to stay in his wolf form, but he wasn't with me, and now with Grace, I was sure he would spend more time as a human to help her.

I didn't have Nikkan to think of answers with, and Grace needed something soon. It was less than one day, and she was already withering away. The only thing I could think of to help her was Red. Even if my mother sent Sera to be my babysitter and forbade me from seeing the wolves, she was still the best answer to all of this. I needed to see her as soon as I could.

It didn't take long to fry the eggs and slather the fresh bread with strawberry jam. Quick breakfasts were my specialty. Nikkan was the one that liked to make elaborate breakfasts with pancakes, eggs, three types of meats along with bread and jam, and anything else he could take as he ran around the forest in his wolf form. The scent of food woke Sera, who was soon kneeling by Grace and checking her over just as I had done when I awoke.

"I doubt that was enough sleep to keep you energized," I commented. She had been up most of the night and barely had shut her eyes before she was up again.

"I'm fine. Technically, I don't need as much sleep now," Sera replied, still looking at Grace. "She isn't fine."

That much was obvious. Grace had a pale complexion during most winters, but her skin was tinged a slight green while she slept more than normal. Healthy people didn't sleep days. Her breathing was shallow, and if you didn't notice her weird skin coloring, you'd think she was peacefully sleeping.

"No, she isn't," I replied as I placed eggs and toast on a plate for Sera.

Sera and I stood side by side, looking down at Grace. I didn't have answers, and it seemed like neither did Sera, but we both wanted to help her, the sooner, the better.

"She's not dead yet," Sera commented.

Leave it to Sera to go there. I wasn't thinking about

the wolves dying. I was more concerned she was going to wolf out and hurt people. That would kill Grace on the inside even if her body stayed alive.

"So, what do we do?" Sera finally asked as she stood and took the cold plate of eggs and bread from me before heading over to my two-seat table.

I joined her.

"I have no idea. I talked to Red, and she said there's no way to break the curse."

Sera shook her head. "But she broke it eighteen winters ago."

I nodded. My thoughts exactly.

"Once I'm sure Grace is doing okay, and I can drop her off with the wolves, I plan to give Red a visit," I explained to Sera.

"I'm not going back there," Grace said in a raspy voice.

Sera and I both hurried over to her.

"Grace, the wolves can take care of you. Protect you and keep you and everyone safe until I find an answer," I explained to her like she was a child, not someone my same age.

Her sleep-lined eyes stared back at me as the corners of her mouth pulled into a frown.

"I'm not going back to the wolves. It would be better for everyone if you just let the tree people kill me. That way, I can't spread the curse, and I can't hurt someone. If I'm not around, that is one less wolf for everyone to worry about."

I shook my head no as Sera looked at her in horror.

"You won't hurt someone. You had a chance last night to hurt Castiel or me, but you didn't. You may be cursed, Grace, but you aren't a killer. The curse can't force you to do something you wouldn't want to do."

Grace looked up at me. I bit my lip to keep from telling the truth that I knew Sera knew also. Sera was trying to sugar coat it. The curse would make Grace into a monster, and yes, she'd have no problem killing Nikkan or me if she was in the change. But Grace didn't need to hear that. Not right now.

"Castiel and I are going to talk to Red and find out how to beat the curse," Sera continued confidently. I had no idea how she did it. No matter what was thrown at Sera, she was always sure. She thought she could do anything, even if she couldn't.

I looked at Grace, but I couldn't turn my eyes to Sera. She wasn't telling Grace the full truth on any of it. I understood why she was doing that, but it wasn't something I could do. I couldn't lie to Grace. The curse would turn Grace into a monster, and there wasn't a cure. Those two things weren't going to change any time soon. I didn't plan to give up, but I was realistic.

Elder had always looked to itself as self-sufficient. They never looked outside the border for help, but I had a feeling this time, we needed more than we could get from Red. She'd already admitted that she didn't know how to fix it. I wasn't sure what the other kingdoms would do, once the wolves spread over the borders, but it might be necessary this time to preemptively seek help if Red could do that.

Red was a political leader, but always private. She treated her kingdom just like her life when she was out in the rest of the world. She listened and analyzed everything, but never showed her cards. I wasn't sure it was time to be leading like that if she genuinely couldn't help the wolves, but her leadership was exactly like her personality. Heck, I grew up with Red as my mother and yet couldn't tell you very many personal details about her. I honestly didn't know if she'd ever been in love or wanted to get married to someone because she kept that all to herself. But in reality, she kept everything to herself. I was pretty sure that if the wolf problem got too bad, there would be no keeping it to ourselves this time.

"We'll take you back to the wolves as soon as you are rested," Sera explained as she continued to talk to Grace.

I nodded my agreement before going back to the food to make a plate for Grace. I brought it back to her as Sera sat on the ground beside her and patted her hand. Grace was still on the verge of crying, but she accepted the food and the support from Sera. She, at least, had calmed from Sera's words, and maybe that's why the future Red lied to her. She could see that Grace needed hope, even if we didn't truly have it to offer.

Sera and Grace continued to whisper as I cleaned up the dishes from breakfast. I lost myself in thoughts rather than listen in. Sera was talking to Grace and planning their fun times after the curse was broken, and Grace wouldn't have to live as a wolf. I couldn't think that far ahead.

I was sure where I stood with the wolves. It was only a day ago that they had shown up at my house, demanding to have Grace back. I know they were acting out of fear and Nikkan's irrational feelings, but it was the first time, ever, I had felt like the wolves didn't want me around.

No matter how much the woods of Elder felt like home to me, I'd never felt like I belonged with the people of Elder. The tree people didn't accept me because of my weird-colored eyes, and the wolves didn't accept me entirely because I couldn't transform into a wolf. But, at least, the wolves never shunned me. They looked at me like an oddity, but I always felt welcome. I wasn't sure that was the case now.

Nikkan had brought some of the older male wolves with him when he came to take Grace home, but he had also brought Micco, their leader. I knew where I stood with Micco. He was like a grandfather to me. Even after their visit, I still knew that Micco supported me and always would. But he couldn't make the other wolves change their minds if they now saw me like the outsider the tree people saw me as.

Elder is made up of two distinct areas, the woods of the north and east and the farm fields of the south. I hadn't tried the farming villages as a place to live, but I didn't know if I could. It was the woods that called me home all the time. Running between the trees and watching the seasons change was part of me. I wasn't sure I could live in a place with few trees, hills, or running water. Every noise, scent, and feeling of the woods was what I needed to survive. This was home, even if I wasn't welcome by any of the people living nearby.

The sun was at the midpoint in the sky by the time Grace felt well enough to stand. I could tell by her tentative steps, that she wasn't going to make the jog back to the wolf village. It was going to be a slow walk, and, hopefully, we'd make it there by nightfall.

"I'll go get Nikkan," Sera said quietly to me as we exited my house. I nodded to her as I offered an arm for Grace to hold as we started our walk.

Grace watched as Sera took off full speed into the woods. She was almost as quiet as I was, but I was still quieter.

"I'm still not sure this is the safest option," Grace

said as she took a few more steps, her strength slowly coming back after sleeping for so long.

"The wolves will know what to do to keep you and everyone else safe. They've dealt with this before. It isn't new to Micco," I reminded her, and that was the truth. Micco wasn't the leader eighteen winters ago, but he was the second in command. He knew what he was doing.

Grace nodded as she gave me a strained smile. I took that as a sign to walk slower, and she slowed beside me.

"And what will you be off doing while I wait to turn back into a monster?"

I tried not to smile at her statement, but how she said monster with such disgust on her face was funny. It wasn't like she thought she'd be scary, but that she'd be a slobbering mess instead. I suppose waking up covered in blood would do that to you, but it was still funny.

Grace caught the smirk I was trying to keep hidden, and she hit me on the chest with her free hand.

"Castiel," she complained with a whine.

I couldn't contain my chuckle as it escaped.

"You talk about being a monster like it's gross," I explained. "But turning into a wolf and running around the forest eating small cute furry animals isn't gross?"

Grace smiled and laughed too.

"Okay, fine. Being a wolf any time is gross." Grace paused a moment and then added, "So you and Sera…."

I had no idea what she was talking about as I stared at her, waiting for her to finish. Grace huffed and then laughed at me.

"You know she likes you, right?"

"What? Not possible. She hates me most of the time, and the rest of the time, she acts like I'm her big brother."

Grace shrugged.

"You like her too."

I sputtered as I tried to come up with another response.

Grace just smiled and nodded to me as she didn't say anything further.

It was impossible. Grace had that one wrong. Sera and I couldn't stand each other. This was the only time I could remember that I could consider Sera as being nice. Most of the time, she was just annoying as she tried to beat me at everything. We might be rivals, but there wasn't anything more between us, and if Grace thought Sera liked me, she was crazy. Sera tolerated me on a good day and hated me otherwise. This whole curse thing was playing with her mind. I was sure of that.

We continued to walk into the woods, toward the wolf village. I knew Grace loved to talk, but she was quiet too. I had a feeling she was more tired than she'd ever admit, but that was part of being a wolf: never show weakness.

As we got further away from my place and into the woods where the chirping of the birds disappeared, Grace's thinking face turned to a frown.

"This isn't going to be over soon, is it?"

I knew that while Grace wanted to believe Sera, but she was smart enough to see the truth. The last curse that made the wolves lose control of their animals took hundreds of winters before it was beaten. It was possible it could take a long time this time around too.

"I plan to go back to Red and find an answer. She was the one that broke it before and the one that can do it again. We just need to figure out how."

"And until then, we will find a way to help the wolves," Sera put in her two cents as she came out of the forest to the path we were walking on with Nikkan beside her.

Nikkan sheepishly looked anywhere but at Grace and me.

"He can take her the rest of the way back," Sera pointed at Nikkan. "He" was better than her usual nickname of mutt. "I explained it all to him, and he knows to keep her safe. Nikkan will take care of her while we search for answers."

I nodded and tried to catch Nikkan's eyes, but he didn't look up from the ground.

Grace questioned me with her eyebrows, and I walked her over to Nikkan, transferring her arm to his arm. Her cheeks flamed red. At least, that was still normal.

"She's not very strong yet," I told Nikkan, even if he wouldn't look at me. "And she needs to take it slow."

"I do not," Grace replied with a pout.

"Yes, you do," Sera replied for me. "The next few days, you will get part of your strength back. It should take several moons before the curse pulls at you again and forces you to change. It will come sooner if you let it, but all Red's papers say you can fight the curse at the beginning. So fight it if you don't want to be a monster."

Grace had fire in her eyes, listening to Sera's talk, and she nodded along with her.

"I can do that," she said, determined but still weak.

I tried to smile with her, but it was hard. I could tell that the animals had left this part of the woods, so she wasn't going to have much to eat as a human or a wolf.

"We will be back as soon as we can," Sera said to Grace, leaning forward in our small awkward circle to hug Grace before we left.

"Keep her fed to get her strength back," I told Nikkan. He nodded without looking at me, still holding a grudge. I was okay with that. He could hate me all he wanted, but I knew he'd keep Grace safe.

"We will be back," I echoed Sera as Nikkan turned to start their walk back to the wolf village.

12TH MARCH

Sera and I spent the night at my place as it was getting close to dark by the time we made it back from walking Grace to the wolves. It wasn't that either of us cared if we traveled in the dark of night, but we both agreed that we didn't want to end up killing any wolves if they got too close. We were both worried about the safety of the wolves, which was strange because Sera never really cared for wolves before Grace. That gave me, at least, a little hope that Elder could change as Red wanted.

I tried to watch Sera and see if Grace was telling the truth about her liking me, but all I saw was the same old Sera. The one that tolerated me and might hate me at times. Grace was just trying to fool me. And boy, had she succeeded. I did smile to myself several times as

I realized I fell for her trick. When she was better, I'd have to get her back for teasing me. I was going to have to come up with something better than her.

We were up early to go back to Azren to see Red. With our super speed-running, we would make it back in no time. I actually appreciated being able to run with Sera since she could keep up with my pace. No other human could do that. We both just took a slice of bread before we headed out. It wasn't hard to eat bread and run. Actually, you could eat a lot while running if you tried, but I would never advise soup.

"Anything we need to bring?" Sera asked as I closed the door to my place.

"Not that I can think of," I replied. I didn't have anything that could help us on our quest. I was hoping Red would be able to think of something.

With our mouths full, we took off on our run. I appreciated that we were both eating, and I didn't have to talk with Sera. It made conversation impossible, and I didn't have to think more about what Grace said.

It was nice that the woods were home for both of us. We could make our way through the foliage and not have to follow the paths most people took, and that would save us time too. Right now, we were working against the clock. I knew Sera said it would take moons for the curse to force Grace into her monster form, but with the lack of food in the wolf village, I wasn't sure she had that much time. The sooner we found answers, the better for everyone of Elder, including Grace.

Unfortunately, in our quiet run, my mind drifted back to Grace, telling me that Sera and I liked each other. Maybe it would have been easier if we were talking. It wasn't that I didn't like Sera; it was just we never seemed to get along. It was partially my fault as

I always found I could do everything just a little better than she could, but it wasn't like I ever rubbed it in her face. Okay, I might have once or twice, but for the most part, I couldn't help that I could do things better than her. Life in the woods just came naturally to me, and as the seasons passed, I had grown stronger and surer this was my place. She seemed to hate me for it most of the time. Hate and like were utterly opposite feelings. I still have no idea why I fell for what Grace said.

Grace had gotten into my head as I kept stealing glances at my running partner. What if it wasn't a joke and she was right. Nothing seemed different, and it admittedly didn't seem like Sera liked me. She was tolerating me just as I was tolerating her. That wasn't a romantic feeling. When Grace saw Nikkan, her eyes lit up, and she always turned some sort of shade of red. I had never and would probably never see Sera blush.

"What?" Sera asked between bites.

I didn't need quiet time to be over. We would likely just start arguing. I needed to put Grace and her rogue thoughts out of my head.

"Did I get some on my face?"

I shook my head no and turned back to watch where I was running. And Grace was so completely wrong. I didn't like Sera in the least. Just because I knew more about her than anyone beside Nikkan, didn't mean a thing. We grew up together. And knowing her favorite things would be expected. I had memorized almost everything about how Sera moved as a way to beat her when we practiced. It had nothing to do with the fact that she was nice to look at when she wasn't mad at me. But that wasn't entirely true either. She was entertaining when angry. But that didn't mean I liked her. Or did it?

I didn't have time to contemplate what Grace had put into my mind any further as we came upon the town. Sera and I stopped at the same time, just outside of town, in the spring foliage. We both knew it was better to be cautious when entering the village than just to run in. The people were jumpy enough before the curse returned; neither one of us wanted to get shot by some nervous townsperson for coming back to town.

Sera sucked in a breath at the sight before us. We hadn't expected to meet anyone on the ground with fear running high, let alone a mob of yelling people. It was very good that we hadn't just run into the village.

"We can't wait any longer," a large man called Raul yelled at Red, who had her back to us. "They will just grow stronger, and more will attack us. If we head there now, we can wipe them all out before this begins again. No wolves, no curse. We won't have to live in fear."

I sucked in my breath as I stared in shock at the tree people of Elder. They were talking about murder. Wiping out an entire race of people. And why? Because they were afraid? What about the wolves? They were just as scared. Maybe even more so. How could the tree people just forget that the wolves were their neighbors, their friends? How had it changed so quickly back to the world I only heard the older generations of Elder speak about? We needed answers to help Grace, but I was beginning to see that we needed answers quickly to help all of Elder.

I moved to go in and tell the tree people to suck it up and deal with it as the wolves had just as much right to live in Elder as the tree people, but Sera reached out and stopped me from moving. Her smaller hand on my arm made me pause, and she nodded to Red.

I tried to stop my thoughts from wandering to what

Grace had told me before, but it was hard with Sera's hand on my arm. I did my absolute best to focus on the mob of people around Red. I didn't fear for her but for them. No one wanted to see Red mad. I knew that firsthand.

"No one will be heading to the wolves," Red said, standing with her arms crossed as she surveyed the crowd in front of her. She had her authority voice on, and her stare down was intimidating. People in front of her shrank back from her glare.

It was strange that someone barely a sapling tall could make grown men cower, but she did just that. Maybe it was the magic of being Red, but I had a feeling it was only my mother. I had never once gotten away with anything growing up. She always knew, and I always was punished. That look from Red could make anyone pee their pants.

"And why not?" someone yelled from the crowd, further back that wasn't as afraid as the front row of people closest to Red.

"Because the wolves are part of Elder," Red replied.

I had been on the receiving end of her glare and didn't blame the guy that asked for blending back into the crowd. Red didn't sound happy in the least. Bringing Elder together had been her goal as the Red, and it was so close. Her dreams for the kingdom were shattered. While I worried that she was against the wolves when she had told me not to spend time with them, I could see that it wasn't Red, but the people, against the wolves. They were easily forgetting the past eighteen winters.

"But they are hunting our children. They will come and snatch them in the night," a woman with a bright green scarf around her head called to Red. "If they don't kill us, they'll change us into monsters. I don't think anyone wants to be around for either of those."

"We are safe in our trees," Red replied, downplaying the concerns. "Stay in the trees at nighttime, and they can't hurt anyone. We've been through this before. We survived for hundreds of winters with the wolves cursed. This is nothing new. Stop being so irrational." Red sounded like she had winters ago when I was a child that needed scolding.

The wolf curse was why more than half the people of Elder lived in the trees. Red had told me once about when she was a child and how people were raised and spent their whole lives never setting foot on the ground. It wasn't the best way to live, but no one questioned it. It kept them safe. Why were they questioning her and their way of life now after hundreds of winters?

It was no different now, except for the guns my mother had stockpiled. I knew that most of the tree people knew about the arms, and it seemed the bolder ones now wanted to use them. Red had never intended for the guns she had bartered from other kingdoms to be used to kill off the wolves. She might have told me to stay away from the wolves, but I knew in her heart that she supported the wolves as much as she could. She saw them as part of Elder, not the enemy, as most of the tree people saw them right now. The guns were for safety only, not mass murder.

"Safe? Safe is when we can walk around our own kingdom without being afraid," a short, balding man towards the front replied. He stared at the ground as he talked, but that was probably the only way he had the courage.

"Yes," the lady from before cheered him on.

Red looked from face to face. I could tell that while she looked strong and intimidating, she was actually sad. All her work was for nothing. One small moment and everything went back to the way it was. The tree people and the wolves hated each other again. The bridge she had spent eighteen winters building was torn down in one night. Her shoulder stooped a little as she looked around and shook her head at the people before her.

"We need to keep Elder safe for everyone, including the citizens that can shift into a wolf. None of you are going off hunting without direct permission from me. The armory will remain closed under lock and key that only I have access to. You can't kill citizens of Elder without being punished, and I will punish each and every one of you that thinks they are above the law," Red informed them.

The people turned to their neighbors and talked. The whispers that I heard were all disagreements. Some were calling for Red to step down. It seemed that many knew that Sera was almost ready to take over. They wanted that to happen now instead of later as they thought she'd allow them to hunt the wolves. They were all upset, and anger was coursing through most of them that weren't afraid of Red and the power she held. The only thing keeping them from outright mutiny was that they needed her. Red was their only true protection.

"Will I be punished for hunting deer?" a young man off to the left wearing a deep yellow hat asked. I couldn't see his face, but he had to be someone I knew. He didn't seem much older than me.

"That's not a reason to be punished," Red replied, falling for his innocent face as he asked his question.

"Then why will I be punished for hunting a wolf?"

Sera huffed next to me and shook her head. She'd seen that coming just as I had.

Cheers went up around the young man. Most, if not all, of the people agreed with him. It was sad to see how much changed in just a few short days. Not even ten moons ago, the tree people of Elder were living side by side with wolves that had moved into Azren. I knew none of them were there now since Red kicked them out, but that didn't change anything. How could someone you viewed as your neighbor now be your enemy?

Red rubbed her head. I don't think she expected that level of hatred from someone younger than me. She had tried to raise the new generation of Elder to love everyone that resided in the kingdom, but it didn't seem to stick.

"The wolf tribes in the north are humans. They may change into wolves, but we all know that they are human. Raul, didn't Cameron help you just last moon cycle when your house burned? He got the water to put out the fire in the middle of the night and then let you live with him while you rebuilt? Now, you want to thank him by killing him and hunting his children?"

The large man turned his red-cheeked face to his feet to avoid her stare.

"And what about you, Michael? Did you take Raven on a date just a few moons ago? Now, you want to hunt her like an animal? So you go on dates with animals? You like animals romantically since that's what you are telling me now?"

The young man turned as red as the older man while the people around him chuckled. Even next to me, Sera was giggling. Red might not have fallen for his innocent face after all.

"We are one Kingdom of Elder, and we need to remember that," Red scolded the crowd like they were unruly children. "The moment we forget that makes us the bad guys. Our kingdom will crumble, and it will be our fault. We are stronger than this curse. All of you need to believe that."

"But what about the guns?" someone near the back yelled. "Why do we have them if we aren't going to use them?"

Red nodded to the man.

"Yes, I have us stocked well with guns. I worried that the curse could come back, and we need to stay safe. We can't let the wolves take the children. They are our future. But we also can't hunt people like animals. The guns are for protecting the city, and that's it. No one will be leaving with a gun to hunt wolves. If I find anyone has done just that, we will go back to the old punishments."

Eyes facing Red all bugged out at her words. Elder was a kingdom that was self-sufficient. Most of the time, people traded for what they needed. We didn't have the latest technology of the other kingdoms, but no one cared. One of the things we really never had was a prison. It was a simple solution. The old punishments were an eye for an eye. If you killed someone, then you forfeited your life. While Red had done away with the laws and allowed people to seek retribution through goods and services, she wasn't joking when she said she'd reinstate it. I knew it was her last attempt to keep control of the mob, and I hoped it would work.

"I've enacted the wards to Azren. Anyone crossing them without first notifying me will be marked and retrieved for everyone's protection. Stay in the trees and don't venture into the woods until Micco and I say it is safe. I'm working hard with Micco to find a solution and keep tabs on our wolf population. I will keep you safe as I have been doing my entire life, but to do so, I need you to follow the rules. They are in place for a reason. We've survived this before and will again."

The people stared at her, and a few nodded.

"I have to keep all of Elder safe. It would do you all best to remember that we are all one nation. And remember your friends that have gone home to face the scariest thing in their life. They didn't ask to be a wolf or to be cursed. All they wanted was to live like everyone else. The wolves you all know are kind and helpful people. I can't begin to list all the things they've done in the past eighteen winters to help the tree people out. Stop acting like they are the enemies. They are our friends, family, and neighbors."

Red had a presence that commanded everyone to look at her. Not a single face was turned away as she talked. She pulled them all in with her words. Red was serious, and they all knew it.

"Start acting like the people I know you are. Keep track of your children, stay in the trees, and remember that your friends are trying their hardest to keep Elder safe for everyone."

Red nodded to the crowd, dismissing them. No one said another word as the crowd dispersed back into the trees.

"Did that about sum it all up?" she asked as she turned to Sera and I still standing out of view in the woods.

"I'd say so," Sera replied as she stepped out of the trees to Red. "But I still wouldn't trust them."

Sera shrugged. I didn't blame her. I didn't trust them either. Red could scare them and punish them, but that didn't mean they would do the right thing. I saw their faces. I had seen their anger and their fear. Those two things were enough to make the most decent man change. They would do things they never would normally do if pushed. I just had to hope the wolves stayed in the north, and the tree people stayed in their trees.

Red shrugged back to Sera.

"They have to be given a chance to be good. We both know that. Now how about the two of you come back home and get cleaned up. I have a feeling this isn't just a friendly visit. You can update me on everything once you get freshened up and fed."

I nodded to Red as I stepped up beside Sera, who was already walking towards the cottage we grew up in. Things were getting scarier for the wolves. Not only did they have the curse to deal with, but now, also the tree people of Elder who had access to guns. The wolves didn't stand a chance if the tree people turned on them. We had a lot to discuss and an answer to find, just as soon as we cleaned up and ate like Red ordered us to. It wasn't quite the welcome home I wanted, but it would have to do.

I wasn't expecting much, maybe a little awkwardness at being home, but Red went full out. After we cleaned up, she prepared a feast for us. There were carrots, squash, corn, noodles, mash potatoes, fresh bread, lamb, beef in gravy, apple pie, cookies, and a cake. It wasn't one of our regular supper meals that I grew up on. I felt a little guilty eating so much while the wolves starved, but I wasn't about to tell Red no. She was more than happy to have both Sera and I home with her; it was a bit strange.

Red was my mother, but she had never been overly motherly. Sera and I were accustomed to helping with meals and doing our share, but Red fussed and made everything herself. I felt like maybe she had been hit on the head and was too crazy to tell us. We'd notice if she went' crazy, right? I'd hoped so.

We spent the meal making small talk. Mainly our mouths were full, and Sera and I could only get a nod in every now and then to what Red was talking about. As usual, it was nothing personal but just about people around the kingdom she had been talking with for the past couple of days. It seemed the whole of Elder knew the curse was back even though it rarely affected the farmers to the south. It was the gossip of the kingdom.

After we ate, we told Red of everything we had done with Grace. She was as disappointed as we were, but that was all she said. It was dark by then, and Red asked to go to bed early. It was very unlike Red. I had begun to believe as a child that she never slept, that the Red wasn't allowed to sleep. I had a feeling Red's powers were fading more than she'd ever admit. I didn't want to broach the subject and let her go to bed in peace before finding sleep myself after our exhausting day.

13TH MARCH

When I woke the next morning, I found Red already awake and in the kitchen cooking. How in the world she thought we needed more food after the feast the night before was beyond me, but I was reassured to see that the faint lines that had marred her face the night before seemed to be gone even if her gray hairs were still there. I searched to see if there were any more signs of her aging, but nothing stood out. Was she getting old because her powers were leaving or because, in fact, she was old? It had been three winters since I last lived at home. That was enough time for her to start going gray.

"Sera is already running the perimeter to make sure no one had the idea to leave town without permission," Red told me as she continued to cook.

I made my way over to beside her and took the

spatula from her hands to take over making the eggs. She nodded to me and then moved to the cupboard to cut up the fruit she had. You couldn't have traded me anything as a child to get me to help her cook. It was beyond my least favorite chore. I'd offer to do the most tedious tasks in the village to get out of cooking, but after living on my own, I was more than willing to help, now that I knew how much time making meals took up.

"Is she coming back for breakfast?" I asked, eyeing up the abundance of food. Either Sera was returning with an appetite or Red was having guests. That wasn't unusual. There was always someone who needed her attention.

Red looked up from the fruit she was cutting up and laughed. I stared in shock at her. Red actually laughed. I could count the times I had heard her laugh when I lived under her roof with one hand. I was back to my theory that she had a serious head injury. My mother never laughed, at least, not that I could remember.

"I guess this is overkill, isn't it?" Red shrugged and went back to the fruit, making the most perfect little slices. "It's just you and me."

I stared at the back of her head more before the crackling noise of the pan brought me back to cooking the eggs. This was more food than Nikkan, and I ate in days, and he had quite the appetite, all wolves did. We both ate a lot, and this was way more. Something was going on.

Red started to hum as she chopped and somehow knew exactly when the eggs were done as she returned to my side with two plates in her hand to scrape the eggs onto. I followed her to the table as she had already placed more food out. Fruit, eggs, bread, pastries from in town, and even sausage. This was a full breakfast, just like dinner had been.

"Are you dying?" I asked.

That was the only thing I could think of that would make Red act so strangely. But that was a stretch. I was pretty sure Red had faced death more times than I could count, and I bet she wasn't giggling and making a feast.

Red gave me a raised eyebrow. Okay, that was a no. But what else could it be? A head injury should have healed overnight and this was definitely still strange Red.

"Really, Castiel. Death? Is that what it means when your mother makes you a meal and is happy to see you return from the forest, not mauled to death by wolves? Can't I just be happy to see you alive?"

No, she couldn't. I had been living on my own for winters now. This wasn't my first return home safe and sound, and she wasn't going to convince me otherwise. I crossed my arms as I stared at her from across the table. What game was she playing now?

"Fine," she replied as she noticed I didn't buy her explanation. "I asked Sera to stay out of the house while we talked, and I figured food would keep you busy and not interrupting me as I said what I needed to say."

There was the woman who raised me, calculated and prepared for anything and everything. I still didn't know why she'd be laughing or happy, but I was getting closer to a reason. Red was always two steps ahead. She had a plan for after her plan, always.

She offered me a pancake I hadn't even noticed when I sat down and waited for me to take a bite. With my mouth full, she finally spoke.

"I know why you are here. I figured most of it, but Sera filled in the holes this morning."

Stupid Sera. Why couldn't she just stay out of things between Red and me? See, we couldn't get along for even one day without me wanting to strangle her. We certainly weren't into each other like Grace wished for us to be.

"You think I'm keeping something from you," Red added, still not eating herself. Instead, she was watching me intensely, reading my every mood, and making calculations about what to do next.

I chewed the piece of pancake in my mouth slowly, so I didn't have to reply. I didn't think— I knew. I had known most of my life that Red kept things from me. She always had and always would. That was just how Red worked. We didn't need to get into another of our famous arguments. It wasn't the time for that. We needed to work together, and I needed her help. I wished I had taken a bigger bite. This was going to be one of those conversations.

I tried my best not to let her words get to me. When wasn't Red keeping something from me? My whole life was her telling me just what she thought I should know — everything else I had to learn on my own. Thankfully, I had Micco and Nikkan to help me, or I'd be wholly dependant on Red. That was probably what she wanted.

"I know I haven't been the best mother, but you have to understand being a mother wasn't something I ever expected to be. I was raised to be the Red. When I was chosen, my parents were so glad that they had another child, knowing that my life would be short and full of danger. They needed a child that would give them grandchildren and take care of them in their old age. I wasn't going to be that. I certainly didn't have time to find love and start a family. That isn't part of the job description for being the Red."

That explained much. My grandparents weren't part of our lives. In fact, my mother rarely even spoke to them, and they lived in Azren. I never really gave it much thought as Red was a busy person, but being that they tossed her aside when she was chosen, that would explain why she wasn't close with them. I didn't entirely blame her for that.

"I have always done this parenting thing as best as I could. I'm sorry I told you not to see the wolves. I know how much they mean to you. Is Nikkan okay? You didn't mention him yesterday."

I grabbed my juice to wash down my food so I could reply. I was so intent on doing my best to eat and keep my mouth shut to keep the conversation going that I wasn't prepared when I'd needed to respond.

"He's doing fine, I guess. He's having one of his fits and ignoring me right now."

Red nodded. She understood that pretty well. Nikkan had been part of my life as far back as I could remember.

"You know how he gets," I added as I reached for a piece of fruit that would be quicker to swallow if she needed another answer.

"He'll get over it, eventually," she replied, and I nodded.

Nikkan had been moody as long as I had known him. Red understood that well. There had always been visits to the wolf village where I would beg to go home early because Nikkan got into one of his moods. It had been better over the last few seasons since he had decided to spend more time as a wolf. That was probably what made him so moody. He was never good about separation from his animal, and his animal wasn't happy to be caged in a house or a village.

"Well, I'm sorry. I shouldn't have tried to keep you from them. I shouldn't have tried to divide you just like our people are doing. I let fear take over and wasn't thinking straight."

"Fear?" I choked out my question.

Red refilled my juice glass, and I gulped it down. Red didn't have fear. That came with the magical powers of being the Red. She was our leader. People feared her, but she never feared anything. She was stronger, quicker, and smarter than anything that might attack her or the village. She was our hero.

"I know you can see that Sera is coming into her Red powers. As hers grow, mine fade."

I nodded. I had seen that much, even if she had never admitted it before.

"And you are what I'll have left when my powers are gone. I was afraid to lose you to the wolves. You've always preferred them over the village, and I was afraid you'd be bitten and become one of them. That I'd lose you."

I stared in shock at her. Red never seemed to care where I was one way or another, growing up. She didn't even stop me from moving out winters ago. I didn't actually think she cared if I stuck around Azren or not.

"I wasn't supposed to outlive being the Red," she continued. "Every other one died before they aged. I'm not prepared to get old. And now, I finally see that I don't want to lose you. I thought I was fine with you growing up, but I'm not. I miss those winters when it was just you and me. I miss the winters where you thought I was so magical and you looked up to me. They went by so fast. I'm just not ready to let go even though I know you are all grown up."

Red was staring at her food as she bit her lip. I didn't

know how to respond. Red was a leader outside and inside her home. She never showed fear or weakness. She always had an answer, and she always did what was right. I did look up to her when I was a child and secretly still did. This wasn't a side I knew how to handle.

I stood up and walked around the table. I bent down and put my arms around the lady that raised me as best she could. Red looked up at me with tears in her eyes before blinking them away while giving me a tentative smile. I sat down next to her now, hoping that she would continue to be honest with me. The bridge she built between the tree people and the wolves might have crumbled, but what we were making now would last. I just knew it.

"I feel like such a hypocrite," Red continued talking once I was seated. "I'm here trying to get the tree villagers to be good to the wolves, and I haven't been. I sent them all back and then tried to keep you from helping them. I've failed the wolves and you too. But I'm not going to do that now. I know we are stronger as one kingdom together rather than apart. We are one people, even if the people of Azren don't see that right now."

I smiled at her. My strong, resilient mother was back.

"Sera explained to me that she thinks I'm holding back, not helping on purpose. What you both need to understand is that while I've kept details to myself, I've never kept anything back that might help us defeat the curse."

"Then what are you holding back?" I wasn't trying to start a fight. I honestly wanted to know what she thought should be kept from me.

Red looked across the room to the open doorway.

"I suppose you want to hear this, too," she called out

to someone.

Sera grinned as she stepped into the view of the doorway. She had been sitting outside, and I wasn't sure how long. I was listening too hard to Red. Obviously, Red had noticed.

I did my best not to glare at Sera as she entered the cottage. This was the first time in a long time that I had connected with Red. I kind of didn't want to share right now.

"Eighteen winters ago, I was barely older than you two are both right now."

Sera joined us at the table and took my previous seat. She reached over to grab a cinnamon bun as Red talked. I did my best to ignore her.

"The curse was in full swing, and almost all the wolves that still spent time as humans were cursed. The curse seemed to hit some time after puberty but wasn't quite as devastating to their health as this round appears to be. Even though they were healthier last time, they were still the monsters people fear now. Wolves would spend each night roaming the woods and killing anything they could find. Any human or animal wasn't safe. It was a different time.

"Things were getting worse, and I decided that it was time to collect everyone from the witches cottages that were the only homes left on the ground. While I didn't doubt the witch magic would hold against the wolves, it was growing harder to protect and move supplies to the cottages. I was making daily runs, and it was getting exhausting to keep both the cottage and the tree people safe. I asked everyone to move into the trees. There was one family, though, that didn't come when I asked, and I went to find them. The wife was almost nine moons pregnant, and she couldn't make the journey to Azren.

They had decided to stay in their cottage until the baby was born."

Sera stopped eating and stared at Red. It seemed that I wasn't the only one Red had never told this story to before.

"I was fine to let them spend another moon there, but I made sure I was always around to keep them safe. In neglecting my duties to the rest of the kingdom, someone very important to me was bitten. In normal times it would have been several moons until he became a wolf and a monster with the curse, but something was different with him. I have a feeling it was because he spent so much time with me. Maybe something with the Red magic. I'll never know because he was instantly a monster, and because he was so close to me, he was the worst kind. It was like all the good in me turned into bad in him. And to top it off, he knew my every move. He knew what I would be doing and when, and he hunted me like there was no tomorrow. He was relentless, and he was dangerous to everyone. He was once my best friend, and he became instantly the king of the monsters. Everyone started calling him the big bad wolf because only I knew who it truly was."

Red took a sip of her coffee and looked outside the window like she remembered a different time.

"What became of him?" Sera asked.

Red shrugged. "He's no longer alive. But that wasn't the point. The point was what happened with the family I chose to protect. He followed me there, and I knew the only way that child would be safe would be to give her my Red powers. While no one around had ever seen a transfer of power, I knew how to do it, and I did. It was then that I marked you as the next Red, Sera. And then I faced my friend. I was prepared to die to save that family, and I refused to kill the one person that always believed in me. The one person that had befriended me and always stood by me. He wasn't the monster he became in the night. He was my friend. And I wasn't going to kill him."

Red had a friend. That just kept repeating in my head as she paused to collect her thoughts more. I couldn't imagine that. Micco was the closest I had ever seen, and she still kept him at arm's length. What she was talking about was way more than that. She'd had an actual friend.

"But then something changed. I don't even know what. The curse was gone and over. I really have no idea or clue how it happened. At first I thought it was something to do with me marking Sera as the next Red, but as time has gone on, I think I was only able to do that because something had changed first. I'll never forget what happened next."

Sera and I exchanged a look as Red nodded to herself.

"I was given a gift I never knew I wanted."

Red finally looked up and directly into my oddly colored eyes that had never made a difference to her. While the people of Elder never really accepted me, Red always had, even if we didn't always see eye to eye. I knew now what she was talking about, even if Sera was confused.

"What?" Sera asked.

"Castiel," Red replied. "Less than a day after I saved you from my friend, two hooded women, whose faces I never even saw, handed me a baby boy wrapped up in a blanket. They told me that the curse was over, and the wolves would be normal again as long as I accepted him and raised him as my own."

Red took a deep breath, and she looked between our

shocked faces.

"I never planned to live long enough to have a family, and yet I was instantly a mother. I saved Sera one day and the next I had a baby of my own. It wasn't a job I wanted or had any idea how to do, but I am thankful every day that I got to be your mother. We might fight about things every now and then—."

Sera coughed, and Red laughed.

"Okay, Castiel and I fight about everything. But I wouldn't want it any other way. I wish I had the answers to help you find the cure, but I know one thing. We will find it. I might not have created you in my own womb, but I did raise you to be the competent man you are. I should never have worried about you with the wolves because we both know there's nothing to worry about. You are strong, Castiel. Stronger than any person I've ever met, and that isn't just physical. You grew more than I could have ever imagined or pushed you to be. You have a strong mind and an even stronger heart. If anyone can find an answer, it will be you. I know it."

I was never good enough, but it seems that maybe that was more on me than her. I had no idea how to respond. I had spent my whole life not feeling I met her standards, and here she was telling me I exceeded them. I was shocked and stunned.

"I'm sorry I wasn't the mother you deserved, but all I can say is thank you for being the son I know I didn't deserve."

I was out of my chair without a second thought and hugging her for a second time in only moments. Red had done her best, and I never doubted that, even when I didn't agree with her. She was a good mom and better than I ever gave her credit for. I could feel the air shifting. There were no more secrets or lies between us.

She had been truthful, and I understood so much more now. She would never know how much I appreciated her. All I could do was hug her. We were going to find the answers together.

14TH MARCH

Red's office was more than a little cramped as I paced around it. Papers were strewn everywhere, and Sera sat facing Red in her chair. I don't know when Sera had moved in, but it seemed like half the mess in the room was Sera's. They both continued to look at papers and pass them back and forth as they talked. I was left in the corner with only room to walk three steps before running into something. The office of the Red wasn't made for two people to share, that's for sure.

Red seemed not to care as we waited for the healer to come, but I didn't have time to wait. She had sent her letter yesterday and gotten a response that the healer would be here in the morning, but it was already past breakfast, and she hadn't yet arrived. I had no idea what morning meant to the healer, but it was getting past morning to me.

I tried not to huff as I stood there, but I couldn't help it. Every moment we spent waiting was another moment my friends could be in trouble. If this healer was as powerful as Red said she was, then we needed her here now. She very well could end all of this for my friends, and she was taking her time.

"Sit down, Castiel," Sera ordered me.

I couldn't help but glare at her. Whatever truce we had going was gone since we had returned to the trees. Sera and I were never going to see eye to eye, and I wasn't about to be taking orders from her. Grace was utterly crazy that there was anything between us but hate, lesser hate on a good day, but still hate.

"We don't have time to wait," I pleaded with Red instead.

Red nodded as she looked over another paper like she was just trying to appease me. How in the world could she just wait? She was as anxious as I was to help the wolves but didn't seem to show it at all. Was she just pretending the day before?

"She will get here when she gets here," Red explained as she continued to work on something that had to be pretty important if it kept her attention.

"She said morning," I pointed out.

"Mal has never been one to run on a time schedule." Red looked up from her paper as she spoke.

With a poof of purple smoke, a dark-haired woman appeared right in the track of where I was pacing.

"You can say that again, old friend." The lady laughed as she shared a look with Red.

The woman looked like she was only a couple of decades old, yet her voice was rich and held the power of someone who had lived much longer. If not for the few gray strands of hair and the knowledge that this had to be the woman Red was waiting for, I would have guessed she wasn't much older than me. She looked like she was barely of marrying age, yet she was the most potent healer Red knew. It was strange to see an older person in such a young body. I knew she was older than she looked but still I stared in awe at the woman who had just magicked her way into Red's office.

Red jumped up from her chair and rushed around her paper-heaped desk to hug the woman. The woman opened her arms to Red. They laughed as they hugged.

"Mal, it's been too long," Red said into the hair of the woman, getting a mouthful in the process.

Surprisingly, the powerful witch my mother had called for help wasn't much bigger than my short parent. They both laughed as they pulled back to smile at each other. It was like I was seeing a completely different person. I almost needed Sera to pinch me to be sure. My mother wasn't the giddy laughing type at all, and here she was smiling and laughing two days in a row.

"You know whose fault that is. I told you any time you wanted; you could come visit me."

"Sure. I'd rather take my chances with the wolves of Elder than the ogres of Arcadia."

"You don't know what you're missing out on."

The eyes of our guest twinkled, and I got the feeling that she wasn't entirely human. My mother didn't explain precisely who or what her guest Mal was, but I could just sense it. Something was different with the mysterious lady before us.

"So, what was so urgent you couldn't tell me in a message?" Mal pulled Red to a small two-seat couch against the far wall in the room.

"We've run into a bit of a problem with the wolves," Red replied. "They seemed to be sick, and I was hoping maybe some of you magic could help them out."

"Sick wolves?" Mal raised an eyebrow like she knew that Red was leaving something out. "I can take a look, but you know my specialty is with two-legged animals, not four."

"We can arrange for them to be on two legs," Red replied, and Mal laughed.

Mal seemed to understand completely without Red telling her more. I had a feeling that Red's explanation that Mal was an old friend wasn't a comment on Mal's age but rather that they had been friends for a long time.

"Do you remember that one time," Mal began, but Red stopped her by placing her hand over the dark-haired woman's mouth as she began to laugh.

I could see there was a history between the two women. Red had mentioned Mal when I was growing up, but I had never met the woman. She was from Red's life before she was the Red. I always had a hard time picturing my mother as just a girl. She was younger than Sera when she was chosen to be the Red and start her training, but for some time, she was just a normal girl. Mal knew that version of my mother. If it were any other time, I would have wanted to get some stories out of the healer.

I had a feeling Mal might be the only person that knew the real Red. She knew her from before the power and responsibility. She knew what Red was like before she had to care for everyone else before herself. I wish I knew that Red. By the way the two of them were laughing, I was more than sure Mal might have been one of the only true friends my mother ever had.

Red had spoken of Mal as a healer, but I could see there was more to that. Her long deep red gown almost sparkled on the lady as she tried to take Red's hands off her mouth. The two of them laughed more as she finally won.

"I've never been introduced to your son," Mal said as she stood and walked towards me. I was still frozen in my spot watching my mother behave very unlike the Red I'd always known

"Mal, this is Castiel," Red replied with a wave of her hand towards me. Her serious face was falling back into place. "He will escort you to the wolves. They won't take kindly to you if you just show up, no matter if you are there to help."

"He can lead me there?" Mal asked, and Red nodded.

"I should go with them," Sera added from beside Red's desk, where she stood looking like she was in as much shock as I was at this side of Red.

"No. He will be fine with Mal, and it's better if just the two of them go. Our energy can mess things up," Red explained what wasn't very clear to me or from the look of Sera's face to her either.

"I suppose you want me to do this sooner rather than later," Mal raised an eyebrow at Red. "Or I could tell them both some great stories of our youth. There's the one with us, the elemental lynx, and that young man...."

Red actually blushed.

"Yes, it would be better for you to head off now," Red interjected before Mal could say more.

"Too bad. I ran into him the other day, and he asked about you." Mal grinned at my mother's red cheeks. "I thought about telling him you are available."

"Castiel, take her to Micco and explain it all to her

there."

I had never seen Red get so flustered. I kind of wanted to stay around for, at least, a little bit more to see something I would probably never see again.

"Young man, if you could take my hand," Mal held her hand out to me.

I had no idea what the lady wanted but did as she asked.

"Now, think of an exact spot you want us to land."

"Land?" I asked.

"Think, boy, and I'll do the rest."

I gave her a quizzical look, and she just waved her free hand as if to hurry me up.

"Close your eyes if you have to. I can't travel places I've never been to. You have to lead us."

She still wasn't making any sense, but I would do whatever she asked if she could heal my friends. As she suggested, I closed my eyes and pictured the village in my head. I thought of standing just inside the wolf village, right where I usually entered when I was coming from my house. I had been there hundreds of times, so it was easy to get a mental image of the place.

"Good enough," Mal said as I felt a tingle come over my skin.

My eyes shot open, and I went to pull my hand back. She smiled at me with what could almost be described as a predatory grin.

"Tsk, tsk. Too late for that, dear boy. Welcome to how I travel."

I was standing in the middle of the wolf village. My stomach heaved as the magic she used seemed to slide off me. I knew that some people could travel that way, but I never heard of someone being taken along for the ride. Still feeling the need to puke, I tried my best to suck it up and stood to look around us as Mal gasped.

"The wolves have been sick for only a short time," I explained as I looked at the nearest person. They were so thin that bones were sticking out where there should have been muscles and fat to hide them. Arms were boney, and collar bones sunken into chests all around me. Everyone we could see looked like they had been starved for moons, not days. The wolves were withering away.

"I swear," I told her as I looked around for someone that looked healthy.

"Castiel?" someone said quietly as I turned around.

Grace sprinted from the nearest hut and jumped into my arms. Her energy seemed to be back, a little bit, at least.

"Let go of her," Mal commanded me before I could respond to my friend.

A blond wolf at our feet looked up at Mal and growled.

"Nikkan?" I said as I recognized my friend.

He obviously didn't like the tone from Mal. His wolf eyes glared at the woman who had indeed come all the way into the forest of Elder to help.

"This is a friend of Red. She's here to help. She's a healer and a pretty great one if you ask Red. She came all the way here from Arcadia."

Nikkan still let out a low growl. Mal was pulling at me to leave the wolves alone.

At least, I hoped she could help. All it took was one meeting, and she was acting like all the other people of Elder. Why was it so hard for people to see that the wolves were just humans too? Grace wasn't going to turn into a wolf and bite my head off right now, at least, not during the day.

Nikkan still didn't seem to agree that Mal was helping

and placed himself between Grace and the healer.

"We need to leave now," Mal told me as she looked around the camp. Her eyes dashed from one person to another. She began to look frantic at all the people that were now staring at us, but she had to expect that much. If you magically poof into someone's home, they are going to stare. "This isn't a disease. This is magic and strong magic at that."

Mal grabbed my arm, and with more strength than I could imagine a woman of her size having, she dragged me toward the outskirts of the village. It was like I weighed nothing to her.

"We didn't get to speak to Micco," I complained as I tried to get my arm out of her grip. I couldn't even move a finger width. She was strong.

"He can explain this more to you. They are sick and need help. That's why my mother called you here."

"Trust me, boy. We need to leave here now before the magic damages us. This isn't a sickness. It is dark old magic. It will attack any being that has a bit of magic in them, not just your wolf friends."

Could the curse hurt us? That wasn't possible. The curse only affected wolves. It had never done a thing to humans. There had never been a single recording of the curse hurting anyone else. The curse was for the wolves. Everyone knew that.

Mal didn't stop pulling until we were outside the village. Nikkan and Grace followed us but stayed back at the glare Mal was giving them. Nikkan returned her glare with a growl.

"If you value Castiel's life at all, you'll stay back away from him until this curse is broken," Mal warned them. Nikkan and Grace stared at me in confusion.

I was confused too. Mal didn't make any sense. The

curse had been affecting the wolves for hundreds of winters before Red broke it. It never once transferred to a human that wasn't a wolf. Mal wasn't letting us explain it to her.

"The curse before affected the wolves," I tried to explain to Mal.

"Because there's magic in their blood," Mal replied as she looked back at the village.

More people had followed Grace and Nikkan to where they stood a few saplings away from Mal and me at the edge of the village. Curious eyes looked at Mal. She was a sight to see as she frantically pulled me from the village we'd just popped into.

I could hear the whispers of the people that were following us, the ones that still had the strength to walk. They wanted to know who she was. Some had heard she was a healer. More than one was looking at her with hopeful eyes. They desperately needed help, and here Mal was dragging me away and leaving them to fend for themselves. Not very helpful.

"I can't fix this kind of magic," Mal stated to the people that stood there watching her. "But I can protect you from hurting others. I can feel the good in all of you. None of you want to harm people, but the curse will make you do that. What I can offer is protection for you and the rest of Elder."

I stared at the small woman. How in the world could she protect all the people of Elder if she couldn't take the curse away? If her magic could protect Elder, then why not remove the curse? I knew very little about magic, but it seemed like they were both on the same scale.

Mal retook my arm and began to pull me back further into the woods. We couldn't see the village from where she stopped, but Nikkan and Grace were following, just not too closely.

"First, I need to call all the wolves to the villages."

She took a step in front of me and began to wave her hands in the air like she was swatting at bugs. I had no idea what she was doing, but after a few moments, she seemed satisfied.

"Next, I will erect the wall you've been trying to build with magic. It will allow things to go through, like the water from the streams or the animals like deer or birds, but it will stop any wolf or human from crossing."

The people behind Grace seemed to have hope in their eyes at the description Mal was giving to them. There was actual hope. I knew the wolves didn't want to hurt anyone, but to be told there was a way to keep everyone safe was something no one could feel until Mal spoke. I wanted to give them hope that the nightmare was all done, but at least this was something. It was a step toward helping all of Elder.

"That will keep both sides from harming each other," Mal said more quietly to me. Red seemed to have filled her in at least a little bit.

I looked back at my friends. This wall was going to keep us apart. Yes, Nikkan had yet to forgive me, but now I wouldn't get the chance to win him back. Until we found a cure to the curse, they would be there, and I would be here. Grace seemed to understand as tears began to trickle down her face.

"Step back, children," Mal said to Grace and Nikkan. They were anything but children, but they knew her order was directed at them.

Mal began to take off her shoes. I had no idea what she was, let alone what she was capable of, but I wasn't going to argue. She was keeping my friends safe from the tree people that seemed to want to hunt wolves now. Mal hiked up her long maroon skirt and dug her feet into the ground. Luckily, it was spring, and the dirt gave way instead of being frozen like it was only moons ago.

I glanced back at my friends. Nikkan was wrapped around Grace's feet, and she had a hand on his head. She looked sad, but Nikkan looked more determined than ever.

"I will find a cure," I told Grace as she didn't try to hide her tears.

She nodded to me but didn't respond.

Mal began to chant. I had no idea why, but it was like I could feel the pull. There was something coming to her. I couldn't see it or smell it, but I could feel it. Mal was pulling more and more of it as she closed her eyes and kept chanting.

"Keep her safe," I told my wolf friend at Grace's feet.

The wolf looked up at me. All the hate and mistrust from the past week were gone. It was Nikkan, truly Nikkan, looking back at me. I knew his wolf side as well as I knew his human side. The look he gave me was all I needed. I knew, without a doubt, he would keep Grace safe.

"And you keep safe, too," I told him.

They were like family to me. I wasn't going to stop until I helped them, but until then, I needed to know they would be fine.

Wolf Nikkan nipped in the air, his way of agreeing with me.

"I will find an answer," I told my friends. "I don't care how long it will take or what I will have to do to find it, but I will help you guys."

Grace smiled through her tears as the chanting of

Mal next to me grew louder. The wind was whipping through the trees overhead and sending gusts down to the ground. I had to pull my hair off my face to still see my friends. Grace was standing holding onto wolf Nikkan as she looked at the lady next to me. The healer was again chanting loud enough to be heard over the wind storm.

I turned to Mal. Her dark, almost black hair was truly sparkling now. I could see hints of red, gold, silver, and bronze in her hair as it stood out from the wind. She didn't notice it as she had her eyes closed while she waved her arms around in concentric circles in front of her. Her rings grew larger, and her chant grew to a yell. Tipping her head back, she continued to chant, her voice rising to almost a scream now. I refused to close my eyes as the wind brought up sand and small twigs into the air. I stared across the way at my friends.

This wasn't a solution. It was a bandage on a wound much more significant than my mother wanted to admit days ago, and hence it was out of control. She didn't have answers, but I wasn't going to stop trying. Nikkan, Grace, and the wolves were as much family to me as Red. I didn't leave family behind.

Mal let out a blood-curdling scream from beside me, and I turned back to her. She fell to the ground as the wind instantly stopped, and everything hanging in the air fell to the ground. I reached down to help Mal back to her feet as she struggled to stand again, but she batted my hand away and stopped trying to get up.

"I'll just rest here," she said to me, her voice gravelly.

"Is it done?" I asked as I turned back to my friends.

I didn't need Mal to answer. There was a fog now between them and me. I don't know how I knew it, but I knew it was magic and the wall Mal had built. It wasn't completely dense; I could see through it. Grace was still there looking back at me, and now there was a large crowd behind her. It was hard to be entirely sure with the foggy wall, but it looked like relief lined the faces of the crowd. It wasn't a cure, but it was better than nothing.

15TH MARCH

After making the wall yesterday, Mal immediately disappeared. I didn't ask her to drop me off back with Red in Azren. What good would it do? She didn't have answers. It was better to stay in the forest and let myself think.

Mal didn't give me much to go with. She said it was a curse and dark magic, not a sickness. So calling any other healers, no matter how insulting to Mal it would be, wouldn't help. The wolves didn't need to be healed. They needed to be uncursed. They needed magic. But where was I supposed to get magic? Mal said it was dark magic. Did I need someone who did dark magic to undo it, or did it need another kind of magic?

Magic was a lesson Red didn't cover when I grew up. Yes, Red had magic. It was what made her the Red, but

I never really knew what that meant. It wasn't like she could do magic; it was more like there was magic inside of her.

No one in Elder studied magic. The few witches we had left all learned in a different kingdom. While some of the stuff we used had been magicked to do what they did, mostly Elder citizens stayed away from anything magic. It was a lot easier to trust what you did with your own two hands rather than magic. I hadn't been taught much of magic beyond the few books that vaguely mentioned it in my childhood education. And I ignored those as I planned to live my life in Elder where magic wasn't needed.

I thought I would head home for the night, but I couldn't. My friends were trapped in an enormous magical bubble with wolves that were going crazy with hunger. I couldn't help them, but I couldn't leave either. There had to be an answer; we just weren't seeing it.

Mal left so quickly I didn't have time to ask her all the questions now swirling in my head. It was as if she were scared of the wolves. That was crazy. She was a healer. She couldn't get the wolf curse if they bit her, and the wolves were fine during the daylight moments. I wished she would have stuck around just a bit more to explain things to me. I was left with fewer answers than before and in a direr situation as my friends were trapped. While I knew they wanted it that way, all the wolves did, they were still my friends, and I didn't feel safe with them where I couldn't protect them myself.

It wasn't the best choice to stay near the wolf village. I couldn't see anything, but I heard them all night long. The wolves were howling and growling enough to wake me, and I wasn't anywhere near them. I feared for Grace and Nikkan. They were just two wolves in a cage full of them. Could they stay safe in all that?

The howls were terrible enough, but what was worse were the human calls. People were still human inside that mess of a village. I could hear screams and calls for help. It sounded like a war zone. Where the heck was Micco? Was he sick too? I knew he couldn't control infected wolves, but it sounded like the whole village was ill.

Micco worried me more as I thought about the older man that was like a grandfather to me. I hadn't seen him any of the last few visits to the wolves. He had been fine when we last spoke, but I saw how quickly the curse took Grace. Was Micco infected, or was he too busy keeping peace in the village? I didn't want to think of the alternative.

I was up before the sun and pacing the magical wall. I wanted to see my friends and know they were okay. I'd stop every five saplings or so and peer through the fog. There was no one on the other side. It was like no one came in this direction because they knew they'd be trapped by the wall.

"It won't change anything," Sera said to me as she came out of the forest to where I was standing. "Mal stopped by on her way home. She told Red the wall is made and will hold against the magic curse. Elder is safe for now."

I shrugged at her. Part of Elder was safe. The wolves weren't part of that. My best friends were in the same place as before, maybe even worse, as they couldn't escape the monsters that the wolves were becoming.

"Safe for who?" I replied.

Sera wasn't there the night before. She didn't know the agony going on behind the walls. Maybe if she'd been there, she wouldn't feel so happy about the situation.

"You know Grace would want it this way," Sera added more quietly.

She was completely right. Grace never wanted to be a monster. Her worst fear was hurting someone else. She wouldn't do that now. But that didn't mean I was giving up. The curse was broken once before, and I would figure out how to do it again. We just had to search every clue we could find.

"Red is waiting at your cottage to speak to you," Sera added, finally explaining why she was there.

I nodded to Sera as I glanced through the fog one last time. I just wanted to see that they were okay, but not a single thing moved where I could see. I had to go on faith and believe that Nikkan and Grace would keep safe. The sounds were gone once the sun came up, both the howls and people crying. It actually sounded peaceful for the moment. I had to take it as a good sign that Grace and Nikkan weren't at the wall. No matter what, they were strong. I had to keep telling myself that.

Sera didn't wait to see if I was following her as she took off back into the woods. I just shook my head. At least some things didn't change.

The wind whipped through my hair as I pumped my arms to keep up with and eventually pass Sera. It felt different than the wind that Mal pulled to us yesterday. Something about that struck me as odd. I wasn't versed in magic; no one beyond the few remaining witches was. So, I really had no idea what Mal did, but I felt it. Like I could reach out and touch it. I had grown up around the wolves and even met a couple of witches, but it never struck me like it did yesterday.

Running through the woods was making my worry ease. Something about being surrounded by trees and the fresh smell of the pine needles made my head clear. It wasn't just my sinuses, but my thoughts were clearer. I wasn't meant to be hiding in the trees like the people around Red. I was meant to be on the ground, even if I didn't have the magical Red powers my mother had. I might not have been her son biologically, but that much I could never deny we shared.

Even as I ran, I kept going over everything. I might have missed something. There had to be a clue somewhere we could go on. If I had to leave Elder to find help, I would do just that. Nothing would stop me from getting the wolves free.

It wasn't like I could suggest to Red that I leave. Elder prided itself on being able to be independent of the rest of the world. I don't recall Red ever asking for help, at least that I knew of. We had all we needed, but what if we didn't. What if we needed help? Would Red be too stubborn to do that as she had been to even see that there was a problem in the first place?

Spring was on the horizon and typically was a season of growth and rebirth. The people of Elder broke their winter slumber, and flowers returned to the trees and the ground. It brought new life and hope. There was none of that now, and it seemed that even nature had been affected as the trees still were bare and the grass brown. It felt like the curse growing in power was sucking not just the life from the wolves but also from the world around them, my world, my home.

Mal had mentioned that it was a dark curse. That was a start. Beyond the werewolves and Red, Elder didn't have magic. People were ordinary humans. If there was a dark curse, then someone had to have cast it. It should be easy enough to track down who could have this kind of power through the history books in Azren, but it would be easier to talk to Red, and she happened to be waiting for me. With magic uncommon to us, just knowing it was magic was a start.

Being raised in Elder meant I knew there were no official records of the start of the curse, but that didn't mean there weren't records on everything else. Elder liked to keep their history. We had a full building dedicated to just that. Several buildings held the books of Elder. We had books that kept track of all trade transactions, books that kept track of all citizens' birth and death records, books that kept a diary of the history of the people of Elder. I didn't study the books much as I never knew I'd need them. But I did now.

After our quick run to my home, I entered my house to find Red had already lit the fire in my cooking stove and made herself a cup of tea. She was staring off toward the window that faced the woods behind my house, lost deep in thought. If she expected to see a wolf, it wasn't going to happen. They were locked away.

"Thanks, Sera," Red said with a nod to her, and Sera stepped back and closed the door, leaving me alone with Red.

"The wall is up," I informed her as I grabbed a cup of tea myself to warm up from my night outside.

"Mmm-hmm," Red replied as she took a sip of tea.

"It seems to be working. Not a single wolf was outside the wall last night." I would have known.

Red nodded again.

"But Mal already told you that much since you sent Sera to come to get me..."

I stopped talking. Red always knew. I had no idea how or why she knew so much, but she did. That's why I was more than a little worried that she didn't know how to break the curse. If she didn't know that, then it was going to take more than I could imagine to find the answer.

"Mal stopped by my place on her way home," Red explained.

I nodded and sipped my tea, waiting for her to explain why she was at my cabin waiting for me. I had learned as a child that she wasn't always great at answering questions. I had to bide my time and sip my tea. She didn't continue talking. I stared for a moment more at her and then couldn't help myself.

"She told me it was a dark curse," I began the conversation while Red sipped her tea like she had all the time in the world.

Red nodded as she stared at me. Her deep brown eyes were studying me, and I had no idea what it meant. I sat there and stared back at her. While she had aged considerably since this curse returned, she still had that authority about her that had made me never outright lie to her as a kid growing up. It wasn't like I could have anyway. She knew everything.

"Mal said I need to keep an eye on you," Red finally explained.

"Me?" I asked.

While I didn't have her abundance of patience and tended to be rash sometimes, I wasn't some hot head like the tree people of Azren that were no doubt biding their time to get their hands on the gun stock Red had been building for many winters. I didn't need a babysitter even if it seemed like Sera was mine these days.

"I just don't see it." Red continued to analyze me.

Okay, I didn't have half the patience of Red. I had to ask.

"See what?"

"Stand up for me and go back by the door," Red

ordered.

I did as she said purely because I had no clue what she was talking about or looking for. I walked back over to the door and turned around.

"Do I need to open it and leave and come back?" I asked. What the heck was Red up to now?

She shook her head and eyed me from head to toe.

"Jump around or lift something up," she ordered.

I had no idea what this game was, but I did it anyways. I jumped a few times and then walked over to my sofa and picked up one of the ends. After setting it back on the ground, I returned to the door and stood where she could see me. What was she looking for?

"Hold out your hand and picture an orange in it." Red was now giving beyond-crazy instructions.

I wanted to call her out on being crazy, but just did what she asked. Nothing happened, but I wasn't sure what she expected.

"I just don't see it," she mumbled, going back to her tea.

I stood where I was and looked at her. Something strange was going on, or she was possibly going crazy. First, the meals and serious, truthful talks, then all the laughing and smiling with her friend, and now staring at me like I had a horn on my head. I really wanted it to be something strange because a crazy Red would be disaster for Elder and my wolf friends. We needed her in the best place mentally to deal with all this.

"You don't have to continue standing there." She motioned for me to join her again.

I crossed my arms across my chest and stared at her this time. I felt it. She wasn't telling me the truth. She had finally told me how I got to Elder, but she just went right back to her old ways. I was sick of it. I wasn't a child and deserved to be treated like the adult I was. I gritted my teeth and finally spoke.

"What the heck is going on?"

Red took another sip of her tea. She nodded to me, understanding that my anger was growing. She knew me well.

"Mal said you have magic. Not a little bit like the wolves, but a lot. Like possibly more than Sera or me," Red explained like it wasn't a big deal.

I couldn't stop my mouth from dropping open. What was she talking about? I was a normal human. Always was and always would be. There was nothing magical about me.

"The people who gave you to me said you were special and would do great things someday, but they never said you had magic. Even now, I don't see it. I don't know what Mal was seeing. Maybe it had to do with being near the wall and the wolves."

I swiped my hand through my hair and just shook my head.

"Do you have magic?" Red asked, peering at me with her all-knowing look.

It wasn't on purpose, but I laughed.

"Mom, you've known me my whole life. I don't have magic. Mal must have seen it wrong. We were in the wolf village and surrounded by their magic. She had to be confused. You are both older than you look. Maybe she's going crazy like you or sensing things as she wants them to be, not as they are."

"Mal's never confused about magic. She's worried that the curse could affect you. She told me that you have to be careful around the wolves. You need to be sure to never let the darkness in."

I just stared at Red. She was definitely going crazy.

I wasn't magical. I didn't have powers. I was just a normal human. Wasn't I?

16TH MARCH

Red left after she stared at me more. I had no idea what she thought she'd see, but I didn't shoot lightning from my eyes or throw fire from my hands. That was never going to happen. I wasn't magical, but somehow, she believed her friend over what she knew was the truth. While she might not have always been very hands-on as a mother, she did raise me. Red, more than anyone, would know that I wasn't magical, but that didn't seem to affect her at all. Red left to go take care of business in Azren. Her parting words were that she believed Mal, and I needed to stay safe.

I don't know how long I sat in my house after she left. I just couldn't believe that she chose Mal over me. I was her son. Wouldn't I know if I had magic? I mean, wasn't that something that would have shown itself during my childhood growing up? If I had any special powers, they weren't very useful, or I must have never had a need for them as I had never used them. Red and Mal were crazy. The both of them. That had to be it.

I had planned to go back to the wall and wait to see if my friends were okay, but Red left Sera with me, and she complained enough to make me stay at my place for the night as she didn't want to sleep outside. Lucky for me, Sera waited outside the whole time I contemplated that my life was a lie. Well, it wasn't a lie, but if what Mal said was true, though I highly doubted it, it meant that my life wasn't what I thought it was.

Sera joined me on the floor and kept unusually silent the whole night. I appreciated that she could do that. Usually, she would have given me her opinion, and we would have spent the night fighting. I needed my rest after the previous night, so I was more than happy to just be in my house in silence.

"Mal's right," Sera told me as she ate breakfast with me. There she was, the annoying Sera I grew up with. "I know you don't want to believe her, but she is."

We were actually doing better than normal, and the fighting was almost non-existent until now. Why was life like this for us? She was like the sibling I never wanted. I guess we couldn't go one whole day without an argument.

"I didn't notice it before, but now that I look at you..." Sera looked me up and down. "I can't see the magic, but I feel it. When I have the full Red powers, I should be able to see it too, at least, that's was Mal said before she left."

Sera shrugged like that was enough to go on. I knew Red was losing her powers to Sera, but was it enough that she couldn't see it and Sera could? I felt a lump catch in my throat. Everything just seemed to be going by so fast. I always knew that Red would give her powers to Sera, and she admitted that it was already happening. But somehow, hearing Sera speak about it made it that much more real that it was happening sooner than later. It was just kind of hard to think of Red getting older and losing that magic that made me not only follow her orders but admire her my whole time growing up. Yes, I fought with Red almost as much as Sera, but I still was beyond thankful Red took me in and raised me. She taught me to be the person I am. Good and bad.

I wasn't sure how I felt about Sera taking over the Red position of Elder, but I knew it was hard to think of Red losing that special spark that made her Red. What was going to be left when the magic was all gone? Would she survive it leaving her? If Red died and my wolf friends were all locked behind a magical barrier, I would have no one left.

I would never admit it to Sera, but she was going to make a good Red. I just hoped it was later rather than sooner. I was pretty sure Elder needed Red more than anything right now. Sera would be a great Red, but we needed the wisdom of my mother. I just wished that wisdom came with answers.

"It would explain a lot," Sera continued, not noticing that I wasn't participating in her discussion. "That's why you can run faster than me and beat me hand to hand."

I almost laughed at that. Sera hated when I bested her in anything, which these days seemed to be about everything we did. That might have been one of the reasons I practiced so much. Beating the next Red was an accomplishment alone, but beating Sera was just fun. I couldn't believe she thought I had magic, but it was a great way that she could accept that I was more skilled than her without giving me any credit. That was a typical Sera move. I hated her attitude, but admired her skill. More than anything, I loved that she still couldn't beat me.

"So, it isn't just that I'm better at hand to hand fighting?" I couldn't help but goad her. She deserved it.

"You aren't better. You are faster."

I rolled my eyes at her. She was just as fast as I was. What was probably the truth was that I had trained harder than her, mainly because I had more time to. I wouldn't tell her that, but it was the truth. Sera didn't just learn about fighting; she had to learn about all the diplomatic aspects of being Red. I got to skip all that and keep training physically. I wasn't sure who would win if she'd had as much time training physically as I had had growing up.

"I'm pretty sure I'm wiser than you, too," I replied, adding more to tease her.

Sera's face turned red as she huffed at my insult.

"Castiel," she warned, wadding up her blanket and throwing it at me.

I couldn't help but just smile. She was so easy to upset. Her competitive side always got her into trouble, as did mine most of the time. If I was honest, Red and the wolves were my family, but Sera fell somewhere in that group too.

I caught the blanket and threw it right back at her.

"Don't make me," she threatened, taking a fighting stance.

I grinned as I jumped the couch and twisted her into my arms, her back to my chest. I had her in a tight grip, proving my point that I was the better fighter.

"Do you want a broken nose?" she threatened.

It wouldn't be the first time Sera head-butted me to get loose. I tipped my head sideways to miss the blow of her head, but instead, she used my momentum to make us both fall to the ground. I turned last moment to make Sera land on me instead of the floor.

"Uff," I grunted as I took her weight. "Guess that supper by Red added a bit to your weight," I teased.

Sera grunted and wiggled until she was turned around on me, face to face. I could feel her arms moving, and I let her. If I wanted, I could have kept her immobile the whole time. Her face was just inches from mine. Her brown eyes sparkled. I knew she thought she was getting the upper hand.

Like lightening, Sera yanked on my arms, pinning them above my head. She grinned at me. I didn't hesitate as I switched our position and had her pinned. I wasn't twice her weight, but even with her Red powers that could throw a full-grown wolf several saplings, she wasn't able to move me.

"Give up?" I asked.

Her grin was now a pout.

"Just admit that my magical powers are better than yours," I teased, wiggling my eyebrows at her. I was giving her an out without admitting defeat.

"Fine, but it's just your powers."

I laughed, and soon enough, she was laughing with me. I reached down and pulled her to her feet with me. We made our way over to get breakfast before we actually started our day.

"Okay, fine. Truce," she said as she took a bite of her bread.

She chewed slowly as she thought, and we sat in

silence.

I would never admit it to her, but I was glad to have slept at home. The howls from the wolves the night before still rang in my head. The misty wall made it hard to see, and nothing came near where I was waiting, but I could hear it. Without food, the wolves would turn on each other. I knew that much. It was killing me to not be there with my friends. I couldn't do anything from the side of the fence we were on.

"But in all seriousness. I'm not joking around about the magic, Castiel. I do feel the magic coming off you. Can you honestly say you haven't felt a change in yourself in the past few moons?"

Sera caught me off guard. She wasn't joking, and she wasn't competitive. She was being serious. This side of Sera was real, and I had to think about what she asked.

Sure, I felt stronger, but that happened every season that passed. I had grown taller and stronger with all the training I had done. Each season was like that. Wasn't that how it was supposed to work? Everyone grew up like that. Wasn't I supposed to get stronger and faster?

"What do you mean?" I finally asked, confused.

"Until a few moons ago, I could, at least, beat you in a foot race every now and then. I haven't beat you once this past moon."

I had to think about that one. Yes, Sera occasionally won, but that wasn't new. Had she really not won in one full moon cycle? I had been so caught up in the wolves; I hadn't considered that. She had won once, but I'd let her. I guess she knew me too well.

"And while it isn't easy for me to admit. I think you are way stronger than I am now," she added.

I still stared in shock at her. Was that true too?

"There's also the fact that the wolf curse was broken when you came here. Red says the curse broke, and then you showed up. What if it was the other way around? What if the curse broke because you were already in the kingdom and on your way to Red?"

Okay, that was one I couldn't even comprehend. I would have never jumped to that conclusion, but it was something we had to consider.

"I think you have magic, Castiel, and not because I can't beat you. I have magic too, but it's nothing compared to you."

Oh great. Sera was on the same side as Red. But this was harder because she had obviously thought about why she felt that way. And she was convincing me.

"I think we need to head into town and see if they have the records on your adoption. Maybe Red doesn't remember something," Sera suggested. "Someone once mentioned that the records are magical. That even if someone doesn't fill out the papers and add their child to the record that it will be there. Even if Red doesn't know who your parents are, the records should have known."

While I still wanted to do more to help the wolves, I did need to know the truth. And if my birth family was magical, maybe they were the answer. Sera was onto something.

"If you are what brought a change to the wolves, we need to figure out how to do it again," Sera explained as she stood up and made her way to the door.

That was one thing I did love about Sera. She didn't sit still long, and she didn't let a problem stop her. I had never once seen anything actually stop her. The girl was tenacious. She was an excellent ally to have in helping the wolves.

“Fine,” I finally replied, putting away the last of our breakfast and following her outside.

Sera winked at me and took off at a full run. Just because I had beaten her in every race for the past moon cycle didn’t mean she wasn’t going to try to beat me now. I laughed. I loved that side of her. No matter how friendly she got, she was never going to be anything less than competitive.

I took off after her and quickly caught up. Sera was right. I was stronger lately, but I had no idea why. I wasn’t exactly sure how magic worked, but I tried thinking all sorts of things as I ran. No lightening, no water or magic balls flying around me, no color changing, or plants moving. I kept trying anything and everything I could think of while we ran, but with my strength and Sera’s newly growing Red powers, we were at Azren before I could try much more.

No matter what Sera, Red, or Mal thought, there wasn’t a magical bone in my body. I couldn’t do a thing magic, and they all had to be crazy. But I did have to give Sera that maybe there was magic in where I came from. That would have made more sense. I might have brought some sort of magic with me when I arrived as a baby. Whoever my parents were, maybe they wanted me to be protected and save the wolves. If we could figure out who I was and where I came from, perhaps we could save them again.

Sera stopped just inside the tree line and peeked out up to the village. I wasn’t prepared to see it so vacant. The people had spent the best part of the past decade moving to the ground, and it was now a ghost village. Not one person was left below the trees. Buildings were empty, and the lights were off. Not a sound came from the town at the base of the tree, and it was almost like even in the trees it was quieter.

Sera stepped out of the trees slowly and waved up to the guard tower that had been unmanned for most of my childhood. Four men stood there and waved back down to Sera. I could see the glint of metal as one man moved. They had guns.

I followed behind Sera as one of the elevators was lowered for us to go into the trees. As soon as it touched the ground, Sera yanked me into it, and it began to rise before I caught my balance.

"New rule is that it can come down, but once it touches the ground, it rises again," Sera explained.

Okay, mental note to myself. Get on elevators fast. Were the tree people that worried? Mal had caged the wolves; they were safe for now.

When the elevator opened at the top of the tree, two guards stood there waiting. Both of them nodded to Sera and I and walked back to their station.

"And they have to confirm every person that enters or leave the trees," Sera continued to explain. "Red made it law that no one can enter or leave without being checked. They are still not completely okay with the wolves, even though they are behind the wall. Some of the people have suggested that it would be a great time to hunt the wolves since they can shoot and not have to get close to them. You know, the normal hotheads that are causing trouble. When I'm Red they'll find they can't talk crap like that. Red is too easy on them if you ask me."

And she would be. Sera was tougher than my mother, but then again, being a diplomat meant you couldn't just boss people around. It was likely Sera would change with time too.

Sera shrugged and led the way on the wooden

pathways between the trees. To someone who hadn't grown up here, I was sure they would be fascinated by the trees. It had taken decades, but the people of Azren had perfected living off the ground. They had running water pumped up to the trees. All the modern conveniences, and you didn't have to worry about a wolf attack.

"To the records building?" I asked, raising an eyebrow at Sera in a challenge.

She grinned back at me. "Race you there?"

She grabbed the nearest branch and pulled herself up into the layer of branches above the houses and buildings. When we were kids, we found you could race in the treetops much better than on the bridges that connected all the buildings. You still couldn't do a straight shot to where you were going as you had to go on branches you could run on, but it was better than the village below. Our competitiveness got us into trouble more than once, but after we moved up a level, we got in trouble a lot less. It might have been that not as many people got caught in our races, but it was still better in the treetops.

I grabbed the same branch behind her and pulled myself up.

"Ready to lose?" I asked her. "Magical being here, after all." I grinned at her, and she smiled back, undeterred by my taunting.

"You've forgotten one thing all-magical being," Sera replied. "When we last did this game five winters ago, you weren't a hulking monster." Sera didn't wait for me to understand what she said as she took off on the branch that she was standing on.

I didn't wait to figure it out either and took off after her. Soon enough, I was being hit left and right by the branches above us. I watched as Sera made it further away from me into the trees. Her smaller stature made it easy for her to run, but not for me. This wasn't going to be a fair run at all. Sera gave one last look behind her at me and gave me a small wave before she jumped to the next branch and kept running. She had the advantage.

I slowed down rather than keeping up with her pace on a branch I wasn't sure would support my weight. I knew perfectly well what it felt like to fall from the trees. We both did. That might have been why we were told we couldn't tree top race by Red as she had to fix us both up. Too bad, we were both adults and grown-up. Red couldn't stop us now. But the darn branches were stopping me.

The nearest trunk rose up another level, and I scrambled up it to get a better view. While we didn't have to follow the bridges between the trees when we treetop raced, we still have to go between branches that supported our combined weight and the pounding of our feet as we ran. As I stared forward, I could see the spire at the top of the records building. It was a straight shot from where I stood. Running below wasn't going to happen, and the branches nearby weren't going to support my weight to run on them at the same time as Sera, but maybe they could support me hanging alone.

I took the nearest branch and bent it down to me. I pulled a little harder, and it didn't break. I had an idea and couldn't help but smile. I took ahold at the branch I was standing on and swung around it. As my momentum carried me forward, I reached for the tree nearest to me. I grabbed that branch as I let go with my one hand. I smiled as I saw the pathway to the record tree was much more direct if I wasn't running. Without any hesitation, I swung to the next branch and the next and the next. With each swing I could feel my body moving faster and my arc becoming longer as I let go of one branch and took the next.

Luckily, as I swung between branches, no one could see me. They would have thought some sort of monster was in the trees. I had to look like a deranged animal as I swung. I was sure Red would be waiting for me to scold me for scaring the whole city if that happened. The records building came up fast as I made an almost direct route to it. Wasting no time, I climbed down to the door and leaned against it to wait.

I wouldn't have much time to catch my breath, and I tried not to laugh out loud. It felt so freeing to fly through the branches, like I was meant to be soaring in the skies. I didn't believe Sera that I could have magic, but maybe she could be a little right that I brought magic with me that stopped the curse last time. Perhaps the people that left me could fly. I could have lived with that.

Sera dropped down in front of me. She was a tiny bit winded from her run.

"How did you....?" She stared at me in shock.

I smiled and shrugged. I wasn't giving away my secret. She'd either use it against me or perfect doing it herself. I wasn't going to chance it either.

"Let's get to looking," I suggested before she could ask more.

Sera sputtered a bit more but didn't say anything as she knocked on the door to the records. A little old lady, whose name I couldn't remember, opened the door. She was at least a head shorter than Sera, but her gray hair piled on her head made her almost as tall.

"Hi, Doreen, we need to access the birth records,"

Sera said with her authority. Doreen nodded and unlocked the door to let us in.

“Thank you,” Sera said, giving the older woman a nod as we walked into the large records building that wove around one of the most massive trees in the village.

I had only been inside the hall of records a couple of times with Red when I was growing up. I really thought there was nothing there for me, rooms and rooms filled from floor to ceiling with books. It wasn’t that I couldn’t read; it just didn’t interest me. I knew Sera had been there tons of times. It was all part of her training to take over as Red. I didn’t need to know or care about all those boring details.

The walls were lined with books of every shape, color, and size, and the hall itself was several stories tall. Sera weaved her way through the tightly fitted shelves, and I followed, trying not to knock anything over. There was so much history in those books. I wasn’t sure any one person had time to read them all, but I knew Sera had read a lot of them.

“I’ve already checked for records on the curse. There was nothing there,” Sera explained as she took another corner and climbed a tight spiral staircase.

I followed behind her, having to turn my shoulders at more than one point since I wouldn’t fit otherwise. This building wasn’t made for people my size. I knew I was larger than the average tree person, but it was a little ridiculous how tightly packed the building was.

The upper level of the record hall had a few more windows that let the light illuminate all the dust in the air. It seemed it had been some time since anyone had climbed so high.

“They are in order by winters, but you know someone always puts things back wrong, so it might take a few moments to find it," Sera explained.

I went to walk with her to the shelf she was going for, but she stopped and gave me the Sera look. It said, why the heck are you following me. Guess I wasn't really needed to help carry a book.

"I'll just wait over there." I pointed to the one waist-tall table in the room by the staircase. There might have been more stands, but I wasn't finding them any time soon since I barely fit in the room.

It didn't take Sera long to come back with a large book. She set it carefully on the stand next to me and began to page through it. The pages were yellowed with age, and beautiful writing filled the inside of it.

"You should be listed here in the first group," Sera explained. "Since you arrived in the winter. These are all the recorded winter births."

"Would that even have me since I was adopted?"

Sera nodded. "Adopted or born to their parents, every single person that was born here is added. It doesn't matter. This book should say that you belong to Red, and you are her responsibility to raise. She would have put it in the book, but if not, it should have automatically been added."

Sera pointed to the list and began to read through the names. She huffed as she turned the page and went through the next list of names. Again, she had to turn the page. After several pages, Sera seemed as frustrated as I felt at all of this. She went back to the beginning of the book and paged through again, slower this time.

"You're not in here," she declared, moving back to the front of the book and looking again. "How can you not be in here? That makes no sense. This is the official record of all the children in town. How would you not be here?"

I nodded to her and made my way back to the stairs. I had no idea why I wasn't in the book. Again, our search led to nothing. I had hoped we could get an answer, but it wasn't going to be that easy. My life was never that easy.

17TH MARCH

The next day, I spent with Sera in the musty old building of records. We had the winter right, so I knew we had the right book. She was convinced maybe it was the wrong book. After searching for additional books, we went through all of those also. While I was ready to move on and explore other options, Sera wasn't.

She was determined to find something, whether it was an adoption or a birth record that I existed. I honestly had no idea what to think of all of it. Maybe it was because Red was the leader that no one questioned her, or maybe it was just that the curse was gone and they didn't care. But book after book gave us nothing. I wasn't officially a citizen of Elder. While I felt like I didn't belong before, now I knew I didn't. Both my mother and the magic that governed Azren records refused to acknowledge I existed.

While Sera wanted to spend more time in the books, I was finished. There was nothing there to find. Sera needed to give it up. We had to look for other clues and search in other directions. It wasn't like this was our first dead end.

The next morning, Red left to go south to the farms, while Sera dragged me back to the records hall. It seemed like life had to go on in the kingdom even if the wolves couldn't move on with their lives. I slightly resented Red for being able to just put them aside for something else. Did she only care about half her people?

It wasn't fair of me to blame Red. She wanted everyone to be safe and to get along as much as anyone. I just wanted someone to blame. Who I really should have accused was whoever cast the dark magic over Elder's shifters to begin with. Since the curse was hundreds of winters old, I was pretty sure the person who cast it was long gone, but what if it was like the Red. What if there was something evil keeping the curse going just like the magic that made Red keep going in each new generation?

After our day of finding nothing in the books, Sera convinced me to spend one more night at Red's cottage. Mainly because she was my personal guard, which she wouldn't admit to, but I knew she was, and she wanted to sleep in her bed. I waited as the night turned dark, and she fell asleep before I took off. I wasn't going to sit around Azren and hope a solution ended up in my lap. The records were a dead end. While the people of Azren felt mildly safer now that the wolves were locked up, my friends weren't safe. I only felt a small bit of guilt for sneaking out in the middle of the night. Sera would be okay, probably just mad that I bested her again.

My run was typical through the first half of the woods. Night animals were out in full force and getting their nightly meals. Owls were hooting, and the possums ran from me as I made small noises so they'd know I was near. Large animals such as the few large cats that hunted near my place were out too. I didn't hear them, but it was like I could feel them.

There had to be an answer that I was just missing. I wished I could have had Nikkan to talk with. While he wasn't one for things such as helping whole groups of people since he was more of the loner type, he was great at coming up with crazy ideas. I knew the majority of them were just plain nuts to try, but at this point, any of his stupid schemes would have been welcomed. I needed a fresh view on all of it. There had to be something.

I was fortunate that my night vision was as good as my day vision. I didn't need to rest or wait as I continued my run past my house. There wasn't anyone waiting there for me, anyway. Nikkan was locked away with the rest of the wolves.

The howls began before I even got near the fence. Their voices rang out in the night air. The wolves were just as bad as the first night in the wall, and I didn't blame them. There weren't any animals for quite a distance; the animals were all staying away, which only made things worse. I knew since I just ran through the woods. I had to imagine all the wolves were starving, and the ones not starving were huddled scared in their homes. It wasn't good for those that already had the curse or those who didn't and were trapped with them.

Trapped wolves were one problem, but trapped, hungry wolves were utterly worse. I knew they had already turned on each other. How far would it go? How long could Nikkan and Grace stay safe? They needed to eat.

I slowed my pace as I saw the shimmer of the foggy fence that kept the wolves in. Even in the dark, it was obvious where it was. I felt the magic of it but still wasn't about to admit that I had magic in me. If I did, it was useless magic, it seemed.

The wall was still holding, and not a single wolf was near it. I could hear the skirmishes beyond the wall, but I couldn't make out a single thing. The fuzzy wall was hard enough to see through, but I knew if there was some sort of movement, I would notice. I began to walk around the wall as I heard the wolves growling at each other. Every now and then, there would be an ear-piercing howl.

There was also the occasional human voice within the fence. I tested the wall more than once, wanting to help the human calls I heard. If they were human, they might not be cursed yet, but just being a wolf condemned them to the same fate as the ones changed by magic. I pressed on the fog wall again. There was no way a human was going through it. I could do nothing for the cries of the people trapped there.

"You can't do anything," Sera commented as she appeared out of the dark.

Of course, she followed me.

"I know that." I hit the wall with my hand. Elder was safe from the wolves, but that didn't mean my friends were safe. Being this close made it more real.

Another human cry came from inside the wall. It was the scream of a man. Part of me wanted to see him and see what was wrong, but another part was thankful I couldn't see him since I couldn't help.

“Nikkan, Grace,” I yelled, hoping to see my friends. Maybe not hoping either if they were locked up safe. But it didn’t sound like much of anyone was safe. “Micco.” I tried yelling for the older man instead. He would be out there in the thick of it, trying to protect those that couldn’t defend themselves.

There were now groans and moans mixed into the snarling and howls of the wolves. Amazingly, someone staggered into view. I didn’t recognize them as they got close. They had dark hair and were twice as wide as Nikkan. It had to be a male.

“Are you okay?” Sera yelled.

We could hear the wolves and people in the village. They had to be able to hear us.

The person looked around and finally noticed us. He looked like he was going to run to us, but before he could take two steps toward us, a wolf popped out of the tree line behind the person and grabbed his shoulder, pulling him back to where we couldn’t see them. The man barely made a sound, like he was resigned to his fate.

“They are dying,” I complained to Sera. “The wolves are killing the humans.”

“We can’t be certain,” Sera replied as she began to pace beside me and occasionally check the wall also.

More yells and cries came from the village. Sera began to pound on the wall as she walked not too far behind me. She might have disliked the wolves before, but she was different now. Grace had changed her. Sera cared.

“I know Grace wanted to keep the people of Elder safe, but she isn’t safe,” I complained. There was nothing Sera or I could do. It wasn’t fair. “What if something happens to her or Nikkan?”

Sera nodded and pounded on the wall. No one else came near the wall, but we could hear it all. Sera wasn't sugar-coating it. She could hear what I heard, and it wasn't good. There was a fight going on within the walls, and I couldn't do a thing to help them. All my training and power was for nothing if I couldn't get within the wall. I knew how much Red feared me being bitten, but I feared losing my friends more than becoming a wolf.

"This isn't fair," I complained as anger started to build inside me.

I pressed my forehead to the wall and tried to see something that would tell me what was going on. Maybe it wasn't as bad as it felt. I doubted that, but I kept a small sliver of hope.

"It isn't," Sera agreed. That was a first, and some of my anger deflated at the thought that Sera and I could agree on something. "But what can we do?"

My anger came back. What could we do? We only got to sit safely behind the wall and listen to our friends die. We were helpless. I hated the magical wall even though I knew it was needed. I hated that they said I had magic, but I couldn't help my friends. I hated that this curse was destroying the people that felt like home to me. I hated all of it.

I began to pound harder on the wall. If I was magical, couldn't I just break it? Could I go save my friends? Was my magic strong enough to keep them safe?

"Castiel," Sera said as she came over and caught my hands. She gently wiped away the blood on my knuckles. "Beating yourself up won't help anything."

I blew out my breath before responding. I wasn't angry at Sera and didn't want to take it out on her. I was mad with the world, angry with the curse, and angry that I was powerless even though the healer and Sera both said I was filled with magic. I never really wanted to be unique or have magical powers, but at this exact moment, I wanted to be able to help my friends. But I was useless.

I turned from the village and leaned back against the wall and slid down until I was sitting with my back to it. It might have been torture to listen to them fighting, but I couldn't leave. I wasn't going anywhere until I knew Nikkan and Grace were safe. I hoped that morning would come quickly, though I knew night time had just begun.

"We can't go in there as it keeps wolves and humans apart. We can't change what we are," Sera explained what I already knew. She continued to stand and scan the woods behind me now. Sera leaned her head against the invisible wall and closed her eyes. "There has to be an answer. We have to be missing something."

I wished with all my might that she was right. I couldn't just accept that we failed. My friends and all the wolves were counting on us. Failure wasn't an option. But man, it felt like we had failed.

"Castiel," a voice called from the other side of the fence.

I scrambled up and looked through the wall.

"Help," she said louder as she stumbled near.

I could see her red hair glowing in the soft moonlight. Her clothing was ripped, but she was still in her human form. I could make out that her arms and face were covered with blood as she neared us and collapsed on the ground in front of us.

"Castiel," she cried as she saw me. "I can't help him." She sobbed more.

Where was Nikkan? I waited for him to appear from behind her, but he wasn't there. I pounded on the wall with my cut-up hands.

"Grace," I yelled, trying to get her to look up at me. I had to know. "What's going on?"

Grace's eyes fluttered between Sera and me.

"He tried to keep me safe, but I can't help him. I can't shift. I'll become a monster like the rest of them. I'm not strong enough to fight the curse. He should never have stayed to protect me. He's dying, and there's nothing I can do."

Grace tried to push herself up to stand, but her legs wobbled, and she ended up back on the ground. She gave up trying and lay down, sobbing. A feeling of uselessness settled in me. I wasn't strong enough. I wasn't smart enough. I wasn't as magical as everyone hoped. I was just me. And I failed. Nikkan was going to die, and I couldn't do a thing about it.

"What can we do?"

Sera looked like she was almost in tears. Her forlorn face was what I needed to find my motivation. I couldn't give up. My friends needed us.

"We have to help her," I told Sera. Sera was pounding on the wall with more vigor now also.

"But we can't go through the wall," Sera complained. "Stupid magic," she shouted at the wall.

A flash of gray caught my eye behind Grace. I could see someone was coming near.

"Grace," I shouted to my friend. Grace didn't move from the ground.

The gray was getting closer. I knew it wasn't my friend. Nikkan was blond, not gray, and this wolf was gray. I could see it nearing Grace, approaching like she was prey. I pushed harder on the wall. Grace was going to die if we didn't help her.

"GRACE," Sera screamed.

Grace still didn't move.

I needed to save her. I needed that magic within me. I needed to protect my friends.

"Magic protect them," I began to chant in my head over and over again. I might not feel my magic or know what it was, but I needed it.

I leaned into the wall and pushed harder. I felt a crack in my hand but ignored the pain. I would never let my friend die right in front of me. I was stronger than that. I was stronger than the wall. If there was indeed magic in me, I needed it now. I needed to be fierce like the black cats prowling in the night. I needed to be scary like the bears that lived far from civilization in the woods. I needed to be fast like the owls that were catching their prey in the darkness. I needed to save my friend and stand up to the monstrous wolves.

More bones cracked in my hands as I pushed. I would save my friend, no matter what. With that determination, magic began to swirl around me. I let out a scream myself as I pushed harder now. I could feel it. There was magic in me that Sera and Mal saw. It was really there, and it was going to save my friend.

It felt like an eternity, but the wolf prowling behind Grace hadn't taken one step as I pushed through the barrier and landed on my hands and knees. The world seemed brighter to me but less colorful. I didn't wait to see what changed as I rushed towards the wolf that was hunting Grace. The wolf looked at me and took off back into the woods but not without me catching my reflection in his eyes. I wasn't a human or a wolf. I had made it through the barrier for one reason only. I was a panther. The magic inside me made me a shifter.

Finish the adventure in God of Shifters

GOD OF SHIFTERS

18TH MARCH

My four feet worked just like human feet. I was actually on four feet! Somehow beyond my wildest dreams, I was a shifter. I had never once been able to transform into an animal, no matter how much I wanted to run fast, soar in the skies, or hunt with my wolf friend Nikkan. There was so much about this ability I wanted to know more about. Why did it happen now? What sort of animal was I? Was I part wolf, but no one knew? I'd seen myself as a panther, reflected in the eyes of a wolf, but how could I be a panther? Panthers didn't live in this part of Elder. I wasn't actually sure if they lived in Elder at all. I scrambled my brain, trying to remember if I'd been bitten and was actually a wolf, a hallucinating wolf, at that.

I didn't have time to contemplate my new ability as I rushed over to Grace. She was still lying on the ground, unconscious. Her eyes were closed, and her breathing was slow, but she was alive. I nudged her with my animal snout, but she didn't move. I was going to have to carry her with me, but I had no idea how to get her on my back as an animal. It wasn't like my sharp claws were made for picking someone up.

Without me thinking about it, my body shifted back to its human form. If I'd had time to contemplate it, I would have worried that I was standing in the forest nude, but just as I became human, another wolf approached us. It wasn't Nikkan, and it wasn't looking to help us.

"Castiel," Sera yelled at me. Her voice was muted, but I could hear her. "Watch out!"

I quickly turned to see her, and she was waving in the other direction from the wolf that had just shown up. I turned that way to see there were two more wolves, and they were both lunging at Grace and me like we were easy meals. I wasn't anyone's easy meal.

On instinct, I transformed to be equal with them, but my new form was larger than they were. I was midnight black, but they could still see me. I was trying to be a giant wolf, but it seemed I made myself a cat instead. My sudden feline appearance made them both stop in their tracks. I hoped it would make them run away like the one did just a moment before, but these two seemed to be communicating as they circled me. There was no way I was going to be able to fight two of them, even as a cat, while protecting Grace.

I needed to be something bigger, something they'd fear. Was it possible to make my animal larger? I mean, I had seen wolves come in all shapes and sizes. I thought their size was a dominance issue, and I felt like I could be larger if I wanted to be.

I felt the magic swirl around me as my body began to vibrate. I wasn't turning back into a human as I stayed on four feet, but I was changing. It seemed like the magic knew what to do, even if I didn't. My body was swelling in size, and my fur was getting shaggier. It was doing what I wanted as if the magic could read my mind. I didn't know how to explain it. It was a part of me, and yet, it wasn't. I couldn't cast a spell but I could shift into another form with barely a thought.

As the magic finished with my new form, I was looking down at the two wolves. My new, shaggy form was gigantic, and I had a feeling I was much more massive now than a cat. I'd fear me if I saw me in the woods. They took one look at me and bolted. That had worked, but I wasn't sure what I was. I didn't feel like a cat now. My limbs were heavier, not as fluid when I picked them up to move. I had a feeling that if I went through the woods, I'd wake half the creatures in it, nothing like the stealthy hunter my cat would be.

Grace moaned on the ground, and I transformed back into my human self. That seemed to be the easiest part. Being human was like breathing. I didn't have to think or will myself to change. I was just that, human. It would have been nice if being human included clothing, but that seemed to be a whole other shifter issue I would have to deal with.

It wasn't that I cared too much about being naked, but Sera was watching from the other side of the wall. I cared if I was naked in front of her. Reaching down to Grace, who had stilled again, I took her jacket off and wrapped it around my waist. Easily, I was able to pick her up, and I brought her to the wall. She hadn't weighed much before, but since she'd been cursed, she'd become light as a feather.

"What just happened?" I asked Sera, who was pressed against the wall as if she was trying to push through it as I had.

"You freaking turned into a bear is what happened," she replied. "Now, get your butt back over here, so I don't lose my head to your mother."

A bear! Well, that answered my question of if I'd been bitten. No wolf bite could transform anyone into a bear...and no one in any of the kingdoms could shift between different animal forms, at least, not until now.

First off, I wasn't even sure I could go back through the wall, and second, I looked at Grace in my arms. I couldn't leave her unprotected. Understanding appeared in Sera's eyes. She cared for Grace too. We both wanted our friend to be safe.

"Just see if you can," Sera suggested. "And if you can pass through the wall, then go back and hide Grace for the night and get back to this side where you are safe."

I hated following directions and hated it more that Sera was right. If I'd had time to argue, I would have, but I wasn't sure how long we'd be alone before another wolf tried to attack Grace. What I needed right now was time to process all of it. And I wasn't going to get that.

"Do it now," Sera almost begged. I could see the worry on her face.

I gently set Grace on the ground and then pushed my hand into the wall. It didn't budge. I didn't precisely remember what going through it felt like, but I knew I'd just gone through it. I wasn't sure how the whole process worked.

"Maybe you need to be angry?" Sera suggested.

I rolled my eyes at her. And why not. It wasn't

like anger was a feeling I could just conjure up like a magician. The healer was right about me having magic, but I wasn't a warlock or anything like that. Sera huffed on the other side of the wall, but there was nothing I could do.

"Say something to piss me off," I suggested, and she stuck her tongue out at me.

Nope, that didn't get me angry.

"Safety and back," Sera commanded. Yes, someday she was going to make a great Red. She already had the bossy part down.

I looked down at Grace, now at my feet. She hadn't stirred at all. How was I supposed to take her somewhere safe and protect her at the same time? I wasn't sure exactly the best way to transport her unconscious body. I needed to be an animal, but then I couldn't hold her. It wasn't like I had arms that could pick someone up once I changed. I had to be smart about it. How could I put her on my back without help?

The noises around me were distracting. While I'd thought it was terrible to be on the other side of the wall, I now knew it was worse to be with the wolves. It was like the foggy wall didn't just diminish sight but also sound. Wolves were growling, people screaming, moans of pain filled the air. It was like a horrible war zone, but they were technically all on the same side.

"Put her on your back first and then transform," Sera told me, coming up with the solution I needed without me having to ask for it. Her mind-reading skills were sometimes appreciated. "You don't change slowly like the wolves; for you, it's like an instant thing. Magic swirls around you, and you are something else. You don't have to worry about her falling. If you change with her on your back, then she'll be there when you are an animal."

I didn't have time to ask more as I heard more animals coming in our direction. Leaning down, I got a good hold on Grace, bent over, and put her on my back like we were kids running through the forest. With the snarls of wolves coming closer, I shifted, looking for the magic Sera talked about.

"Not a bear," Sera complained her voice now louder in my animal form. "You need to be a wolf. Blend in. If you are a bear and walk into camp, even those that aren't cursed yet will attack you. They'll think you are coming to hurt them. Be a wolf and stay safe. Please, Castiel. Stay safe."

I gave her a nod with my now furry head. I would never admit it, but I was glad one of us was thinking straight. All this new shifter stuff or just having magic at all was messing with my head.

I looked down at my wolf paws. I was a deep brown color. No one in the camp would know me, but, at least, they wouldn't attack on sight. The scraps of Grace's jacket were at my feet. I owed her a new one.

"Stay safe," Sera repeated, more quietly this time as she looked into my animal eyes.

I stared back at Sera. It was as if I could feel emotion from her like she was afraid. Sera afraid? Never! That girl looked danger in the eye and didn't blink. Either it was just the way she was or the power of the Red, but I had never seen Sera afraid once. My wolf, though, was saying otherwise. Sera was afraid.

I nodded my wolf head to her as I couldn't speak any reassurance. I would stay safe. And I would keep my friends safe. Sera nodded back to me.

The village was right in front of us now as I took off. I didn't have time to waste as I ran back through it. I wasn't sure how I was going to find Nikkan, but then it came to me. Somehow my wolf nose knew exactly which scent was my friend. I hurried through the fighting and craziness of the village to find him.

Wolves were fighting wolves; some were just fighting themselves. Snarls, growls, and howls filled the air. Blood and more covered the ground. I had a feeling this wasn't only from this night's activities. Part of me was sad when I saw wolves going in for the kill on their fellow wolves. They would regret it in the morning, and I didn't have the time or ability to help. I wanted to stop it all, but Grace and Nikkan came first. I was saddened not to see Micco in the mix. I worried about the older man.

Nikkan's scent grew stronger, and I knew I was closing in on him. My friend wasn't too far away. I could also tell that it wasn't just his scent from his fur, but his blood I was smelling—fresh blood.

I rounded another home and found what I was looking for. Sure enough, Nikkan's golden wolf was on the ground. Several wolves were still attacking him, and it looked like he didn't have sufficient energy to take them all.

'Nikkan,' I wanted to shout at my friend.

The blond wolf looked up at me and left an opening for the first wolf to attack a second time. The attacking wolf's muzzle was covered with Nikkan's blood as it dove in for another bite. It only took a moment for Nikkan to recognize Grace on my back, and his fighting spirit returned. He rolled over and used his hind legs to push the wolf away. The second wolf then lunged for him, and Nikkan maneuvered this time for the second wolf to hit the first wolf. Yips and growls followed as the two wolves attacking Nikkan now were looking at each other as the enemy. I stepped forward and gave a growl myself, and as soon as they saw me, they both retreated. They seemed to be fighting two against one, but a fair fight wasn't their concern.

Nikkan let out a low growl. He wasn't happy with me carrying Grace, but I had no way to tell him who I was.

How the heck was this supposed to work? It wasn't like I could turn human in the mess that was the wolf village. I would be food for any nearby wolf. The only reason they weren't attacking Grace on my back was that I had her. I was sure of that. I was still healthy and strong, too much of an opponent for most of them to easily take on, so they left me alone.

I wanted to scream at my friend, Nikkan, it's me, Castiel.

But it was impossible without being able to talk.

My frustration began to build as Nikkan growled at me and was looking for a way to get Grace from me. How could he be such an idiot? Did it look like I was going to harm Grace? Really? I was carrying her. If I wanted to hurt her, she wouldn't be on my back.

"Nikkan, stop," I screamed in my head at my friend. "It's me, Castiel."

His growls immediately hushed. I stared at him for a moment before cautiously taking one step towards him.

Images flashed in my mind. Nikkan and Grace were inside a hut, both human, as howls began outside. Wolves beat against the door to the home. Grace was scared, and Nikkan shifted. Wolves broke into the house, and Nikkan defended Grace as she ran. He tried to follow, but it was too much. Several wolves attacked him at the same time.

I was seeing exactly what happened but from Nikkan's perspective.

‘Can you hear me?’ I asked cautiously.

Nikkan said the wolves could communicate in wolf form, but he never said it was in words. In fact, I think his only reply on that subject was that it was complicated.

Wolf Nikkan nodded his head.

‘We need to get Grace out of here. She passed out by the wall and was being hunted. We need to get out of here now before someone else attacks.”

More memories passed to me. Grace was standing with Nikkan as he begged her to transform. She repeatedly told him no. She was too afraid of losing control. The curse was getting stronger each night. She wouldn’t transform as long as she could hold out.

I figured that much. Grace was pretty stubborn. It was strange to be seeing my friend’s images, but it felt natural like it was how we were supposed to talk. I had no idea how to send him images, but it seemed like he understood me.

‘We need the quickest way out of here,’ I commented, trying my best to get my ideas across to Nikkan.

Wolf Nikkan actually rolled his eyes at me before nodding for me to follow him. I didn’t waste any time and kept close to him as he limped his way out of the village. We made it without any more wolves chasing us. They all probably assumed that Grace was our meal, and they didn’t want to fight two to one.

Nikkan led us further into the wolf territory and away from the wall. I knew Sera was going to be mad at me, but it couldn’t be helped. I was going to make sure my friends were safe before anything else.

As soon as we left the village, we slowed our quick pace to a walk. I was thankful for that as it was easier to keep Grace on my back the slower we moved. She didn't stir at all as we made our way into the woods.

The whole place was quiet and empty. It was strange to be in a forest that should be teeming with life and not hear a peep. It was as if the life of the great forest of Elder had been sucked out of it. It was dead. Nikkan didn't seem to notice or care as he kept his lead, occasionally looking back at Grace. But I cared. This forest was my life. I didn't want to see it die.

While I didn't like it, the quiet forest made perfect sense. No animal in its right mind would want to be around the crazy wolves. I didn't want to be around them. They were tenacious and fighting, but worse, they were cruel. Wolves in a pack only fought for dominance. Now, it didn't seem to be the case. I wondered if Micco had any control of his wolves anymore. Did it matter that he was alpha?

Nikkan kept his pace and kept leading us for what seemed longer than possible. The wall had to end at some point, but so far, we hadn't found it again. I felt terrible knowing that Sera was probably going crazy outside the wall, but there wasn't anything I could do about it. I could pass through the wall, and she couldn't. At least, I hoped I could still go through it.

Nikkan finally slowed as we neared the mouth of a cave. I wasn't sure what time it was, but the sun was going to rise soon, and we had been up all night, trudging carefully through the woods.

Images came into my mind from Nikkan. He wanted me to put Grace down by the mouth of the cave.

'Sure thing, puppy,' I wanted to say back but had no idea how to convey that in images.

Nikkan yipped at me like he got my message, and I placed Grace on the ground. Nikkan walked over and lay down beside her, sharing his warmth with her human form. She was shivering.

I hadn't thought about that. It was a cold spring night, and I wasn't feeling it in the least. My nice furry covering seemed to be good enough for me to ignore the elements.

Nikkan lifted his head and nodded to her other side. I moved in to keep Grace warm as well. I was slightly worried that the wolves would be able to find us, but Nikkan relaxed and was quickly snoring. That had to mean it was safe.

Part of me wanted to leave my friends and go find Sera, but I still couldn't do that yet. I needed to speak with them and know what was going on before I went back to Sera and my mother. I needed to know what I could do to help. Without another thought, I closed my eyes and drifted off to a warm sleep beside my friends.

Birds chirping brought me back to consciousness not too much later. Some sort of animal sense had alerted me that morning was coming, and now, it was here. I lifted my animal head and looked at my two sleeping friends. They were more exhausted than I was. I stood and stretched. It was actually much more comfortable to sleep in my wolf form than human form on the ground all night.

Using my new sense of smell, I made my way over toward the interior of the cave, following a weird odor. As I neared, I caught the scent clear as day. Someone, or rather, something had marked the cave with pee, and it smelled horrible. Human pee was bad enough, but to smell it with my super animal senses was awful. I gagged.

"Doesn't smell too great, does it?" Nikkan asked as he walked past me naked. He made his way into the cave and pulled out a bag from behind a rock. A piece of clothing landed at my feet.

I changed back into human form and pulled on the pants while Grace still slept.

Nikkan had pulled on his own pair of pants.

"So, when did you get bit?" Nikkan asked as he dug through his bag more. He pulled out a sweater and went over and laid it on the still sleeping Grace like a blanket to keep her warm.

"I didn't," I replied and watched his reaction. He paused and stared at me. He didn't reply, so I had to continue. "And I'm not a wolf."

At that, Nikkan burst out laughing.

I waited for him to finish before I took off the pants I had just put on and transformed into a bear right in front of him. Nikkan had always been more the show than tell type of person. He wasn't going to believe my words since, even to me, they sounded a bit outrageous. Nikkan stopped laughing and stared at me. I sat down on my haunches and stared at him. Raising an eyebrow, I challenged him to say something. I let it sink in a moment before turning back into my usual self and slipping the pants back on.

"Yeah, so not sure what I am, but I'm not a wolf. Well, I can be, but it isn't that simple. Really, man, your guess is as good as mine."

While most people would have been afraid, especially in Elder, where the only magic was with the wolves, Nikkan just grinned at me.

"That's great. I'd give my right arm to have those powers. If I had that ability, becoming a legend would be simple."

I wasn't sure that was what I wanted, but I could see the wheels turning in Nikkan's head. Being famous was something he wouldn't mind. Growing up as the son of the Red made me know that it wasn't anything like he expected it to be. And besides, I didn't want to be a god of anything. I wanted just to be me and help my friends. But it seemed likely that I'd need to learn more about my background to do anything to help them.

"Were you able to pack food in that sack or just clothing?" I asked, getting away from Nikkan's new dreams as he thought about my unique abilities. I wasn't a performing monkey, and I wasn't joining Nikkan's grand circus plans that I knew were brewing in his mind.

"Just clothing. There's no food around the village, and if I was able to sneak something out here, it would attract the wolves."

That made complete sense. I nodded at him.

"I'll go get some breakfast," I commented as I saw Grace still sleeping on the ground. "We can talk more when I get back."

I didn't wait for Nikkan to agree. It was already daylight, and the wolves would all be sleeping, exhausted from their terror-filled night, both the ones in human form and those forced into their wolf forms. The woods were safe for now.

"Fine, but don't be gone too long; otherwise, Grace will worry."

"Sure, blame the sleeping girl. Good one," I jabbed back at him. It was great to have him as my friend again.

I wasn't exactly sure where the fence around the wolves was, so I took off heading east. If I ran into it, then I'd deal with it then, but until then, I kept my ears and eyes open for something we could eat. I was looking for anything. Berries, plants, or an animal if I could find one, but the woods were stripped clean of everything and anything. There were berry bushes I passed but no berries on them. Typical tuber plants had the tops thrown on the ground from someone else finding and eating the roots. And the animals had basically vanished. I needed to get a better view and sense of all of it.

I didn't hesitate to change forms, and soon enough, I had a wingspan wider than a sapling is tall. My golden-brown feathers ruffled as I gave a hop and took flight. I was beyond thankful that the ability to change animals also came with a natural ability to be one. I didn't have to learn how to fly; I just knew how.

Once I got above the tree line, I took in the view. It was a sight to be seen, and I wished I could share it with my friends. There was nothing but blue sky above me as I caught an air current and held my wings out to steady myself. I floated in the air. I didn't have to do a thing. Part of me wished I could stay up there forever. It was simple up in the sky. There was the sun and the clouds, but nothing beyond that: no noise, no distractions, no worries.

I flapped my wings in two powerful strokes and broke free from the air I was floating on. Soaring in the sky and watching the ground pass below was a surreal feeling. I was a man, and yet I wasn't. I was flying.

Continuing my journey east brought me to the wall. I didn't hesitate as I flew through it and luckily didn't crash into it. The ground was still a bit below me, and it would have hurt to hit it at the speed I was going, but I didn't need to worry. The wall let me right through. As a man, it stopped me, but as a bird, it didn't. The wall was keeping wolves and humans apart, and I had a feeling that I couldn't cross as either of those. Right now, I wasn't either.

With a few more flaps, I brought myself closer to the treetops. As I found one larger branch protruding in the woods, I landed softly on it. It was a great vantage point to see all around me and the ground below. I wasn't sure when I set out how I was going to hunt as I didn't have a weapon on me, but now I knew it didn't matter. I was the weapon.

I waited, sitting perfectly still. It was strange not to have to move. My sense of sight told me all I needed to know. I could see further than I ever could imagine; I could see more colors. It was a strange feeling yet comforting. It felt natural. I sat on the branch perfectly still and waited.

It didn't take long for prey to arrive. I didn't hesitate as I swooped off the branch, nose-diving to the wiggling creature on the ground. It didn't stand a chance as my talons tore into the creature. I landed with a thud on the ground to see if I needed to do more. I wasn't about to fly around with a half-dead creature. While I ate meat, I understood it was still a life. The animal deserved respect and not to spend its last few moments alive, being terrified.

Transforming into my human skin felt natural as the tingles coated my body, and I instantly was standing on two legs. Reaching down, I could tell the rabbit I had found was dead. That was enough for me. I needed to return to my friends and make sure they were safe before I headed back to Sera and tried to figure out what more we could do.

Before I could change back, I noticed a brown piece of cloth hidden just where the rabbit had come from. I reached down and pulled it loose. It was a pair of trousers. The wolves occasionally hid clothing, so it was blind luck that I had found it. At least, I thought so until a piece of paper fluttered off it.

I glanced at the note and then back at the pants. Someone had left them for me. The note was addressed to me and told me that it was a present. Who in the world was leaving me a present in the middle of the woods? Who would know this was where I would be? It was like magic that someone would know that I would be there at that exact time. I glanced around the forest. There were no humans within my sight or hearing distance. Whoever left it for me did so more than just a few moments ago.

Not wanting to make my friends wait any longer, I rolled the pants up and placed them by the rabbit. Someone with foresight had to have left them, but I didn't have time to explore the area and look for a clue as to who it might have been. We needed to eat, especially after last night.

Transforming and flying back was as simple as it was the first time. I was worried that the weight of the rabbit and pants would throw me off, but it didn't. I also wasn't sure what the barrier would do, but that was simple too.

When I arrived near the camp, I could see that Grace was up with Nikkan. I didn't want to attract any wolves to the area, so I sat down further away from them. Slipping my new pants on first, I made my jog back to my friends.

Nikkan had a fire going and was ready for the rabbit I handed him.

"I'm not really understanding all this, but thank you, Castiel, for helping us," Grace told me as I sat down next to her and the fire. It looked like Nikkan had filled her in on me.

Being an animal was definitely warmer than being human. It had to be all the long fur. But I couldn't complain too much. The fire was keeping us all warm as Nikkan expertly skinned and placed the rabbit above the fire to cook.

"I do not understand it much myself," I admitted. Grace smiled shyly and nodded.

It was crazy to see her shy again, but then again, Nikkan was with us. The confident girl that was giving up her human life only days ago seemed like a dream. She was back to being the red-faced girl I grew up with. I really didn't mind, though. After the first night of them behind the wall and no news of what happened, I was grateful that my friends were just alive.

Nikkan sat down and took Grace's hand in his own. She was still a good shade of red but happier than I had ever seen her before. Nikkan shrugged at me.

"When you are faced with every day being your last, you kind of have to make a move," he explained, which made Grace turn a deeper shade of red. "Don't waste time wondering if something is right or not. We have to live in the present and be happy now as we don't always have tomorrow."

I laughed. When did Nikkan get sentimental? I was more than happy to see my two friends, finally admitting the truth. In all this darkness, they still had hope.

"So yes, explain it more," Grace said, changing the subject. "What are you?"

That made me laugh more. "Um... I'm Castiel..... pretty sure I'm human....male, at that, if you want to check," I teased.

Grace's cheeks went back to red as she covered her eyes, thinking I was going to get naked. That was more

Nikkan's style, not mine. I was only teasing.

"I meant the animal thing Nikkan was trying to explain. He said you could turn into a wolf, but you aren't a wolf." She peeked through her fingers at me and removed her hand once she saw I was still sitting... and still had my pants on.

I nodded. "So far, I've been able to turn into any animal I want to be."

Grace's eyes bugged at my admission. It seemed that Nikkan hadn't really explained it much at all to her.

"Anything?" she asked.

I nodded again.

"How about a mouse?" she suggested.

I hadn't tried yet, but it seemed likely. I stood up and thought about being a mouse. My body shrunk, and soon Grace seemed like a mountain beside me. Her face pinched into an oh as she looked at me. I transformed back into myself as Nikkan grabbed Grace's face to stop her from looking at me. I completely forgot about the whole naked part of being cursed.

"Oops," I said as I made to cover myself.

Nikkan dropped his hands from Grace's face as his mouth hung open in shock. The pants I had found in the woods while hunting were still on me. It seemed maybe someone was looking out for me after all. I grinned at my friend without a single way to explain it. Being a shifter just got a whole lot easier. One shifter problem down and one more to go. I was feeling more than a little optimistic.

While I wanted to head right back to Sera and show her that I was okay, I couldn't. My friends were both injured, and I couldn't leave them to fend for themselves. I hoped that one good night's rest would be enough to allow me to go find Sera and prove to her that everything was fine. She wasn't serious about my mother taking her head, but I knew she was worried; both of them would be.

After spending the day playing with my new transformation powers, yes, I could shift into any living creature, including a fly, we made plans for the night. Grace could feel the power of the moon and the curse calling to her. She was having trouble keeping human, so we decided it was better if we were all wolves. Before night fell, we all transformed. As she shifted on her own accord, she had control over her wolf or at least seemed to. We weren't sure how long her control would last, but she had it for now.

Nikkan's camp was the perfect place to spend the night. We were able to take shifts and keep to ourselves the whole night. It allowed us to rest and recover as Nikkan and Grace were both still recovering from their injuries. The food I had caught helped, but they needed more. All the wolves needed more.

It would be a great time for the kingdom to come together as one, but the tree people were still unrealistic. They would rather let a race of their kingdom die, than risk helping them. I didn't understand their position before the curse returned and even less now. The wolves were all trapped behind a wall to keep them safe, and the tree people still didn't want to help the wolves in return.

While we could hear the howls and the voices of anguish, we were far from the mess of the village. It seemed likely that we were the only ones trying to stay away on our own. I had expected more people to leave, but Grace and Nikkan had explained to me that as a pack, it was hard to do that. Nikkan had an easier time leaving because of all his time spent with me, and Grace was able to latch onto that. Being a lone wolf was hard, but it seemed we had our own little pack going on, so that made it easier for both of them. Everyone else was more or less stuck in the main pack.

19TH MARCH

Finally rested, we were able to wake at a normal time and had the energy to go about our day. We headed back to the village as humans to see how we could help and gather supplies for the next few nights.

I tried my best not to gasp as we reached the edge of the village. We had only been gone one night, and it had changed more than I thought was possible. What was once a nice little bustling town was now a war zone. Blood and dirt splattered nearly every wall. People lay around in various stages of death. We passed more than one person who was never going to recover and probably wouldn't last another night. We'd run through it the day before, but it hadn't really registered in the way it was registering now.

It was hard to walk by people and not stop to help. We didn't have the supplies to help, let alone the time. Another moon was coming tonight, and it was hard enough to keep Grace from being pulled by the curse.

"I'm going to go find Micco," Nikkan said as he took Grace's hand and pulled her with him. "We'll come back to the wall to meet with you and Sera."

I nodded to my friend as he took off to the west, and I continued south through the village. I tried not to look too hard at anyone I passed. There was bound to be someone I knew, and it was hard enough to just walk through it. If there was someone I knew, I'd have to help them.

As I made it to the southern edge of the village, I happen to glance at the hut I was passing. There was a small person sitting by a severely injured older man. The person was dutifully bandaging the man and didn't notice me. I stopped to help, and the person looked up at me. I stared in shock. It was a young boy. He couldn't be more than seven or eight winters old. I froze in my place. All the carnage I had seen had consisted of adults. I'd assumed the children were locked away somewhere safe.

The curse couldn't affect young children. It wasn't until they reached maturity that the magic would take them too. Nikkan's family had sent his younger siblings away days ago. I didn't expect there to be any left.

"Are you the only one here?" I asked.

The boy looked up at me with big sad eyes. He shrugged.

"Micco came last night and helped my sister escape, but he could only carry one person at a time. I made her go first because she's smaller than me."

"So, Micco has a safe spot for you to go to?"

The man the child was tending started to cough, and he tried to sit up.

"He said he was going to get them somewhere safe, but I think he's fighting the curse like the rest of us. I hope Tilly is fine."

I needed to find a way to stop the curse, but at the same time, I just couldn't leave the boy in the village. He wouldn't last the night. There would be no reason to stop the curse if there were no youth left. While I wanted to go back and look for more clues, I was needed more with the wolves.

"Wait here," I told the boy. I needed to let Sera know that I would be back to Azren as soon as I could, but first, I needed to get the children to safety.

The boy looked to me and nodded. His father tried to thank me, but I stopped him.

"Save your strength for tonight."

The man nodded.

Before my friends could return, I took off running to the wall.

Everything swirled together in my mind as I ran. I was a shifter, but that still didn't help me break the curse. I knew why the healer told me to stay away from the wolves. Maybe it was possible the curse could happen to me also. But I really didn't care. Being cursed could end my life as I knew it, but at the same time, I couldn't just turn a blind eye to the wolves like the rest of Elder was doing. The wolves needed help, and I was going to help them, no matter whether it put my life in danger or not.

I didn't fear death. Death was part of life. Growing up in Elder had taught me that much. But I did fear failing to keep people safe. I may not have been born as a citizen of Elder, but it was my home. I was going to do anything possible to keep it from falling apart, even if the cost was my life.

Outside of the village, I turned into a large cat that could cross the barrier and picked up my running speed. It took almost no effort to run through the woods in my lithe four-legged form. One thing was for certain; I was born to be able to do this. I understood my life much more now that I realized that.

Maybe it was Grace and Nikkan finally getting to me or maybe something else, but when I rounded the last tree and saw Sera standing just outside the wall, searching the forest to see me, reality hit me. I bounded through the barrier without a second thought. Sera turned around to face me and didn't fear the animal pouncing at her. In one motion, I transformed back into myself and continued onto where she was.

"Did you..." Sera began asking, but I didn't let her say anything else.

Reaching forward and cupping her head in my hands, I pulled her to me as I stepped forward. I think the shock of my boldness stunned her as I pressed my lips to hers, but it was only a moment before she was kissing me back. Her arms wrapped around my neck, holding me to her as much as I was holding her to me.

"Castiel?" Nikkan's voice called, breaking us apart.

I leaned my forehead on Sera's. Life was too short the play the games Grace and Nikkan had played for over a season. I wasn't sure what would happen, and there was death all around the village. I planned to come home unscathed, but that wasn't really my choice. I needed to live in the present.

Even if I had denied what I truly felt, I understood it now. Sera was the girl I had always been watching. I knew everything about her and how to push every button to make her mad, but I also knew how to make her smile, those real ones she saved just for me. While I acted like I hated her, that was just easier than admitting that I liked her. I wasn't going to lie to myself or her now.

"I'll meet you in Azren tomorrow," I told her quietly, really wishing we had time to finish our kiss Nikkan so rudely interrupted.

"Tomorrow?" Sera asked, still slightly stunned by my actions.

"There are kids left in the village. I need to make sure they are safe before I leave."

Sera bit her lip and nodded. I knew she could never object to saving kids.

"Nikkan and Grace agree that there must be something to do with me that will help all this, but there will be nothing left to save if the kids all die."

Sera looked to my lips, and I could tell she wasn't finished with our kiss either. That made me grin.

"I promise to be there tomorrow."

Sera nodded, still not saying a word. I dipped my head down for a quick kiss before letting go of her and shifting back into my cat form before she could protest.

I jumped back through the barrier and to my friends, who were both staring at Sera in shock.

"I'm not making the same mistake you guys made," I commented after I was back in my human form. "I'm not going to play the game of who likes who for many, many moon cycles."

Nikkan grinned and punched me in the shoulder.

"Then what the heck are you doing on this side of the wall? Your girl is over there." Nikkan pointed to Sera, where she stood, still watching us.

"I'm not heading back with her. I will fly over to Azren

tomorrow after we make it through tonight and get the children in town to safety."

"Children?" Grace looked confused. "They were supposed to leave with Micco. I thought that's why we couldn't find him."

"I found a kid in town. His father said he thought the curse had taken Micco. No one is coming back for the ones left. We need to save them."

Grace gasped.

"We need to get the remaining kids to the caves. We can keep them safe there."

Nikkan nodded.

"I'll gather supplies if you gather the kids," Nikkan replied.

"We can put them in the trees---"

"Just like when we were kids," Nikkan finished for me. I nodded, and my friend took off.

One of my first times in the village, I had wandered away from Red because I was bored by her meeting with Micco. I came across Nikkan. He wasn't the nicest to me, but he was beyond curious about how people lived in trees. It was one of his main obsessions. Every time I returned, he'd ask me more and more questions. Finally, one day, I returned to find he had made a tree village himself. It wasn't the most stable thing. In fact, it was downright dangerous, but it was his interpretation of all I had told him, made of course, with blankets.

I turned back to Sera before we left to go back into the village. She stood on the other side of the wall, the wind blowing her hair in her face, but she was still watching us. She raised a hand to give me a nod before she turned and ran back into the woods towards Azren.

"I'll go this way, and you go that way. Tell them to meet over at the Yael house and bring only what they can carry." Grace took charge like I had never seen before.

I hurried back to the hut where the young boy waited. We needed to work fast. I wasn't sure if we'd have enough time to get all the children into the trees before night came, and the wolves came out.

One by one, I looked in every house I passed. As other children joined us, it went quicker as we were able to look into several houses at the same time. By the time I had made it around to all the houses I could find, Grace had gathered fourteen kids with her. Combined with the eight I found, we had more than I expected. How the heck had they made it through the nights?

"Okay, everyone, we're going on a hike," Grace said cheerfully. "It's going to be boring and tiring, but we need to keep moving as a group. No one gets left behind."

"And then we have to work quickly to make camp," I added. This wasn't going to be all fun and games, even if Grace used her cheerful voice.

"Will my mom be alright?" a little girl asked. Her dress must have been blue at one point but was now covered in blood and mud.

"I hope so," I replied. "But more than anything, she wanted you to be alright. My friends and I are going to do our best to make sure you are alright. Your mom will be happy if you are safe."

The girl nodded and reached for my hand. Without hesitation, I took her and tossed her onto my back to be able to walk faster and lead the other children away. She was by far the smallest child and would slow us if she walked. This made her feel safer, and we could move quicker.

We took off, and in no time, Nikkan was able to catch up with us. We were lucky that we were with wolf children, as most of them spent their days running free in the woods and didn't have any trouble keeping up. I couldn't imagine any of the tree people being able to make the trek we were on. Most of the children had left the village feeling down and distraught from the last few nights, but I could see their spirits lifting the further we got away from the camp. Memories of their depressing nights would haunt them for seasons to come, but we were now giving them hope.

"Castiel," one of the older boys called to me. I slowed to let him walk beside me.. He looked over his shoulder at Grace and Nikkan as they walked with the children behind us.

"Samuel, right?" The boy lived a few homes down from Micco. I had seen him many of the times I had come into the village.

"Yes." He nodded at me. "Um... I was wondering." Samuel looked back another time at the kids behind us. "Are they safe?"

"They?" I looked at the gaggle of children marching through the woods. I would do anything to keep them safe, but could I actually say they were safe?

"Grace and Nikkan," Samuel clarified. "Are they cursed yet?"

Oh, were the children safe from my friends? Everyone knew I was human and safe, but they didn't know about Grace and Nikkan. That was a tricky one. I wanted him to know that Grace and Nikkan would do all they could to help keep them safe, but he also needed to know that any of the adult wolves were susceptible to the curse, and he needed to be on guard, not only for them but for other wolves that might show up. "Neither one has succumbed to the curse yet," I explained carefully. "But that doesn't mean that they or any other wolves are always going to be safe. That's why we need to get you all away from the camp and then Nikkan, and I'll make you beds in the trees to spend the night in."

The boy nodded. I wasn't sure if he understood that I was protecting my friends or not, but he had to know nowhere in the wolf village was safe.

"We're sleeping in the trees?" the little girl on my back asked.

"Yes, it's the safest place to sleep," I replied. And it was. That was why the tree people lived up there. It wasn't because they hated the ground or anything.

After what seemed like much longer than I had thought it would take, we made it to our cave. Everything was just as we had left it. Grace and Nikkan got busy making the hammock beds, and I headed out to hunt food for the children.

Hunting was much easier when you could leave the barrier. I had no idea how the wolves were going to continue their lives inside the barrier. They were out of food, and I couldn't hunt enough for a village. But I could hunt enough for twenty-two children. I returned with a deer, and the older children all came to help as Grace prepared it to cook over the fire.

Nikkan was ready with all the beds by the time I returned, and we quickly went to work climbing the two largest trees near the cave. One by one, we tied the hammocks to the tree. To be on the safe side, we nailed the two boards Nikkan brought with him to give extra support to the middle of the hammock beds. It wasn't the safest way to sleep, but we were out of options. The tree people were right about one thing; the trees were the only place you could go to avoid the wolves.

As the night neared and the children were all fed, Nikkan and I boosted and arranged all twenty-two children in their hanging hammock beds. As the last one was slipped into the fabric cocoon, I sat down on the branch holding the beds as near as possible to the truck of the tree. Nikkan stayed below with Grace.

Grace was losing control of her wolf every day. I could see the strain that staying human was having on her, but she didn't want to scare the kids. As the moon rose higher in the sky, I could see that she was visibly having trouble with her human form. All of the children were asleep as I hopped down to the ground.

"Grace," I said quietly to my friend.

I could see her nails were already elongated into claws. She growled back at me.

"Nikkan, she needs to complete the shift," I told my friend.

Nikkan just grunted as Grace elbowed him in the gut.

I held my hands up to indicate I wanted no argument from her.

"Grace. Shift."

She blinked her eyes. I could see the wolf in her.

"I can't," she gritted out. "What if I lose control?"

"Then Nikkan and I will stop you," I replied. "We won't let you hurt the children."

Grace glanced up to the beds. We made sure the strongest wolf wouldn't be able to jump up to where the children slept.

"But…." Grace gasped as her body started to change on its own.

"I'm changing with her," Nikkan said as he began to rip off his clothing.

As was I. Without a moment passing, I went from two feet to four feet. I met Grace eye to eye as I shifted at the same time as her. Her reddish wolf growled at me. Wolf form or not, I wasn't about to let Grace boss me around, so I leapt forward and pinned her to the ground. Nikkan gave me a growl as I stared down at Grace. I didn't acknowledge him. I was too busy telling Grace I was in charge.

"Hold onto your wolf," I told my friend. "And don't fight me."

She whinnied beneath me and turned her head, baring her neck to me. I knew she was in control and let her go. We had won this night from the curse, but I wasn't sure how many more she had left. She was fighting it, but it wasn't something she could continue to fight. The curse always won. The question was, could I save her before it made her into something she could never forgive herself for becoming.

20TH MARCH

I woke the next morning and found my two wolf friends curled around each other. I had already told them I was leaving at first light, but now I had to pause and smile at my friends. Only moons ago, they would have claimed it was for warmth, but at least now, they were admitting the truth. While I wanted to stay behind and help keep the children safe, it was time for me to get back to Azren and maybe admit a truth myself.

Without any pause, I shifted into a large eagle. Feathers sprouted on my arms as bones broke and rearranged in the places they needed to be. There was no pain or waiting as it happened. One moment I was a man, and the next, I was a bird. I had no idea why it was easy for me when I had seen more than one wolf struggle changing. For the wolves, it took several moments and even up to many breaths during the first changes. It wasn't like that for me, and I had no idea why.

With a powerful push from my wings and my legs, I launched myself into the air, taking flight. It took several more powerful wing strokes to get me high enough into the air to allow me to soar. By holding my wings out, I floated on the breeze and didn't have to use a single bit of energy. It would be easy to get lost in the air. The blue sky had always called to me before I could become a bird, but now, it was endless. I could go wherever I wanted, and I'd be there in no time. This was beyond my wildest dreams. While I wanted to stay in the air for fun, I turned myself south and headed off towards the capital and my waiting mother.

To get down from the sky, I pulled my wings in closer and began my descent. While I still had my own mind and the memories inside it, I didn't need to wonder what to do. It was like when I was an animal; I just knew what to do. I could fly without flying lessons and had a feeling if I turned into a fish, I could swim just as naturally. The power thrumming through me made me wonder where I came from more than ever.

As the city came into view, I landed on a branch just above my mother's office. Easily, I shifted into my human form and was thankful for my magical change of clothing. I wouldn't have to walk around Azren naked, and whoever left them for me deserved a big thank you.

I let a few people walk by before I hopped down from the tree. I didn't need to scare anyone. They were already on high alert. I didn't want to get shot.

No one noticed me as I was above them instead of

on their level. Without wasting any time, I was walking into Red's office. I expected to see Red there waiting for me, but I stopped in my tracks when I found just Sera. She turned around and looked up at me from her desk that now faced my mother's desk.

My heart hammered in my chest as I wondered what I should do. The last time I saw her, I was more than a little impulsive. I didn't regret my choice, but I wasn't exactly sure how to proceed now. I had thought the feelings seemed to be mutual, but that could have just been me caught in the moment. Drying my hands on my magical pants, I swiped one through my black hair. While I wasn't flying as a human, I felt like the wind was still whipping around my body.

"I was beginning to wonder if you really were going to come or if something more happened," she commented, standing up.

I couldn't read her. Was she happy or sad to see me? Was she annoyed? She didn't seem to be, but I just couldn't be absolutely sure.

"Red already left to go to the archive building."

I turned to leave the office, but Sera grabbed my arm before I could leave.

"Not the hall of records," she said, not letting go of me.

I turned and found we were only standing a breath apart from each other. She bit her lip as she looked up at me. Bossy Sera, I could handle, but Sera looking at me like she was right then was something I had never expected. Sera smiled as she turned but didn't let go of my hand.

"We have three archive buildings where we keep records beyond normal Azren records. Red wasn't sure why your adoption wasn't recorded, so she went to go see if the archive building had anything that could help us."

Sera walked over to one of the trees that supported my mother's office. It wasn't a large space, but at the same time, it was close to the size of my home. If it had been built around a tree like many of the homes, one tree would be enough to support it, but being that it was the office of the Red, the room was held up by three trees, so that the middle was completely open, and she was able to hold meeting it the room with everyone able to see her.

Sera pushed on the tree, and a door snapped open.

"What in the forest is that?" I asked as I could see into the hollowed-out tree. There was just a small space; I doubted it could fit more than one person in it. This was new.

I had spent my youth exploring my mother's office. There wasn't really much for me to do at times, and being that Red was always busy in her office, I often was in here with her. When she'd leave the room, I couldn't help from looking around, trying to find things I wasn't supposed to know. I had never seen this tree room before. Guess there was still more to discover after all.

"Only the Red can open this door," Sera told me, explaining my thoughts. She had caught me more than once on my hunts through the Red's office. She never tattled on me, but she always gave me her classic Sera disappointed face. "It can be used to travel to ten different locations in Elder. Sometimes the Red needs to be somewhere quickly, and horses or running just aren't fast enough. We need to head to the archive near the border with Oz."

Sera's words made sense, that is, the actual words she was speaking, but what she was saying didn't make a bit of sense. She still held my hand and tugged me into the small space inside the tree. Once we were both stuffed into the tree, we didn't have any room to move. She turned to be able to close the door and pressed herself back into me. Her head was just below mine, and I could smell the shampoo in her hair.

"We're pretty sure that even though you aren't the Red, the tree will let you pass as it does us," Sera told me as she reached up with her free hand and tugged the door all the way shut.

"Pretty sure?" I asked. That wasn't reassuring.

Sera didn't answer. Great, she was talking in riddles and not sure. It was beginning to sound a bit dangerous.

It was dark in the tree. I had no idea what we were doing, but I trusted Sera. I heard a click before it felt like the floor was falling out from beneath me. I grabbed ahold of Sera's waist as we fell quickly but then stopped. She made a thumping noise, and the door pushed back open. I followed Sera out into the bright light and stopped to gape. I knew where we were, and her words made a bit more sense. We were in Red's office on the southern edge of Elder.

I stepped out onto the dirt floor and looked around. My eyes weren't playing tricks on me. We really had traveled several days' worth of running in moments.

"Red said to meet her at the archive," Sera explained, not letting me have time to absorb what had just happened.

Pushing open the office door, Sera marched out of Red's office and into the morning sunlight of the fields of Azren. I knew there were caves nearby, but we never spent too much time here when I was growing up. The farmers needed little from Red and were happy with their simple way of life never being interrupted. Red was needed up in the forest more than anything to help with the wolves, so I didn't see much of the farm fields of Elder.

Sera waved to me as she took off running. While it seemed a race was in order, as it was every time we ran someplace, I had to keep pace with Sera, and I wasn't sure where I was going. Sera took the pace as fast as normal, but it wasn't a problem for me. She easily cut through fields and went off the pathway more than once. It seemed she was better versed in this area of the kingdom than I was.

Not too much later, we entered a small cluster of trees. Sera slowed down finally, though I could see nothing that would make her do that. As she rounded a hill, I caught the slight sense that there was more to this cluster of trees than the plants. Sure enough, Sera made an exact turn onto what looked like it could be stone steps, very miss-matched steps, but steps none-the-less. We climbed down, and I followed behind her. The pathway narrowed, and we slid between some huge stones. Anyone passing by wouldn't have seen the opening, but I did now that we were going through it.

The path led us deeper into the hill, and the air chilled as the walls were no longer interspersed with trees but more and more solid rock. We hadn't gone down more than a few saplings, but it was enough that we were underground a bit, at least, under the forest that was above us.

Sera didn't say anything as we walked, and I didn't either. I wasn't too worried, though. It was strange to see her after my impromptu kiss at the wolf village, but it wasn't now. Some things with Sera were just natural, and this was one of those times. Besides, I wasn't sure what exactly to say to her. Deep down, I did have feelings for her, but I wasn't sure how deep her feelings were. But for the moment, it didn't matter.

"We have the archives here to keep them dry," Sera finally spoke as we reached far enough into the cave that I figured we'd need light soon, but as she walked around the corner, I noticed that we wouldn't.

Above us, the cave was open to the sky. I could see the blue, but all around, under the ledges, I could see containers. Red wasn't too far away as she sat on a boulder with a container at her feet. She held some paper in her hands.

"This is the papers from The Vale for the winter you came here," Red indicated the papers at her feet. "So far, I've been through The Echo and found nothing. I also made it through The Floris Observer and found nothing either. Sera, can you look through the Arcadia Chronicle and, Castiel, The Arboria Weekly, while I finish The Forge Hart?"

I sat down and took the box she had stacked at her feet that she had motioned for me to take. She had boxes upon boxes of the newspapers from different kingdoms. From the look of the very filled cave, it was likely she had papers from all the kingdoms. I never thought much of Elder not having a paper, but I didn't realize that they kept the ones from everywhere else.

"It helps us to keep track of what is going on in other places, but we only keep notes and the papers from what might affect us back in Azren. The rest of the papers are stored here," Red explained to me as I gawked at the room.

"And before you ask," Sera continued for Red. "We purposely don't have a paper because we prefer to have no other places keeping up with us."

That made perfect strategic sense. I nodded to Red

and Sera before I opened up the first paper and began to scan through it, not exactly sure what I was looking for.

"You had to come from somewhere," Sera explained as she took her box and began to do the same. "Red came early to sort through and find all the editions from around the time you were born."

I glanced around the cave. There were boxes stacked all over. I had no idea how they knew where to find what, but I trusted that both Red and Sera knew.

"What exactly am I looking for?" I asked as I finished the last of the paper in my hand without a clue.

Red smiled at me. "These papers might give us an idea. We need to see if there is any mention of male babies in other kingdoms whether they are adopted like you or any children that went missing."

I nodded. If I did come from somewhere and made the newspaper, that wasn't going to be a good finding. How would it go over diplomatically if Red was accused of kidnapping and raising a child from another kingdom? That easily could lead to war. I know she'd never do that. I was certain she told us the truth of how I came to her, but that didn't mean anyone else would believe her.

The paper in my hand was labeled, and I had to think hard. We didn't use the same system to name our days, and I tried to remember what day I was looking at. As I looked at the pictures in the newspaper, I could see everything was summer. I didn't need to look that far ahead. I needed something in the wintertime. Quickly I paged through the front pages until I found winter papers and began to skim through them.

We all three sat in silence as we read. Page after page were things I didn't care about, nor did they matter. I really didn't care at all about people who would work to line walls with gold. How silly did you have to be to use your energy for that? Gold didn't keep the cold out. You needed solid, sturdy walls, not gold-lined. While I could relate to their mountain-dwellings that seemed quite like the tree villages, I couldn't relate to the extravagance. I kept reading but was sure I wasn't going to find any clues. The world outside of Elder just never seemed practical to me. And this place wasn't an exception.

"Sera told me about your magic," Red finally commented as she closed her box without finding anything to mention to us. She picked up another box and opened it. "I always knew that you were destined for great things." Red gave me a smile, but it wasn't a happy smile.

"I wouldn't say that," I replied with a shrug. "This magic in me doesn't help my friends. It doesn't help the wolves. I'd rather have the ability to cure people than shift into animals." Though now that I knew how it felt, if given a choice, I would miss my ability, but I'd still choose to help my friends.

Red shrugged and gave me her all-knowing look. While I didn't stop the curse or save my friends with being able to change into any animal, I did kind of help them the past couple of nights. I had kept Grace safe and got the children to safety.

"There are kids behind the wall," I blurted out. Red had to know the truth. She was sentencing the wolf children to die.

"I know. Micco was setting up a safe place for them." Red was back to glancing over her paper. She already knew. How did she not tell anyone?

"But he didn't," I added. "I helped Nikkan and Grace

round up all we could find, and we put them in the trees."

Red looked up at me, alarmed.

"What do you mean, Micco didn't help?" Her voice wavered. I knew Micco was a close friend of hers, but I wasn't sure if she was more alarmed that he didn't help and something could be wrong or that there were children in danger.

"I didn't see him. The kids said they waited for him, but he never came back."

Red bit her lip as she glanced back to the entrance of the cave.

"Let's work until lunchtime and then head back," Sera suggested, as she could also see that Red was upset by my words. I was glad to see that we weren't going to just leave this as another unanswered question.

I looked back down at my paper as both Sera and Red went back to theirs. I glanced through each column and found nothing as I had in the last edition. I had a feeling there was nothing to find, but I needed to be sure. If there was a lead to where I came from, that would be helpful, maybe give us a clue as to why the curse stopped when I came to Elder as a baby.

I continued to scan everything. It was boring to read over what didn't make a single difference to me. It was interesting though to see actual pictures of the birds they used to fly around on. I had never traveled to Arboria before, but now with my new ability, I would be able to travel anywhere. I stared harder at the birds and wondered if I could transform into one myself. So far, I had only tried animals I had seen with my own eyes, but this was something that might be a bit of a fun challenge. I studied the picture more.

"A baby boy," Sera read from over my shoulder. "It

isn't about a boy being kidnapped, but isn't it strange that the king and queen of Arboria had a baby boy around the time Red took you in?"

I wasn't sure what she was talking about until I looked at the column next to the picture I was studying. There was a much larger picture of a king and queen with an infant in their arms. I quickly scanned the writing next to it. Sure enough, in the winter I came to Elder, the King and Queen had a baby boy. I scanned the article. It mentioned nothing about an adoption, but it did say it was quite a surprise. No one knew the queen was pregnant. He was currently the crown Prince. Prince Fallon. I had heard of the name but knew nothing of the guy.

Red was now standing and looking over my shoulder too.

"I've met him before." Red finished the article and nodded. "He's been to Elder once. I'm pretty sure he hated it here."

Sera laughed with Red. But I could completely understand. Arboria and Elder were two different worlds. I was more than sure I'd hate it in Arboria too.

"We need to head back and deal with the wolves," Red said as she placed her paper back in the box.

She then carried the box over next to the cave wall and added it to a pile. I grabbed my own box, taking one last look at the Prince's birth announcement before taking the box over to Red. She took it from me and put it in a different pile. There must have been some sort of order I didn't understand.

We left the sort of cave and trekked back across the fields. Red didn't cut through the freshly growing corn like Sera did before, so it took a bit longer to get back to her office. She walked in silence the whole way, and I felt like she didn't want to be interrupted in her thoughts.

As we went into her office, she finally spoke.

"Then, we were right about his magic being accepted by the trees?" Red asked Sera. Not where I thought she was going to go with questions.

Sera looked me up and down.

"He seemed to come through whole. I guess that's a yes."

Whole? Was there any question of going through the magical tree not whole? And they both let me do it? Heck, they didn't warn me? Typical Red and future Red.

"Good," Red replied as she walked over and opened the tree door. She stepped inside and shut the door. I didn't know anything happened. How could I have missed her doing that as a kid? Maybe she never did it in front of me because I would have asked.

Sera didn't wait as she opened it again. Without a sound, Red was completely gone. Because of our lack of magic in Elder, it always surprised me when I saw something like that. I tried to keep my face neutral, but it was strange to see magic. Maybe I hadn't' seen enough of the world because Sera and Red didn't bat an eye. Sera turned to me and tapped her foot.

"Waiting for an invitation?" she asked. "Would you like it on paper or just sung?"

I smirked at her teasing. "I'd prefer it in a dance."

Without a second thought, I grabbed Sera and twirled her around in a circle, making us end up in the small secret tree space. My back hit the tree wall with a thud, and Sera bounced into me. I kept my arms around her, making sure she didn't hit the tree walls at all. I grinned as she looked up with flushed cheeks.

"That was the perfect invitation," I teased.

Sera huffed and turned back around, pressing her back into me. She yanked the door shut, and we were left in complete darkness again. Before she could touch the wall and send us back to Red, I bravely dipped my head and kissed her jaw just under her ear. My feet dropped as Sera made contact with the tree and sent us back to Red.

We stood in the dark tree with Red right on the other side. Sera twisted in my arms without opening the door. I could barely make out her face in the pitch black, and that was probably only thanks to my animal abilities. I wanted to be able to see her eyes and judge what she was thinking, but as she pushed up on her toes to kiss me, I didn't have to wonder. All that thinking about if she liked me too was very much confirmed.

I don't know how long we would have stayed there in the dark tree, but the knocking on a door made us both pull apart. Sera turned and pushed open the tree door to find Red answering her office door.

"They are all gathered," a man's voice said from the other side of her door.

"Who is gathered?" I asked from behind Sera as we approached Red.

Red didn't answer as she left, and we followed as expected. Sera didn't seem to know what was going on either, but that didn't matter. Red's always had been like that. Some things in life never changed, and I was actually grateful for that.

The tree people had built an amazing system of homes all several saplings off the ground, but one problem you encountered when you build a bunch of connecting buildings was that there is very little space to have a meeting of all the inhabitants. I could tell what Red had planned as we walked further towards the middle of the village. There were several stories of bridges that went around the trees, and there was one favorite spot that Red always liked to talk to her people from. Red walked far enough that anyone who wanted to hear her could.

"Thank you all for coming here on short notice," Red started as she looked around at the faces gathered. It wasn't all of Azren, but it was a lot of them.

"We need to talk about the wolves."

A few people groaned, and a couple more glared, but most of the faces waited for her to continue. I wasn't the only one used to waiting for Red to say what she needed to say.

"Right now, they are trapped behind a wall. They chose to build a wall to keep the rest of us safe. They chose to isolate themselves. While I understand your fear of the wolves, I need everyone here to think hard about what is going on. The wolves are citizens of Elder, just like every one of you. They are humans, even if they can turn into wolves. They are our friends, family, and neighbors. They are a part of this, all of this." Red gestured around the city.

Faces stared back at her, but surprisingly, no one was complaining. Days without any attacks seemed to have quelled the majority of the people's fear.

"We need to think of what we can do to help them," Red continued. "Every night, more and more wolves succumb to the curse. Yes, you are all safe here, but they aren't safe there. The wolves are attacking each other, and many are dying. Even worse, are the children. Micco told me he had plans to keep the children safe, but Castiel was brave enough to enter the wolves' territory and help all the ones he could find. There are still children left unprotected beyond that wall."

Women gathered, all looking shocked. I was sure many of them were picturing their own children in the same place as those lost children.

"As many of you know, children can't get sick. It isn't until they come of age that they can get the curse. So those children are sitting there with their parents, waiting for them to turn on them and attack them, if they have parents left. These children are innocent. The wolves are innocent. All they've ever wanted to do was be part of Elder. And you have all turned your backs on them."

Red now looked from face to face, and many turned from her stare.

"I'm ashamed to call myself a tree person."

There were a few gasps from the crowd, but most of them nodded along with her.

"If this was happening to your mother, your brother, your children, how would you feel?"

I could see that she still affected the people of Elder. Even if her Red powers were draining and going to Sera, Red still had the power of her voice and reasoning. Red was still the leader that had been running Elder for many seasons. Red was Elder.

"I expect more from you," she concluded before turning back to Sera and me.

That was our only cue to move out of the way, and Red left the tree people citizens of Elder sitting in the safe tree bridges stunned. I wish I had more time to see what was coming next, but I needed to head back to Nikkan and Grace and check on the children. I had been scolded more times than I could count by Red, and I knew what it felt like to get her look of disappointment. Even the people scowling seem to be ashamed as they should be. Red couldn't make them be better people, but that didn't mean she has to sit silently and let them continue to act like they were. I couldn't be prouder of Red as she walked away without a single look back. She would forever be the Red in my mind.

Red packed as many supplies on me in my bird form as she could. I wished I had time to carry more, but I didn't as night was falling, and I needed to make it back to my friends. For the second night in a row, Grace had to fight for control of her wolf. I was certain we almost lost her before she submitted to me, but luckily enough, she did, and we had a restful night; no wolves tried to come out to where we were. Grace was losing her battle with the curse, but I wasn't going to give up on her.

I felt slightly guilty after my mother's impassioned speech. Here I was hiding off in the corner of the wolf territory, and the wolf village was in chaos. I knew the sleeping children above me needed me to stay and protect them, but it was still hard to hear the pleas of people and the howls of the wolves.

21ST MARCH

When we woke the next day, it was like the horrible night hadn't happened. I could pretend we were just camping, and Grace sure did keep it cheerful enough for the children to do just that, but the older children knew the reality just as Nikkan, Grace, and I did. The curse was destroying the wolves.

"Can we go back today to check on them?" one of the older kids asked.

It was obvious that they had also heard all the howls. I didn't blame them in the least for being worried. They had left behind parents, grandparents, and older siblings.

"We can't go back until it's safe," I answered before Nikkan could. He would have said the same thing.

"If we can make a safe zone here, then maybe some of the parents, if they aren't cursed yet, could come here," Nikkan suggested. "They could live on the ground away from the children but still be able to see and talk to them. We could build a real house for the kids, like the tree people have."

That sounded like a good enough idea to me, but I wasn't sure how to execute it. I had built my own place, but that was on the ground. I wasn't really versed in how to build treehouses. Azren was safe and secure by the time I was born, and I wasn't sure how to do that from scratch. It was a whole city in the trees, and I didn't know where to start to make one house. I couldn't think too hard as Azren took too many seasons to count to build, but we had to start somewhere.

"How about I head back to the village and pick up supplies, see what I can find," I suggested.

Nikkan nodded.

"I'll come with you."

"I can stay with the kids," Grace added.

"But wouldn't it be easier if they had your help too?" Samuel asked.

He was the oldest of the kids. He probably didn't have too long before he was old enough to be cursed also, but for right now, he was safe from it.

"I can take care of the camp. It isn't like anyone is going to come and cause trouble right now. It is day time." The boy had a point.

I looked at my friends. We weren't going to be gone too long, and it was daytime. And besides, I could fly back in only moments if we needed to help.

Nikkan nodded like he was on the same thought path I was.

"Okay. You keep the younger ones to the trees just

in case, and we will be back by lunchtime."

Samuel nodded to Nikkan and then to me. I could see the boy was confident enough. He would be fine.

Nikkan, Grace, and I took off back to the village. Where I could normally run back in record time with my new endurance, I took it slow for my friends. Grace was still a bit weak from her fight with the curse, and Nikkan was the ever-attentive boyfriend. He carried her part of the way despite her protests.

"So, you didn't get to a chance to tell us if you found anything," Nikkan began as we got out of sight of the kids. I had turned back one last time to be sure they were fine, and they were.

"We didn't find much. It seems Red keeps newspapers from all the kingdoms. We went through them, and the only thing we found was that a Prince from Aboria was born around the same time as me."

"Could he be your twin?" Nikkan asked.

Grace burst out laughing.

"Not possible. They are as much alike as night and day." She tried to keep her laughter down but still found it quite funny.

I shrugged. I knew very little about Prince Fallon. I had no clue what he looked like.

"How do you know that?" Nikkan asked as I raised an eyebrow at Grace.

"He's in all the magazines we import. Haven't you seen him before? He's that really good-looking guy with a crown. I'm sure you would have seen him at the magazine stand. I think he's always on a cover or two every moon cycle."

"Good-looking?" Nikkan asked. I could see the jealousy on his face.

Grace laughed again.

"Not as good-looking as you." She grabbed his arm and twined her fingers with his. That seemed to appease my golden-haired friend.

"What do those magazines say about him?"

I didn't think I was related to him as I could picture the guy Grace was talking about. I never knew his name, but I was vaguely aware who Prince Fallon was, and we looked nothing alike, but I had to wonder if there was some sort of connection. He was the best lead I had so far. It wasn't like any mysterious babies adopted seasons ago would just be roaming around the forests of Elder so I could ask them.

"What's he like?" I asked. Grace seemed to know more than the newspaper I was reading.

"Handsome, but not as handsome as you," she added again for Nikkan. "And he seems to know it. He doesn't go anywhere without women throwing themselves at him. They say he's the most eligible royalty as he doesn't have any siblings and will inherit the throne outright when his father wants to be done. You can't imagine how many girls want to be a princess that's guaranteed to become queen."

Nikkan made a gagging face behind Grace's back.

"What does he do for a job until he becomes king?" I asked. I had heard that some royals had other jobs or trained with their military. If I remembered right, the King of Aboria wasn't much older than Red, and he was likely to rule for quite a few seasons.

"Job? Does Prince Fallon work? I doubt it," Grace replied with a flutter of her eyelashes. She might have said Nikkan didn't need to be jealous, but I could understand that look on her anywhere. She had a crush.

"No job?" Nikkan asked, puffing out his chest as if

that made him a better candidate for Grace.

Not that my friend could say much. Nikkan spent most of his time as a wolf sleeping around my house. We made most of the border runs together, but that was about all Nikkan would do as a job. Not that it meant much. Most people in Elder didn't have traditional jobs, at least, not the people living in the forests. We had enough stuff to get done each day just not to go hungry or cold. Jobs were an afterthought or a talent.

"Then what does he do all day?" I asked. I wanted to understand this Prince Fallon better.

Grace shrugged. "Not much of anything, I suppose. All the pictures I see of him are when he is at parties. He seems to do those a lot. And he must like them. He's always smiling."

Okay, I really had nothing in common with the Prince of Aboria. But that didn't mean I was giving up quite yet. It was possible what I needed to do was meet this prince. Maybe he could tell me where he came from and give me a better clue as to where to look. Adoption by a stranger wasn't that common in Elder. Most people knew who their parents were, even if they weren't raising them. Maybe it was wishful thinking, but I felt like I needed to talk to this prince.

"Even if he's handsome," Nikkan drew out the word while his nose wrinkled in disgust. "He doesn't sound like he provides much. A pretty face can't catch you a meal or build you a home."

I nodded. That much was true.

"And that's why I'm with you and not running off to Aboria to try to catch the eye of a prince," Grace said as she patted Nikkan's arm.

I had to agree with Nikkan. The prince didn't sound like much, but he was a lead. If I didn't find any new answers here in Elder, I was going to have to look further into him.

We all three stopped talking as we came to the village. I didn't think it was possible that it could be in more disarray than before, but it was. At least a quarter of the huts were torn down or burned. Off to the west, I could see there was smoke, possibly from a burning hut.

People littered the street. As we walked into the village, I could tell most, if not all, were still alive, but that was likely due to the magical wolf that resided inside them. Wolves had much faster healing, so even if they were fighting and getting hurt, they weren't dying, yet.

It took every part of me not to stop and try to help. The children needed help first, and then we could look at the rest of the people. When they had a safe home, we could turn to helping the cursed.

"What do we need?" Grace asked, trying not to look around either.

"Nikkan and I'll try to find as many boards as we can; you look for nails and hammers," I directed her.

"And blankets," Nikkan added. "They could use more blankets. I saw that little curly-haired one shivering this morning. They don't have fur to keep them warm like us."

"Once you get what you can, head back to the camp. Don't wait for us. I don't want them alone any longer than they need to be," I told her. "Nikkan and I'll probably have to make several trips to carry what we can find."

Grace nodded and kissed Nikkan's cheek before heading off into the village.

"I figured that the wall we didn't finish would be the

best place to get boards."

Nikkan nodded his agreement as we began to walk to the edge of town. It would be easier to skirt around the town than go through all the carnage that blocked the streets, so we took the longer route around town.

As we approached the wall, I could tell we were right. Unfortunately, with just two of us, it was going to take a bit of time to haul all the unused wood to our camp. Nikkan and I stood before the stack of wood.

"We should probably take the trimmed boards first," I assessed. They looked like the floor of the tree houses in Azren.

"Or we take it all," Nikkan suggested. As usual, Nikkan was crazy ambitious.

I had no idea how he planned to pull that one off. He motioned to a cart nearby. Together, we could probably pull the cart back to the camp, but we still could only fill it full enough that we could pull it. We were strong, but not that strong.

"We still can't take it all," I told him.

"And why not? Is your animal form just for show, or could you be an ox and actually pull this thing?"

I nodded to my friend. I hadn't thought of that. While my new animal form very much felt like just a part of me, I hadn't thought to do more than run as a wolf or fly as a bird. He was right.

"Then, let's do this."

I paused.

"But you better not let anyone try to eat me!"

Nikkan threw his head back and laughed. I wasn't exactly sure if that was a yes or a no.

We first loaded up the cart. When we got as much on it as possible, I moved to the front of the cart and stared at it. I wasn't exactly sure how to make it work, but we would. I let the change take over my body, and I was instantly an ox. I looked back with my changed eyesight at my friend. He was grinning that his wild idea was actually going to work. I moaned at him to hurry up, and he quickly harnessed me to the cart.

It was a slow trip back to the camp as we couldn't take the direct route through the trees, and we ended up leaving the cart further away than we would have liked, but Nikkan and I managed to bring a full cart of boards to the camp in one trip. Now, we just needed to figure out how to make a treehouse. But that was going to have to wait. I needed to hunt on the other side of the wall and get food for the children.

I expected a quick trip to catch something and bring it back, but that wasn't going to be the case when Sera showed up.

"Feeding time for the cubs?" she asked as she found me gutting a deer.

I had been lucky and found an animal big enough that it would feed them for days. I was going to have to use my bear form to carry it back. I nodded to her as I worked, my arms were covered in the guts of the animal.

"What's the plan to do next?"

I finally looked up at her. I didn't have a plan. I was at a dead end. We thought I was possibly part of the key to stopping the curse because the women who brought me to Red told her that, but if I couldn't find out where I came from, then I wasn't any help. I shrugged before going back to the animal in front of me. I had too much to get done and not enough time. Twenty-two children depended on me to get them food and keep them safe. I didn't have time to figure out any more about how to save them from the curse. I was failing.

"You're not giving up, are you?"

"I can't give up if there's nothing to give up. I'm a ghost. I'm not a citizen of Elder."

And that was the truth. I wasn't in the record books. I was no one. At least, helping the wolves and the children survive gave me a purpose. What was I otherwise?

"Nothing? You really think you are nothing?"

"According to Elder, I am." I stood up and looked down at her. She crossed her arms across her chest and huffed at me.

"Really, Castiel? I thought I knew you better. The Castiel I know is strong and wouldn't let little things like this get in his way. Guess I was wrong about you." Sera threw her arms in the air and marched away.

I tried not to watch her go, but it was too hard. Her receding form faded into the trees. I knew I'd upset her, but it was the truth. I didn't know what to do next. I wanted to help my friends, but I didn't know-how. Helping the kids gave me something to do until I could get more crazy ideas out of Nikkan. When I ran out of thoughts, he was always there to give me more. That's why I needed to go back and be with him and Grace. I just needed a few nights to reenergize and think, and I would be back.

Camp and hungry children were waiting for me when I returned to my friends. Grace took the deer from me and instantly went to work, making it into a meal. When she took the meat that she could use tonight, Nikkan took the rest and wrapped it enough to keep it from spoiling until we could finish using it tomorrow.

Night came too quickly, and our fed wolf children were tucked in their hanging beds. I was exhausted from our day and my fight with Sera, but I knew what was coming. The curse was growing quickly in Grace.

Grace was worried before she turned, but she couldn't stop it now. She had to turn. The pull of the night was too great. I turned with her, and Nikkan tried to keep up, but as soon as she was a wolf, Grace took off into the woods.

She took off on a hard run, heading north of the village. I didn't wait for Nikkan and took off after her. Grace ran fast, but I was faster. When I finally caught up with her, I had to tackle her to the ground. She yipped and growled at me, fighting back. I could see that Grace wasn't in control. The wolf staring back at me wanted to kill me for stopping her.

'Grace,' I pleaded with her, "Come back to us."

The wolf growled and tried to buck me off her, but I wasn't just stronger; I was also larger than her. I had to press harder to keep her to the ground and worried I might hurt her, but the opposite wasn't an option. I wasn't going to let her go free and hurt herself or others, even if she wanted to. I wasn't going to let my friends down.

Grace growled at me again.

'Grace, please. Fight it. I know you can.'

Grace bucked more beneath me, and with her twisting and wiggling, she was able to move her head close to my foreleg. Clamping down, I felt the pain but ignored it. I wasn't letting go that easy. Grace shook her head and then suddenly stopped. I felt the images come to me in a rush.

Grace was sorry and regretted hurting me. She was back in control. I stayed where I was until she looked into my eyes. Slowly, she faced me, and I could see my friend in her eyes. It was one more night, but she was still in control. The curse hadn't won yet.

Slowly, I let go of my friend, ready to stop her if it was just a trick. Grace nodded to me, and I motioned behind us.

'We need to head back to Nikkan. You left him in the dust.'

Wolf Grace gave a little chuckle and nodded to me as she took off in front of me back the way we had run. I didn't give it any thought as we picked up our pace to head back as to why Nikkan hadn't caught up with us. Yes, cursed Grace was fast, but she wasn't fast enough to outrun us completely. And Nikkan wasn't a slow wolf.

Grace howled as we neared and saw the scene before I did. Nikkan was on the ground as four wolves took turns jumping in and biting him, taking chunks of his fur and skin with them. Grace didn't wait as she charged forward. I knew our odds weren't the best with four crazed wolfs against three as it was, so I changed my form. I wasn't going to fight fair. My size grew as I neared, and long brown fur covered me. I could feel the power in every step as I neared my friends.

I didn't wait for an invitation as I swiped at the nearest wolf. One powerful hit and the wolf went flying. It hit a tree and whimpered. It wasn't long before the other three wolves knew what they were facing, and all turned to me. That was fine with me. I was ready for it. As each wolf moved, I was able to get in a hit. Even if the wolf got a scratch or bite on me, it wasn't enough to stop me. It wasn't a fair fight. I was four times the size of them in my bear form. When the wolves had enough for the night, they turned and ran back the way they came, and I slumped to the ground beside my friends. It was going to be a long night.

22ND MARCH

We spent the rest of the night, keeping Nikkan safe as he healed, and running the attacking wolves away from the tree where the children slept. If I had to guess, it would be they came because of the meat hanging in the tree with the children. I could have brought the meat outside the wall, but it was too late to matter much. They already had the scent. It was daylight by the time we made it to sleep.

When I woke, I found Grace and the older kids were already stripping the meat down to be smoked. Being that the scent would attract the wolves, I thought it was better if I went to the other side of the wall to dry it. This time I would be proactive. While they finished, I went over to start a pit for the fire on the other side of the wall.

Physical activity was great to keep my mind off everything, but once I had everything ready and got the meat from Grace, I had nothing to do but sit by the fire. Which, unfortunately, left me way too much time to think.

I needed to keep following leads and coming up with a way to save my friends, but it was getting harder. Grace wasn't going to beat the curse much longer and what would happen to Nikkan when it took over. I knew she could fight it after her next change, but as it came more often, she would lose more often. She would be a monster, and she wouldn't hesitate to attack my friend. How in the world could I protect them when I knew he wouldn't fight back. If there was one thing I knew, he loved her and would never hurt her, no matter the monster she became. That didn't leave me with options. If I wanted both of them safe, I had to either find the answer or stay here for the rest of my life and protect them.

The smell of the smoke was a comfort of home. It was the woods, and I was alone in nature, and it felt like the only place I ever wanted to be. I spent the rest of the day smoking the meat that we would save for the children. I wasn't sure how long it would last them, but it was better than nothing. It would be easier if we had help getting food to the wolves, but Elder didn't seem to be coming to the aid of the wolves as they should have. I would just have to keep working double-time to get them fed and safe and find a cure.

The forest on this side of the wall was everything I could remember of life in Elder, but the opposite side was nothing anyone wanted to experience. I felt for the wolves trapped there, but I was just one person. I could only do so much. My friends and the children were my priority.

As I checked the meat again, I heard Sera approach. She joined me at the fire and inspected my work.

"For the kids," I explained.

Sera nodded.

"You're a good man, Castiel," Sera finally spoke. "I know this is stressful, and you don't have time to think about all this, but what you are doing is worth it. Those kids are safe because of you."

I nodded. I had no idea how she knew I needed the encouragement.

"But others aren't as lucky. I feel bad that I can't help the ones not cursed. They either are being attacked and fighting for their lives, or hiding. None of those sound like great options. Can you imagine spending the rest of your days living like that?"

"That's why we need to keep looking for answers. I went back to the papers yesterday and spent the day looking through them. It seems like the only lead was the one you found, Prince Fallon. I think it's worth going and meeting with him."

I nodded. I knew it was, but what was I supposed to do? Leave my friends? Would they be there when I got back?

"I can't leave them right now," I finally replied.

Sera nodded as she understood.

We sat down on the ground near the fire and just waited. The meat was almost done, but that only solved one very small problem for a very short time. They would need more food and soon. They would need warmer clothing next winter, and you couldn't exactly keep children in hanging beds all day. They needed to be able to play and be children. I was giving them none of that.

That was what my life had boiled down to. Problem after problem. I thought it was bad when I had to deal with Red, but this was much worse. I never in a million winters expected things to turn out like this.

Sera reached over and took my hand in hers.

"It may seem hopeless, but I know you'll figure it out. You always do. You are the strongest and smartest man I know. If there is an answer, you can find it."

And just like that, my heavy heart was lighter. Sera was reminding me of the truth. I didn't give up. That wasn't in my nature. I'd deal with one thing at a time, but I would find my answer. I would help my friends and the wolves I called family.

I let go of her hand and put my arm around her. I pulled her close and kissed the top of her head.

"Can you watch the meat while I go back and help Nikkan build more? We're trying to build a treehouse for the kids, so they don't have to hang in beds all day to stay safe."

Sera nodded as I stood and pulled her up too.

"Once I get a safe structure for the children, I can leave Nikkan in charge of them so I can go explore my options more. See what else I might have missed."

Sera smiled at me.

"There's the Castiel I fell for seasons ago."

I paused. Seasons ago? Really? I thought she hated my guts. Boy, was I wrong on that one, but I was never going to tell Grace that. Girls were so confusing, and yet they seemed to understand each other perfectly.

Sera let out a laugh.

"Go help the world. That's what you're best at." Sera yanked on my hand, pulling me down so that our lips could meet again before she pushed me back and stepped to the fire to tend the meat.

I just shook my head. No matter what, Sera was still Sera, pushing me around and calling the shots. I doubt she could be any other way as neither could I. I didn't need to save the world. Just my friends.

Without a second glance back, I took off into the woods and made it to the camp in no time. I actually wondered if my running speed had increased. Was that possible?

"No, no," yelled Nikkan from the tree where he was sitting. The teenage children were staring back up at him from the ground. "We can't use that board. I need the other one. They all need to look like the boards in the tree village, and that means they need to look like the one over there."

I stared at where he pointed and had no clue what he was doing.

"This would work a lot better if we knew how to do it," Grace grumbled as she stood next to me and watched Nikkan let out a frustrated growl. "Besides you, Nikkan is probably the only one still in his senses that had been around the tree village enough to try to replicate it."

I grew up there and wasn't completely certain how to replicate it.

"Sera's tending the meat," I explained as Grace looked me over. "It should be done by before nighttime."

"Good, because I'm pretty sure that won't be." Grace pointed up to Nikkan.

With one last chuckle, I climbed the tree to join my friend in his building pursuit. Neither of us had a real clue about how to build a treehouse, but it was better than nothing. It couldn't be too hard, right?

The afternoon passed quickly as we hammered and pushed the boards into place. It wasn't much of a house, but it was a walkway under the hanging beds of the children. They seemed to appreciate our work, even if we didn't know what we were doing. Before dusk, I was able to help get the children settled for the night before I could make a quick run back to Sera.

Cracking of bones brought my attention back to the trees around me. It was too early to change, but I assumed Nikkan wanted to beat us this time. I turned to tell Grace to wait for him to finish and found her red wolf growling at me.

"Nikkan," I yelled for my friend. He had gone down to the river to fill the canteens for the children. "Nikkan!" I yelled again as my friend's red wolf lunged for me as I scrambled down the tree.

I ducked out of the way, and she went flying over me. I didn't wait to see if she was going to attack again. Her wolf was out for blood, and I was the only thing she could attack.

"Pull the rope up," I yelled to Samuel. We were lucky all of the children were already up there. Samuel was going to have to get them in all their beds. I had to deal with Grace.

"Nikkan!" I gave one last shout. "Tell him I'm going after Grace," I instructed Samuel.

"I will. Be safe," he yelled back.

While Grace went north the night before, this time, she headed right back to all the action, the wolf village. I changed into my wolf form.

'Grace,' I yelled, mentally to my friend. As expected, there was no response.

I picked up my speed as I chased her. I needed to get to her before she got with the other wolves.

'Grace, come back,' I tried again.

Nothing worked. The red wolf that was my friend

kept straight on her path to the village. I wasn't sure what to do next. I needed to keep her safe, but I didn't want to hurt anyone else.

While trying to come up with my options, I didn't need to think any further as a pack of wolves jumped out at Grace. She viciously bit into the first one she could reach. I watched as another one was going to attack her back. Even cursed, they were working together. Actually, they were working more together than they normally would.

I didn't wait to be invited to the brawl as I jumped into it and defended Grace. She turned and nipped at me, but luckily, she was distracted by yet another wolf attacking her. Grace bit at him before sliding out of the wolves that had been circling her. Now, they were circling me and waiting to attack. I didn't have time to deal with them. I needed to get to Grace.

As I tried to see how to get out of the group, all the heads turned to the new wolf joining the group and growling at everyone, Nikkan.

"Go get Grace; let me deal with these," I told him.

Images from Nikkan came back to me. He wanted me to get Grace as he claimed he wasn't fast enough.

'Yes, you are.'

Nikkan shook his blond wolf head.

'And you are still injured from last night.'

Nikkan sent back images to tell me he was fine, and he wanted Grace safe more than anything, even his own life. I wanted to argue with my friend and planned to do just that when he jumped into the circle of wolves and pushed me out of the way. He wanted me to leave now.

I looked back at Nikkan. He kicked off the wolf that tried to bite his back legs. We didn't have time to argue more or keep trading places. I knew how stubborn my friend was, and I had to let him be. He'd made up his mind, and I wasn't going to change it. The more time I spent trying, the more likely Grace would be hurt.

'Stay safe,' I told him before taking off after Grace.

I followed her scent into the village. It was a wreck, but I didn't have time to inspect what I was passing. I ignored the wolves around me and tried my best not to see the blood that was splattering the walls of the huts. It was bad in the daylight but worse in the dark. It was complete chaos.

Grace had gone into the village and roamed around. I wasn't sure if she was looking for something or just wandering. As I finally caught sight of her red coat, I took off faster, jumping the fighting wolves and knocking one from a human that had been unfortunate enough to be outside his house.

The night was dark, but the wolves were all out. Something about the new moon seemed to make the curse stronger. From what I could see, either the cursed wolves were hurting other wolves, or they were hurting themselves equally or at the same time. Either way, they were all being injured. The super healing of the wolves could only go so far. I was afraid of what morning would bring.

Grace ducked from my sights, and I chased her into a home. I didn't expect her to attack when I entered, but I should have known better. Grace wasn't in control of her wolf, and I had just cornered her in a house.

She jumped on my back, and her claws raked into my unprepared body. I could feel the scratch bleed, but I didn't have time to contemplate what to do next. I just acted on instinct and flipped her off me. She flew into a pile of wooden boxes by the doorway and yelped. Sitting back and ready to pounce again, I expected her to take off. Instead, she stood and growled at me.

"I don't want to fight you," I called to her, hoping there was at least a bit of sanity left in her.

There wasn't. She jumped at me, planning to clamp down on my forepaw. I twisted and caught her neck with my mouth instead. I didn't want to hurt her. I didn't want to draw blood, but she wrestled under my paws, and I knew I was cutting into her. She wasn't giving me a choice.

"Come back to me, friend. Come back."

Grace continued to twist in my paws, forcing me to hurt her further. If I let go, she was just going to attack, but I didn't like this either. I was staying safe, but there was no way for me to keep her safe.

The stupid curse was ruining Elder. My friends were trapped not just by a wall but by their wolf. It was supposed to be a part of them, a way of life. But it wasn't. Instead, it was taking over their lives. This wasn't Grace. She bucked under me, snarling; she wasn't my friend. But she was still there. I knew she was. Her human side wasn't gone. Grace wasn't gone, but this curse was trying to destroy her.

I hated everything about the curse. The people of Elder didn't deserve this. The wolves didn't deserve this. Grace didn't deserve this. I wanted more than anything to save her, to save the people I loved.

Grace growled and bucked at me. I loosened my grip on her throat, and she tried to bite me, making my sharp teeth scratch against her. If needed, I was going to hold her in this house until morning came, and she returned to herself. I just didn't know how much of her would be left. I had already marked her up more than I ever wanted.

"I'm not giving up on you, Grace. Never."

The wolf stopped for a moment, and I looked in her eyes. I wanted more than anything to see my friend, but when the beast below me snapped at me and caught my shoulder in her tight jaw, I knew for tonight the curse had won. Grace wasn't in control. She wasn't coming back to me until morning. I pushed more of my body weight into her to keep her in her place.

'I'm sorry, Grace, but I'm not letting this curse win. We're going to beat this curse. I'm going to change things.'

And with that thought, my body started to tingle from my toes up to my head. It felt familiar but more like when I changed forms.

Crap. This wasn't the time for me to be testing any of my powers. If I changed into something smaller than Grace, she was likely to eat me on the spot. The tingles continued, and I saw my human form starting to take shape. That was at least better than turning into a mouse, which would be supper for my hungry friend.

When the tingling stopped, I waited to be bitten by her. I already felt the blood dripping down my back and my shoulder where she had cut me the deepest, but I was sure I was scratched from head to toe. I knew she would attack. But something was strange. She hadn't attacked.

I looked down to see I was pinning a very human Grace to the ground. I scrambled off her.

There was only one reason a wolf turned human, not on their own. When they died. No matter the form they died in, their bodies always returned to human. There was Grace lying on the dirt floor as human as she could get. I had somehow killed Grace.

Nikkan was going to kill me. He was going to be devastated. Grace was dead.

I reached down and took her lifeless body into my arms. I tried not to cry. She didn't deserve to die. She didn't deserve to be cursed. She was young and had much more life to live. This wasn't fair. I hugged her body close to me.

"I'm sorry I couldn't protect you," I whispered into her hair. I had failed. Life wasn't fair.

The world was losing a great spark of life with Grace. She was kind, compassionate, and strong-willed. She was going to make Nikkan happy for the rest of his life, and now she was gone. I wasn't sure what I did, but she was gone. Nikkan would never forgive me. I was never going to forgive me.

Nothing could have prepared me for the onslaught of guilt that hit me. All I wanted to do was save my friends and the wolves, and I couldn't even do that. All this magic was inside me, and it wasn't good for a single thing. I was useless.

Grace gasped in my arms, and I almost dropped her in shock.

"Castiel?" she said with a hoarse voice like she hadn't spoken in days.

"How is this possible?"

I knew she couldn't answer me, but I just didn't understand.

"You're alive."

Grace didn't open her eyes.

"Seems so," she whispered as she wiggled her fingers.

I could see why she wasn't moving as her body was dripping as much blood as mine was. After another glance at her body, I could tell she was cut, bit, and scraped probably twice as much as I had been.

"And you're human."

"That too," she added as her eyes finally fluttered

open. "What's going on?"

"I have no idea," I replied. "But we need to shift and get the heck out of here. The wolves are going crazy tonight."

Grace sat up and shook. Nothing happened. She looked at me and then closed her eyes in concentration. Her entire body shook again; then, her eyes snapped open to me.

"I can't change." Panic laced her voice.

"What?" I asked. That was impossible. She had been born a wolf. She could never be cured.

"I don't know why, but I can't change." Her eyes darted to the open door. She was food for the cursed wolves. It wasn't safe anywhere in the village.

I didn't have time to contemplate why this was happening, but without her wolf, we couldn't leave the village. She would be eaten before we made it a house away.

"Then, we need to find shelter right now."

I turned back to the open door. When we had entered, wolves were running past. More than one caught sight of me when we tangled, but luckily, no one entered. They would be coming back. I didn't need to take any chances with the very human friend I now had.

"Now," I repeated as Grace tried to stand.

I didn't wait. I scooped her into my arms and pushed further into the small house. I aimed for the middle room, which I knew it would be the hardest to get into. Luckily, she had chosen a home that had more than one room, as many didn't. I set Grace in the middle of the room and started to stack everything I could find in front of the doorways. Throwing some blankets at her, I went back to barricading us in the room.

"Cover up with the blankets, and hopefully, the

scent of your blood will be less. I'm going to transform and stand guard."

Grace nodded to me as I turned into a large bear. I took up the remaining space in the room and sat down with my back to the doorway, hoping my girth and scent would keep the wolves away for the night; otherwise, I wasn't sure her miraculous change would be worth it if she didn't make it through the night.

23RD MARCH

I kept guard as Grace finally dozed off to sleep. It sounded like the animals had moved their arguments elsewhere, and I was able to get some sleep also. I was pretty sure if a wolf tried to enter, I was big enough to block their way. Perks of being a large bear.

When morning came, I still wasn't sure if it was safe for us to leave. Grace huddled in her blankets and watched me with big eyes, still not saying anything. I was slightly worried she was in shock from last night.

"Grace," I spoke quietly and slowly. "I'm going to transform into a mouse and go take a peek. If it's safe, we have to go find Nikkan. He took on a pack of wolves to keep you safe. Don't let anyone or anything in. I'll be able to go out and in without needing to open the door."

She nodded.

My magic swirled around me as I shrank down into a mouse. It felt the same as the night before when I was made human without trying. While Grace couldn't shift, I was still able to do it. I didn't understand it, but it was my magic.

In my now much smaller form, I found a crack in the doorway and took off. The house was completely silent. I could hear Grace breathing as it was the only sound. As I neared the open front door, I kept to the shadows. This was the tricky part. I wanted to see what was going on, but I didn't want to be seen as a snack for anything that was out there. Pausing to take a deep breath, I moved forward, still in the shadows, but far enough out into the doorway to look around.

The world was much different in my much smaller form. Everything was huge and looked distorted. My mouse senses told me that the world was fine, even if mixing my mouse impressions of my surroundings with my human brain was getting everything all tangled together. I know what objects I was looking at, but with their new size, my brain didn't want to accept it. I guess I needed to stick with larger animals until I was more used to it.

I looked around the empty street. Red painted walls and the ground. I could see a few humans lying naked and not moving. They had likely been a wolf when they died, just like I thought Grace had. I sat very still and listened to everything around the house. There was nothing to be afraid of. It seemed like the wolves had all fought it out the previous night and were either dead or resting now.

Grace was waiting for me when I entered. She was fully dressed when I appeared in front of her.

"We need to find Nikkan now," I told her as I grew to my full human size and was tossing the blockade from the doorway. "It doesn't look good out there."

I looked Grace over.

"Can you shift now?"

She shook her head. What in the world was going on? Could being in a near-death experience change a shifter? Would it come back?

"Okay. Let's move this stuff and get out of here."

Grace joined me and moved the last few pieces blocking the doorway as I looked around the room. I dug through a few of the boxes we had moved and looked in a chest. There was a large dagger, or it could have been a small sword. I took it as I grabbed Grace's hand. I'd have to return it later, but for now, we needed a way to stay safe in human form.

"Stay behind me," I told her as I pulled her through the house.

I kept alert as we crept through the house. My mouse senses said there was nothing, but my brain was having a hard time believing that. There were wolves all over the place the night before. We couldn't be alone now. And with the children in the woods, I sure hoped the wolves hadn't taken off during the night. I knew the kids would stay safe where they were, but they'd be terrified.

The wolf village was too quiet and covered with fine white dust. Since the curse had come back,, the village was always filled with, at least, moaning. Right now, the place was silent, and that didn't sit right with me.

I had thought the white sparkle from the dust was just my mouse eyes, but I could see it was fine snow. The unexpected spring snow shower didn't hide the carnage of the night, but it made me feel like the world was starting over. I stayed on alert but had hope.

Grace stayed behind me as we made our way back through the village. I wasn't sure where to find Nikkan, but I was going to the last place I saw him and would go from there. We didn't make it all the way there when Grace called out, and I spotted the blond wolf lying on the ground. It looked like he was still a wolf. I wasn't sure why Grace wasn't. Just one more mystery to figure out.

Wolf Nikkan tried to push himself up on his paws but fell back to the ground. He didn't have the energy to do it.

"Save your energy, friend," I told him as I scooped him into my arms.

Nikkan gave me one whine but accepted my help. Had he been human, he would have punched me, but as a wolf, all he could do was bite, and I knew my friend wouldn't bite me in case he turned me into a werewolf. I was more than certain he was too injured to protest further.

"Let's get him back to the camp and the children," I told Grace. She nodded as her eyes filled with tears while looking at Nikkan.

I began to walk back out of the village when we heard some noises in the south. I changed my course. When I was as close as I would get with my injured friend, I sat him on the ground.

"Watch over him, and I'll be right back."

I handed Grace my small sword, and she held it with both hands. She might not be trained like I was, but I knew she'd defend him with her life if needed.

The trees were dense and let me creep further near the conversation I heard. There were men yelling at each other, which was a good sign. If it had been wolves snarling, I would have left, but men I had to see. And one voice was familiar.

When I finally could see, I didn't hesitate to step out of the brush.

Micco was standing and facing three large men that were all yelling at him. I approached the group from behind Micco.

"We got lucky last night," one was yelling.

"We can't count on something like that happening again," another added.

"If we hadn't all been knocked out, who knows what would have happened," the first continued.

"Enough," Micco growled, his wolf seeping into his human voice. "While last night was hard, it will get better. We all know this. The curse was the hardest during the first winter season when it happened long ago. We just need to weather this out." Micco stopped talking when he heard me approach. He turned to me.

"How in the world did you get in here?" he asked.

I smiled and hugged the man that was like a grandfather to me. I was happy he survived. I didn't know where he was in the fighting, but it seemed he was no worse for the wear.

"We have a bit to catch up on," I replied as Micco hugged me back. "I'm just glad to see you alive."

Micco gave me his hearty laugh as he pulled back.

"You think a curse can beat me? Ha." The old man was as tough as you could get. Though he did look like he'd seen better days.

"What happened last night?" I asked about the argument I had walked in on.

Micco scratched his head.

"We have no idea. One moment we were all running around fighting, and the next moment we woke up, and it was morning time. Once people started to change back, no one could explain what happened. It was like something knocked us all out cold. Some people woke human."

Maybe the bodies we saw weren't dead, after all.

A thump landed at our feet, and I took up a defensive stance in front of Micco. He reached down at the package at our feet and undid the twine on it. Opening it up, he found it filled with white bandages. Another thump landed, and I could see where it was coming from, the wall. I left Micco and the wolves behind as I made it to the wall.

I stopped in shock.

Behind the foggy wall were hundreds of people. In front, Sera stood next to Mal, who had her hands on the wall. She was chanting as more people tossed packages through the wall.

Mal nodded to Sera, and Sera walked over to the wall. She held out a hand to touch the wall, but it didn't stop her. She pushed through and ran over to me, jumping into my still shocked arms. She just went through the wall. Was it still there? I didn't have time to process it as Sera pulled my face to hers so that she could kiss me. Sera pulled back and grinned at me.

"What's going on?" I asked as Mal walked through the wall also. I could still see the foggy wall. Behind her, tree people followed with bags and some pulling carts.

"I asked Mal to change the wall and allow humans but not werewolves to walk through. It will still keep Elder safe from the wolves, but we can come through. This way, we can help during the day and get supplies to everyone," Sera explained. "If we take care of the wolves, you can search for the cure."

I looked behind her. The normally scared tree people

were walking out toward the village with their packages, stopping at any wolf they found. Many bent down to help injured wolves stand; others just dug through their bags to hand the wolves food or drinks.

"We've brought food, clothing, and medicine," Sera said over my head to Micco behind me. "And I brought builders to the other side where you have the children. We need to get over there and let them start working. It will probably take them at least four days to get a small structure up in the tree, but they've vowed to come back every week until there is a place for the wolf children to stay safe. They are safe now. The tree people want to help, and I thought this was the best way. You can count on us to keep everyone safe."

I didn't care who was watching. I leaned down to Sera in my arms and kissed her again. Tree people cheered at us as they passed, but I blocked them out. I had no idea how she did it, but Sera brought the two sides together for me.

When we finally broke apart, I took her hand in mine and walked over to the old healer.

"How is this possible? I thought the wall had to keep both wolves and humans apart."

Mal shrugged. "That was all I could do. I didn't have the ability to see the difference between a human and a wolf-human."

"But you see it now?"

Mal grinned. "I didn't make this possible. You did."

How was that possible? My magic wasn't the kind that made walls like Mal. All I could do was transform. The wall didn't let me through as a human, and I didn't try to change that. I always went through the wall like an animal. We had tried to walk me through it like a man, and it didn't work. What was she talking about?

"Last night, you used your magic to change Elder. Sera already had the tree people and me here to help, but this wall was all you. You can see the small difference between the humans and the wolf humans, and that was what was needed to make the wall this way. I'm glad you finally accepted your magic, Castiel. Your mother will be proud."

I hadn't noticed that the people came without Red. Sera squeezed my hand.

"She had some visitors and told me she couldn't leave."

Visitors? Who was coming into Elder when we had a problem with the wolves? Most people would run the other direction. While we tried to keep things to ourselves, there were sure to be reports going around the kingdoms about the wolves.

"Let's go get those builders in and going on the houses," Sera suggested, not elaborating further.

We said our goodbyes, and Mal was gone in her poof of smoke.

"We better go get Nikkan and Grace."

I led Sera into the woods, where I left my friends. Sera took one look at Nikkan and scooped him into her arms. He didn't protest this time as she marched back near the wall.

"Miller," she yelled at a passing man. "See that he is fixed up and don't let him shift until he heals."

"What is wrong?" Grace whispered, staring in shock at the people pouring through the wall.

"He's injured more than it seems. I could feel at least half a dozen ribs are broken, and there are some deep gashes under him that need stitches."

Sera set Nikkan down on the clean shirt the man just put on the ground. I could see the blood blossoming beneath my friend.

"Will he be okay?" Grace asked.

Sera stood up as Miller began examining Nikkan. She pulled Grace into a hug.

"He will be. I promise."

Grace let out a sob that she seemed to have been holding in probably all night. I decided to walk over to Nikkan and let the girls have a moment.

As I turned to leave, I heard Grace gasp behind me, and I turned around.

"Did I do that?" she asked, pointing to me.

I looked down at my chest. There were scratches and bite marks, but they were already scabbed over and healing. It seemed the wolf-accelerated healing was very accelerated in me. I shrugged.

"Not your front, your back," Sera explained as Grace began to sob more. "You're a bit scratched up."

I tried to look over my shoulder, but I didn't see anything. Instead, I rotated my arms, and I felt some blood trickle.

"It doesn't hurt," I told Grace honestly. "And I'm pretty sure I gave back as much as you did." I pointed to her arm that I had to bite more than once to keep her from running away or biting me.

She looked at her wrist and nodded. It wasn't much, but she did feel a bit better.

"You and Nikkan stay here and get better," Sera told Grace, and Grace nodded before she dropped down beside my best friend. "And we can go check on the children."

Sera reached for my hand and pulled me into a run toward the children's camp.

I smiled at her next to me before increasing my speed to be in front of her. I would never get sick of running through the woods of Elder. While it was still quiet in the wolf area, it felt like home. The trees had little leaves growing, and the air was fresh once you got away from the village: the wind, the smells, the crisp spring air. I was as home as I ever would be.

Before we made it to the children and our camp, I halted in my tracks and threw out my arms to catch Sera. She laughed as I picked her up and twirled her.

“They really are going to be fine, aren’t they?” I asked what I already knew. “Thanks to you.”

Sera grinned. “I didn’t do a thing except lead them through the woods at nighttime. This was all you and Red. She made them believe, and you gave them a way to help. The two of you are truly the leaders of Elder.”

I gave her a quick peck on the forehead.

“I would have given up if it weren’t for you. Thank you.”

Sera grinned at me.

“You wouldn’t have, Castiel, because giving up isn’t part of you. Never has been or ever will be.”

24TH MARCH

It was hard to leave my friends, but I knew they would be fine and I needed to find out where I came from, who I was. I'd been thinking about visiting Prince Fallon of Aboria for a while and now seemed the best time to do it. The children were safe, and the wolf tree home was growing with the help of the tree village builders. I didn't have the cure to the curse, but the wolves were going to be fine. My friends were going to be fine. Red and Sera had seen to it. Elder had seen to it. I was truly inspired.

Grace was completely human. She could pass through the barrier where Nikkan couldn't. I have no idea why she was changed, and no one else was. I wasn't sure if it was me that did it, but she was now free of being a wolf. Nikkan insisted she move to be with

Red in the tree village, but Grace had other plans. She was staying with the children in the treehouse. She was going to take care of them when their parents couldn't.

Micco was now very busy but in a much happier way than before. He had a village to run, and it was no longer on the verge of dying. The wolves had hope again, thanks to the tree villagers, who finally understood what being part of Elder meant. Life would go on now, and people didn't have to hide in fear on either side of the wall.

I wasn't sure what I was supposed to do now, but the visitors in Azren were waiting for me. The easiest way to travel would have been to transform into a bird, but Sera was with me, so we decided to race home, for old times sake of course. I might have let her beat me, just this once.

Sera told me to meet her in Red's office, but I was stuck outside the door. I wasn't sure I wanted to know who the visitors were or why they were here. I had enough to deal with as it was. I didn't need anything more. I turned away from Red's office door and found my favorite branch. I climbed up into the tree that gave me the best view of the village and Red's office at the same time. I wasn't sure how much alone time they'd let me have before Red came looking.

I was happy for my wolf friends; I really was. But something was keeping me from being completely happy. Maybe it was the fact that the magic of Elder refused to name me as Red's son, or maybe it was that helping the wolves didn't make me part of them. I was still different.

As a child, I thought if I could change into an animal, I would fit in. Now I could, but I still didn't fit in. I knew I needed to find a cure; that was my priority, but when

I came back, what would that mean. I still was stuck not being either a tree person or a wolf. And what did the magic inside me mean? It allowed me to transform, which was the best feeling in the world, but I had no idea where or why I had it.

Things had been simpler before the curse. In one moon cycle, my whole life had changed. I worried that if I went away, it would all change again, and I wouldn't be able ever to come home. No matter how I felt about the people, the woods of Elder were my home.

I sat in the trees and listened to the people that walked by below. I loved the tree that Red's office was built with. It was a mighty oak tree that stretched up above most of the other trees. It was strong and resilient, just like my mother. What would she be like when I returned?

"Will she die when the power of the Red is all in you?" I asked Sera.

She thought she had snuck up into the tree with me, but I knew she was there. My current spot wasn't just my own favorite spot.

"I hope not," Sera replied, taking my hand in hers. "I don't think I can do this thing alone."

I smiled at her as she moved next to me instead of being on the branch overhead.

"You could do it with your eyes closed. Elder isn't going to know what hit them when you are in charge."

She blushed.

"Is that why you don't want to go down there and see who came all this way to talk to you?"

I shrugged. It was only one of many reasons.

"Because you know she's not going to let you sit up here all day. Eventually, she'll drag you down there and probably embarrass you as much as she can. She's still the Red and your mother."

That sounded like something Red would do. Sera would probably offer to help.

"You both know I can just turn into a bird and fly away. I'm not the poor defenseless human that you two can boss around anymore. I have magic." I snapped my fingers like something would happen. I was certain nothing would, but it would have made a great effect if it had.

"No one has ever been able to boss you around, Castiel."

I laughed at that. She was right. I hated bossy people and often times did the opposite to spite them. Except with Sera. I knew when not to do what she said because she was trying to trick me into something. She never caught on, but when she was lying to me, she'd raise her left eyebrow just a little bit.

"Let's go see who these people are," Sera suggested; at least, I was going to call it "suggested" because if she was bossing me, I'd have to sit still.

I gave her my *are you serious* look, and she laughed, tugging on my hand to come down from the tree with her.

Sera walked into the office without knocking. It was her office, too, after all. I followed behind as Sera went and sat down at her desk by Red. I moved off to the side of Red's desk and leaned against the wall. I crossed my legs at my ankles and looked over the guests.

The first impression told me they weren't from Elder. When the one closest to me turned to me, I tried my best to hide my shock. Golden-ringed eyes peered at me. She eyed me up from head to toe and then back to my matching eyes.

"Triplets?" she whispered.

I had no idea what she was talking about. The other one, who had been in conversation with Red, didn't turn to me but finished what she was saying.

"If you can just show me where I can post a letter. You know how parents can be," the red-haired girl told Red.

I had to keep from laughing. Red had no idea of how caring parents could be. Hers had a baby to replace her once she became Red, but I doubt that ever made it into any of the papers. Red just nodded to her.

I wasn't sure where they were from, but they weren't from Elder. I could detect a slight accent on the girl, and I wasn't sure where to place her. I tried to remember all the places I had visited with Red.

"This is my son, Castiel, whom you have been asking about," Red said, turning to me. Her voice was neutral, but her eyes were watching the girl like a hawk. "Castiel, this is Princess Azia from Draconis and Princess Blaise from Atlantice."

I nodded my hellos but still had no idea why two princesses from other lands would want to see me. And their eyes were a bit disconcerting. I crossed my arms over my chest and stared at them. Season after season with my mother was paying off. I didn't need to make the first move.

Princess Blaise covered her laugh with a cough like she felt the uncomfortableness in the room but didn't have a response.

I stared longer at the two girls and had more questions than anything. They didn't look anything alike. One was a dark blonde, and the other was a redhead, their faces held different angles, and their height had to be off by more than a hand's width. But those eyes. Their eyes were just like mine.

"We will take our leave," Red said as she stood and looked at Sera.

I shook my head to my mother.

"I need to pack. I'll take them back to my place to talk. Did you find a guest house for them to stay before they leave?"

Red nodded to me as Princess Azia spoke.

"We don't need lodging. We plan to leave after speaking with you."

I nodded to her before walking over to my mother. She raised an eyebrow at me as she heard exactly what I had said. Sera had her impartial mask on like my mother taught her, but I could tell she was happy at what I said. That was one thing I'd always like about Sera. She wasn't afraid for me to go off in the world. In fact, she encouraged it.

Leaning down, I hugged Red, and her mask slipped for a moment. My mother was looking back at me with her smiling eyes before she went back into the role of being the Red.

"How long do you plan to be gone?" she asked, as an interested leader would be in the case of a citizen going abroad, not as a mother looking after her child.

"I'm not sure. I need to meet with Prince Fallon and see if he has any information. It shouldn't take me more than a day or so to get to him." I wasn't sure what to say in front of the princesses, but I wasn't about to tell them that I could transform into animals. "I'll come right back no matter the information to discuss with both of you, of course. If he doesn't have what I need, we'll have to come up with more leads."

"You might need more than a day or two," Sera added. "He might need a little convincing to talk to you."

I nodded. That, I could agree with. Prince Fallon did

not seem to be the kind that would want to deal with a guy from Elder. I had nothing to offer him.

Red nodded to me as I turned to leave. I opened the door to the office and motioned for the two princesses to follow me. As I turned to close the door, Sera stopped me.

“Stay safe,” she said quietly, looking up at me with much sadder eyes like she just understood what it meant that I was leaving.

“I’ll be home before you notice,” I replied. I planned to fly to Prince Fallon. I knew it wouldn’t take too long to go across Elder and Arboria. Sera nodded.

I knew she was in her Red mode along with my mother since we had guests, but I didn’t care. I wasn’t the carefully controlled ruler-to-be of Elder. I was and always would be just myself. And with that thought, I wrapped my arms around Sera and dipped her back as my lips met hers. She grinned as I set her back up on her feet.

“Castiel,” she said my name as she had many times before, and I finally understood her tone. She wasn’t mad at me; she was exasperated with me, in a good way. I grinned as I looked past her into the office.

“I’ll come back soon, Mom. Don’t worry. I’ll find an answer, and if it isn’t there, I’ll keep looking.”

Red sighed and shook her head. She wasn’t mad at me either. They both knew that I wasn’t going to change.

The two princesses were watching silently, but I didn’t care. They came here for something. I’d hear them out and send them on their way.

The walk back to my place was like going as a snail. It was slow. I missed running with Sera already. I had to wonder how long the princesses had been traveling.

At this pace, they had to have been in Elder alone for days, maybe a moon cycle. They were that slow.

They talked quietly behind me, but I didn't particularly listen. I was using my better senses to look around my forest. I hoped my travels to Arboria would only take a couple of days, but I had a feeling the prince was going to be hard to deal with as Sera expected. Men like him always were.

My house looked just as I had left it. It wasn't anything you'd bring a princess to, but they came to me, so they'd have to suck it up and deal with it. I really didn't have time to deal with princesses. I needed to find my answers and keep looking for the cure.

I opened the door and held it back for them to enter. The dark blonde one stopped before going into the house and looked up into the tree my house was built against. A small purple dragon swooped down and landed on her shoulder before she entered the house.

A dragon. A real-life dragon. I had never seen a dragon before, and now, I kind of wanted to try being one for a little bit. I could fly to Arboria as a dragon, but that would probably get me attacked on sight because dragons weren't local to Elder or Arboria.

The princesses looked around my meager place and decided to sit together on the couch. The red-haired one...Blaise... openly gaped at the room.

"Is this really where you live?"

I ignored her tone and went about deciding what to bring.

"What? It's a fair question," she continued in her accent that screamed, not from Elder.

"While it isn't as impressive as the tree village, I built this place completely on my own over three winters ago. Everything from the walls to the couch you are sitting on, I built. So, sorry, princess, if it offends you."

I went back to looking around but soon decided I didn't need to take anything with me. I planned to travel as an eagle to fly there quickly, so it wasn't like I could carry much anyway.

Grabbing a chair from the table, I pulled it over to sit facing the two girls.

"We didn't mean to offend you," Azia told me.

I shrugged, neither agreeing or disagreeing with her. I was used to the other kingdoms talking about us. We didn't use the latest technology, but that didn't mean we were backward. The people of Elder chose to live this way. I was beyond certain neither girl had lived a moon cycle in the woods alone, yet almost every citizen of Elder could do that without breaking a sweat. Different kingdoms valued different things. It didn't make one wrong or right, but just different.

Red was born for her job with dealing with other kingdoms. I could barely stand others and their judgment of us. The people of Elder were happy with their lives, so why did it matter to anyone else?

"Let's get on with it. Why are you here?" I would have rather kept waiting and let them talk, but I didn't have time. I needed to talk with Prince Fallon and find out where he came from. He was the best lead I had, and I was going to act on it once I got these girls on their way.

"How much does Red tell you about the other kingdoms?" Blaise asked. "Since you aren't her successor. That was the girl there, Sera, correct?"

"I mainly keep out of it as much as I can, but I have met some of the official leaders and know the basics. It isn't much interest to me. As you said, I'm not ruling the kingdom, ever."

The princess nodded.

"Three months ago, things started to change in Draconis." Azia said.

The weather was strange, people were fighting, the dragons...well the dragons felt a shift in energy. Then my mother went back to sleep. We haven't been able to wake her. I decided to head to Urbis, but—"

"She found me first because we started to have problems too. My mother turned back into a mermaid," Blaise interjected.

"Before we could go to Urbis, we heard there were changes here, and we came to see if it was all related," Azia continued.

"And it seems we are. I didn't imagine having a sister but a brother too. It's amazing," Blaise added in apparent delight.

"Brother?" I asked. What in the world were they talking about?

"Our eyes. Don't you see that you are just like us?"

Okay, they were right about that, but it didn't make me their brother. And how were they sisters? They looked nothing alike.

"I thought twins, but now I see it's triplets."

I was getting dizzy looking between the two as they kept throwing information at me that made no sense.

"We don't have triplets in Elder. Twins occasionally, but anything more than that doesn't happen unless it's in animals," I replied. I really didn't know what they were talking about.

"So, you were born here?"

I bit my lip. These two girls were strangers and princesses at that. They knew nothing of me or our ways. I wasn't really sure I should be giving them any information. The blonde seemed to understand my hesitation.

"We were both adopted. I might be Queen Briar Rose's daughter, but she didn't give birth to me. Blaise is also adopted. One night over eighteen years ago, we were given to our mothers. We know nothing more. Are you eighteen years old also?"

"Yes, I'm eighteen winters."

"Which would make us triplets," Blaise added excitedly. "I can't believe we found another golden-eyed person here in Elder of all places."

"Or I could be your cousin for all you know," I added, but in reality, any relation was more than I could have ever expected to find. And they were right about the eyes. I had never seen my eye color before, except on the two of them.

"We need to head to Urbis together and see if we can find out what is happening," Azia explained.

I shook my head no to that.

"But we need to stop at Floris first. If this is going on all over, we have to check on Princess Lilian. I need to be sure she's okay."

"Floris first," Azia relented.

I shook my head as the pair of them bickered.

"I'm not part of your little adventure, no matter what my eyes look like. I mean, come on. I look nothing like either of you two in any other aspect."

Azia was tall for a woman, but not huge. She was willowy, and despite the purple hooded jacket she wore and the sword at her side, not to mention the dragon she carried around with her like a designer purse, she still looked like a princess. The shorter one, Blaise, was worse. Her red hair didn't look anything like Azia's and her wide eyes even less. Blaise also had more curves. Side by side, they were nothing alike beyond the color of their eyes. My black hair and olive skin tone was a stark contrast to the fair-skinned princesses. I saw nothing of me in them.

While it would have been a great dream to find family, I didn't think I was theirs. It was impossible. We lived in different kingdoms. And while the two of them were almost neighbors, I was far from it. Who would have three babies, drop two off together, and then take the third halfway across the world?

Princess Azia cocked her head to the side as she studied me. She had that look like Red that I recognized all too well. She was thinking. I didn't need to be analyzed by a princess. I was pretty sure Urbis had nothing to offer me. I needed a cure for the curse the werewolves had, not for sleeping like Queen Briar Rose.

"What would convince you to come with us? I'm more than certain you are meant to be with us. I can't give you an argument why, I just know it," Azia finally told me.

"The people of Elder are my home, and I need to help them. I understand wanting to help your mothers. I need to help my wolves. But I don't think we're going in the same direction unless you can tell me where you came from before you were adopted." That was what I needed to know; what I needed to ask Prince Fallon.

"We don't know, but we think Urbis," Azia replied. "That's why I want to go there, among other reasons."

"But we are going to visit Princess Lillian in Floris first to make sure she is ok. Blaise added, shooting a look at Azia. "I know Lillian isn't related to us, but she is a friend of mine. I need to know she is alright."

"I'm sorry that you've come so far for nothing, ladies, but I have my own trip to deal with. Before you came, I was just about to head out to Arboria to see Prince Fallon.

"Why would you want to see Prince Fallon?" Azia eyed me curiously.

"I want to find out about..."

"Your birth?" she answered before I could finish the sentence. "That's pretty much what we are doing too. What if I told you that after we check on Princess Lilian, we could go to Prince Fallon and get the information you need?" Azia suggested. "Then, it would be worthwhile for you to come with us."

That was a bit enticing. I could look along the way for more answers, and fresh ideas wouldn't hurt anything. But as I looked at the two disheveled princesses, I wasn't sure how many moon cycles that would take. It wasn't like my friends would get better while I was gone. The moon would still call to them. Worse even, it meant I would be traveling between kingdoms at a slow pace and protecting the princesses. They probably just needed me as a bodyguard.

"As enticing as it is to be your male escort through the villages, I still have to decline. How long has it been since you left home? One, two, six moon cycles? I can't be away from Elder for seasons. And I don't have time to travel around protecting two princesses, no offense."

Azia smiled at me—like genuinely smiled.

"None taken. Let's make a wager."

"A deal?"

"Yes, how about we have a little sword fight competition. If I win, you join us going to Floris and then Arboria, and Urbis. That should take three months maximum. If you win, then we leave and let you go on your way."

Was she serious? She was thin and a princess, how was she going to fight me equally? Was she setting herself up to fail? Or was she? I knew very little about the next generation of the monarchies of the kingdoms because they were all within a few season cycles of my own age. From what I heard of Prince Fallon, he did nothing but party and lived lavishly. While a bit dirty, I could tell the princesses both lived fancy lives also.

"Okay, deal."

Azia went outside, and I followed behind. Blaise stood in the doorway to my place, and the dragon landed on the ground beside her. I really wanted to try being a dragon. Was flying as one different than a bird?

"You like her?" Azia asked.

"I've never seen one before," I replied honestly.

I wasn't about to tell her I was going to transform into one as soon as I could get away from them just for a little bit, see if my magic extended into animals that came from other places

"She won't stop our fight if I get the upper hand?"

Azia smiled. "No, she'll stay out of it."

"Good." I knew perfectly well my wolf friend would jump in a dual. It was the nature of being a wolf. We watched each other's backs.

I took up my sword.

"Ready when you are."

Azia took a sword from her hilt. It was beautiful with the hilt shaped like a dragon with ruby eyes. I had never seen workmanship like that before. Such a typical thing for royalty. I was sure she thought with her better, magnificent sword, she'd beat my plain Elder sword. That was probably the main reason I didn't know the next generation. After meeting all of them at some point in my childhood with Red, I knew from a very young age; I didn't fit in. I didn't remember meeting these two princesses.

I waited for Azia to make the first move, but she just stood there. Why would she bargain with me with a sword fight if she didn't really want to fight?

"Are we starting?" I asked her.

I couldn't just strike at a princess, no matter the reason. I did have a moral code. I kept my sword up. I could do this all day if she wanted.

Her sword came towards mine in a slow arc, and I easily blocked it. Her hit was either testing me, or she was wielding a sword too big for her. That often happened with women when we first started to train them in Elder. They thought a bigger sword meant they would be able to keep up. That wasn't how it had to be done. You didn't need to be bigger with the most muscles; you needed to be smarter. Someone must have missed teaching the princess that lesson.

I made a quicker swing at her, and she just managed to block it. This wasn't a fair fight, but at least I'd be on my way. Two more hits, and I'd have the sword from her hand. I moved in to swing again and didn't notice what was happening until she had taken me down on my back, and my hand was trapped to the ground with her boot.

Azia grinned at me from her position above me. She wasn't the weak princess she pretended to be. She had skills.

I smiled as she offered me a hand to stand. It wasn't often I was beaten, but she was going to be a fun challenge to train with. If I was going to have to go around from kingdom to kingdom, I was going to learn a thing or two or three.

As our hands met, I felt the tingles of magic slide through me. Azia smiled more. Was this what she was talking about?

"While you don't want to admit it, Castiel, I know we're connected."

Okay, she was right. I could feel that. My magic hummed beneath the surface like it was happy they had found me. Maybe wandering around the kingdoms would be helpful, after all. As she said, I was sure I was connected to these two princesses. It was time for a new adventure and answers for my people. I wasn't coming home until I helped them, and I was certain I would be a whole new man when I did. It was time to say goodbye to Elder for a little bit and hello to the rest of the kingdoms.

TERMS USED

Vocab:

Winters- one year

New moon- one month

Moon cycle- one month

A moon- one day/24 hrs

A season- 4 months

A sapling- 5 feet

Grab the Next boxset in the Kingdom of Fairytales series

MEET THE TEAM

The Kingdom of Fairytales Series was a team effort. Below are the people that made it possible:

EQP Management: Rhi Parkes & J.A. Armitage

Our authors: J.A. Armitage, Audrey Rich, B. Kristin McMichael, Emma Savant, Jennifer Ellision, Scarlett Kol, Rose Castro, Margo Ryerkerk, Zara Quentin, Laura Greenwood and Anne Stryker.

Our Editor
Rose Lipscomb

Our Beta Team
Nadine Peterse-Vrijhof
Diane Major
Kalli Bunch
Stephanie Woodwood

Our Proof Reader
Tina Merritt

And to all the wonderful people who loved the world we created and reviewed our stories.
Thank you

READING ORDER

SEASON ONE
SLEEPING BEAUTY
Queen of Dragons
Heiress of Embers
Throne of Fury
Goddess of Flames

SEASON TWO
LITTLE MERMAID
Queen of Mermaids
Heiress of the Sea
Throne of Change
Goddess of Water

SEASON THREE
RED RIDING HOOD
King of Wolves
Heir of the Curse
Throne of Night
God of Shifters

SEASON FOUR
RAPUNZEL
King of Devotion
Heir of Thorns
Throne of Enchantment
God of Loyalty

SEASON FIVE
RUMPELSTILTSKIN
Queen of Unicorns
Heiress of Gold
Throne of Sacrifice
Goddess of Loss

SEASON SIX
BEAUTY AND THE BEAST
King of Beasts
Heir of Beauty
Throne of Betrayal
God of Illusion

SEASON SEVEN
ALADDIN
Queen of the Sun
Heiress of Shadows
Throne of the Phoenix
Goddess of Fire

SEASON EIGHT
CINDERELLA
Queen of Song
Heiress of Melody
Throne of Symphony
Goddess of Harmony

SEASON NINE
ALICE IN WONDERLAND
Queen of Clockwork
Heiress of Delusion
Throne of Cards
Goddess of Hearts

SEASON TEN
WIZARD OF OZ
King of Traitors
Heir of Fugitives
Throne of Emeralds
God of Storms

SEASON ELEVEN
SNOW WHITE
Queen of Reflections
Heiress of Mirrors
Throne of Wands
Goddess of Magic

SEASON TWELVE
PETER PAN
Queen of Skies
Heiress of Stars
Throne of Feathers
Goddess of Air

SEASON THIRTEEN
URBIS

Kingdom of Royalty
Kingdom of Power
Kingdom of Fairytales
Kingdom of Ever After

BOXSETS

AZIA
BLAISE
CASTIEL
DEON
ELIANA
FALLON
GAIA
HALIA
IVY
JAKON
KELIS
LYRIC
URBIS

www.ingramcontent.com/pod-product-compliance
Lightning Source LLC
Chambersburg PA
CBHW020246030826
48979CB00030B/2635/J

* 9 7 8 1 9 8 9 9 9 7 4 3 7 *